I0667044

Praise for Promise For Tomorrow

"The author skillfully blends science fiction and romance, resulting in a balanced but suspenseful plot. The multiple plotlines serve to increase the tension leading to a grand climax in which all is resolved. I really enjoyed this novel." *Fallen Angel Review: Five Angel Review*

"PROMISE FOR TOMORROW, a rousing delight of a read. Danger, deceit, betrayal, love, and surprises both good and bad, abound and surround them all. An excellent story of an intriguing culture and a paradise that should remain unspoiled with dreamy style and colorful prose. Get it, read it, KEEP it." *Romance Reviews Today*

Romantic Times: Awards Promise For Tomorrow 4 ½ Stars. It also made the "TOP PICK" list of books.

Praise for Forget About Tomorrow

"This action-filled thrill ride is full of romance and suspense. Readers will delight in this fast-paced, engaging novel." *Romantic Times Magazine*

"Ms. Kreger has a talent for drawing out the action in such a way as to keep the reader on their toes until the very last page. It is full of more twists and turns than you would find on a roller coaster… I highly recommend it!" *Coffee Times Reviews*

Other Titles by Liz Kreger

The Tomorrow Series
Promise For Tomorrow
Forget About Tomorrow

When Darkness Falls

LIZ KREGER

Copyright © 2015 Erin Krueger
All rights reserved.
ISBN: 1939328233
ISBN-13: 978-1-939328-23-6

No part of this work may be copied or distributed in
any way without written permission of the copyright holder.

This is a work of fiction and all names, people,
places and incidents are either used fictitiously or are a
product of the author's imagination.

DEDICATION

I met Liz about thirteen years ago at a Milwaukee WisRWA meeting, but it seems longer. We quickly became friends, and not because we discovered that we had both had a mastectomy, but we just clicked – though I think anyone would click with Liz. She shone so brightly even then. I admired her writing, and when there was an opening in the online critique group that I belonged to, I invited her to join us. There were eight of us: Allison Brennan, Maya Banks, Amy Knupp, Janette Kenny, Karin Tabke, Michelle Diener and me. None of us wrote in the same genre, and it didn't matter.

She was so vibrantly alive, not a cancer victim but a cancer warrior. In all the years I knew her, she rarely complained, and when she did, it was with humor. In my mind, I see her with a smile, talking about her daughter, her 'little darling'—and still wanting to go over her manuscript for one last revision.

Despite her long battle with cancer, she was happier than many healthy people I know. She was an inspiration on how to live. She will be missed, yet she's still alive in the hearts of the many people who loved her. Including me.

Edie Ramer

This isn't the way it should be, but this book is dedicated in loving memory of the author herself. Liz fought cancer for eighteen long years, and I was proud to know her for twelve of those years. In fact, every writing conference I ever attended in the US was with Liz as my roommate. I'm so grateful to have had those times with her; fun, exhausting, exhilarating times that highlight how alive she was, how vibrant.

Even as she lay in her bed at the hospital, just weeks before cancer took her for good, we spoke on the phone and talked about her visiting me in Australia.

Her never give up, never surrender attitude to life is reflected in the courage and determination of the characters in her books, and she was as beautiful and magical as any of them. I will miss you, Liz. You truly were a warrior.

Michelle Diener

Liz Kreger was one of the most fearless people I've known. Fearless and determined. For most of the twelve years I knew her, she was fighting cancer. But she didn't let fear overcome her, no matter how many hits she took from the disease. She was determined to live life on her terms and to keep on fighting.

When a lot of people would've set aside nonessential pursuits like writing, Liz became more motivated than ever to create new stories. Our writing group decided to pool our efforts in order to publish this last book for her, and I knew there could be no better tribute to our eighth member. As Liz's health was failing, I realized, as the copyeditor, chances were high that I would be the last one to go through the story with a critical eye before it would be published. I wasn't sure what to expect, because I hadn't previously laid eyes on it.

Liz blew me away with this story. Editing it was bittersweet—I was bowled over by her talent and the way she swept me into her world. And I was so saddened that there won't be more Liz stories to come. Because she was good.

What I love most about this story is the way Liz herself shines through in it. There are expressions in the writing that I can hear coming from Liz's mouth, in her voice. The ideas inherent in the complex fantasy world she built show hints of Liz's take on life and the world we live in. And perhaps most poignantly, the main character, Riona Northstar, encompasses a lot of who Liz was, even though I suspect Liz didn't plan it that way. Riona is a fighter. She's selfless, inherently good, and willing to fulfill her duties even when she'd like nothing more than to sit back and soak up the peace of the world around her. I imagine Liz longed for peace from her battles, but she didn't complain, she didn't stop fighting, and she never used her health as an excuse for anything. Riona's backstory includes a fight, when she was a mere human, against breast cancer. Given the license to "play God" the way we writers do in our fiction, Liz made her character conquer the disease by becoming immortal. I only wish she could have given herself that power so that those who loved her would still have her with us today and so that the rest of the world would have more compelling, wonderful Liz stories to savor.

Amy Knupp

Two things stand out to me about Liz. First and foremost, she loved life. She was vibrant in personality, enthusiastic in everything she did, and completely down-to-earth. Like Horton the Elephant, Liz said what she meant and meant what she said. I loved that about her. The second, and probably the most important thing, was that Liz loved her family. She glowed when she talked about Erin, her pride and affection shining in her eyes or through her emails. Liz loved fully. She taught me to embrace life because every day is a gift that should never be wasted.

Allison Brennan

Every time I sat down to write my dedication to Liz, I sat dumbly staring at the flashing cursor. I mean how was I supposed to put into words how special she was? What a fighter she was? How by sheer willpower she beat cancer's ass for almost

2 decades? How much I loved and respected her?

As a writer one would think it would be a no brainer to string the words of praise together, but there simply are no words in any language adequate to embody the beauty that was Liz.

But I'll try to do her justice. Liz's energy was always bright and her eyes sparkled with a joi de vivre matched by few. And she was so happy to be alive. As often as she was in treatment and as many times as the bitch cancer tried knocking her off her ass, Liz met it head on refusing to let it get her.

Liz had more tenacity in her than a prize fighter. She was more courageous then a Congressional Medal of Honor recipient. Ever cheerful, she was positive, outgoing and loving. A giver who never had a bad word to say about anyone.

Her smile was warm and her laugh infectious. She was a true warrior princess, a woman who did not acknowledge the words, give up or defeat.

She never forgot my birthday or to offer words of support even when she was not feeling well. She was more concerned about making sure everyone around her was ok than she was concerned about her difficulties.

Liz embodies the true measure of goodness. She was not perfect, but I never saw her as anything less than amazing. The light of the world is dimmer without her sunny smile and happy presence. I miss her greatly.

Karin Tabke

Years ago when I was asked to join a group of progressive unpublished writers like myself, I had absolutely no idea that each one of those seven smart, diligent and talented women would make a major impact on my life in a very positive way. That's when I met Liz Kreger online, and I immediately liked her as a person and an author. In her writing and as a fellow critique member, her ideas were original and honest. She possessed a unique imagination, took feedback with an open mind and gave the same, telling it like she saw it in a manner that always helped and never offended.

Liz glowed with love and never forgot a birthday or holiday, never letting slide what so many of us do in this hectic world. Each time she was diagnosed with another round of cancer, I admired her courage, confidence and fortitude, knowing I couldn't have been that composed if faced with the same. "Never give up," she told me when I fell to my lowest and my inner drive dwindled, and then she sent me a lovely pendant inscribed with those words that I wear to this day. My heart hurts just trying to express what she meant to me and how much I'll miss her. She was a true friend. I admired her, loved her and will cherish my memories of her.

Janette Kenny

Writing is a solitary job. Writers are, by nature, reclusive creatures, living more in their minds than they do in reality, always creating stories and characters, thinking of distant, far away places and making them come to life on the pages of a book.

I met Liz almost from the inception of my decision to attempt a career in fiction writing. We met online, our communications via email or message board. There were eight of us. All in the same places. All starting out and trying to get that first break. Our first contract and the launch of a career in writing.

And from the very beginning, Liz was a strong, charismatic personality. Unflaggingly cheerful and supportive, never one to doubt or become mired in perceived failure. You see, Liz was a survivor many times over. She'd dealt and defeated cancer many times before I met her. And during the thirteen years of our friendship, she would battle cancer again. And again.

At first, my breath caught when she told us that cancer was back. I thought surely no one could survive it again. And my heart ached for her, for her family and for the daughter she loved so very dearly.

But Liz hadn't survived the beast for as many times as she had to ever go down lightly. She cheerfully waded into the fray and I was astonished by just how strong and courageous she was. She kept us updated, and never did she express doubt or fear to us. She made her treatment and the highs and lows funny and amusing. Attacking life with the wit and charm that was so much a part of who Liz was.

During the thirteen years of our friendship, it seemed she was always battling health issues in one form or fashion. When attending a writing conference, she fell, and her bones, weakened by the repeated rounds of chemotherapy broke and yet she attended the rest of the conference in a wheel chair. Just further proof of her indomitable spirit.

Liz taught me so much during the years of our friendship. After awhile I no longer got that churning in my gut or the knot in my throat that usually accompanied the news that cancer was back. I believed her invincible. She'd proven time and time again that she wouldn't go down without one hell of a fight.

She taught me courage. The deep abiding kind, to face down one's worst fears and come out triumphant. She taught me patience. She taught me friendship and love. She taught me faith in the absence of anything to believe in. She taught me to live every single day and cherish it as the true gift it is. To never take anything for granted and to live—and love—holding nothing back.

She taught me to tackle life. And my demons. My doubt. My insecurities. She made me a stronger person just from knowing her and witnessing her triumph in the face of adversity time and time again. She taught me to never say quit. Never to surrender. Never to give up.

I learned so much from Liz and my life was enriched just by knowing her. And having the gift of her friendship. One I will be forever grateful for.

The last time she let us know that cancer was back. Again. I didn't worry overmuch. I took it in stride and told myself, she'll beat it. She always does.

This last time she didn't. I'm heartbroken and I grieve the loss of such a wonderful role model. She leaves behind a legacy, her daughter, who will always know her mother loved her with every breath in her body. She leaves behind friends, who will always honor her memory and keep close her spirit and her will to live.

To say she is an inspiration is an understatement for which there are no other words to replace it with. She was the epitome of strength. A more courageous, strong-willed woman I have never known.

This book, published after her passing, is her final gift to us all. She worked hard to finish when she knew her time was fast approaching. And so we, her friends, took up the mantle, collected her words so the rest of the world could share in the same gift we enjoyed for so many years.

It's with a heavy heart, that I bid her farewell to her in her parting gift. But knowing that she lives on through the pages of her final story brings me comfort because when I want to feel her, all I have to do is open her book and visit her through the pages.

Good journey, my friend. You loved dearly and you were dearly loved. I take heart in knowing you are now looking down on us from heaven and that you are never far from our hearts or minds.

This is our, your friends', final gift to you so that your legacy will live forever. Go with God and dance among angels. My life was blessed to have had you in it.

Love always,

Maya Banks

Chapter One

It was time to go home.

My final task was complete and I was finally free. I was tired, so very tired. After better than a hundred years on the road, I wanted nothing more than to lie down for the next hundred years and sleep. Do nothing. Think of nothing. No more duties. No more obligation.

The warmth of the fire toasting my feet was a small comfort on this chilly evening. The smell of burning applewood nearly drowned out the scent of tobacco, bodies that hadn't seen soap in weeks, and the smell of the meal served earlier. The main taproom of the Crossroads Inn was a little overly warm, but it was a welcome change from the conditions I'd endured these past years.

Glancing over the patrons scattered throughout the sizable room, I marked each. Some I recognized from the last time I'd passed through Memis, and others were new faces. All appeared well known to the proprietor.

Allowing my glance to continue around the room, I noted the small changes and additions to the taproom. Rich rosewood paneling covered the lower half of the walls, while white plaster rose above it, portions covered with murals of hunting and wildlife. I'd created most of them over a hundred years ago and made them masculine to fit the decor. The preservation spell was still active. It was good to see they were still there, just as rich and vivid as the day I'd created them. I was rather proud of this work.

A long bar ran along the width of the room, lovingly polished to a rich patina. The proprietor, Master Sherwood, served the half-dozen patrons seated along its length. He was a big man, bald, with a pair of gold-rimmed spectacles perched on his nose. Despite his size, much of his bulk was muscle. Few people would mess with Amos Sherwood more than once.

I automatically checked the proximity of my weapons. One could never be too careful in this day and age. The numerous small throwing blades strapped into the caisson crossing my chest were comforting, as were the straps that held longer sheathed knives high on my thighs. My sword, fashioned to resemble the long-ago katana, was belted at my waist, and a longbow was propped against my chair, the quiver of arrows within easy reach.

About to raise my mug of warmed ale to my lips, I was momentarily distracted by the opening of the door, which brought with it a gust of chilled wind. Pulling my cloak closer, I huddled farther down into my chair, making sure my hood concealed my face. The last thing I needed was for someone to take note of my Sithi features or the white hair streaked with golden-brown. I didn't feel like throwing up a glamour. It wasn't necessary here at the Crossroads Inn. Or, I should say, it'd never used to be necessary. Times changed, as I well knew.

For the most part, the people of Memis were tolerant of my presence provided I didn't flaunt my heritage. This way we could all pretend they were within their Church strictures if they ignored the Sithi in their midst. A little hypocritical, but, hey, it worked for me.

Stretching my feet closer to the flames, I ignored the closing of the door, allowing myself to become mesmerized, lulled into a soothing semi-consciousness as I blocked out the sounds and smells of the taproom. The flames danced in the grate, sparks swirling upward to wink out. A part of me relaxed into my comfortable chair, while another part was fully cognizant to my surroundings.

Mine wasn't the only chair positioned before a hearth big enough to roast a cow. There were three others, but only one was occupied by a graybeard mumbling softly into his mug of ale.

The gloom of the early evening and the steady patter of rain against the windows fit my mood perfectly. There was going to be a storm later, a bad one. My senses warned me that this was not a night to be traveling, which was fine with me. I was perfectly happy within the comfort of the inn. The low murmur of voices blended in with the shuffle of cards and click of the chess pieces. There was no music tonight. No dancing. It was a night of quiet solitude.

I cradled the mug in my hands but made no move to raise it again. Mulled wine might have been a better choice on a night like this, but right now I really didn't care. I was tired. The only thing I wanted was a place to warm my sorry butt. If I managed a little bit of a buzz, that was fine with me. Although it would take considerably more ale to get a Sithi drunk. Something in our metabolism pretty much put the kibosh on our getting sloshed.

Staring into the flickering flames, I contemplated my next move. It was well past time to return to the Lake Country and pay my respects to my ruler in Minneson City. Queen Tesina and I could exchange our usual barbs, I'd push my luck with some smart-ass comment, and she would once again try to banish me from the court, which I would, of course, ignore. I'd hang around the court long enough to piss her off some more, and then I'd head for my home.

A small smile curved my lips. Sounded like a plan to me.

I'd been away for far too long. After better than a hundred years, I didn't even want to think about the condition of my home right now. Without renewal, a preservation spell only went so far, and this many years of neglect would be stretching it.

Perhaps Dylan had returned. My brother's son had gone

missing several years before I left Minneson City over a century
ago, and I hadn't heard anything from or about him since. I was
beginning to worry. He was a difficult man at best, but as the only
living relative leftover from my human life, I tended to be a little
overly protective. Something that annoyed him to no end.

The booted step crossing the length of the taproom distracted
me from my thoughts, and I turned my attention on the
newcomer, watching as he approached Amos Sherwood. His
cloak was soaking wet, drops of water falling to the floor with soft
splats. No one else would be able to catch the sound, but my ears
were far superior to those of a human.

Despite my desire for solitude, I turned my head slightly to
watch the small figure as he stopped at the gleaming bar and
dropped a backpack onto the floor. Amos paused in his polishing
of a pewter cup.

"I've come seeking aid, sir." The voice was young, a faint
tremble betraying anxiety. I returned my attention to the fire.
None of my business.

Queen Tesina was sure to have received word concerning
Dylan by now. Getting the information out of her might be tricky
since she knew how worried I was about him. She might withhold
any news out of sheer spite.

"I was told that one of the Sithi folk frequents this inn."
Desperation colored the young voice and jerked me back to the
present.

This time my pointy little ears did prick up. From the depths of
the hood, I turned once again to look at the small figure standing
at the bar. He was leaning forward, hands braced on the rounded
edging, knuckles whitened with the force of his grip. From this
distance, I could see a thick golden ring on one finger, but I
couldn't quite make out the inscription. It was the custom among
nobility to wear a ring to identify their house. A faint touch of
curiosity stirred within me. What would a young noble be doing

in a modest tavern such as the Crossroads on a night like this? And from all indications, alone. And looking for a Sithi, of all people. Not a smart thing to do here in Memis, where the Church frowned … hell, despised, anything to do with Sithi.

With an effort, I quashed the germ of interest but kept my attention on the pair.

Amos Sherwood resumed his polishing, setting the cup on the shelf behind the bar, which already held a number of similar mugs. He glanced in my direction before he smoothly removed an empty mug from under another patron's hand and returned it filled.

"You heard wrong, lad."

From the shadows of my hood, I watched as young shoulders slumped in despair, and I realized something. This was no lad. Opening my senses, I used a touch of magic to confirm my suspicions. Yep, definitely female. Curious. It wasn't uncommon for a young woman to wear the clothing of a boy, but I did notice that the plain cloak was of a fine material, the hose well fitting and snugged into a pair of well-crafted boots. Judging by the amount of mud edging the bottom of her cloak and marring the shine of those boots, the girl had traveled far today. It had been raining for much of the afternoon, and the material was nearly soaked through, dark gray at the shoulders, then lightening where she'd been sitting a mount. There was a bulge at her waist. At least she was smart enough to travel while armed.

Over the girl's head, Amos glanced my way for a second time. Our eyes met for a brief instant, and he raised one bushy brow. I shook my head, a slight movement.

No. I'd been gone from my lands for too long. The last thing I wanted to do when I was so close to returning was get mixed up with some human drama.

The barkeep gave the girl a *sorry, can't help you* shrug.

I turned back to the fire. I'd been coming to the Crossroads Inn for centuries. The Sherwoods had established it better than six hundred years ago and passed it down, always keeping it within the family. They appreciated my patronage and, in the past, valued my defense of the inn. Centuries ago, I'd placed a spell on the premises designed to alert me should the need arise. Times weren't always this peaceful, and there was always riffraff roaming the countryside. They knew my aid would be extended to them when needed.

Since not everyone was tolerant of my kind, the arrangement between us suited me. We'd learned caution in our association.

Which begged the question of how someone knew to look for one of the Sithi here in Memis. Amos and I didn't advertise my patronage of the Crossroads Inn, and seeing how it was only in the last few months I'd begun visiting this inn again after a decade-long absence, someone was pretty well informed.

A slight movement to my left showed the graybeard nodding off, his chin drooping against his chest, his breathing deep and even. I leaned forward to catch his mug before he could drop it and set it on the stone hearth. He also appeared to be a seasoned traveler. Very well seasoned. I tried not to draw too deep of a breath. My sensitive nose told me he hadn't seen a bath in a good number of weeks. His cloak was dry and of a fine wool but showed signs of long use, stained in numerous places. The gray, nearly white hair was long, tangled, and blending in with the full beard that covered the lower part of his face and trailed over his chest. His eyes were closed, but there were fine lines radiating out at the corners. Despite the gray hair, it was difficult to guess his age.

I'm not sure what, but something made me open my senses to him. There was a strong taste of power to him. Sithi power. Not an ordinary old man. A mixed blood, possibly a wizard. Interesting. I'd never seen him here in the inn before. Memis was a small town where most of the inhabitants knew each other. Odd that not one but two strangers had appeared. Both on the same day as I.

Watching the old man for another moment, I heard a soft snore and smiled slightly. Nice try, but he was as alert as I was. His feigned sleep would fool most everyone, but I wasn't just anyone. I was a full-blooded Sithi. One of the eldest. An ancient.

"Sir, can you tell me where I might find the Sithi folk?"

"Look, lad. The only way you'll be findin' Sithi in Florida is if they be passin' through. The Church don' look kindly 'pon them, so they don' tend to linger around here."

"But I've come so far. I couldn't enter the Lakeland without a guide. I tried, but the mists kept turning me away."

Damn! The little fool must really be desperate to attempt to pierce the mists of our lands. To do so without an invitation and a guide was suicide. Humans risked madness and death if they persisted.

I was going to be stupid and do something, wasn't I?

Against my better judgment, I got to my feet and crossed the taproom until I was standing next to the girl. I'd deliberately left my mug behind and gestured to Amos to provide me with a new one. He gave me a long, questioning look before he turned and drew a fresh drink from the tapped barrel behind him and set it down before me. Resting my elbows on the bar, I cradled the brimming mug between my hands. Amos cast a final glance at the girl before he moved to the far end of the bar to give us some privacy. Now that I was this close, I could feel the despair radiating off the small figure at my side. There was no mistaking her desperation.

"Dangerous thing, lad, to seek the Sithi folk," I murmured into my mug, turning far enough to study the girl. I could now see that her ring was of a thick gold, the insignia of an eagle etched into it. I recognized it.

This was getting worse and worse. Not only was she a

Newland noble, but she was a member of the Sterling family. Far from home and deep within Florida territory. This mystery was deepening and captured my interest despite myself.

I was careful to keep my features concealed within the shadows of my hood. I considered casting a glamour to conceal my true features, but the energy expended would further tire me. My Lady granted magical strength in times of need, not for unnecessary disguises.

The girl glanced at me and away. The hood of her cloak fell to her shoulders, giving me a glimpse of a pale face, dark smudges under large blue eyes. Her posture screamed of exhaustion as she slumped against the bar beside me, dropping her head into her hands for a moment before she scrubbed her hands through her shorn hair.

"I don't know what to do anymore," she whispered even as she raised her head to peer toward the door, her expression fearful. "Finding the Sithi was my only hope."

"What's so important that you seek the Fair Ones?"

My question regained her attention, and she darted another glance at me, trying to see past my hood. "Are you with the Church?"

Despite myself, I snorted. Finally, she was showing some caution. If the notion wasn't so laughable, I would be insulted. Yeah, right. Me, with the Church. They'd sooner burn me at the stake than welcome me with open arms.

The Sithi and the Church didn't see eye to eye. Ever since the Lady had supplanted their One God in the grand scheme of things, the Church took a dim view toward my kind. The Church of the One God kept a tight lid on their secrets. Particularly the one where their One God was no longer the deity in charge. He'd had his chance with this world. Now it was his sister's turn. And for the past thousand years, She'd done a damn fine job.

Not that I had anything against the One God. Hell, I used to worship him myself. When I was human. But I'd made my choice, and while I may have had a few … scratch that … many second thoughts, deep down, I don't regret choosing to follow My Lady.

"No. I'm not with the Church. I'm merely a traveler like yourself." Only half my attention was on my words. Something distracted me, something wrong. Extending my senses, I sent out a probe, casting about for the dark miasma I detected beyond these walls. Something I hadn't felt in centuries.

I turned toward the heavy oak door, my guard up. My nostrils flared, but I couldn't catch the scent of anything beyond the woodsmoke, spilled ale, and the other usual smells associated with the inn. But my skin crawled with an instinct of wrongness. A wrongness that grew with every second.

"I—Get down!"

I shouted out the words as the door burst open. Dark shadows, accompanied by the driving rain, flowed into the room, moving with a lethal grace.

I shoved the girl down even as I flung off my cloak and drew my sword from its scabbard with one hand and a knife the length of my arm from the sheath on my thigh. Crouching, I faced the shadows. Their shapes were insubstantial to the mortal gaze, but my Sithi eyes saw their true selves. Misshapen, they appeared to be the size of a grown man, but it was a form of glamour. They were actually taller than I was, topping me by a head.

Unaware that their disguise had been compromised, they ignored me, their full attention on the girl cowering behind me.

I flung out my free hand, and my power arced out, the light of My Lady covering the creatures and collapsing their disguise. Audible gasps and screams sounded all around me as they were revealed. Enormous, their muscled bulk was nearly naked. Their only clothing leather trousers. The color of mud, most of their exposed flesh was covered with hair too sparse to be called fur. Their faces were shaped wrong, nearly smooth and without individual features. Their eyes slits of red, almost no nose, and a gap for a mouth. I caught a glimpse of sharp teeth.

Skori! The Cursed Ones.

My presence took them by surprise, and they cowered back from my Sithi light. That instant of hesitation was their fatal mistake. Using the skill born of centuries of practice, I swung my sword in an arch and neatly beheaded the first one, black blood spewing in an arc to paint one of my murals. Without waiting for the body to fall, I turned my attention to the second, twisting on my heel to rip my short knife in an undercutting arch, and neatly disemboweled it. Black blood and intestine spurted from the wound, an acrid smell filling the room with an unspeakable stench. The sound the creature made as it fell was nightmarish.

Before I could whip around to face the third, the graybeard at the hearth came to life. Snatching up a staff from where it rested against his chair, he swung it out before him. A bright blue light flared from the clear stone in the tip and caught the third Skori full in the chest. As the light sank into it, the creature writhed in agony before it was consumed.

I didn't spare the old man much more than a glance before I turned my attention toward the door. These had been the vanguard. More Skori were coming. At a distance still, but moving at an abnormally swift pace.

Not good.

I focused on the night, pausing only long enough to wipe my weapons against the leather trousers of one of the dead before I re-sheathed them. Looking over the sprawled bodies, I opened my senses to assure myself they were all dead. You couldn't always be too sure with the servants of the Dark Brother. Unless the wounds were fatal, they were able to heal most anything.

I glanced around to find the girl still crouched beside the bar, her sword clutched in her hand. So, not completely clueless. Blue eyes were wide with terror as she stared down at the dead creatures littering the floor. Amos was just coming around the end of the bar, a mug still clutched in his hand. Beyond cries of alarm, the other patrons of the inn hadn't had time to move, everything had happened so quickly. I reached down and grabbed the girl's arm, pulling her upright. The Skori had focused on her. She was the target of their hunt.

"Come, we must leave here," I whispered as I steadied her. She wrenched her gaze from the dead creatures, raising it to my face as my words penetrated her shock. When I was sure I had her full attention, I turned to Amos. "Creatures of darkness, Amos. There are more approaching. We will lead them away from your inn. The Lady bless you, my friend."

Without waiting for his response, I paused only long enough to snatch up the rest of my gear from where I'd left it beside the fire. A quick glance around found that the wizard had vanished without a trace. No time to track him down. Yanking the girl with me, I hurried through the oak doors as she fumbled to re-sheath her sword. I hated to leave this mess for Amos to clean up, but the sense of wrongness grew. If we moved quickly, we might outrun it. Maybe.

Plunging into the night, I ignored the driving rain. I raced across the worn cobblestones that separated the inn from the stables, my footing sure as I supported the girl when she slipped on the rain-slick stones. We were both soaked in seconds. A quick glance showed black clouds roiling overhead while lightning streaked across the sky, followed by the growl of thunder.

This was not normal. My senses had predicted a storm, but nothing of this magnitude.

The storm was a herald. Something was coming. Something that needed the shroud of night.

The stable doors were closed tight. I paused only long enough to lift the latch and push them open. My horse nickered as she sensed my presence, rousing the other animals bedded down for the night. Only a small lantern illuminated the dozen or so stalls within the stable. The scent of straw and manure was heavy on the air, sweet and sour at the same time. The pounding rain beat against the slate roof, but the sound was soothing within the warmth of the stable.

"Which is your mount?"

"The third stall," the girl said, her voice a thread of sound. A glance at her showed a grayish tinge to her face as she swayed on her feet. Impatience ate at me. There wasn't time to cater to her trauma. Callous of me? Probably. But the things that were approaching weren't going to wait on human hysterics. They were definitely going to add to them if they caught up with us.

"Stay here." I pushed her down onto a bale of hay and headed for the stall she'd indicated, snagging the tack balanced on the stall door. The girl wasn't going to be of much use in saddling the horses. Her gelding was a nondescript dun but with fine formations. He was built for speed and endurance. Both of which we were going to need. Unfortunately, it looked like he'd already been well used today. There was a feel of weariness about the beast.

Nevertheless, I wasted little time in saddling her mount and leading him out of the stall. The inn grooms had brushed him down and watered him earlier, but he could still use a good night's rest. Unless I found a replacement, that wasn't going to happen. I eyed the other three horses occupying the stable, but other than a pale gray, none of them possessed the fine lines of her gelding. I started toward the gray.

"You aren't thinking of stealing my horse, are you?"

I whirled around, my sword in my hand in an instant. In the faint glow of the lantern, I saw the graybeard standing at the entrance of the stables, backlit by a flash of lightning. Water ran down his face and into the tangle of his beard, dripping from his cloak onto the stone floor. A saddlebag and other gear were slung over one shoulder while he held a tall staff topped by the now-dull stone in the other hand.

He stood still as I gleamed with magic, my power building a defense against any attack he might offer. It was disturbing that I hadn't heard, or sensed, his approach.

A well-trained wizard, then. Adept at concealing his presence. I eyed his staff with caution even as I answered him. Although the stone was dull, it didn't mean he was defenseless.

"The thought crossed my mind."

"I'll have need of her if we are to escape those foul creatures."

"We?"

"Yes, you'll need my help."

"Will I?" I allowed my skepticism to show and lowered my sword slightly, caution radiating from the pit of my stomach. I wasn't about to put up my weapon until I was certain of the direction of his alliance. Wizards were tricky. The reasons behind their actions weren't always clear.

And they didn't necessarily act in your favor.

"You need to get this girl to safety. I can help."

"You think so?"

"I know what's chasing her."

The girl, who had been silent until now, roused from where she'd been slumped on the bale of hay. In the faint light, her eyes were haunted, her face devoid of all color, but grim determination straightened her shoulders.

"Those things … they were after me, weren't they?" To give her credit, there was no longer a tremor in her voice. Her gaze was steady as she watched me sheath my weapon. "You're the Sithi I was seeking."

"So it would seem."

"The innkeeper knew."

"He knew."

She drew a deep breath and got to her feet, coming forward to take the reins of her gelding while I tied her pack to the saddle. She ran her hand over the horse's neck, calming it with a soft touch. Perhaps the effect was beneficial to them both.

"For the past month, I've been traveling, searching for the Sithi."

I wanted to ask why but refrained. My head went up, a hound sniffing the wind. No time. I glanced at the wizard.

"If you're determined to accompany us, old man, get your horse ready. We're leaving here with or without you."

For a man of his aged appearance, the wizard moved with surprising speed. He had the gray saddled and was mounted by the time I'd led Mysteria from her stall and gotten her ready. The Sithi horse danced with eagerness as I led her to the open stable doors, directing her through with a gentle hand. Her head tossed with impatience and pulled against the reins. She sensed what was closing in on us.

The storm hadn't let up in the short time we were in the stable. If anything, the rain came down harder. Lightning flashed across the sky, followed almost immediately by thunder. The girl's horse shied, but Mysteria and the wizard's mount never flinched. I led my horse into the rain, her footing sure on the sleek cobblestones.

We were again instantly drenched. It wasn't like we could get any wetter, and we were in for a miserable night. In more ways than one.

"Mount up," I directed the girl, waiting until she scrambled into the saddle and took up her reins. I grabbed hold of the bridle and led the gelding until we came to the stone bridge that spanned the river. During the summer, you could wade across the short expanse of water, but now, with the spring rains and the melt-off from the mountains, it ran high, the water black on this stormy night.

The roar of the river concealed our passage over the stone bridge. No need for stealth, but the fewer who marked our departure, the better. The citizens of Memis were a good lot, for the most part, but there were several families who would take coin to divulge information on anything out of the ordinary. Not that the creatures following us would offer currency. They tended to kill first and ask questions later.

It didn't take long to pass beyond the borders of town and into the surrounding farmland. In the murky darkness, it was difficult even for me to see the fields, lying fallow now but soon to be planted with the spring crop.

The road leading north was wide and normally hard-packed, but the rain had turned the surface slick with mud, the hooves of the horses sinking with a sucking sound with each step. Not that I had any intention of remaining on this road. It was too obvious. About ten miles distant, I knew of a smaller road that branched off the main thoroughfare and led into the dark forests. Not many people chose that route. Particularly at night. Vicious creatures inhabited these ancient forests. Or so it was whispered.

During the final days of the Great Waste, some enterprising survivors had thought it a humane gesture to free the animals from the zoos. Since then, this continent had become a natural habitat for exotic animals originally from Asia and Africa. Tigers were not an uncommon sight, along with the normal fare of wolves, cougars, and other smaller carnivores. In the Plains of Jordan—once Kansas, Nebraska, and Oklahoma—gazelle, impala, zebras, and wildebeest had turned the breadbasket of America into an African savannah to be shared with vast herds of buffalo and native antelope. I'd even seen a herd of elephants in what was formerly Southern Texas. It was amazing how easily these animals adapted to the North American continent in a thousand years.

Dangerous as it was, though, for my purposes, this route would have to do. Not ideal, but with luck, our trail would be faint, and if the creatures following us had trackers, our scent should be washed away by the rain. Maybe. Hopefully.

Our horses moved swiftly through the night. I made sure we alternated between a fast walk and a trot. The last thing I wanted was for one of them to come up lame when the necessity of speed became imminent. Within the hour, the storm gradually decreased until it died to a steady drizzle. My eyesight allowed me to see that the dark clouds were moving to the south. A few stars emerged from the remaining tattered clouds. Was this a sign that we'd lost our pursuers? Hard to tell. I'd been viewing the unnaturalness of the storm as a cover for the creatures of darkness.

None of us spoke until we reached the turnoff a short time later. The gelding was holding up fairly well, while the wizard's mare showed no sign of lagging. I pulled up and glanced behind us, sending out my senses and searching for anything abnormal in the night. Everything appeared … no. I closed my eyes to better concentrate. There! My senses touched something foul. It was distant but unmistakable.

The Skori were still on the trail. Damn.

"Come," I said as I turned my mount into the dark forest. I gathered a minuscule portion of my power and created a ball of light. I held it aloft in my hand, and it illuminated the narrow trail ahead of us. We had to travel single file. I led, the girl followed, and the wizard brought up the rear. I still wasn't sure about the wizard, but I'd rather he stood between the girl and the creatures that followed us. Whatever his reasons for accompanying us, I could sense no evil in him. Wizards were able to mask their true nature from most Sithi, but I was an ancient. None would be able to fool me.

However, just because I sensed no evil in him didn't mean he didn't have his own agenda. One that didn't necessarily mesh with mine. Wizards were loyal to their One God. No one else.

The forest closed around us, the trail so narrow that, at times, low branches brushed against us on either side. Rotted leaves left over from the fall muffled the hooves of our horses, each step sending up the scent of decay to mingle with the freshness of rain. The trees grew thick enough to shield us from the remaining drizzle. I could hear the girl's breathing behind me, quick and frightened. She had reason to fear. The dark creatures had not stirred from the north in hundreds of years. The followers of the Dark Brother had always appeared content with the North Country.

Curious that none of our Rangers had reported activity. Word would have flown far and wide had there been a hint of the Skori on the move. It also made me worry for them.

"Where are we going?" The girl finally found her voice. Mindful of the inhabitants of the forest, she kept it low.

"North for now. I want to get out of Florida and into Newland. From there … you tell me. You are the one seeking the Sithi." I turned and glanced back at her. She sat in her saddle straight, her hands sure on the reins. An experienced rider. Good. "Would you care to tell me why?"

"I need to find a Sithi named Riona. No one I spoke with could tell me where to find her, so I decided to seek out the Fair Folk, hoping to get a message to her."

My mind blanked for a moment as I stared at her without speaking. Life was full of curious coincidences. Normally, I didn't believe in them, but every once in a while, Fate—or my Lady— decided to step in and deal directly with the lives of mortals and immortals.

Had My Lady led this mortal to me? Possibly. One rarely knew the workings of my deity.

"I am Riona Northstar, girl."

I watched her face as I gave her the name I now went by. Saw her shock and heard her gasp. My glance went beyond her to the wizard, but he met my gaze with calm. He betrayed no surprise.

Had he known?

"Then you are the Sithi I seek." Hope came to her pale face. Excitement animated it. "I'm told you are a friend to Newland. That you are a friend to the Sterling family."

"You heard correctly, child. Although I have not seen King Ambrose for a number of years, he holds my best regard."

"My name is Merry. Meredith Sterling, and I need your help."

Now it was my turn to feel shock, although I knew no such emotion crossed my face.

Damn, this was one of my direct descendants.

Chapter Two

I should have sensed the girl's connection to me. Meredith Sterling was my great-great-great-whatever-granddaughter. I stared at her for another moment, then turned to face the darkness of the forest once more. I'd had centuries of practice controlling my expressions, but this time I wasn't too sure that I'd succeeded. Certainly the glimpse I had of the wizard's face revealed an expression of thoughtfulness.

"Why do you need the help of a Sithi?" I asked without turning my head. The forest was quiet enough that my words were clearly audible above the muffled horse hooves. An owl hooted somewhere in the night, a rustle in the undergrowth where a forest inhabitant crouched in silence as we passed. The wind had died along with the rain, the drip of moisture almost soothing after the fury of the storm.

"Someone or something is killing my family."

Her words caused me to pull Mysteria to a halt, twisting around to face the girl. My mount danced a few steps as she caught my agitation. I ran a soothing hand down her neck until she calmed.

"What are you talking about? Ambrose has four sons and evidently one daughter. The last time I saw your father, you hadn't even been born yet."

"Perhaps …" the wizard said quietly. I glanced toward him to see him staring over his shoulder. "We should discuss this when we have the leisure. I believe our trail has been picked up."

Damn! I cast my senses out, reading the night. The wizard was correct. The Skori had left Memis and were even now setting off down the north road. It wouldn't take them long to locate our trail. Now that the rain had stopped, it would be asking a lot that they missed our turnoff.

"We have to move faster," I said as I put my heels to my mount. Mysteria sprang forward with eagerness, surefooted despite the dark trail. The other two horses followed, catching my urgency. The trail widened and narrowed at intervals, at one time forcing us to dodge low branches that would have swept us from our saddles. The gelding kept the pace fairly well, but he was beginning to lag. His breathing was labored, and he'd stumbled more than once. Drawing on my magic, I felt the warmth of power fill me. With its liquid rush, the night didn't appear as dark and oppressive. Everything came into crystal clarity, a good many of the shadows fading. Drops of water trembled on individual branches, the beauty of nature amplified. The slight breeze was a soothing cacophony that blended in with the beat of our horses' hooves.

Unfortunately, the downside of the infusion of power was that it also allowed me to better feel for the dark creatures behind us. They hadn't reached the turnoff yet, but I sensed perhaps a score in this hunt. And they were moving fast.

This pointed to a single-minded determination to achieve their goal. A goal that apparently involved the girl riding so silently behind me. Merry hadn't said a word since revealing her family was being killed off. That gave me much to think about. Who had been killed? Her brothers? King Ambrose? No, word of the king's death would have flown on the wings of a hawk. I would have thought the death of any of his heirs would have been equally newsworthy. Yet I had heard nothing. Then again, I'd only recently returned from the depths of the southern swamps. Didn't exactly get much news down there.

The thought of harm befalling his sons sent a pang through me. I'd known those boys since were small. The eldest, Edmund, was perhaps fifteen the last time I'd seen him. A bold and clever lad. A fitting heir to his father. At thirteen, Lionel was the next son, quiet and studious. Connor was the most daring of the four boys. At the age of nine, he'd enticed his brothers into countless escapades that were always somehow pulled off. Roderick had only been five the last time I'd visited my descendants, and already a lively lad.

They didn't know, of course, that they were of my line, nor had I ever enlightened them. That was the past. A past I'd left behind over a thousand years ago. Yet somehow I always managed to keep tabs on the Sterlings. They'd been leaders since the survivors had emerged from the dust of the plague, starting with my husband, Ian.

He'd led the ragged band of survivors through those first nightmarish years, keeping us together and reconstructing a healthy society of humans.

With the country of Newland in need of a governing body, the Sterlings had created a monarchy and ascended the throne over eight hundred years ago. They'd proved themselves fit and able rulers, for the most part. Personally, it had been a proud day for me. I'd been there for Henry Sterling's coronation. He'd proven to be a good king and had the good sense to marry a strong woman who made an effective partner and queen. Ian would have been pleased.

"How close are they?" The wizard's words jarred me out of my memories, and I gave myself a shake. Now wasn't the time.

"They haven't reached the turning yet." I wasn't about to count on their missing the trail. Using a thin stream of power, I fed it into the gelding, giving him a much-needed boost of energy. With a toss of his head, he renewed his mile-eating pace, easily keeping up with Mysteria. I monitored the wizard's mare for a moment, but there was no need for aid. The wizard must have been doing that himself.

We couldn't keep this up for long. This pace would eventually kill the horses. But right now, it was far more important to keep ahead of that which pursued us.

A howl rang out through the night. A howl of triumph. It was a sound to freeze the blood in anyone's veins. They'd found our trail. The gelding reacted with a nicker of fear, throwing his head up and nearly yanking the reins from Merry's hands. Even Mysteria quivered.

The forest seemed to hold its breath for a moment, and the inhabitants went still. The stillness of a rabbit against a predator. Of a mouse before an owl. The hope that whatever hunted it would never notice it and pass on. We did not have that luxury.

I tested the air.

"They're gaining on us." The quiet words coming from the wizard weren't a question. I glanced back. He was stroking a hand through his beard as he watched me. He was remarkably calm considering what was pursuing us. The Skori had not been seen this far south in more than nine hundred years. That was the last time the Dark Brother had become impatient with the success of his Sister and sought to supplant Her. We Sithi had dispelled his forces then, and if he was making another bid, we would dispel them again.

"Yes. They're moving incredibly fast. There is no way we can outrun them." I knew there was a river ahead. If we could get across it, we might be safe. The clean wash of river water might deter the creatures.

But time was against us.

I turned to concentrate on the trail ahead. My light illuminated the twists and turns as we rode deeper into the dark forest. This was a portion of an ancient wood. Old even before my human time. It was probably part of a national forest once upon a time ... just outside of Memphis, Tennessee. It had been preserved then and, after the upheaval, had grown ever more potent. There was an old magic here. A magic made even more powerful after a thousand years. A hush filled the air, as if the ancient wood was holding its breath. Or waiting.

We Sithi had no fear of the old forests. It was through our efforts that the ancient wood had been preserved and the newer flourished. Centuries of manmade pollutants had nearly destroyed much of the forests in North America. Our Lady had entrusted us with dispersing the toxins and the restoring the deep woods to their former glory.

Was there enough gratitude remaining in this wood to protect us from the creatures tracking us? Only one way to find out. We came to a slight clearing, a mere widening of the trail, and I pulled to a halt.

Low, a breath of sound, I began to sing, almost too soft to be heard by human ears. I used the language taught to us by Our Lady, a language unheard in eons. I sang of the might of the oak, the suppleness of the willow, the strength of the elm. Of roots sunk deep into the rich soil. I sang of the calm found in the deep pools and the beauty of the meadows adorned in wildflowers. I reminded the forest of what we Sithi had done for it and what we would do in the future. I gave it full honor and pledged my protection. And I begged. Begged for its aid, for its protection.

I sang for long minutes, unmindful of my audience of two. At last my voice fell away to silence. I glanced back and, in the glow of my magic, saw the bemused expression of the girl and the look of admiration given to me by the wizard.

I ignored them both. Had the forest heard me, or was it so deeply asleep that we were going unnoticed? I drew a breath to try again ... then froze.

A groan sounded all around us, the low rumble vibrating the

ground below us. A shiver of movement ran through the leaves, shaking loose droplets of water.

"What is that?" Merry's voice was fearful as she shook off the lingering effects of my song. She tried to look around in all directions at once. The low moan came louder, the rustle of branches as thousands upon thousands of trees reacted. Exhilaration filled me.

I had awakened the forest.

Putting up a hand, I waited in silence. There was no reason to believe the forest would respond to my plea. The ancient woods cared nothing for the fleeting lives of humans and tolerated the Sithi because of our abilities granted to us by Our Lady. We did not make the mistake of instilling human emotions on the inhabitants of the forests. They were alien to mankind. We understood them better, but I would never presume to know their way of thinking. That was impossible.

In the pause, I heard the arrival of the Skori. Suddenly, they were all around us. The horses reacted with fear, dancing in a tight circle as red eyes gleamed at us from the darkness.

I drew my blade. My elven eyes saw them clearly. Saw their massive, heavily muscled yet misshapen figures. They were more animal than human, but human was what they once had been. These were the beings who'd chosen to follow the Dark Brother. The king of lies and destroyer of beauty.

Merry screamed with fear as one pressed closer, its gash of a mouth opening to give a slathering growl of pleasure. Waves of rancid anticipation flowed from it, the red of its eyes gleaming and reflecting the light of my elven glow as its attention centered on the girl.

The wizard moved his mount to guard Merry's back, controlling his horse with ease while he set the butt of his staff in his stirrup, its tip glowing blue. As the light increased, I allowed my elven magic to flare brightly, intent on blinding the creatures, if only temporarily. The combined glow revealed their hideous appearance in stark relief as they stepped into view from between massive tree trunks. Hands that ended in claws reached forward in savage glee, until the light hit them. Shrieking, they flung up their arms to protect their eyes, backing into the shadows once more. I knew the reprieve was temporary. Before long, they would gather their nerve to attack in force. They were too eager to reach Merry.

But as they faded between the trunks of the trees, there came another groan from the forest. The sounds of something solid hitting flesh came from all around us. Increasing the power of my light, it revealed the impossible. The trees were closing in around us, crushing the creatures that huddled in their shadows. Howls and shrieks rose all around, many cut off with a sickening wet sound. The acidic smell of their blood flooded the air around us.

The horses danced around in a milling panic. I controlled Mysteria with the use of my knees as the trees came alive to defend us. Even as I watched, two trees slammed together with a Skori between. Blood and gore spurted from between the trunks like a grape squeezed between two fingers.

I dimmed my light so that Merry would not witness the dark creatures being crushed to death by the broad trunks closing together. My eyes had no trouble picking out the motion of the trees as wide branches swept down to slam into one creature, crushing it, while another was neatly beheaded. The remaining few turned to flee but were caught up in the branches and torn to pieces.

It was a sickening sight, even by my standards. I'd seen a lot of death during my long life, but this caused my stomach to roil. Still, I could find no pity within myself for these beings. They would have spared us no such pity as they ripped us apart.

As far as I could tell, none escaped. The sudden silence that descended was broken only by the creak of branches and the rustle of leaves as the trees resumed their stance. We were surrounded by a solid wall of wood, except for the trail ahead of us, which was clear, widened to allow the moonlight to fall on the smooth surface.

"Come." My words were loud in the sudden silence as I turned my mount toward the beckoning trail. I had no doubt that any creatures remaining in this forest would soon be destroyed. The forest would not tolerate the presence of such foul beings within its borders.

As our horses cantered from the site of the carnage, I could hear the trees closing behind us, cutting off the trail and eradicating any trace of our passing. Merry's quickened breathing was audible, but to give the little human credit, she didn't panic. This had been a sight that no mortal had ever seen before—hell, few Sithi had witnessed such an event. I suspected Merry might be in shock, but we would have to deal with that later.

As we rode, I lifted my voice to sing my gratitude to the ancient forest. My song wove through the trees, the new leaves rustling in the windless night. This time there was a sense of listening as the pure notes melted into the surrounding trees. Never before had I felt so in tune with such an old wood. The weight of its years pressed in on me and made me aware of how young I was when compared to the mighty forest. It was a humbling experience.

I sang for a long time, allowing my voice to fade away as we reached a clearing that led toward a wide river. The moonlight revealed the swift-moving water, the recent storm and winter runoff causing it to overflow its banks. I glanced around the clearing. It would make a good place to spend the night, but despite the knowledge that no Skori remained in this forest, I'd feel better once we had the width of the river between us.

This thought no sooner entered my mind than the wild river appeared to calm, its racing water slowing to gently run over rounded river stones. The moonlight reflected off the now-quiet river, and I smiled. The forest had granted us one last boon.

"Amazing." The word was murmured by the wizard. I glanced over at him and found his attention on the water. He'd pulled his cowl up around his head, and I was hard-pressed to see his face within the shadowed interior.

"Who are you, old man?" Asking the man's name earlier hadn't seemed important. Now that the immediate danger had passed, I'd prefer to know who I was allying myself with.

"Merely a traveler, my lady elf."

"Hardly a mere anything, my lord wizard." I allowed sarcasm to enter my voice. "The power you harness goes far beyond those of a normal wizard. I suspect you're the one they call Finnegan."

His smile was faint, a mere twist of his lips, but he acknowledged my guess with an incline of his head. Now this was interesting. The exploits of Finnegan were legendary. From the western coast of Cascadia to the eastern shores of Newland, his name was whispered, his many feats spoken with awe. I'd heard of his defense of humans over the years and even admiration from my brethren. Something rarely given to a human.

For whatever reasons, I'd never met up with the man. Hardly surprising given the many places I'd been assigned and the fact that I'd just spent the last twenty years in the Everglades of what was once the state of Florida, doing what I could to restore that land to its once-pristine environment. Centuries of storms had reclaimed much of the land that mankind had drained for its use, reducing the Sunshine State to a spit of swampland that extended into the Southern Sea.

"So, what was the great Finnegan doing wasting time in a nondescript inn in the middle of a country that would just as soon throw you in a deep, dark cell?" Which was true. The Church held wizards in high contempt … nearly as high as it held the Sithi. Anyone who didn't kowtow to the party line was suspect, as far as the Bible thumpers were concerned, and wizards were near the top of that list, despite the fact they worshiped the same One God and labored on His behalf.

"I could say I was expanding my horizons."

"But …?"

"I, too, heard rumors that the Crossroads Inn was frequented by a Sithi. You are a difficult people to locate when you don't wish to be found, My Lady Riona."

"I seem to be very popular lately," I murmured before I turned my attention back to the river. It was at a shallow flow now. Safe to cross. Best do it now while the forest was feeling generous. I urged Mysteria forward, guiding her over the now-exposed river stones and into the frigid water. She moved easily, having no trouble seeing by moonlight. The other two horses followed suit. The water barely came up to her forelocks as she daintily sidestepped the larger stones. I was just as glad to avoid another drenching. Our cloaks were still soaked from the earlier storm, and I personally wanted to get dry before we rested for what remained of the night.

Which wasn't much, I decided as I monitored the position of the moon. Dawn was only hours away. I stole a glance behind me at Merry. She'd been riding in silence. Way too quiet. I'd have to do something about that. The main thing right now, though, was getting to the other side of the river. No doubt the river would resume its wild course once we crossed.

Mysteria reached the far side, moving swiftly up the bank and onto dry land. There was a fair-sized clearing before the forest began once more, sparse grasses blanketed by last year's leaves providing a measure of cushioning. The branches of the surrounding trees were leafed out enough to provide some shelter for the night and hopefully had kept much of the earlier storm from drenching the ground. It was as good a place as any to camp. I motioned Finnegan to come closer.

"We'll spend the night here." I shot a glance at the girl. She took no notice of her surroundings, sitting her horse without moving. The gelding stood still, his head hanging low as exhaustion caught up with him, a shiver wracking his body as reaction to the Skori attack swept over him. "I don't like the way Merry is behaving. She's in shock and needs rest."

"I agree."

"After tending the horses, I plan to look around a little bit. I wouldn't suggest leaving this clearing."

"After what I witnessed in the forest? No, my lady, I'm not about to wander far." There was a thread of amusement in his voice as he dismounted. His mare was in far better shape than the gelding, but she, too, showed signs of strain. "Will the forest allow a fire for the night?"

"I believe it will, if it's a small one and well contained."

"Not to worry. I'm not about to incur its wrath." He moved to Merry's side and urged her down with a gentle hand. The girl moved stiffly, seemingly unaware of her surroundings. She still hadn't said a word.

I noted her condition as I dismounted. Yep, she was in shock. However, I needed to ensure our safety before dealing with Merry Sterling.

I secured my glowing elven light at a point above our heads before removing my gear from Mysteria. She wouldn't be much use in the reconnaissance of our surroundings. Besides, she, too, needed time to recover. Sithi bred though she might be, she still suffered from the effects of our wild ride from Memis. Murmuring softly into her ear, I ran my hands down her neck and over her back, using my magic to check her condition. The saddle I used was light, far lighter than those used by humans. A Sithi-bred horse was trained to respond to the thought pattern of her rider. The only other gear I used was a bridle, and this I removed to give her more comfort. Patting her on the neck, I released her to allow her to find fodder.

I moved to Merry's gelding and relieved him of his burden, setting her gear down on the grass. I murmured senseless words to him as I ran a soft cloth over him, using my magic to relax him and heal the ordeal of our flight. He was still skittish from the creatures we'd encountered, but he calmed under my hand.

Giving him one last wipe, I released him to follow Mysteria, trusting that she would keep him near. The wizard had already tended his mare, allowing her to join the other two horses.

"I'll be back shortly. I want to get a feel for our surroundings. See what you can find to build a fire ring." I paused to give weight to my words. "We don't want to upset our host with an uncontrollable fire."

"No. I saw how this forest dealt with unwelcome intruders."

"I'll bring some deadwood back with me." A slight smile curved my lips before I looked at Merry. My smile died. She was sitting in the grass, staring out into the night. "Guard her, wizard."

"With my life."

I gave him a long look, gauging his sincerity. I could detect no subterfuge, but it was hard to tell with wizards. I'd have to trust him. It was important to know what might inhabit this wood besides us. Its ancient awareness might not detect what I would consider a threat.

Without another word, I turned and walked into the darkness of the trees. Enough moonlight filtered through the branches to allow me to see as clearly as if it were day. Sithi eyes were similar to those of a cat. Our pupils expanded to gather in every stray bit of light and gave us the ability to see in near darkness. Only with the true absence of light were we as blind as any human.

I traveled easily through the dense undergrowth, avoiding branches and brackets with the skill of long practice. As I ran, I sent my senses outward, detecting and cataloguing every life-force within the vicinity. The natural inhabitants of the forest were unperturbed by my presence. Deer paused in their grazing to stare after me as I passed. From an overhead branch, an owl followed my passage, his intended prey forgotten. I found signs of fox, martens, numerous rodents, and once, even the still-foreign presence of a Bengal tiger. I carefully pinpointed its location. Tigers were unpredictable at the best of times. Fortunately it was a good distance away and showed no interest in our little party. Picking up a sense of its emotions, I got the impression that it had sensed the dark creatures and was intent on heading in the opposite direction.

Making a circuit of approximately a mile surrounding our camp, I could find nothing of threat. The forest was still awake. I could feel its attention on me as I traveled through it. If I had to put a name to its emotion, I would say it was more curiosity than anything.

I slowed as I neared the river. Pausing at the banks, I could see that it had resumed its natural volume, the low roar of rushing water drowning out the other sounds of the forest. I stared toward the far bank. It would be impossible for anyone or anything to cross the river when it was this swollen. There would be no pursuit from that direction.

Turning my attention in the direction of the camp, I could see the flicker of firelight through the trees. Over the rush of water, I had no problem detecting the low murmur of Finnegan's voice as he spoke to Merry. She made no response that I could hear.

I stood in the dark watching for a good half an hour. It wasn't that I distrusted the wizard. Yet. He was an unknown factor. I'd learned long ago to be sparing in my trust of anyone or anything. Finnegan had his reasons for being in that tavern tonight. And I suspect that Merry had a lot to do with his presence.

It was time to get some answers.

Locating a supply of reasonably dry deadwood, I returned to

the clearing. I deliberately made no sound as I approached, yet the wizard betrayed no surprise when I suddenly appeared on the other side of the fire.

It made me wonder at his abilities to read the life-forces around him. When a Sithi bred with a human, there was really no telling what talents were inherited. In the past, a few wizards had displayed magical abilities so close to those of an elf that the difference was evident only through the absence of the physical features.

"How is she?"

"You were right. She's in shock. The appearance of those things was one thing. Seeing the forest come alive was another."

"I was afraid of that." I squatted down in front of Merry. Even by the firelight, she was pale, her pupils dilated and fixed. The poor kid. She couldn't be much more than seventeen or eighteen. Far too young to have witnessed that which would have affected someone many times her age.

I called forth my magic and moved to take her face between my hands. The gleam of elven light bathed her pale face, revealing her vacant stare and unresponsiveness. A motion from the wizard drew my attention before I could touch her.

"Allow me, my lady. I'm human. She should react to my magic more easily than yours."

Actually, with my familial connection, I probably had a closer tie with Merry Sterling, but still, he had a point. It was true, some humans did respond more easily to human magic rather than Sithi. Chances were good he had more than a touch of Sithi blood in him, but he was human enough for his magic to work better on a mortal than mine. I'd have to do some deep searching to find out whose line mingled with his human blood. Difficult to do if I didn't have his cooperation.

"Very well, Master Finnegan. I need Merry to be coherent. I want answers before we go farther."

He nodded and waited until I moved out of the way. I watched carefully as he took my place and rubbed his hands together, generating the glow of magic. Not the same method as mine, but effective. He took both her hands in one of his and placed his other hand on her head, resting his palm against her forehead. Closing his eyes, he began murmuring a prayer to his One God, allowing the flow of magic to run from his hands into her. The glow traveled up her arms and passed over her chest, spreading from where his palm rested to encompass her head. For a moment, they both shimmered with the wizard's blue power.

An impressive display. I'd not seen such power in a human in centuries. Could be that most of the stories surrounding the wizard Finnegan hadn't been exaggerated.

For the count of a dozen heartbeats, neither moved. Then Merry drew a deep breath, and her eyes widened as animation returned to her face. She stared into the elder face before her, tears filling her eyes as full awareness returned to her. Her sharply indrawn breath was a gasp of sound, and a sob escaped her.

"What were those things?" Her words were faint, trembling to near incoherence. This was a delicate moment. Finnegan had retrieved her mind from whatever dark corner it had fled to, but too much backlash could send it right back. Her consciousness had reacted in self-defense, shutting down rather than accepting. Merry must have led a very sheltered life. That she'd traveled from Canada City to Memis without incident was incredible. And that she'd attempted to enter the Lakelands pointed to a determination to succeed.

I knelt beside Finnegan. Her gaze moved to my face, seeking something ... some reassurance, perhaps.

"They are called Skori." I kept my voice calm, careful to reveal nothing in my expression. "Normally they live far to the north. We have Rangers monitoring their activities, but evidently they somehow managed to slip past."

"The trees …"

"Protected us." I took her hand. She had to understand. One way or another. Her cold fingers tightened around mine in a death grip. I could feel the remnant of the wizard's magic flowing over her. It reacted and then melded with my own. It was a familiar magic. Something I needed to analyze later.

"The forest holds no tolerance for such foul creatures, Merry. I asked it to give us aid, and it did."

"It came alive."

"Every forest is alive, child. That is something to be grateful for."

Closing her eyes, she drew a shuddering breath, and then her grip eased. I relaxed a fraction. She was past the worst. There was acceptance.

"Rest now, child." I urged her toward the blankets Finnegan had set out near the fire and made sure she was comfortable. The flickering flames cast shadows over her still-pale face, enormous blue eyes staring up at me. "We have a long way to go."

"You'll come with me to Canada City?"

Kneeling on the damp ground beside her, I considered the whispered request. I'd been gone from my lands for so long, and I was so very weary. Did I really want to involve myself with humans again? No. Personally I'd had enough of them to last me a couple of lifetimes. But looking into her shadowed eyes, seeing the desperation there, how could I refuse? She was descended of my line. I wanted to ask what she'd meant when she'd said earlier that her family was being killed off, but now wasn't the time. She'd just gotten over a double shock of seeing a horde of Skori descend upon us and then witnessed the forest come alive. It was enough to drive anyone to the brink of madness. She needed time to recover before I began questioning her.

"I'll come."

My simple answer appeared to reassure her. Relief replaced the desperation, and she smiled slightly before closing her eyes. Her hand curved under her cheek like a child, but the other gripped the edge of her blanket in a show of tension. I waited several minutes until her hand relaxed and I knew by her even breathing that she'd fallen asleep. Exhaustion had taken its toll.

I glanced over at Finnegan and motioned him out of earshot. Just in case. "That was a large band to have traveled this far south without detection. Any thoughts?"

"They had help."

I inclined my head. "Agreed. The question is … who?"

"Much as I hate to implicate my own people, the Church?"

"Unlikely. Bishop Langley is an ambitious man, but I doubt he'd condone aiding the minions of the Dark Brother."

"You might be surprised, my lady Riona." Finnegan shot a glance at the sleeping girl and lowered his voice further. "Bishop Langley has changed much in these past dozen years. He has been casting a covetous eye toward Newland. The Church is strong there, but he personally has little hold on that country. I believe he sees himself as the savior of the uneducated masses who openly consort with the heathens."

"Heathens meaning the Sithi, of course."

"Of course."

In my opinion, Bishop James Langley had always been a fool. But even fools could be dangerous. And misguided. If the Dark Brother had somehow managed to influence the head of the human Church, there was no telling what He could accomplish. Of the three siblings, the Dark Brother was the most dangerous. The One God was benevolent, for the most part, with bouts of occasional petulance. If you could call forty days and forty nights of rain a tantrum. My Lady Goddess was practical where her dealings with mankind were concerned. She had created us Sithi to return and maintain the natural balance of the world after her brother's debacle with the industrial age.

But the Dark Brother, or Dark Master, as he was also known ...
I shuddered. He was pure evil. So far, his two siblings had
managed to keep him in check for eons. I didn't know all that
much about him, but when I'd been human, he'd been the Satan
of my religious belief. Now that I'm more educated in the higher
deities, he was in a class of his own. The Skori who followed him
were a dim reflection of his true nature. I considered it fortunate
that the Sithi far outnumbered the Skori and that the humans were
even more populous. The followers of the Dark Master were
dangerous, powerful creatures, but their magic was weak when
compared to ours. What they lacked in magical ability, they made
up in animalistic strength and sheer brutality.

Was Bishop Langley in league with the Dark Master? I'd been
absent from the world of humans for so long I'd lost touch with
their present politics. Twenty years ago, Langley had been a rabid
advocate for the eradication of the "heathen Sithi" and of the
wizards, whom he called "half-breed abominations." However,
he'd kept his attentions focused on the country of Florida, which,
for the most part, tolerated our existence provided we were subtle
when passing through.

"Do you know what Merry was talking about when she
claimed the ruling family of Newland was being killed?"

"The Sterlings have always been a friend to the Sithi and to the
wizards. All four sons of King Ambrose have either been killed or
have disappeared."

I felt his words like a blow to my heart but was careful to
betray no reaction. I'd known those boys since they were children
...

"There is rumor that the slaughter was done by the Sithi."

"What?"

"A rumor put out by the Church, I suspect."

What a surprise.

"What actually happened?" I asked.

"Three have been slain by … something. Most likely by the Skori." His voice was steady. His dark eyes went to the sleeping girl, and something that could have been tenderness crossed his lined face before he erased the expression and continued. "All on the same eve, as far as I know. Roderick was home with his wife and two sons. None survived. Lionel was hunting in the deep forest and his body found by his companions, torn to pieces as if by a wild beast. They say his wife and son have disappeared, and I can only assume they were also killed. Edmund, Ambrose's eldest son, was cut to pieces and delivered to his father in a basket."

"What of Connor?"

"No one has heard from him. I suspect he is dead as well."

I watched his face. I didn't bother using my magic to probe the validity of his words. He was too tightly shielded to allow me to see into his heart. Our flight had blown his grayed hair into a wild mass, mingling with the heavy beard to conceal much of his expression. Only his dark eyes revealed his emotions. They burned with a combination of worry and anger. Anger for the loss of four members of the ruling family? What was his connection to King Ambrose's sons?

I turned my attention on Merry, watching her as she slept. She was too young to shoulder this responsibility. I nodded in her direction.

"Where was she?"

"Merry lived in the castle and was closely guarded. About a month ago, she slipped away in search of help. The help of the Sithi. She believes only the Fair Ones can save her family, and her country." The wizard paused and appeared deep in thought. The flickering light from the fire chased shadows over his face, both concealing and revealing at the same time. "There are dark happenings around this country lately, my lady. Whispers of betrayal and murder. People have gone missing, never to be found, and too many unexplainable sightings of unspeakable creatures … no doubt these Skori, as you name them. I suspect they are the cause of much of this unrest."

"And there has been no investigation?"

"Some. King Ambrose was in the midst of tracking down some of these rumors when his sons were slaughtered."

I almost flinched but restrained myself. I had to put aside my personal feelings for the Sterling family. Staring out into the quiet darkness surrounding us, I catalogued the normal sounds found in a night forest. We were safe for now, but what would happen when we left the protection of the forest? That had been a large band of Skori roaming the countryside. It would be foolish to assume they were the only band on the loose.

"How did King Ambrose react to the death of his sons?"

"It's said he's slipping into madness. The king speaks of his sons as if they're on a journey and he expects their return any minute."

A heaviness gripped my heart. Ambrose was a good man and a strong ruler. He'd held Newland together for the past forty years and was a friend to the elves. We were always welcome in his court. Not that any, other than myself, had entertained his court since he'd come to rule. To my knowledge, my people had been avoiding contact with humans for several decades.

Ambrose certainly kept the Church under control within his lands. I had no doubt that the minute he received a hint that King Ambrose's mind might be gone, Bishop Langley would waste no time in moving in and turning Newland into a country of the same zealous bigots as Florida. The Church had a firm hold on Newland's neighboring country and wasn't about to pass up the rich pickings of Newland itself. Like sharks with the scent of blood in the water, they would attack in a feeding frenzy.

Something I had to prevent.

Chapter Three

I had no choice but to help Newland.

My name was once Rowena Kathryn McAllister. It was the name I was born with. My True Name. Way back when I was still human. Once the Great Plague had finished ravaging the land, the survivors had done what we had to do to live. We married, had children, etc. I'd met a man named Ian Sterling and, despite everything, managed to fall in love again. I'd lost a husband and two children to the plague. I never thought I could find love again. But with Ian … he was special. I was devastated when I'd learned he'd chosen to remain human while I was destined to become Sithi … and immortal. Watching the man you love slowly age and eventually die … well, that was something I never wanted to experience again.

Deep down inside, a part of me remembered what it was like to be human. Most Sithi chose to forget their origins, but it was something I could never do. To do so would be an injustice to the love I'd shared with Ian. To the love I'd had for our children and grandchildren.

I'd remained at his side while I'd slowly changed in appearance and attitude. Many of my kind had immediately fled the world of man when the change came, but I had not been able to bring myself to desert my husband and our three children. Ian had never turned from me, not even when my hair had gone from its former blond to the changeable locks of the Sithi. When my eyes had lost their warm brown and become aquamarine blue. When my ears had become pointed … although he had made more than one Mr. Spock joke from the old *Star Trek* series. I, in turn, had been forced to watch my beloved husband grow old, feeble, and eventually die. Ian had lingered far longer than most humans. He'd been well over ninety-five when he'd passed to his human paradise.

My Lady had permitted me to remain with my family far longer than she'd allowed others to. Most of my new people had been ostracized by those who were once their family and friends and had retreated beyond the mists of the Lake Country. Their tasks had been revealed by Our Lady, and they'd set out to accomplish them. I was late in taking up my duties, yet I'd never been chastised over it.

After Ian had died, I'd known I could no longer stay. The pain of losing Ian was a foreshadowing of what I would experience when my children aged and died. They were all adults by that time, married, with children of their own. I was a great-grandmother when I'd finally left and joined my brethren in the Great Lakes region that we had claimed for our own.

Even now, after nearly a thousand years, the pain was still there. Not fresh, not sharp, but there. A memory that was sometimes bittersweet.

The wind picked up, and I turned my face into it, automatically deciphering the scents it carried. Other than the lingering stench of the dead Skori, there was little to cause alarm. I also realized that the forest was going back to sleep. We could only remain here for the night. Then we had to travel. We could not count on the forest to defend us a second time.

I sensed a change in Merry's breathing and knew she was awake. Glancing down at her, I found her watching me, all signs of sleep vanished. When she noticed my attention, she sat up, tugging the blanket around her shoulders, hunching closer to the fire. Without a word, I threw more wood onto the small blaze, building it to dispel any lingering chill.

Automatically, I opened my senses to her, feeling her kinship to me despite the centuries that separated me from my children. I was also a tad surprised to sense that, at some time in the distant past, an elf had dallied with one of my descendants. I got a faint sense of the elven blood coursing through Merry's veins. Greatly diluted but present.

"I have to believe my brother Connor is still alive." Her voice was so low that anyone without my ears would have had a hard time hearing her. "Perhaps if one of his sons lives, my father will return to his senses."

Her continuation of my conversation with Finnegan also showed that she'd been awake and listening to us. At least for the last five minutes or so. Her brief rest appeared to have done her some good. There was no sign of lingering shock.

"Does your father know you're gone?"

"I doubt my father is aware of what day it is, much less my absence." Bitterness coated her tongue. "Normally I am closely guarded when I'm in the castle. Or I should say … *was* closely guarded. I was a valuable asset and not allowed off my leash. My father planned an advantageous marriage for me. At least until the court erupted in confusion surrounding my brothers' deaths. Then with everyone running this way and that, and with Austin Branigan whispering poison in my father's ears … well, I just left. Someone had to find help."

No mistaking the cynicism in her voice. Couldn't say I blamed her. Evidently, as the only daughter of a prominent house, she was slated as the marital sacrifice to cement political relations with another kingdom. It wasn't an uncommon practice, and personally I didn't like seeing it done to one of my kin, but who was I to protest? They had no idea who I was or what my relationship was to them. And that was the way I wanted it kept.

For now. I'd seen instances where a human family was able to trace their roots to a Sithi ancient. Most of the time, the attitude it generated wasn't a pretty sight.

Looking at her, I thought Merry's father would be hard-pressed attracting a suitor for her at the moment. Evidently she'd taken a blade to her blond hair when she escaped her father's castle. It lay in uneven layers around her thin, pale face, giving her an almost elfin look. Blue eyes too large for her face had shadows under them, and they looked bruised and haunted. Her mouth was pulled thin, lines bracketing both sides. There was beauty here, but well hidden at present by the defeated air surrounding her.

"You're a long way from home, young Meredith Sterling. Do you think your father has sent out search parties?"

"My father no longer cares for anything."

"So you took it upon yourself to search for that help?"

"Someone had to."

"Or someone had to stay and run a country." My words were meant to provoke. I was curious to see what reaction I could draw from this young woman. "With your brothers gone and your father unfit, you should step up."

"Who would listen to me? I have barely reached my majority. And I'm a woman." I could see her temper flare. Good. Anger was far better than listless acceptance. "Two strikes against me already."

"Since when is being a woman a hindrance from ruling? Newland has had queens before. Some brilliant queens."

"Austin Branigan runs Newland now."

"Austin Branigan." I knew that name. Granted, it had been a long time since I'd last been in Newland, but I seemed to recall a young man, short, heavy. He stood out in my mind because he was always lingering about the throne room, inching close to the rich and powerful. He was from a minor family, noble, but low on the status level.

"A man who has managed to insinuate himself into King Ambrose's good graces," Finnegan said. He was seated on a log he'd pulled closer to the fire and was extending his hands toward the warmth of the flames. "He is now the king's chief advisor. Or I should say, King Ambrose's only advisor. He has found reason to dismiss all the others."

"Austin Branigan is a toad of a man who views himself as indispensable to my father," Merry said in a disdainful tone. Obviously no love lost there. "My father hasn't made a move without his counsel for the past three years. I've tried warning him against Branigan, but he pays no heed."

Which probably wasn't good. Apparently Ambrose neglected his only daughter in favor of his sons, seeing her as only a political tool and not the resourceful young woman I saw before me. Weary, yes. Bedraggled, no doubt. But she'd been clever enough to make it as far as Memis before the Skori had caught up to her.

Question was, when had the creatures of the Dark Master picked up her trail? She'd mentioned attempting to gain access to Sithi land, and that was a couple of hundred miles to the north. Had they been loitering outside our lands? Or had they gone looking for the girl? This could be a bid to wipe out the Sterling family. Their demise would send Newland into a state of turmoil. If King Ambrose's mind was already compromised, this would finish it.

But to what end? Was this a plot by the Church? A bold move on their part, if it was. And how had they gained the ear of the Dark Brother and, in turn, the Skori? This was becoming a disturbing mystery. Or was it something darker? I had to confer with My Lady for answers. She would know if her dark sibling was active in the world again.

But first I had to point something out to my companions.

"You could be queen, Merry."

She stared up at me as if I'd taken leave of my senses.

"But I do not want to be queen!" The words burst out of her, anger choking her voice. "I know nothing about ruling my people."

"You've already made a start, young Meredith Sterling. You see them as *your* people," the wizard put in quietly from his position across the fire. He'd been silent after his comment regarding Austin Branigan.

I slanted him a look but said nothing, allowing Merry time to think on my words. If Connor was dead, then Merry was the logical heir to the Newlandian Kingdom.

"The foes of your country were meticulous in dispatching the sons of Ambrose," Finnegan said after a moment. "It has all the makings of a long-planned campaign. We must assume Connor has also been killed. His body has never been found."

Which didn't bode well for Merry's avowal to remain unencumbered with the burden of rule. She flinched at Finnegan's blunt assessment of her brother's death.

"We will go to your father, Merry," I said. "Perhaps I can clear his mind enough to continue his rule while he trains you to take his place."

"Did you not hear me, elf? I do not wish to rule."

Mentally, I flinched. I'd once been in her position. The Sithi had required a ruler, and I'd been selected. Merry's words were an echo of those I'd uttered nearly a thousand years ago when I'd rejected the rule of the Sithi. Tesina had eagerly stepped up to accept the station. My relief had been short-lived as I'd felt the disappointment in My Lady. I'd never sensed her rebuke, but I knew her disappointment.

Shaking off the memory, I speared her with a cold look, instilling a hint of power in my voice.

"There is nothing wrong with my hearing, child. But if you do not step up to take control, Newland will fall into a battle for succession … something that hasn't occurred in five hundred years. You cannot be mired down in petty squabbling. Now is the time for strength. If what the wizard says is true, then there are outside powers influencing these events. If the army of darkness is gathering, it will roll over your country and destroy it. I doubt it will stop there. The Plains of Jordan will be swallowed, as will Cascadia and, yes, even Florida. The Dark Master cares nothing of the world of man. He sees only his own power and the power of his followers. Never forget that."

Shame colored Merry's cheeks, visible to me even in the light of the fire. Her glance dropped to her knotted fingers. After a long silence, she looked up and met my gaze. Her eyes were awash with tears but steady.

"I know, Lady Riona. I know Newland must be ready. But it has been centuries since we've had a queen. Will the people follow me?"

I concealed my relief. She no longer battled her fate. Would that I be so fortunate.

Mentally, I called on My Lady for guidance. There would be time later to contact Her for answers regarding the Dark Master. Right now I needed a hint that the path I was choosing was correct.

I heard Merry begin to speak, but Finnegan made a sound for silence. I blocked both of them out of my consciousness, concentrating on my internal magic. Drawing on the power of nature, I felt all awareness of my surroundings recede as my request was answered. The scent of flowers swirled around me, and peace settled over me as the loving presence of My Lady welled up within. A hint of the future swirled past my sight, blinding me for an instant, then a veil covered my eyes, and the Vision drew stronger. I saw a slightly more mature Meredith Sterling standing upon an escarpment, a crown upon her brow. She held a raised sword in her hand as she commanded the defense of the castle. Armored men and women crowded the battlement, spears and bows at the ready. The Vision opened further, and I could see my people standing side by side with the humans. At Merry's signal, arrows flew true, striking into the heart of darkness. Two small figures shrouded in a cloak stood at Merry's side. I couldn't tell if they were male or female.

The Vision faded and reformed. This time, the hordes of darkness were overwhelming the defenders of the castle. Bodies lay everywhere, both human and Sithi. Broken. Mutilated. Horror swept over me as I watched the scenes unfold, still misty but unmistakable.

I saw those same small figures, concealed within their cloaks standing in the background, watching the carnage. As if feeling my presence, as one, they turned toward me. Within the hood of the cloak, I saw the face of a young girl and a young boy, both staring out at me, their eyes familiar. Piercing. They were the eyes of Merry.

The second Vision faded, but they had both been strong. The stronger the Vision, the greater the possibility of it coming to pass. But which was the true Vision? Had it been the same children in each Vision? The triumph over evil or the defeat of mankind? And who were those children? That they appeared in both Visions pointed to high importance in the reality of my Seeing.

Merry could be a strong ruler, but the war with darkness could overcome her. Despite the love and loyalty at her back, she could fall. In the presence of her own children. Would the children aid mankind, or would they be the instruments of its defeat?

I felt my blood freeze in my veins as the possibilities crowded my mind.

"The people will follow you," I said at last, and the veil cleared. That much I was certain of. It was with an effort that I kept the tremor out of my voice. This had shaken me more than I cared to admit. I wanted to say more, but did I dare? How much was likely to come to pass? "You carry Sithi blood within your veins, Merry.

That will help you persuade your people."

"Sithi blood!"

"Weak, yes. But present."

Now it was her turn to fall silent. How could I tell her that despite her best efforts, it was possible it would not be enough? That there was a strong likelihood that she would fail and humanity would be overrun by the scions of the Dark Master?

Any peace I'd achieved in the past few decades was shattered as I stared into the dying fire. The consumed wood glowed red and black, seeming to breathe with each stray breeze. The night had fallen silent. The inclement weather had encouraged the nocturnal creatures to seek shelter while the recent evil presence ensured their continued absence.

War was coming. One way or another. The uneasy peace and prosperity of centuries was tethered on the edge. Ready to fall.

An iciness entered the forest as night dew covered the meadow, the chilled moisture encouraging the closeness of cloaks and blankets. I found new sounds in the night. The stamp of the horses as they settled in what remained of the night. The rushing river only meters away from us. An occasional rustle disturbing the undergrowth. The whistle of the wind weaving through the nearly bare branches of the trees surrounding us. My ears caught the near silent passage of an owl as it hunted, the quick drop and faint squeak of a captured mouse. The spring was too new for insects, so the quiet pressed close to us.

Despite my distraction, my mind kept circling back, worrying over the matter like a dog over a bone.

How much of the Vision was true? The future was never set in stone. I had to remember that. The many skeins of possibilities changed with each road we chose. Would humanity fall if Merry became queen? Was she not only the catalyst but the downfall of her people? And most likely the downfall of my people since we had aligned ourselves with mortals? And what of those children?

Twins. Their skin had been pale. I'd made out a few locks of hair, pale with brown streaks. Sithi hair.

So many questions with no answers. For the first time in a very long time, I felt the shiver of fear travel down my spine. It was an emotion that did not sit well with me and one I found unacceptable. One way or another, war was coming to mankind, and fear would only hinder me.

Out of the corner of my eye, I caught Merry's smothered yawn. Leaning over, I tossed another log onto the fire. Sparks danced skyward to be lost in the dark, mingling with the vast array of stars overhead. There was a tinge of color in the eastern sky.

"Rest. Both of you. I'll stand watch."

"Wake me at my turn," Finnegan said as he slid from his log to the ground, using it as a pillow. He pulled his cloak around himself, his face half-hidden by the hood.

"No, I have little need for sleep. There isn't much night left, so take what rest you can. We must start for Canada City in the morning. Every day that King Ambrose fails is another day lost."

Finnegan merely raised the edge of his hood long enough to give me an inscrutable look before he dropped it and made himself more comfortable. Even with my superior senses, it was difficult to read the wizard. Merry made a feeble protest, but exhaustion got the better of her. With a nod, she curled up in her blanket. For a moment longer, her eyes reflected the flickering flames of the fire before her lids drooped, and she soon fell asleep.

I continued to watch her for a while longer, feeling my face soften. Such a heavy burden to drop onto those slender shoulders. Life sometimes wasn't fair. Less so for her. The future wasn't going to be easy for her, but I had no choice but to place my faith in her. Meredith Sterling could make a great queen. But if another aspect of my Visions was to be believed, she could also be the destruction of mankind.

I could only hope that the second Vision was only a possibility and not a true conclusion. And what of the children? There appeared to be a likelihood that any child she bore would be her salvation or her downfall.

The Lady willing, we'd be strong enough to hold back the coming darkness.

Chapter Four

Dawn broke over the horizon, pearling the sky with the promise of a clear day. The fire did little to stave off the chill, but I felt little of it. The avian activity increased to greet the new day, flashes of color darting through the trees and bushes, lingering to inspect our presence before moving on. Their calls filled the air with sweet music. A natural sound. A reassuring sound.

I'd had much to think about during those hours of my watch. Uppermost in my mind was that I hadn't seen myself in the Vision I'd had last night. If it was a fight against the Dark Master, I should have been there, on the escarpment with Merry and my brethren. Was it a harbinger that I might not be alive when that Vision came to pass? Or was I somewhere else, fighting another battle? The uncertainty was disturbing.

In the past, I'd cheated death so often that I liked to believe I was destined to be occupied elsewhere if and when that battle commenced.

Centuries ago, when the plague had taken most of humanity, it'd been an equal opportunity killer. Didn't matter if you were rich or poor, black or white, young or old. It'd taken over ninety-five percent of the world's population. None of the survivors knew how it had started, and I guess, in the long run, it didn't matter. Our society and planet had been balanced on the edge of a sword for the hundred or so years before the plague had been unleashed. It'd been a matter of time before some manmade disaster hastened the end of world as we'd known it.

Had My Lady caused that little germ to escape whatever lab it had been contained in? Who knew? I'd never asked. Didn't want to know. Either way, I should have died centuries ago, but I was one of the survivors … which was, in itself, a miracle.

I'd been diagnosed with breast cancer just months before the world went to hell. I always figured once I survived the plague, I'd go belly up because … quite frankly, humanity was too busy struggling to survive to care about the cancer treatment of one woman.

My pre-plague treatment had been a lumpectomy, chemotherapy, and I had been on a weekly infusion of Herceptin to keep my cancer under control. But once the plague struck the world, my follow-up visits to a doctor and continued treatment had been low priority. The few remaining doctors were too busy dealing with cholera, dysentery, and a dozen or so other lovely diseases that had broken out in the aftermath.

With so many bodies all over the place, we'd been forced to dig mass graves to get rid of them before they rotted in the hot August sun and added to the virulent cocktail of diseases springing up. It'd been imperative that we clear our own little space of paradise to avoid the diseases that accompanied the stench, the uncertain drinking water, the spoiling food supply.

Just when you congratulated yourself on surviving the plague and the accompanying diseases, you began to wonder if the dead weren't the lucky ones.

I'd never forget what one of the surviving doctors told me when I'd approached him about some way of monitoring my cancer. He said that I should probably just put a bullet in my head and save myself the trouble of dying slowly. Nice, huh?

Not everyone had been so callous. With Ian's help, I'd found a doctor—sorely overworked, of course—who'd gone over my prognosis with me. Ian and I had broken into my oncologist's office and gotten hold of all my records and films. Dr. Milken had looked over everything pretty thoroughly, as far as I could tell, and just shaken his head. He'd told me that without the proper treatment, there was no telling how long it would before my cancer returned.

In the days, weeks, and months that had followed, I'd given serious thought to that bullet on more than one occasion. By this time, I was married to Ian and had just given birth to twins, Marissa and Marcus. Despite the uncertain future, despite the suspicion that my cancer had returned, I'd decided that I was going to live life to the fullest. There was just something about surviving an earth-shattering plague that makes you appreciate the little things in this world. I had a husband who loved me, two beautiful children, and an uncertain future. A future that had become moot in the course of one night.

The night of the Dream. I used a capital D when I referred to the Dream because it warranted it. Every adult survivor had fallen into a deep sleep one night about three years after the last traces of the plague had died away, and we'd all dreamed the same Dream. Didn't know if this happened all over the world, but I could only assume it had. Every survivor that I'd spoken with about that night had agreed that the Dream had begun the same way.

It started mildly enough. A walk down a stone lane, walled in by a misty fog that allowed no sound, sight, or smell. Something kept me walking. There was no fear, no anger, really no emotion that I recall. Serenity, a sense of peace infused me as I walked until I came to a triple split in the road, which continued a short distance to three doors. They all stood out in stark relief despite the mist.

The first was enormous, made of plain white marble shot through with streaks of silver and gold. It was beautiful, dignified. A door that beckoned you and made you want to pass through.

The second door was completely different. Still of marble, this one was as black as night with streaks of reds and golds running through it. It at once fascinated and repulsed me. This door spoke of power and decadence. The third and final door of marble was a beautiful green, carved with trees and flowers so lifelike that I expected them to sway in a breeze.

In the Dream, I stood staring at the doors, each one compelling in its own way. I don't really know what made me choose the green one, but my feet carried me closer to it. A glance over my shoulder showed the white door pulsing with peace and tranquility while the black door was a temptation beyond imagination, of promised domination. The longer I stared at it, the stronger the compulsion became to desert the green door and open the black. Dark promises whispered in my ears. Power beyond imagination, my every desire fulfilled. Wrenching my gaze away from the black door, I conquered its allure, stretching out my hand to place it on the intricate carvings before me.

Needless to say, I had chosen to follow My Lady. We'd all discovered later upon waking that the greatest power of mankind was its ability to freely choose. There were those, the majority of mankind, who'd chosen the white door and remained human, the followers of the One God. There were fewer, like myself, who'd chosen the green door. We'd slowly evolved into the Sithi people we are today. Our life had become one of labor as we'd restored this world to its primeval self. Following the plague, the Industrial Age had crumbled, and the power of Our Lady had restored the earth to an agricultural purity. Our reward was magic and immortality.

The fewer still who chose the black door had evolved into something dark and evil. I wasn't sure if the humans who'd chosen the dark way were naturally flawed in some way or if the Dark Master had promised them riches and power. I confess that I'd felt that power myself from where I'd paused before the black door. If I had hesitated long enough, would I have become one of the Skori that now inhabited the far north?

I'd never know. I liked to think I would never have fallen to such a fate, but I honestly couldn't say for sure.

While our change had been gradual and gentle, the Skori change had been quick, brutal. When they vanished into the night, it was usually on the heels of murder and mayhem.

The sun broke over the horizon, stirring me from my past. A past I didn't dwell on too often. Movement from my companions drew my attention. Merry sat up and stretched while Finnegan grimaced, working a knot out of his shoulder and muttering something under his breath about the hard ground and old bones.

At some point during the predawn hours, I had attempted to delve into his origins without success. The old man was adept at concealing his ancestry. If the knowing look he slanted in my direction was any indication, I suspected he was aware of my attempts. And was amused by them. No matter. He would have expected me to try. Far be it from me to disappoint him.

The one fact I'd been able to learn was that he was strong in magic. Unusually powerful, even for a wizard. That told me the Sithi in his background was an ancient. "Curiouser and curiouser," to quote a long-dead author.

"How do you feel?" I asked as I left my position next to the wide trunk of an oak tree.

"Old."

With a slight smile, I poured him a cup of tea that I'd begun steeping earlier. The brew was strong and fragrant. He cupped his hands around the tin mug to absorb the heat before carefully sipping.

Bending, I rummaged through my pack until I came up with a packet of trail mix. Setting the bag aside, I continued my search until I unearthed three oranges. There were few remaining orange trees in what had once been the state of Florida, but I'd used a spell to carefully preserve them when I'd first begun my work in that region. I'd seen cultivated groves of orange trees in Southern Cascadia, but the great distance made procuring the fresh fruit difficult. I preferred my private stock. "Here."

I tossed one piece of fruit toward Finnegan, who caught it deftly. Cradling it carefully in his hands, he raised it to his nose and breathed in deeply, savoring the citrus scent.

"A rare delicacy, my lady Riona. Thank you."

"Just Riona, please. I was fortunate to locate a few trees to the far south. You won't find another orange grove outside of Southern Cascadia."

"What are these?" Merry had freed herself from her blankets in time to catch the fruit I tossed to her. "I've never seen them before."

"It's called an orange. You peel off the outer skin and eat the sweet flesh inside." Finnegan was already peeling the large fruit, carefully setting aside the thicker skin. "Save that part. Dried, it can be used in cooking."

I merely raised a brow and set aside my own peelings. Somehow the wizard didn't strike me as the culinary type. Merry watched us for a moment and then turned her attention to her own fruit. The look on her face the first time she bit into a section was one of surprise and delight.

"We have to move out immediately after eating." Wiping my fingers on a bit of grass, I parceled out the trail mix. It wasn't much of a breakfast, but it would do until we broke for lunch. "I'm uncomfortable lingering here in Florida."

I glanced around the peaceful setting of the glade. It was beautiful this early in the morning as the rising sun burned off the lingering mist. A faint shading of green covered most of the foliage with the harbinger of spring. The song of countless birds mingled with the sound of the rushing river.

At that moment, I should have been at peace with the world.

This was what I was created for. This delicate balance of nature. With the absence of industry, the world had returned to a more leisurely, agricultural pace. Nothing mechanical worked in the Garden of Eden created by My Lady.

But like every Eden, there was a snake hidden somewhere.

I felt edgy. Something wasn't quite right. I checked the horses, but they were fine. Physically, the gelding had recovered, for which I gave thanks. There should be no wild ride into the night today, but I really didn't want him pulling up lame on us.

Somehow I found myself at the riverbank, staring back over the expanse of water in the direction we'd come from. My elven senses told me nothing threatened us from that direction, but there were times when I had to distrust my senses and go with my gut.

"Saddle up," I said without turning. "We must continue."

Without another word, I kicked dirt over the embers and packed up my remaining gear.

"Make certain the fire is well doused," Finnegan said to Merry as he began saddling his mare. "We don't want to incur the wrath of the forest."

Without being asked, Merry picked up a cup and ran to the river's edge. It took her three trips before she was satisfied that the fire was out. After what she'd seen the night before, I couldn't blame her for her caution with the forest. I could have told her that the forest had once again fallen into its slumber, but sometimes a little respect for the unknown was not a bad thing.

We were packed up and mounted in short order. I gave our campground one last glance to make sure nothing had been forgotten. I noted that the orange peelings were gone. Finnegan must have been serious in wanting to use them in cooking. Odd. Well, the man had been around for a very long time … longer than a normal human life-span. Sithi blood reacted differently when mixed with humans. Some gained powerful earthen magic;

some gained a longer life span. Evidently Finnegan had acquired both.

I turned Mysteria toward the forest. During my reconnaissance during the night, I'd found a deer track that led in the general direction we needed to go. The road leading north we'd used on the other side of the river had vanished as if it had never existed. No doubt courtesy of the forest. Our trail would be all but nonexistent. The knowledge felt right.

As I led the way into the trees, I sent my senses outward, locating and marking every forest inhabitant. The creatures of this wood had little fear of man. The centuries had instilled more of a caution. The population of mankind was still considered sparse … nowhere near what it had been a thousand years ago, but it was My Lady's plan to avoid the gross overpopulations of centuries past. Mass starvation was a rare thing now, at least on the North American continent. Mortal families were rarely larger than three or four children.

This was again through the intervention of My Lady. As the One God had once encouraged large families to better serve and worship him, My Lady interfered with the reproductive capacity of humans. Not common knowledge even among the Sithi and certainly unknown to the humans. I doubted the knowledge that the Goddess caused birth control would sit well. Particularly with the Church. As a result, we had a manageable population.

I wasn't sure what the reproductive habits of the Skori were, but I suspected they bred as rarely as we did. At least I could hope. We would have been overrun by now if not.

It was rare for the Sithi to have children. Being long-lived as we were, our population would swiftly overtake those of the humans if we had the same reproductive capability. It was a delicate balance and one that we did not rail against, for the most part.

I would have liked to have another child, but even after a thousand years, I was infertile. Not that I'd mated often since the death of my last husband, but the few relationships I'd entered into had not yielded a child. Something inside me mourned that fact, while another part of me knew it was just as well.

My work was not yet finished. I hoped the complete restoration of the Everglades would be my final obligation to My Lady, freeing me to do as I would.

Until She found something more for me. I had no illusions that My Lady did not have something lined up for me. She was a hard mistress but a fair one. I suspected that this quest with young Meredith Sterling might be my next assignment. Whether She was as of yet aware of it or not. I thought about it for a moment. Given the Vision My Lady had sent, She knew.

The dense forest caused the deer trail to weave this way and that in a drunken manner, at times nearly disappearing when we came to a ravine or a creek bed. More than once, we were forced to detour or backtrack to find a more accessible route. The trees grew close together, slowing our progress as we maneuvered through the heavy undergrowth.

More than once, I almost wished the forest hadn't erased the road, but that thought was fleeting. The safety of Meredith Sterling was more important than the ease of our journey. Or so I tried telling myself as I cursed under my breath when a branch caught my cloak and tore a hole in it. Sithi woven it might be, both waterproof and durable, but it wasn't impervious to damage.

The morning chill left the air as the sun climbed higher. Still early spring, this far south, the temperatures were comfortable for traveling. When we came to an open meadow, we paused only long enough to rest the horses and enjoy the warmth of the sun on our faces while partaking of a sparse lunch.

Within the heavy wood, the sunlight dappled through the thin foliage to hit the forest floor, creating a primeval beauty that managed to take even my breath away.

The afternoon began to melt into evening before I started to search for a likely place to camp for the night. I knew we weren't far from the edge of the forest. By the middle of tomorrow, it should melt into a more gentle wood, and then farmland would appear. I estimated that despite our slow progress, we'd traveled perhaps twenty miles.

Once we reached the main roads, our pace would pick up, and we should make far better time. It was better than eight hundred miles to Canada City, and factoring in minor delays, we should get there in just under three weeks.

Provided, of course, we didn't run into any more Skori. I wasn't optimistic we'd seen the last of them, but I hoped to avoid any more encounters.

"We'll stop here for the night." I'd found a clearing that looked relatively comfortable. There were several large boulders that would provide protection from the night wind and, at the same time, conceal our firelight. The sun was sinking behind the tree line, purpling the sky and lengthening the shadows.

Dismounting, I waited for the others to follow my action before attending my mount. The horses would find plenty of fodder here, and they wouldn't have far to go for water, I thought as my ears caught the gentle gurgle of a nearby steam.

"I'll gather firewood," Merry said as she set her gear down beside a boulder. She straightened to allow herself to stretch out the kinks that the daylong ride left before she turned toward the edge of the trees. She seemed to have recovered from her numerous shocks. I sent a silent prayer of thanks to My Lady. Whether through Her intervention or that of the One God, the girl appeared back to normal.

I sent out a probe to ensure there was nothing threatening in the immediate vicinity, but other than a wolf pack to the north of us, I detected nothing.

"Stay close." I glanced at Finnegan and he nodded. He'd see that no harm came to Merry. It came to me that I was beginning to trust him. "I want to look around."

As I'd done the night before, I made a wide circle of our camp, checking to ensure no hidden dangers lurked nearby. The wolf pack sensed our presence but displayed little alarm. If they'd been nervous about something, I would have investigated more closely. At this time of year, when the bitches whelped, they'd be extra wary of any danger.

That reassured me enough to complete my circuit and return to the campsite. Finnegan was setting out bread and cheese while something simmered in the pot he had positioned over the fire. My nose detected beef, various root vegetables, and herbs. It smelled delicious. Perhaps the wizard did have some talent in the kitchen.

"All clear?"

"Yes." I relaxed my guard and squatted beside him, watching as he crumbled dried oregano into the stew. "Smells good."

"I find that cooking relaxes me."

"To our benefit."

Merry snorted with laughter from her position on the other side of the fire. It was a testament of her character that she'd overcome her fear and boded well for the future. From what I could tell, the girl led a sheltered life within the walls of her father's castle. Even if she had been worldlier, there was little that could have prepared her for the Skori. After so many centuries, few humans had ever seen the dark creatures. Those who had rarely survived.

While the stew simmered, I stood and circled the camp, setting wards to protect us from magical attack. It was a precautionary move since I could detect no threats. Call me paranoid, but despite my many years, I still did not know the full scope of the Dark Master's power. I'd rather be prepared.

I leaped up onto the highest boulder, turning slowly so that everything came within my view. For a long moment, I stood watching the sun vanish over the horizon. The purple sky slowly deepened into true night. Countless stars appeared in the heavens overhead, sparkling with jewel-like clarity. That was one thing I didn't miss about the Industrial Age. The pollution that had hidden the stars for decades. Humans from a thousand years ago would be hard-pressed to recognize the beauty of the heavens now.

My throat tightened.

"What are you doing?"

Merry's question made me glance down. She stood just below me, her cloak wrapped around herself against the freshening wind.

"As much as I trust my Sithi senses, there are times when my eyes like reassurance."

"Can you teach me?"

I raised a brow at her, a little surprised.

"You said I had some Sithi blood in me. Can I learn to read the air around me?"

An interesting question. And one I hadn't considered before. Was it possible to teach a human to trust that sixth sense? Most already possessed it in varying degrees. What we'd once called sensitives and psychics. But it was a talent that was largely ignored by mortals.

"I doubt you are able to learn such a skill. You either have it or you don't."

Her face fell, and I felt a thread of remorse wind through me. I didn't have to be so blunt, but it was the truth. Unless you had the natural talent, trying to learn it was useless. Her Sithi blood was so diluted over the centuries that it was doubtful she was strong enough to read the wind.

I leaped down from the boulder, aware of Finnegan's interested stare. I raised a brow to him in silent challenge, and he shrugged, turning his attention back to the stew.

"Come, sit here." I chose a place across from the fire, deliberately within earshot of Finnegan. The wizard would be able to follow our conversation no matter what distance I put between us. So why bother?

Despite her disappointment at my answer, Merry took a seat with ill-concealed eagerness. It occurred to me how little I'd bothered to talk to her since we'd met two nights ago. Had I been so wrapped up in my solitude for this past decade that I've forgotten how to relate to mortals? I could use the excuse that the danger pursuing us did not make for casual conversation, but I knew that was untrue. It had just never occurred to me that Merry needed companionship and was perhaps more than a little curious about Sithis. Most humans were. Few dared to ask questions.

"Ask me what you will. What do you wish to know?"

"Everything."

"That's a tall order, young Merry."

She was silent for a moment, looking down at her laced fingers, then her head came up, and she met my gaze straight on, determination in every line of her body. "You say I'm going to be queen of Newland one day. I need to know about the Sithi and the Skori."

Of all the questions she could have asked, that was one of the last I would have expected. And a tough one. There were things that I could not reveal to mortals. Things that Our Lady forbade us to discuss. Our true origins, for instance.

She must have sensed my hesitation, because she leaned forward, her expression earnest.

"I have to understand all the beings in this world, Lady Riona. How can I protect my people if I have no knowledge of those who may threaten them?"

"A very good point," the wizard murmured from his position. I shot him an annoyed glance, which he met with unconcern.

"Perhaps you'd do well to answer a few questions, Master Wizard," I shot back at him.

"Ah, but given your age, Lady Riona, I'm sure you're far more knowledgeable, if not to say eloquent."

I stared at him for a full minute. So he knew I was an ancient. I really couldn't say if I was angry or amused. Either way, the man had a lot of cheek. There weren't many who'd tweak the nose of a Sithi, so to speak.

Even Merry stared at him with shock, her gaze darting back to me to see what my reaction was to his provocative words.

Amusement won out, and I began to laugh. It felt good. Come to think of it, I couldn't remember the last time I'd laughed. There weren't many things in the Everglades to illicit laughter, and my task had been too arduous to leave much room for amusement.

"You are a brave man, Master Wizard," I said at last as my laughter died. "I'll give you that. It takes either a brave man or a foolhardy one to comment on a woman's age, whether she be Sithi or human."

I turned to Merry. "As for you, Meredith Sterling, I can only tell you this. Human, Sithi, or Skori … we are three different species. You saw the Skori and know what they are capable of. I cannot tell you their origins, nor the origins of the Sithi. It is not my place to say. But …" I put up a hand when her lips parted to interrupt. "If I receive permission from My Lady, I will tell you what I can. This I can say, the Sithi are friends to humans. We may be distant and elusive, but that is of necessity. I can give you my word that the Sithi will ride with mortals against the threat of darkness."

"Is the darkness coming?"

Her question was quiet, solemn.

"Yes," I answered with equal softness. I had to be honest with her. "One way or another, it is coming."

We all fell silent. A shiver ran through the night as the

nocturnal creatures also went quiet. Only the crackle of our fire and the wind could be heard over the sudden hush.

"Now I must question you, Meredith Sterling," I said after a long moment. "What can you tell us about the rumors your father had been investigating?" I moved just enough to put a man-high boulder at my back, crossing my legs to get comfortable. I pulled my bow and quiver closer, checking the condition of the feathers on the arrows and my bowstring. My preservation spell was still intact, and neither had taken any damage in the rain. Nothing short of a fire could damage them. Not my favorite defense, but effective.

Merry hunched closer to the fire as the flickering flames threw shadows over her face. She did nothing to hide the pain that flared. I was almost sorry to see the momentary happiness fade from her expression, but I needed to know what I was letting myself in for.

"There wasn't much to go by. As Master Finnegan said, it was mostly talk of disappearances and strange creatures seen in the night." She bit her lip before continuing. "I hid in the doorway behind my father's throne room one afternoon when a delegation from a village north of Yorktown came to petition my father for help. One villager claimed to have seen an animal the size of a bear attack a man on horseback, killing both rider and animal." She twisted her hands together, a quiver entering her tone. "After seeing those Skori, I believe his story."

"And what was King Ambrose doing to check the validity of these stories?"

"It was odd. Father would appear determined to send out a squadron to look into these matters, and then, in the next breath, he would change his mind and do nothing."

"How long has this been going on?"

"Perhaps a half a year. The stories began last autumn, just after the crops were harvested."

"And when were your brothers killed?"

"Just after the Christmas holiday."

"With the new year." Did that have any significance? We'd managed to retain the same count of months and days from the old days. The year had changed to reflect the beginning of the New Age. We were now in the year of Our Lady, 1021, N.A.

Finnegan's description of the brutal way the brothers had been killed did not indicate a ritual or an offering to the Dark Master. This went way beyond a warning to cease making inquiries.

Four brothers. Four sons of a powerful king. What was the connection? To throw Newland into turmoil in order to make picking it off more easily? Chaos was an effective tool of darkness. Yet all evidence pointed to the fact that the Skori weren't satisfied with just going after the sons of King Ambrose. I glanced at Merry.

They wanted her as well.

Was the entire Sterling family the target, or were they after one particular Sterling and just being thorough?

"Merry, how old are you? On what day were you born?"

She looked confused. Even Finnegan gave me a look askance. "I just turned twenty. Born one minute after midnight on the first day of the new year."

A chill ran down my spine as I did the quick calculation. She was born on the first of January, 1001, one minute into the new millennia. Oh one, oh one, oh one, one oh oh one. Did that have some significance? Coincidence? I doubted it. I wasn't really big on coincidences.

"What if …" Even after all my years of practice with concealing my emotions, I still had to stop and clear my throat. "What if the Skori had the wrong target?"

There was a moment of silence. Even the wind seemed to hold its breath.

"You're saying that Merry's brothers were killed while those creatures were seeking one specific Sterling." Finnegan's words were quiet. The wizard leaned forward, intent, eyes eagle-sharp on my face. "How would they have known? The Skori, as far as we know, are brutish creatures with little thought beyond death and destruction. Someone had to command them, point them in the direction of a specific quarry."

I drew a deep breath as I controlled my expression. I could be wrong. Lady, I hoped I was wrong. But My Lady had controlled the world for over a thousand years. Merry had been born on the cusp of the new millennia by the reckoning of the new calendar. Somehow the Skori had known about a child born on that day. Had they been searching for Merry Sterling these past twenty years? Being creatures of the dark, they had little sense of passing time, so perhaps they'd discovered, or had been informed, that a member of the Sterling family was the child they sought and had been systematically killing each member of that family in search of the correct one.

Which meant that the Skori had been sent specifically to kill Meredith Sterling.

Chapter Five

We got an early start the next morning. I managed a decent night's sleep, waking only three times to do a brief circuit of our camp, to make certain my wards were holding. Although my stamina was extensive, it wasn't limitless. I did need sleep once in a while.

Merry was quiet as we broke our fast and saddled up. After last night's revelations, she appeared to be in a thoughtful mood. A mood I didn't want to break. She had to come to terms with some heavy stuff and would in her own time. Our conversation the night before had ended shortly after she'd revealed her date of birth. I'd had too much to think about and wasn't ready to share my hypothesis.

Something told me that it was imperative we put miles between us and Memis, a feeling I'd learned to heed in the past. We could head straight for Canada City, but that would take us through the mountains. Not easy traveling at this time of year when springtime storms sprang up unexpectedly. Swinging north made more sense since that would take us through what had once been Kentucky and along the borders of the Lakelands. There would be a measure of safety there.

As I swung up into the saddle, I waited until the other two were ready before turning my mount north.

"We'll go a little north before turning east."

"A little out of our way, Lady Riona," Finnegan said as he

settled himself in the saddle, checking to make sure his gear was secure. He had his hood pulled up over his head, concealing much of the matted hair. Seeing his face in stark relief, I could almost see past the tangled beard to the man beneath. Almost. The thought crossed my mind that the wizard was making an effort to disguise his appearance. Cut the hair and shave the beard and even I would be hard put to describe his features.

"It will make for easier travel." Shaking off the fanciful thought, I concentrated on the matter at hand. "I'm hoping that the closer we travel to the land of my people, the less likely we'll be to come across the Skori."

"But they're dead, aren't they?" Merry directed her gelding to fall in beside Mysteria.

"Do you honestly believe they are the only Skori hunting party to come out of the north?" My words were harsh, but I didn't want her becoming complacent. Not when our lives rested on vigilance. "These creatures are determined, Merry. Never mistake that. Once a hunt begins, they do not stop. They will not stop."

"Until the fox is run to ground," she said quietly. Her face had paled, but a spark appeared in her blue eyes. "I will not be the fox, my lady Riona."

I smiled. Pleased to see the backbone in the girl.

I allowed the smile to turn both sly and cold. "Not a fox, Merry. A wolf that will turn and fight to the death."

Mysteria danced around in a tight circle as she caught my mood. I allowed her to frisk for a moment before soothing her with a light touch on her neck.

"Never forget that, Merry. The Skori will show no mercy, so do not expect any."

"If they are what killed my brothers, I know that already." Her lips trembled once, then firmed. "I loved my brothers, Lady Riona. They were overbearing and, at times, infuriating, but they were also noble and good. They did not deserve to die the way they did. I would see them avenged."

"Good." This time I gave her a look of approval. "Hold that fire in your heart, child. The road will be hard, but we will prevail."

The night's rest had done her a world of good. Determination blazed from her eyes, imbuing her face with a strength that had been missing these past two days. In fact, with the early-morning sun falling on her face, I could see the true beauty of her features. Delicate, with the shadow of her Sithi blood, she was compelling in an innocent way. An innocence fast melting away. Her experiences of the past month had done much to remove any naïveté, but that was only for the best. Merry needed to be ready for what lay ahead. If my Vision was true, she would lead the armies of humans and Sithi against the inhabitants of the north.

I had no doubt they would invade. The question was when and where. I had no time line. The northern border was vast and heavily wooded. I could only pray that we had some warning of where they would strike. It was the fact there was no word from the Rangers that worried me most. Their silence was ominous.

We left the forest as the sun edged toward the western horizon and the shadows began to lengthen. The thinning woods gave way to meadow, which in turn gave way to farmland. The road we followed was hard-packed from decades of use.

I was pleased to see fields begin to dot the land. Furrowed dirt this early in the spring, but soon the fields would be sprouting with countless crops. Once the home of tobacco and prize thoroughbred horses, this land's purpose was now more practical cattle farming and grain.

The need for survival had pretty much done what the anti-smoking laws of the old world never could. Tobacco was still grown in some regions but not many. There wasn't a big market for it. As for the horses, they'd evolved into the more practical workhorses necessary for farming. Only the very rich possessed the finer breed that had once won millions in races.

"The soil in this part of Florida is very rich," Finnegan was saying to Merry as we rode. "Much of the corn and barley is produced for the region here."

"I seem to remember reading somewhere that there is a vast grotto near here."

"What was once called the Mammoth Caves," Finnegan confirmed. I glanced at him in time to see his gesture to the east. "During the Great Waste, countless masses attempted to go deep underground to escape the plague. Unfortunately, their would-be refuge turned into their grave. I'm told that centuries ago, the Sithi went down into the caves and cleared them out. Is that correct, Lady Riona?"

"Yes," I said quietly. "I was one of the Sithi who removed the remains of the humans who perished there. It was … unpleasant. My people then restored the caves to their pristine condition. It is now a rare individual who ventures into their depths."

Both Merry and Finnegan fell silent, for which I was grateful. A newly turned Sithi, I had joined my brethren in removing the thousands of bodies from the caves. We had still been close enough to our human roots to be sickened by the sight. The nightmares had lingered for years. Curious that Finnegan knew so much of that history. Few alive would. And certainly fewer yet who weren't Sithi. The man was an even larger enigma than I'd suspected.

I shook off the memory and concentrated on the road ahead.

We kept a distance between ourselves and the farmhouses. Still, there were workers in the fields, and more than one farmer paused in his labors to watch us pass.

"Few people must come out of that forest," Finnegan murmured as yet another farmer stopped to stare at us. The young boy with him dropped his hoe and began running toward us until the older man called him back with a sharp word.

"Not very trusting," Merry added, twisting in her saddle to

stare back at them. I followed her glance and saw that the boy was now running toward the distant farmhouse as fast as his short legs could carry him. To report the strangers? More than likely.

"No," Finnegan answered when I remained silent. "The Church encourages its citizens to report anything unusual. I have no doubt that a rider will be dispatched to carry news of three travelers leaving the dark forest."

I merely pulled my hood farther over my face. No sense in advertising to the good citizens of Florida that a Sithi was passing within its borders. As it was, we were going to have to stop at the next village to replenish our supplies and, with luck, find a bed for the coming night. I had little doubt we'd find a village ahead. There were too many farms along this way for there not to be one. I was hoping for a sizable one that might allow three strangers to pass through without too much fanfare. The smaller the village, the looser the tongues.

I was also hoping to be long gone before any representative of the Church arrived.

Unfortunately, the village that appeared over the next crest was small, perhaps twenty houses clustered on a cleared space a short distance from a creek wide enough to step over in drier seasons. Right now it was swollen beyond its banks and bordering the road along which we rode. Much more rain and it would sweep up and over the lane.

"You take the lead, Finnegan," I said quietly when I saw faces peeking out of windows from behind curtains. Some remained visible, while others ducked out of sight. "That looks like an inn up ahead."

I gestured toward an ancient elm near the center of the village, its branches sweeping wide to encompass one of the few two-story structures on the green. Whitewashed walls were framed by wide wooden beams, and going by the thickness of the thatch on the roof, the inn had been here for a long time.

A few chairs were positioned under the sparse shade of the elm branches, a half barrel turned upside down to provide a table for board games if the patrons were so inclined. The chairs were empty, but I was willing to bet there would be drinkers later, when the day's labor concluded.

The sound of steel hitting steel rang out, and my eyes picked out the smithy positioned on the far end of the village. The stereotypical burly blacksmith was out front, feet spread wide as he brought a huge hammer down on what was destined to be a scythe. I gazed at him for another moment. Despite popular myth, iron had no effect on my people. Still, there were those who persisted with the belief. Particularly here in Florida.

I returned my attention to the inn just as the owner appeared at the doorway. With the warming weather, the windows were open to take advantage of the freshening breeze. In several of the second-floor windows, curtains fluttered, and one or two faces appeared to watch the scene below.

"My good sir." His tone jovial, Finnegan drew his mare to a halt before the innkeeper and dismounted. "I wonder if we could trouble you for a meal and beds for the night for myself and my daughters."

I slanted Finnegan a sharp glance. His voice might be light, but he'd instilled a quavering note that added years to his age. His whole appearance changed as he hunched in on himself and ran fingers through his beard, making it bushier than ever. His eyes crinkled with wrinkles that had been absent only minutes earlier. If I hadn't seen Finnegan move with the spryness of a youngster, I'd guess him to be a doddering old man.

Who was I to dispel his act? If he thought an elderly gentleman garnered more respect than a vagabond, more power to him.

"Of course, of course." The innkeeper smiled wide at the prospect of paying guests. "We have plenty of rooms available. I can even offer you a private sitting room if you wish."

"Only two rooms, good sir," I murmured from within my hood. I wasn't about to let Merry out of my sight.

Gathering my magic, I threw a glamour over myself before pushing back my hood and bestowing a warm smile on the innkeeper. The man gaped at me before rushing forward to assist me in dismounting. With my magic tied off, I wore the guise of an attractive human female, delicate and pale. He would see only pale blond hair and the blue eyes similar to Merry's.

"Of course, my lady. Please come in. I'm Master Baldwin, the proprietor of the inn and mayor of Tinsdale."

"Tinsdale. Is that the name of this village? How charming." I accepted his help in sliding from Mysteria. It was doubtful anyone from this out-of-the-way flyspeck would recognize a Sithi-bred horse, much less the style of her riding gear.

"Been here since the Great Waste, my lady," he went on, pride evident in his voice. A glance over his shoulder and he turned a shade annoyed as he paused in his gallant aid to shout behind him. "Hillary! We have guests! Have the girls prepare two of our finest rooms. Tomas! Martin!"

He returned his attention to me, rubbing his hands together. "Tinsdale used to be much larger, of course, but … well, you know …"

"I know." I smiled again as he trailed off. Funny how uncomfortable humans got when speaking of the Great Waste.

Merry dismounted from her gelding without any help and stood swaying with weariness. It had been a long, hard ride today. I suspected she would welcome a soft bed tonight. I knew I would.

"Tomas, Martin, come take the horses," Master Baldwin called out to the two young men coming around the corner of the inn. They were obviously brothers, both tall and wiry, their clothes plain but well kept. There was a distinct resemblance to Master Baldwin in their features. One was sucking on the end of a piece of hay while the other made an awkward bow to us before taking charge of our horses.

I paused to whisper in Mysteria's ear, urging her to allow the handlers to tend to her. Otherwise she'd be more than likely to take a chunk out of one of the men. My companions trooped into the inn behind Master Baldwin, but I stayed to note where our mounts were being taken, then glanced at the houses a short distance away. Several curtains flicked closed as some of the watching faces behind them ducked from sight. Possibly nothing more than curiosity, but I marked which houses hid watchers before I continued after the others.

The inn's great room was small by any other standard than those of a village, but it was clean and well kept. The sizable hearth was empty, but with the spring weather, there was little need for a fire during the day. The evening would cool enough to warrant the warmth of one. A bar stretched the length of one wall, its surface gleaming with a recent polishing. The shelves mounted on the wall behind it held a dozen or so mugs and tankards. Two casks of what was probably ale and cider sat in holders, ready to be breached with the coming evening.

The smell of bread baking permeated the air along with other savory scents. My mouth watered at the prospect of a well-prepared meal.

"Hillary!" Master Baldwin yelled again as he started toward the door leading to the back, where the kitchen was no doubt to be found.

"Don't shout, man. I'm right here." A large woman descended the stairs, her graceful movements belying her size. "I was seeing to the rooms."

Mistress Baldwin's face was plump but kindly, dark eyes shrewd as she looked us over. Although we were travel stained, she had no trouble determining the quality of our clothing. Her gaze fell on Merry, and she bustled forward with a look of concern.

"You poor child, you're plumb worn out. Sit here, and I'll bring you something warm and bracing." Mistress Baldwin urged Merry into a padded chair, fussing over her before taking her cloak. "Get these people something warm to drink, Master Baldwin, and be quick about it."

Without waiting to see if her husband followed her instructions, she turned to Finnegan and me.

"Father," I said to Finnegan before she could speak, "perhaps Millie should rest before dinner."

I had to smile at his start. If he wanted to portray an old man, I was willing to play the daughter. Ironic, given that I was far older than he.

"Yes, yes, that would be best." Whatever his thoughts on my subterfuge, Finnegan continued the charade readily enough and turned toward the lady of the house. "My daughters are unused to such hard travel, Mistress. We'd like to rest and freshen up before enjoying that wonderful meal I smell cooking."

"Of course, the poor dears. Your rooms will be ready in just a few minutes, and you can freshen up. I'll have dinner sent up to the private room in an hour. Would that suffice?"

"Admirably, my dear lady."

Master Baldwin reappeared bearing a tray with three steaming stoneware mugs balanced on it. He set it on the table beside Merry's chair and stepped back. Taking the seat on the other side of the table, I opened my senses to him, searching for any intention of harm. There was a hint of nervousness and more than a touch of worry in his aura. These he kept well concealed behind his jovial manner. I turned my attention on his wife and found little other than open friendliness and defiance. It was an odd combination.

I passed my magic over the drinks, but other than heated cider, they held nothing harmful. I nodded to Merry before picking up one of the mugs, warming my fingers against the stone surface. Mindful of the heat, I took a cautious sip, pleased to find the cider a good quality. Its tart, fruity flavor was laced with cinnamon and sweetened to cut any hardness the winter storage might have caused. I always had enjoyed a good cider.

"Let me check dinner. Master Baldwin, if you'll join me?" Mistress Baldwin gave us one final glance to ensure that we were comfortable before she made an imperious gesture for her husband to follow her. Merry began to say something, but I put one finger to my lips for silence. Tilting my head, I tuned out all other sound until I picked up the voices of our hosts just beyond the great room.

"I don't care what the Church has decreed, Peder. I refuse to report each and every stranger who comes through Tinsdale." Mistress Baldwin's voice was hushed as she spoke with her husband in the hallway leading to the kitchen. "These people seem harmless enough. Merely an elderly gentleman traveling through with his two lovely daughters. What danger could they possibly pose?"

"But what if Brother Morris discovers that we allowed strangers to pass through without informing him?"

"They came down the Woodland Road, didn't they? I've no doubt Dennis Thural has already sent his boy to report their presence. By the time that dim-witted boy returns, these good people will be well on their way."

"Dim-witted he might be, but young Karl is sure to get to the monastery and back by the morning."

"Not without a horse, Peder. I noticed the Thural mare down at the smithy this afternoon. She was to be shod, and I'm thinking Master Thornton hasn't gotten around to her yet."

Okay, so we had until midmorning or later to put miles between us and Tinsdale. Interesting that the Church wanted a report on every stranger passing through. They never used to be so paranoid. Under normal circumstances, they were satisfied with the number of their human worshipers and generally limited their actions to denouncing us heathens. I remembered when the Church had tried to convert us in the past. That hadn't gone over very well.

"Well, if you're sure it's safe," the innkeeper continued, sounding more than willing to be convinced. "I don't mind saying we can use the money these travelers will pay us for lodging and supplies."

"Just you keep that in mind, Peder Baldwin." The woman's voice was firm, and I had to smile. There was little doubt who ran this household. "It was a long winter with few guests. Ever since the bishop's decree, it's been a right struggle."

"That it has, Hillary. That it has."

"Well, I had best be getting a warm dinner ready for these folks. You see to the private room. Also check on Cynthi and Maddi to make sure our guests' rooms are ready, or those girls will get what for."

When I heard Hillary Baldwin's footsteps fade toward the kitchen and the return of Master Baldwin, I turned my attention to my mug. A glance at Finnegan showed him staring at me with a raised brow. I shook my head. I'd explain later.

Finishing her drink, Merry also gave me a look of inquiry, which only showed she was more cognizant of her surroundings than she let on. Good. I wouldn't have been surprised to find her asleep already, but the girl was alert to everything around her.

"Well, sir," Master Baldwin's tone was cheerful as he rubbed his hands together with satisfaction, "I can show you to your rooms if you'd like to rest for a spell. We have a private dining room for your use when you've a mind to enjoy my wife's cooking. Folks come from miles around to sample Hillary's peach cobbler. Won first prize at last summer's fair over in Campbellsport."

"I'm sure it will be delicious, Master Baldwin." Finnegan set his empty mug down and stood. "Come, girls. We'll take a moment to shake the travel dust off ourselves and then see if Mistress Baldwin's offering is as wonderful as it smells."

"You go ahead, Father," I said. "I'll be right with you. I want to check Mysteria's leg before it gets too late. She may have been favoring it."

"Pish, Mistress," Master Baldwin said as he waved his hand. "I'll have one of my boys take a look at her. They have a way with horses."

"Thank you, Master Baldwin, but I'd feel better checking myself."

Without giving him time to object, I stood and made for the door. It wasn't my mount's leg I was interested in. I wanted to question a few people about this decree of the Church. I had no doubt that Master and Mistress Baldwin could give me some answers, but they were too guarded to reveal much. The simpler the mind, the more likely I was to get my questions answered.

Chapter Six

Rather than go through the kitchen, which surely led straight to the stables, and past Mistress Baldwin, I went out the front door. I preferred to avoid the proprietress as she'd no doubt have her own questions for me. She struck me as a shrewd woman who allowed little to get past her.

The sun was sliding to the west and the shadows deepening with the descent of night as I followed the gravel lane that led behind the inn. The stables were already well lit with lanterns on either side of the open double doors. I could see inside, where the two young men were attending our mounts and making them comfortable for the night. They'd already finished Finnegan's mare, and one of them, Tomas, was leading Merry's gelding to a stall.

Mysteria stood still as Martin ran a brush over her withers. I could hear him talking softly to her, calming her with the measured strokes of his brush. Her ears flickered back and forth as she appeared to be listening, which she probably was. My mare had a good instinct when it came to humans.

Refreshing my glamour, I entered the stables. Sensing my approach, Mysteria swung her head toward me, alerting Martin. He stepped away from the mare and made an awkward bow.

"Mistress. What kin I do for you?"

"I'm just here to check on my mount." Going to her head, I stroked my hand down the side of her neck, smiling as she butted her head against my chest. "I thought she was favoring her front right leg earlier, and I wanted to make sure it was taking no heat."

Martin looked down at the leg in question, surprise on his face. By human standards, he might have been an attractive young man with his dark brown hair and hazel eyes. He was the slimmer version of Master Baldwin and very obviously his son, with similar features and manner.

"I din't notice anything, Mistress." He bent and took Mysteria's leg in his large hands, running gentle fingers over the tendons and muscle. "No swelling and no heat, Mistress."

"Perhaps I was mistaken." I gave him a smile as I sent a slim weave of magic toward him, just enough to loosen his tongue. It was a draining practice, dividing my power into two streams, but I didn't have time to obtain answers the conventional way. "Father is concerned about brigands when we continue on tomorrow. Have you heard of any in the area?"

"No, Mistress." Tomas reappeared after bedding down the gelding. Similar in looks to his brother, he was a hair shorter and a bit stockier. "The Church makes sure there ain't no trouble wit' robbers."

"Really? That's good to know." I widened the weave to encompass the second brother as I continued to stroke Mysteria's neck. The weakening drain was immediate, but I steeled myself to withstand it. "I heard the funniest thing when we were in Memis. They were saying that the Church was waylaying strangers and questioning them."

"Well, Mistress …" Martin began when his brother cut him off, my weave making him stumble over his words.

"Not waylayin', exactly. Just wantin' ta know who is goin' where and the like."

"Jes bein' careful this days, Mistress," Martin went on when his brother paused. "There's lotsa talk goin' around." He darted a quick glance around the stable and lowered his voice. "'Bout monsters."

"Monsters!"

"Now, Marty. Don' you go scarin' the lady. Ma will have our hides if we give the guests a fright." He turned back to me, giving what he hoped was a reassuring smile. It didn't quite cut it. "We ain't seen nuthin' like that, Mistress, but Brother Morris, jes' last month, he came to Tinsdale hisself to warn us to be careful and to report any strangers passin' through."

"How very odd," I murmured. "Do you think he means any strangers or anyone who looks like monsters?"

"Well." Tomas scratched his head with one grimy finger before he glanced toward his brother. "He jes said strangers, din't he, Marty?"

"Yep, strangers. Oh, and them Sithi folk. Remember? He said to report if we sees any of them elfs."

"Oh, yeah, Sithi folk, too. Said them heathens had t'be stamped out or God would smite us. Smite us … is that the right word, Marty?"

"Yep."

Stamp us out, huh? The Church couldn't be very bright or they'd know we were pretty much the only thing that stood between humans and the Skori. Most humans didn't even believe in the existence of the dark creatures. They thought they were boogeymen created to frighten young children into behaving. Wrong. Big-time wrong.

"And what are you supposed to do if you come across one of the Sithi folk?" I asked more out of curiosity than anything. There were very few ways to contain one of my people, and I wondered if they had a clue. Knowing our True Name, our birth name, was the most effective way to neutralize our magics, if only temporarily. "I mean, are you supposed to capture them or something?"

I kept my tone ingenuous, gazing up at the brothers without

guile. Secure within my disguise, I had no qualms with using my magic to encourage these mortals to talk. I was still well within the rules of My Lady to do no harm to humans unless under dire need or to defend myself. That was why it was draining to use my power in this fashion. While doing the work of My Lady, I could move mountains, but when not in direct service to Her, the effort was like trying to push a heavy stone uphill.

"I don' know. Brother Morris din't say anythin' about catching a Sithi, did he?"

Marty looked perplexed as he thought it over. He and Tomas exchanged glances and shrugged.

I wondered if this was the work of Bishop Langley. It sounded like something he'd order. If what Finnegan said was true, Langley may have gone off the deep end. Question was … how deep? The good bishop wouldn't be the first man of the cloth led into temptation by the Dark Master.

"As long as you don't think we have anything to worry about." I nodded to the two brothers and made my way back to the inn. Not a heck of a lot of information, but some. I suspected I wouldn't get much more out of the other members of the Baldwin family. They seemed to be a decent lot.

"Is everything well with your horse?"

Mistress Baldwin was at the back kitchen door just as I was about to circle around to the front of the inn. She must have seen me leave the stables through the window overlooking the courtyard.

"She's well." I changed my direction and approached her. Secure in my disguise, I gave the woman a smile. "I was worried for nothing. Your sons handle horses very well."

"They do seem to have a magic touch with them."

Was it my imagination, or was there a touch of emphasis on the word *magic*? I saw nothing in Mistress Baldwin's expression to hint at a double meaning, but still, she was a shrewd woman. I'd be stupid to underestimate her.

"The world could use a little magic now and then."

"That it could, Mistress, that it could. Now." She was all business once more and gestured for me to follow her into the kitchen. "I believe your father and sister are already in the dining room. I've got my girls serving dinner to them."

"Wonderful. I'm starved."

I trailed after Mistress Baldwin as she led me down a short hall to a door through which I could hear voices. Inside, I found Finnegan and Merry seated at a long table, the meal spread out before them.

"Now just you call if you need anything else," Mistress Baldwin admonished as she cast an assessing glance over the table. Giving a nod of satisfaction, she withdrew. Even after her footsteps receded down the hall, I waited another couple of seconds before going to the door and cracking it open. The dim hallway was deserted.

"I've already checked," Finnegan said as he helped himself to the sliced roast beef. "No one is listening, and I've set wards to warn of anyone trying to eavesdrop."

"Good." Closing the door, I dropped my disguise with a sigh of relief. I must've been far more tired than I'd suspected. The strain of holding my glamour left me feeling slightly light-headed.

I glanced around before joining them at the table. The small room afforded a comfortable privacy, its walls paneled with a dark wood, broken up by brass wall sconces. The lit candles gave off a soft glow and revealed simple decorations made of wood, a shelf of fine china plates. A small hearth occupied a portion of one wall, a fire burning to ward off the chill of the coming evening. Looking out the small window, I was almost surprised to see how little time had passed since I'd ventured to the stables for information. The sky was still a deep purple streaked with reds and golds, but already, stars were appearing overhead.

Merry was making headway into her meal, her entire concentration centered on the heaping plate in front of her.

She looked up as I took a seat.

"I asked the two chamber maids a few questions while I was putting our stuff in our room," she said as she paused long enough to take a sip from her mug. Mulled wine, if I wasn't mistaken. "Don't worry. I was careful."

"Did you learn anything useful?"

"Not much. They were far more interested in talking about the other boys in the village and the spring festival that's being planned for next month."

"Pity. When it comes to gossip, maids are usually a fount of information."

"One of them, Cynthi, did say that few people use the Woodland Road when coming to Tinsdale. She thought we were very brave to venture into the dark forest. She said there were all sorts of stories of the creatures that live in there."

"Superstition." It had to be. The forest would not tolerate the Skori within its borders.

I helped myself to roasted potatoes and just a bit of the beef. Sithi didn't eat much meat as a rule, but every once in a while, I got a taste for it. It was the latent carnivore in me. The caramelized onions and carrots looked a little wrinkled, but it was spring, and these were no doubt from last year's harvest. Sweetened winter squash and freshly baked bread dripping with butter rounded out the meal.

After the last few days on the road, it was a feast for all of the senses.

"There will be someone reporting our presence to the Church by morning," I said as I bit into the warm bread. There was nothing quite like bread straight out of the oven. Forget those feeble imitations clogged with preservatives of centuries past.

I dribbled a bit of honey on the slice before consuming it, the rich flavors exploding in my mouth. "When I listened to the elder Baldwins earlier, they indicated that one of the farmers we passed would send someone to a monastery some distance from here. Because the boy will need to go on foot, we'll be hours down the road by the time he returns."

"Any idea why the interest?" Finnegan paused in his meal to watch me. In the better lighting of the room, I could see that his eyes weren't black at all. Rather, they were the rich brown of dark chocolate. One of the few delicacies of the past that I missed with a passion. I supposed I could have gone in search of the cocoa tree in the far south of what had once been Mexico and South America, but my duties to My Lady always kept me on this continent. Pity.

I shook off the stray thought.

"While speaking with the stable hands, they said something about the Church warning of 'monsters' and wanting to be kept informed of all strangers passing through."

"Monsters?" Merry asked.

"The rumors your father heard could not have been exclusive to Newland, Merry. No doubt there have been sightings of Skori within the borders of Florida. They may not know what they're dealing with, but at least the Church has the sense to alert its followers of the dark creatures."

"Langley is no doubt taking advantage of the rumors to strengthen his position," Finnegan said.

"Could be."

"But he's the head of the Church." Merry abandoned her plate for a moment as she frowned over our words. "Bishop Langley has no need to panic his people into following him."

"Just because he's already powerful doesn't mean he won't move to consolidate his position, Your Highness," Finnegan explained as he helped himself to more sliced beef. "Newland is run by a monarchy, while Florida is under secular rule. Leadership in a monarchy is inherited, but with the Church, it is an appointed position."

"And with any position of power, it is not always the most deserving who leads." I paused long enough to pour myself a glass of mulled wine. The spices infused in the dark red wine perfumed the air, mingling with the savory scents of the meal and even complementing the faint smoky smell of the small blaze burning merrily on the grate.

It was a comfortable respite from the night and day of hard riding and frightful events.

"It's doubtful this interval will last," I said as I leaned back in my surprisingly comfortable chair and rested my drink on my stomach. "We should take advantage of it while we can, but we must continue in the morning. I suspect Brother Morris will not be long in arriving to view three outsiders."

"No, the novelty of strangers coming out of the old woods will be enough to bring him to Tinsdale." Finnegan followed my example and relaxed back in his chair, combing his fingers through his matted mustache and beard. "I was speaking with Master Baldwin earlier while waiting for Meredith to come down." He smiled briefly. "He told me that Tinsdale rarely receives visitors. Evidently, because it's surrounded on three sides by the forest, other than merchants, few venture this way."

"What about those things?" Merry asked. "Those Skori? Will those things come here?"

A good question. If there were more than one hunting party, they may yet pick up our trail. Which would lead them straight to Tinsdale. A troubling thought. I would not repay the hospitality of these people by bringing those creatures down on them.

"I could lay a false trail when we leave." For this task, I should have enough strength. Surely My Lady would approve of the use of my magic for this need.

"Will you accept my help?"

I glanced at Finnegan with surprise. For a wizard to make such an offer was almost unheard of. Possessive of their secrets, few shared their magic with a Sithi. To allow one of my people within the sphere of his power would be an open invitation to delve the man for his full potential. Plus it was extremely intimate. Sexual, even.

For a moment, I tried to see beneath the matted beard and wild hair to the man below. It was as much a disguise as my earlier glamour. High cheekbones, bronzed where his skin had been exposed to the sun. The wrinkles didn't extend beyond his eyes, making me reassess what his age might be. Younger than I'd first supposed. It was his eyes, though, that were the most arresting. The deep chocolate-brown was intense, piercing, framed by long, dark lashes. He had beautiful eyes.

I stared at Finnegan while he returned my gaze with steady self-assurance. Either he was strong enough to ward off any attempt to probe his power or he was confident that I would not be so presumptuous to attempt one.

Trouble was, how could I resist? I was already curious about him. For him to issue this open invitation. Well …

"No, Master Wizard. For this I have the strength. If I should need help, I will gladly accept it." What was I saying? To be handed an opportunity to freely examine the magic of a wizard was priceless, yet here I was turning him down. Pitiful, Riona. Absolutely pitiful. Queen Tesina would have my pointy little ears for passing this up.

Still, the man had a right to his privacy. For him to even make this offer revealed the degree of trust he had in me. What I'd done to earn it was still in question.

Finnegan nodded, a slight smile just visible through that jumble of beard. I got the feeling that I'd given him the response he'd expected, which of course pissed me off. Since when had I become predictable?

Tossing back the rest of my drink, I stood and cloaked myself in my disguise. I allowed my eyes to glow turquoise-blue at Finnegan for an instant before I dimmed them. Just to let him know I was irritated. Petulant? No doubt. But I was better than a thousand years old. I was allowed a snit once in a while.

"Merry? You ready to turn in?" Taking a grip on my emotions, I made sure none of my pique sounded in my voice. A glance at the girl showed a hastily stifled yawn behind her hand. I had to smile, my annoyance gone. The poor child was exhausted.

Turning back to Finnegan, I gave him a regal nod. As I led Merry from the dining room, I heard the wizard's soft voice just before I closed the door.

"Sleep well ... Riona."

Chapter Seven

This time when the clouds gathered, I sensed nothing inordinate about them. Springtime in the mountains spawned numerous storms, but just to be on the safe side, I cast out to determine if this one was natural. To make sure it concealed nothing harmful to us.

It was an ordinary storm. Good.

Leaving the Tinsdale Inn was difficult. The proprietors had made our stay pleasant and comfortable, with Mistress Baldwin fussing over us. I wanted to get an early start, but by the time we ate a large enough breakfast to satisfy Mistress Baldwin and negotiated for supplies, the morning was well along.

With subtle questioning, Master Baldwin revealed that the east road was the most traveled, but there was a second, more indirect route that led north toward the border and then east into the mountains. Without prompting, he encouraged us to use that less-traveled route rather than the other. I suspected Brother Morris would be coming along the east road later today.

Too many questions might have raised suspicions, so I had no idea where or how far away this monastery was. Estimating the time it would take the boy to arrive at the monastery assured me we could still avoid this Brother Morris.

"Thank you for your hospitality, Master Baldwin, Mistress Baldwin," Finnegan said in grand tones as he handed over a small bag that clinked with coin. "I truly cannot say the last time I've slept so soundly."

I hid a smile. What a liar. Our rooms had been side by side, our beds sharing the same wall. I'd heard the old man's restless pacing for a good portion of the night. I knew this because I, too, had been awake for much of the night, sitting in a hard chair beside the one window, watching every shadow for movement or for anything out of the ordinary. What little sleep I'd managed was enough to refresh me.

Fortunately, Merry had slept deeply.

I glanced at the girl as Finnegan continued to praise the quality of the inn. She looked far better than she had two days ago. The shadows were nearly gone from under her eyes, and her stance showed a sense of purpose. The weak sunlight penetrating the clouds revealed the true beauty of her face. Delicate with a vein of steel running through it. Still growing into her beauty, Merry would be a stunning woman in a few short years.

"I must say that I would not hesitate to stop here again in the future, Master Baldwin, nor would I hesitate to recommend your accommodations to my associates."

"Father," I said in an effort to move this along. "We really must be on the road if we're to make any distance before nightfall."

"Yes, yes, child. We'll be leaving shortly."

I nearly choked at his *child* crack. The dirty look I shot him was met with a distinct twinkle in his dark eyes. Apparently, it took more than a peeved look from an elf to worry a wizard.

Finally, after a little more verbal delay, we were on our way. Allowing Finnegan to take the lead, I made sure Merry was between us as I brought up the rear. Before the road curved to the north, a glance behind showed the Baldwins watching our departure. When she saw me turn, Mistress Baldwin raised one hand in farewell, her face set. I was aware of her regard until we passed out of sight around the bend.

We followed the east road for perhaps a mile before we came

across the smaller, less-used route Master Baldwin had mentioned.

If we were still followed by the Skori, I didn't want to inadvertently lead them to the quiet community of Tinsdale.

"Hold up a moment," I said as I drew Mysteria to a halt. Closing my eyes, I centered myself to access my magic. Forming a picture of the three of us in my mind, I drew in a measure of our scent, careful to include the essence of the horses. I cupped my hands together, and a dim light began to glow through my fingers. When it reached the strength I needed, I opened my hands and allowed the light to escape. A small ball of energy flashed down the east road, a decoy to lead any pursuers in the wrong direction. Now my only hope was that the Skori would be far more interested in following our trail, false though it was, and avoid any unwary travelers coming down the east road. Sighing, I breathed a prayer to My Lady. There was little else I could do.

Now I watched as the clouds gathered. The sun had vanished some hours ago to shroud the day in a false twilight. The breeze picked up strength, carrying with it the heavy scent of rain. Lightning flashed high in the steel gray cumulonimbus clouds, leaping across the sky in a pyrotechnic display. I waited, counting slowly until the rumble of thunder confirmed that the bulk of the storm was still some ten miles away. It wouldn't take long to reach us.

Damn. I wasn't looking forward to another soaking.

We'd been following the secondary road from Tinsdale, making pretty good time. The forest surrounding us wasn't an ancient but was at least a thousand years old. Possibly one of the first to be restored by my brethren. We tended to concentrate on what flora already existed in the area and expand it to swallow the towns and cities decimated by the plague. Using the considerable powers bestowed upon us by Our Lady, houses, buildings, roads, whatever was man-made had been either demolished to dust or hardened to form boulders. A few places, like New York City, had become a miniature mountain range butting up against the ocean. Rather than bring down all the skyscrapers, we, in a joint effort involving over a thousand Sithi, had hardened the concrete buildings and reshaped them into a mountain range. It was, in my opinion, one of our most spectacular efforts.

If someone were determined enough, they could enter the warren of caves that now snaked through the burrows of what used to be New York City. They'd find chambers of breathtaking beauty, but nothing manmade. The interior of the buildings had been metamorphosed into glittering chambers of stalagmites and stalactites. Rivers of water ran throughout the system and continued the transformation into a beauty yet unseen by mortal eyes. Evolution a la Sithi.

For the most part, mankind was unaware of the engineering marvels they'd once created and taken for granted. With the end of the Industrial Age, nothing mechanical worked, oil products were useless, and humans had lost the ability to split the atom and create weapons of mass destruction.

My Lady wanted to keep it that way. Many Sithi had been alive during that era, and we'd never forget the countless times the world had teetered on the brink of utter annihilation. I had no doubt that if the plague hadn't wiped out the majority of humanity, we would have done it ourselves within the next decade. Mankind was, if nothing else, suicidal that way.

"We should take shelter," I called to Finnegan, who was gazing upward with a slight frown on his face. Another flash of lightning lit up the sky directly overhead, followed seconds later by the rumble of thunder as it vibrated over the land. "We have to get off this road."

If we remained on the road, we were sitting ducks, not only for a thorough soaking but for a lightning strike. The vegetation bordering the road was scrub, for the most part, the heavier wood set farther back.

"What about going back to Tinsdale?" Merry asked as she easily controlled her gelding. The horses were beginning to spook.

"We're too far away. Besides, it's not safe. Not with the possibility of the Skori still out there."

Or the arrival of Brother Morris, for that matter. Skori might be the more dangerous of the two, but I never discounted the trouble members of the Church could cause. We could not afford the delay.

"I agree," Finnegan said as he peered through the gloom at the road. We were at the top of a slight hill, completely exposed to the elements, but the route curved downward and entered a tract of woods. The trees grew closer to the road, affording us some scant protection. With few leaves in the canopy, it was doubtful we'd escape a soaking. "We'll press on and watch for shelter."

The words were no sooner out of his mouth when a fat raindrop struck him on the top of his head. Finnegan's upward glare earned him another drop square in the eye. It would have been humorous if I weren't busy pulling my hood up to protect my own head. With a thought, the pale olive-green of my cloak switched to a darker gray. A better color to blend in with the elements.

The raindrops fell in quick succession, the hiss growing in volume until it drowned out everything else. The wind picked up, the force of it pressing our cloaks against our bodies and threatening to whip our hoods back. The day seemed to bleed into night, and the road ahead of us became a shadowy ribbon of mud.

"Let me take the lead," I shouted to be heard over the wind. Without waiting, I urged my mount forward, pulling alongside Finnegan. It was useless trying to travel without light. With a gesture, I formed an elven light and held the glowing ball in my upright palm. I was forced to release my grip on my hood, and the wind caught it and flung it back. Rain pelted my face and head, drenching my hair and sending a wash of cold water down my neck. A shiver ran along my spine; I regulated my body temperature to better ignore the discomfort.

Suddenly the storm was in full swing, and the time for searching for shelter had passed. Waiting it out under a tree was not an option. Other than some scraggly pines, these woods offered no protection. Ahead, I could see another clump of trees. These looked a little denser.

I tried to tell myself the inclement weather was good. Even if my false trail failed, the storm made it impossible to track us. But was I being foolish? We had seen no sign of the Skori since we'd left the ancient wood, and I was confident that none had survived its wrath. So why was I so convinced they still posed a danger to us?

Call it a hunch or just call it instinct. I'd relied on it often in the past, and my gut feelings were rarely wrong. We were still being hunted.

The visibility of my light only extended perhaps a dozen feet ahead. Within minutes, we gained the comparative shelter of the trees, for all the good it did us. The road was a sea of mud, the slick substance making travel even more dangerous. The wind whistled down the corridor formed by the wide trunks, driving the rain into our faces but offering a measure of protection from the lightning. It continued to flash overhead, immediately followed by thunder, causing our horses to dance in nervous excitement. Even Mysteria.

The electricity in the air hampered my ability to scan ahead for danger, so the figure that appeared in the middle of the road surprised me. One moment the lane ahead of us was empty, the next, a man atop a horse stood in the middle of the mud-slicked road. Mysteria tossed her head with alarm as the accompanying roll of thunder followed the flash of lightning.

I pulled her to a halt, signaling my two companions to do the same. Quickly, I dimmed my elven light and whipped a glamour over myself. Despite the gloom, my eyes easily picked out the man. He was tall and lanky, his height evident even mounted on a horse.

I moved Mysteria forward until she blocked Merry, whose gelding danced with fear. She handled the animal well, her hands steady on the reins as she allowed him to dance in a tight circle before bringing him under control. I quickly sent out a scan for any other intruders but found nothing. The man appeared to be alone.

Returning my attention to the motionless figure, I studied him with care. His cowled hood concealed his face, and the rest of him was covered by a heavy cloak, which appeared weighed down by the rain.

"You there!" the man called, lifting an arm in greeting. I tensed, but there was no sign of a weapon in his hand. Instead, he held a lantern, its dim light doing little to hold back the gloom. "Are you lost?"

"Not lost." Finnegan took the lead while I continued to scan for other intruders. Call me paranoid. "Merely travelers caught in the storm."

The man raised his other hand and lowered his cowl. The next flash of lightning revealed a human with average features. An oversized nose dominated his face, but we were close enough for my eyes to pick out his balding head, the fringe of remaining hair plastered to it.

"Let me offer you shelter," the man called out, moving his mount closer. I felt Finnegan stiffen, and he shifted his staff until it was held at the ready. I waved a hand.

"Keep to our disguise," I said in a low voice. "I sense no threat coming from him."

"Do you live nearby?" Finnegan did not relax his grip on his staff, moving it slightly until the tip was toward the figure.

"Just over the hill."

"How did he know we were here?" Merry asked in a soft voice.

I glanced her way, but she was staring at the stranger, her face set in an expression of distrust. Like me, she ignored the wind as it whipped her cloak behind her. Water dripped down her face, plastering her shorn hair to her head. Unlike me, she was shivering in the chilled air, her skin taking on a bluish hue.

"This is hardly a night for someone to be out riding on the off chance of coming across travelers," she continued.

A good point. What was the man doing out in the middle of a storm? The wind whipped my cloak around me, strong enough to lift the sodden material. For an instant, my hair blew into my eyes, and the rain lashed against my face. I knew my glamour was firmly in place; my persona of a young mortal female should easily protect our mission.

"I was just returning home myself," the stranger went on as if he'd heard Merry's question. "I saw your lantern and thought you might be in trouble. Please," he continued. "Let me offer you shelter."

"What do you think?" Finnegan asked me in a low voice. "We cannot continue much farther in this storm."

I thought about it for a moment longer, allowing my elven glow to fade completely. It was fortunate the stranger had mistaken it for a lantern. Finnegan was right. It was useless trying to go on tonight. The storm was growing fiercer, the wind snapping bare branches and sending them flying. I glanced upward in time to see a fork of lightning spear down and strike some distance away. The smell of ozone flooded the air.

"We'll stop," I said. Common sense won out, but I distrusted anyone who just happened to be out on a night like this. Deep down, I had a bad feeling about this. "But we must have a care."

"Of course." Finnegan raised his voice and called to the man even as he urged his mare forward. Merry and I followed close behind. "Thank you, sir. We will take you up on your kind offer."

"This way." The stranger pulled his hood back up over his head and turned his mount, starting down the road he'd come. As I watched, his horse stumbled in the mud, then scrambled to regain its footing. The lantern swayed with the gait of the animal, vanishing and reappearing with each gust of wind. It was a wonder it stayed lit.

"What do you think?" Merry raised her voice to be heard over the storm. She darted a quick glance at the shrouded figure before urging her gelding closer to Mysteria. My horse snapped at the gelding when it crowded in close, and I pulled her up sharply.

"I think we should keep our eyes and ears open."

"Maybe we should continue."

"We cannot, Merry. The storm is growing worse. It will do us no good to risk injury."

A particularly strong gust of wind whipped into us, powerful enough to take my breath away. The day that had started out so mild now bordered on the verge on freezing, the rain reaching with icy fingers to penetrate our clothing and steal away any remaining warmth. A shudder ran through Merry's small frame, her lips tinged blue. Even in the near darkness, I could see the pinched misery in her face.

My desire to find shelter had more to do with her safety than mine or even the wizard's. Much more time in this weather and we'd risk Merry coming down with hypothermia. She didn't have the advantage of being able to regulate her body temperature that I had. Which I also suspected Finnegan of having. I'd been monitoring him. He appeared to feel the cold as little as I.

We'd traveled only ten minutes when, through the trees, I saw lighted windows ahead of us. A promise of shelter and warmth. As we neared, I could see that the structure was three stories high, perched on a low hill, and surrounded by a stone wall that, from this distance, looked to be perhaps ten feet tall. Sporadic flashes of lightning showed that we were approaching from the back. I could see the stables through a break in the wall, the gates standing open in invitation.

I sent my senses out questing, searching for any hint of threat. The electrical activity in the air really messed up my probe, but I detected nothing out of the ordinary. Everything appeared normal.

Was it too good to be true?

We followed the stranger in through the gates, the hooves of our mounts just audible on the cobblestones that made up the courtyard within the walls. The effects of the storm lessened as we gained the shelter of the stone walls. The rain still poured down, but the buildings and walls blocked much of the wind's fury. A stone walkway covered the entrance of the stables, stretching the length of the courtyard to the mansion beyond. It was a relief to find shelter from the rain. Mysteria pranced for a moment, shaking water out of her face before she quieted.

There were more lights inside the courtyard, lanterns carefully shielded from the wind, their flames flickering wildly and throwing shadows over everything.

I continued to scan, careful to keep myself between Merry and the stranger. I noticed Finnegan hadn't put up his staff yet, evidently prepared to counter any attack. I liked a man who was ready for a fight. The value of the wizard was growing with each moment.

"Please, be welcome."

I returned my attention to the stranger, watching as he dismounted before doing the same. As far as I could tell, he was unarmed and showed no sign of threat. On foot, he was shorter than I'd first assumed, swathed from head to knee in a plain brown cloak that ended at the top of mud-splattered boots. He'd pushed his hood back until his face was visible, his features unremarkable.

Two young men came running from the stables, bowing to the man before one of them hurried to take his mount. Okay, a nobleman, then, if this subservient behavior was any indication. Both young mortals were tall and had the look of men well used to hard labor.

One took the bridle of Finnegan's mare, waiting patiently as the wizard dismounted. Finnegan untied his pack, slinging it over his shoulder before allowing the groom to lead his horse into the open double doors of the stable. Two more young men arrived to take Mysteria and Merry's gelding. They both attempted to hand us down from our mounts, but I avoided their help to swing from the saddle.

I was unwilling to have a human touch me while I was alert to danger. Ignoring the groom, I gathered up my gear, pulling my longbow from the strap that held it secure to the saddle. I'd unstrung the bow when the rain had begun. A wet bowstring did no one any good. Smoothing one hand over Mysteria's neck, I whispered to her, instructing her to allow the grooms to take her to shelter. After giving her one last pat of reassurance, I turned to follow our host as he led the way toward the mansion, using the covered walkway.

"Carry my gear," I told Merry in a low voice. Without waiting for her consent, I handed her the pack I'd taken from Mysteria's saddle. "I want my hands free."

She took it without protest, juggling the packs until she found a comfortable balance. I kept my cloak over my sword. No need to advertise I was armed. I kept my longbow, using it as a staff as I fell into step behind the men. The stranger and Finnegan walked side by side, the wizard towering over him by a full head. Merry and I brought up the rear.

"It's a wicked night to be traveling," the man was saying to Finnegan. "Have you traveled far?"

"Just from a village a day's ride from here."

"Tinsdale." The man nodded, and I stared at him, alert. He didn't appear to notice the sudden tension in the air. "It's the only village from the direction you were traveling. You've come a long way despite the weather."

"Your offer of shelter is greatly appreciated, sir."

"Please. Call me Brother Morris."

Chapter Eight

F innegan's only reaction was a slight hesitation in his step before he continued walking beside the monk. Merry's gasp was audible to my ears, but I didn't think anyone else heard it. I shot her a warning glance and slipped my hand inside my cloak to touch the hilt of my sword, muttering a curse under my breath.

What were the chances of meeting the one person we were most trying to avoid? I didn't like coincidences. They made me nervous. My grip tightened on my staff.

"Ah, excuse me a moment," he said as he halted. "I meant to inform my men that the road to the west is washed out."

With a nod toward us, he returned to the stable entrance, gesturing to the groom who lingered outside the doors. The three of us watched him as he fell into an intense conversation with the man. It was impossible to read the monk's expression in the flickering shadows cast by the lanterns. Even my acute hearing could not pick up the low conversation from this distance.

Without thought, I began to gather my magic. Maybe he was telling his man about a washed-out road. Or maybe he was instructing him to warn others and to take us prisoner. Power thrummed through me as I turned my focus inward.

A hand on my arm stayed my instinctive defense.

"Wait," Finnegan said softly. He kept his grip on my arm but watched the monk. I could feel the touch of his hand through the damp material of my shirt. Very warm. With my power coursing through me, I caught his scent. It reminded me of open sky and the warm sun. Masculine. Funny the things you notice at the most inopportune moments. "He has no way of knowing who we are."

"Are you willing to bet on that?" I ignored my reaction to his touch as I kept my voice just as low. The rumble of thunder overhead concealed our words even from Merry who stood a scant meter away.

"No, but I'm going to advise caution. There are four rather burly stable hands that I can see, and I caught a glimpse of another man over there in the doorway." He gestured to the far end of the walkway, where the shadows nearly concealed a door. I could see a darker shape standing just within. "Can you sense anyone else?"

I hesitated. My power pulsed and throbbed, but I subdued it, redirecting it to send out a new probe. The electrical charge in the air did not completely conceal the man in the doorway, nor the fact that there was at least one other man besides the four grooms within the stables. The numbers did not look good for us. I could not risk injury to Merry on the off chance that this Brother Morris knew who and what we were.

"There is another within the stable. And"—I closed my eyes —"yes, another mortal just beyond the man in the doorway. He is armed."

"A monastery like this houses a number of people, Riona. There is no telling how many. Can you disable them all?"

Unfortunately, he was right. I was good, but I didn't want to cause unnecessary harm to anyone. Plus, I could not say with certainty that I'd located every threat. Who was to say there wasn't someone with an arrow trained on one or all of us? I might not die of natural causes, but a well-placed arrow could still end my life.

For now, I would wait and watch. This Brother Morris had thus far offered us no threat. Perhaps he didn't know who his guests were. At present.

Automatically, I checked the strength of my glamour, making sure it was firmly in place. I'd allowed it to slip while we were battling the elements, but now I was careful that none of my elven features were evident. I would continue my masquerade of a young mortal female. With luck, we would be deemed harmless travelers and be on our way in the morning.

If not, I would use my time here to mark out each inhabitant and prepare our defense should it prove necessary.

We stood sheltered from the weather by the walkway, Merry shivering in the chilled late afternoon. She was soaked through, and hypothermia was still a very real danger. We had to get her out of those wet clothes and warm.

Brother Morris finished his conversation and returned to our side. I watched the groom reenter the stables, showing no further interest in us. A tiny part of me relaxed. A very tiny part.

"Thank you for your indulgence. I wanted to see about getting that road repaired as soon as possible. The passage there is treacherous, and I did not want other travelers injured. Please, come in." He seemed to notice Merry's pinched features for the first time. "Good heavens, child. You're freezing!"

"I'm fine, Brother Morris."

"Nonsense. Come in, come in."

He urged us along the walkway toward the monastery. As we neared the structure, it was easier to see it for what it was, a bastion of the human religion. A regular fortress of thick stone that no doubt had stood for hundreds of years. Many of the windows were lit, warm beacons to push back the darkness with the promise of comfort and safety. Staring at it, I could see that the stone was bare and unornamented. I knew it would appear cold and barren during the daylight hours.

Either illusion could very well be misleading.

I placed myself beside Merry, probing the shadows, but the

figure that had been here moments ago was gone. The second man I'd detected was farther down the hall, moving away from us. My ears caught the soft tread of his footsteps as he retreated. There was something odd about the measure of his steps, a sound almost too light to be human, yet not Sithi. I would sense the presence of one of my brethren. The thought briefly crossed my mind that it could somehow be Skori, but I immediately dismissed it. I'd be able to sense if one of the dark creatures were anywhere near.

The hallway was wide, dim, with lighted wall sconces positioned every third meter or so. The flooring started with unadorned paved stone until we reached a heavy wooden door studded with iron. The latch was also of iron and creaked slightly when Brother Morris opened it. His gaze lingered on me only an instant, but I felt his examination.

Wondering if this was some sort of test, I deliberately brushed my hand against the iron latch. Why humans persisted in believing Sithi were adversely affected by iron was beyond me. This door leading in from the stables must be a defense against my kind. Or so they believed.

The chamber we entered was vast and high ceilinged. A wide stone staircase vanished into the overhead shadows. There were whispers of sound everywhere. The soft murmur of voices accompanied by a piano, singing hymns somewhere deep within the building. The distant hiss of rain against countless windowpanes. The sputter of a candle within one of the wall sconces as it burned itself out.

All these things I heard and catalogued, alert for something, anything that was out of place.

"Visitors are always welcome," Brother Morris was saying as he led us through the great hall. "The halls of God are always open."

"We do so appreciate the shelter."

I only half heard Finnegan's response. I was listening to the sounds around me. Merry walked at my side, saying nothing, but her head was constantly turning, keeping everything and everyone in sight. Water still ran down her face and dripped from her hair. Out of the corner of my eye, I saw her wipe the water out of her eyes. She saw my glance and edged closer.

"What do you think?" she asked in a low voice.

"Nothing suspicious as of yet," I replied just as softly. "Stay alert."

Brother Morris held the door open for us, and we entered ahead of him. This room was smaller, more intimate, and comfortable. Rich fabrics covered many of the chairs, and thick rugs cushioned the feet while concealing the hard stone below. Tapestries covered the walls while thick velvet curtains hid the windows from view.

Rain lashed against the glass, a pattering sound that made me glad that we were indoors. A fire burned in the large fireplace, the heat welcome after the chilling we'd received for much of the afternoon. There was a peculiar smell in the air, an incense not unlike the church incense I remembered from my youth. Not unpleasant, but pungent. I wrinkled my nose, automatically dispelling the slight dizziness that swept over me.

I heard a soft gasp come from behind me and turned in time to see Merry collapse to the ground. Finnegan was already on the floor, sprawled in a boneless manner that told me he was unconscious.

My power, held in abeyance, flared at my call. Fury fed my magic, building it to an inferno. I glanced around and found my target. The monk stood at the open doorway, a cloth pressed over his face. Fresh air swept in through the open door, dispersing the drugging incense, but the scent had done its work. I felt disorientated, off balance.

"Hold, Rowena Kathryn McAllister."

The utterance of that name froze me, and my magic sputtered and failed. Shock flooded my senses, and I was rendered temporarily helpless.

My True Name! This mortal knew my True Name. His use of it dispelled the magic I wielded, as if snuffing out a candle. The effect was temporary, but his knowledge of that name allowed the incense to invade my senses, cloud my mind. I fumbled as I reached for the sword strapped at my side, managing to pull it free.

I saw a hint of movement out of the corner of my eye and struggled to go on the defensive. The blow to the side of my head took me by surprise. As I dropped to the carpeted floor, I clung to consciousness, my mind whirling.

Fool! You stupid fool! Trusting a priest was beyond stupid. Trying to brace my hands under my body, I turned my head in time to see the second blow coming and then nothing. Everything went black.

I was dreaming. I knew I was dreaming because I knew that I'd been rendered unconscious by the monk or his accomplice. But it didn't feel like a dream. It had a misty, unreal feel to it.

Like … a shiver traveled down my spine. It was like that first walk so long ago when I chose to follow My Lady. I halted on the stone path and looked around, although there was little to see beyond the wall of white. Yes, this was the same lane, the same feel to the mist surrounding me, pressing in from all sides. At the same time, I wasn't alarmed.

Where was I?

Knowing there was little else I could do, I continued walking, placing my feet carefully. Curious, I put my hands to my hair, pulling it forward so that I could see the pale golden tresses still streaked with winter white. Then I touched my face, finding the angular shape of my cheeks and chin, the delicate shape of my ears where they came to a slight point. I was still Sithi. This wasn't a dream of my past. Was this a dream of the present?

I didn't know how far I walked before the mist thinned enough to allow me to see a circular clearing some distance away. Huge, it appeared to be paved in white marble. As I drew near, it seemed to glow. There was no sunlight, but the white marble reflected light that emanated from some unseen source. I hesitated before I stepped upon it and looked around. The mist surrounding the clearing concealed everything beyond. It unsettled me. It felt more like an arena than a clearing. Or a coliseum.

A feel of eyes watching me sent fear racing up my spine. Something, I wasn't sure what, warned me of peril, and I left the clearing, stepping back onto the paved stones I'd just traveled. Backing up, I allowed the mist to enfold me once more. It made my view of the clearing uncertain, but somehow I knew I should not be seen.

My caution was rewarded when three figures appeared on the marble clearing. One second, the arena was empty, the next it was inhabited. From where I stood, it was difficult to make them out. Two were tall, broad of shoulder, and obviously male. The third was a head shorter, slender, and shapely. All three were garbed in long gowns, but from this distance, I could only make out that the woman was dressed all in green while the two men were in white and black respectively.

Fear stabbed through me as realization flooded my mind. These were the three deities. The gods of the Sithi, Skori, and mortals.

I should not be here. This was a scene not meant to be witnessed by a mere Sithi. I tried to turn to follow the path away from the clearing, but something stopped me. I could not move. I could only stare at the figures before me, relying on the mist to conceal my presence. Never had I felt so naked, so exposed. Sweat beaded my brow, and I pressed my lips together to halt the sob of sound that would have escaped.

The distance and the encroaching mist did not allow me to see their features, but I could hear them perfectly.

"You will recall your minions, Brother," My Lady said, her tone hard and unyielding. Her back was to me, but her posture was stiff with anger. "This is my era. Your people were allowed to exist because of the choices they made nearly a thousand years ago. They are to be confined in the north. That was the agreement."

"I will send my Skori wherever I choose, Sister." The tone of the Dark Master was smooth, amused. Sinister and sensuous at the same time. As if her anger was of no consequence. "Your weak Sithi are no match for my people. They are a nuisance that will be driven out."

My Lady started toward her brother, her movement threatening.

The third figure, clad in white, stepped between them. "You know the laws, Sister. Soon, a thousand years will pass, and our followers will once again be given the right to make a choice. Just as they were given the right in the beginning."

"That is for your humans to choose, Brother. Not my people."

"And were your Sithi and your Skori not once human? They retain the same rights." His was the voice of reason, gentle and pacifying.

"Our brother has not earned the right to his millennium, Yahweh. Look what happened the last time he interfered and tried to take a millennium. You will recall, Brother, what he did during your era with the black plague? He could have destroyed mankind."

The figure in white cast a glance toward his brother, who merely shrugged. I could still see them in shape, but their faces were unfocused. It was a dizzying effect.

"I seem to recall some interference from you as well, my dear Danae," the Dark Master said. "With your druids."

"My druids did not threaten the very fabric of the universe."

"Regardless, with the new millennium, choices will be made," the One God said, making a gesture that said the matter was settled.

"No! My time has come," the Dark Master interrupted, his tone menacing. "I have been denied far too long, and I want guarantees, not choices. The numbers who choose to worship me are dwindling."

"Which only goes to prove that humans are not predestined to evil, Brother." My Lady's tone was smug. "And that is why you will never truly rule over them."

It was the Dark Master's turn to take a threatening step toward his sister. The mist ebbed and flowed around me, and I continued to stand frozen. My breathing quickened until I was almost panting. This explained so much! Every thousand years, there was a struggle for control between the three siblings. The One God had had control for the first two millennia of modern man, but with the failure of the Industrial Age, it was deemed My Lady's turn to correct the mistakes of her brother.

But now the Dark Master was demanding his turn. The thought was enough to freeze my blood. What the Dark Master would do to our world did not bear thinking. Darkness and evil would rule, and everything that was good would vanish forever. I could see why his siblings were unwilling to allow him his turn.

"You know our laws, Brother. When you can prove that humans will embrace the evil of your soul, then you will rule." The One God, Yahweh, his sister had called him, was speaking again, and I strained to listen. "Until then, our sister's rule appears to be successful. Far more successful than my own."

"Thank you, Brother." My Lady inclined her head to acknowledge his words, pride in her voice and in her motions as she gestured toward the black-garbed being. "All the more reason to demand that our brother restrain his Skori."

"He has one year to change the course of events, Danae." Yahweh's words made My Lady stiffen. "When the girl gains twenty-one years of age, the question is moot. This is your one chance, Brother."

"Yahweh ..."

"It is as we agreed when you gained control, Sister. No more argument."

My Lady gave a toss of her head, her outrage evident in her stiff posture. How I wished I could see her clearly. Never had I put a face to My Lady. But now I had a name. Danae. It was a beautiful name. Graceful and majestic. I felt honored to have it revealed to me.

Without warning, the two brothers vanished from the clearing, leaving My Lady alone. Although I was certain I was hidden, she turned and looked straight at me. A smile curved her lips. I realized it was she who'd brought me here. To witness ... what? An explanation for the events that were unfolding? A warning to prepare me for the future?

"*Of course.*"

The voice sounded in my head, letting me know that My Lady was aware of everything I did.

"*You must guard Merry Sterling, my child,*" her voice continued. "*At all costs.*"

Although she faced me, I still could not see her face. To look upon the visage of my deity would be an honor I'd never dared contemplate. How I wished I could.

As if hearing my desire, the mists cleared for a moment, allowing me to view the most beautiful woman I'd ever seen. Her cheeks were high, like those of the Sithi, her skin flawless. Eyes the clearest blue of a mountain lake smiled down at me. Her hair was a rich russet, falling about her shoulders and down her back in a luxurious wave. It was held away from her face by a circlet of gold, leaves and flowers adorning it, pulled back to reveal ears that rose to a delicate point.

My knees almost buckled. The Sithi were created in her image! It was a stunning revelation. I'd always thought we were a mockery of the human image of an elf, but we were actually modeled after My Lady.

"I will guard her, My Lady." My voice was rough with emotion. I dared not use her given name. It was an honor I was not bestowed. One I had not yet earned.

"*I brought you here to witness this meeting, Riona,*" she continued as she came closer to where I stood. The mists cleared further, and I dropped to my knees without conscious thought, bowing my head to stare down at the paved path. It wasn't fear that had me shivering. Not exactly. More a sense of feeling unworthy. Her bare feet came into my line of vision, and I felt a hand under my chin as she raised it until I met her gaze.

She withdrew her touch, and I felt cold without the warmth of her fingers against my chin. Bereft. "*My brother, Yahweh, does not understand the danger our sibling presents. He is a forgiving god, and has allowed our brother countless opportunities to prove himself. But each time has ended in disaster.*"

Her eyes were gentle. Sad. The purity of her features made a mockery of everything I'd ever thought beautiful. This close, I could see that she was dressed in a gown of rich velvet, the emerald material molded to her figure like a second skin as it fell to the ground in graceful folds. There was nothing provocative or sensual in her garb. It was a style popular during the Middle Ages but fashioned of far superior material. A torque of gold glittered at her throat, the design intertwined with leaves and flowers, matching the circlet around her head.

"Are we pawns in an ongoing battle between you and your brothers?" I don't know why I asked this. It was suicide to question a deity, but I had to know what we were up against. The meeting revealed a significance to the coming year, and somehow Merry was the key. I wasn't sure how a twenty-year-old girl could be so significant, but the deities made it clear that everything depended on keeping Merry alive. Did her death signify the end of the present era? Did it leave the next up for grabs?

"Not pawns, child." There was nothing in her tone to indicate anger at my boldness, but still I bowed my head once more. Cripes. One did not piss off a deity. Not if one wanted to live to see another day. *"We love our people. Each in our own way. Even my dark brother. But I cannot deny that there is a degree of sibling rivalry between us."*

"Merry Sterling holds the key, doesn't she?"

"Yes. She is the turning point. She must find the strength within herself. No one but she can discover what that strength is." My Lady smiled down at me, reaching out once more to lay her hand against my cheek. Her fingers were cool on my skin.

"You are her guide, Riona. I bid that you keep her safe until she achieves her destiny."

"What is that destiny?"

"I cannot say. You will know when it happens, child." My Lady tilted her head to one side as if listening. Her expression hardened even as she began to fade from my sight. The mists swirled up to sweep me away from her. The loss of her touch caused me to cry out in protest, but she was gone. The eerie fog closed around to blind me. From somewhere far off, I caught her final words.

"Awaken, Riona. You're in grave danger."

I came awake with a jerk.

Chapter Nine

Consciousness was slow in coming, even with My Lady's urgent warning echoing in my subconscious. My head hurt. Badly. I didn't want to regain consciousness. I yearned to wallow in the memory of My Lady's beauty. Her grace. The last thing I wanted right now was to return to the world of mortals.

But her last words and the urgency instilled in them forced me back to the present. Gathering my strength, I clawed my way through the darkness until I could see light through the closed lids of my eyes. I rested that way for a moment, trying to get my bearings as memory relived my last moments of consciousness.

The drugging incense. The priest. The unexpected attack that had knocked me out for who knows how long.

Brother Morris had to have known who we were from the very beginning. He'd known we were coming down that road and had lain in wait for us. The question was, how could he have known?

The thoughts whirling through my head weren't doing anything for my headache. I tried to calm myself long enough to think, to determine where I was, if I was alone, and where my companions were.

There was something dry and matted at the back of my head. Blood. Quite a bit of it. I'd been unconscious long enough for my wound to close up and heal itself, leaving me with a blazing headache. Delving within myself, I realized the priest had hit me hard enough to leave a good-sized gash at the back of my skull.

Very Christian of him. Fortunately for me, Sithi healed fast, otherwise I'd be history. Literally. The wound had closed up before I could bleed to death.

I realized I was rambling with myself. Not like me at all. The blow must have scrambled a few brain cells. Either that or I wanted to avoid giving thought to the Vision My Lady had bestowed upon me. It answered so many questions and raised a hundred more.

Concentrating, I took stock of my surroundings. The stone floor was cold under me. There was a sense of a small space. A cell, then. I'd been there for a while. Long enough for the cold to permeate my bones. Still without moving, I regulated my body temperature and kept my breathing even and shallow. Casting about me, I could sense no other people in the cell with me.

Where was Merry? Finnegan? They'd been incapacitated by the incense before I had. Worry and fear ate at me.

Something else crashed down on me with the force of a bolt of lightning. Brother Morris had known my True Name! That was what had frozen me and drained me of my magic for the fatal instant before he'd struck.

Such a thing was impossible. No one in this world should know that name. No one but …

Another Sithi.

The thought sent a spike of cold fear through me. No, none of my brethren would betray another.

Would they? the little voice inside my head whispered, birthing a kernel of doubt. A Sithi guarded her True Name, the name she was born with, with great caution. To reveal your birth name was to give another temporary control over you.

I tried to think which Sithi would know my True Name. Dylan, of course. My human brother's son, he'd known me all his life, but he would not betray me. Never. Only a few others knew my name. Queen Tesina. She and I had been friends once upon a time.

Before her insecurity and jealousy ate at her and she'd begun seeing me as a rival rather than a companion. Still, I could not envision Tesina betraying me. There had been lovers over the past thousand years, but other than one or two … No, my True Name was known only to a handful of Sithi and never to a human.

Using care, I sat up, sweeping the mass of hair from my face. When I felt steady, I knelt. I was still dressed in my fawn-colored trousers and overcoat, a line of blood running down over one shoulder. My white shirt was a mess, both from blood and the filth of the floor. I was surprised to find that I still possessed my dagger. I would have thought that would be the first thing they'd relieve me of. My gear was missing, of course, as well as my sword. No surprise there.

The sound of footsteps outside the cell alerted me, and I came to my feet in one lithe movement. I was not going to be found kneeling on the floor like a supplicant. I reached for my magic and found it easily within my grasp. My skin glowed with power as I prepared a nasty surprise, waiting until the cell door opened and the figure of Brother Morris was framed in the space. I was about to strike but noticed what he held in his outstretched palm. Merry's ring.

A spike of fear formed in my gut as I tamed my magic and held my defense. I withdrew to the shadows of the cell to conceal my expression, but I knew magic still glowed faintly around me. I wasn't about to release my power completely.

"Please do not do anything foolish, elf," Brother Morris said as he watched me. He displayed no fear. He had changed from his wet cloak to a plain brown monk's robe, belted at the waist and falling to his ankles. Low boots were visible below the hem. "I left instructions that the girl and the old man were to be killed if I do not return within fifteen minutes."

"That's very Christian of you."

"When dealing with abominations, one must think beyond

what is expected of me by my God."

It always amazed me that humans seemed to think they knew the inner workings of their deity. The One God I'd observed would never have condoned murder of innocents in His name. But that was for Brother Morris to sort out with his deity when one day he stood before Him in judgment.

"Why are you doing this?" My head ached, and it was difficult to think straight. With a short prayer to My Lady, I felt some of the pain ease. Gratitude infused me, and I stood a little taller, topping the monk by a foot. I was still effectively hobbled and rendered incapacitated. Given opportunity, I have no doubt that My Lady would judge me justified in destroying this human, but I would not, could not risk harm to my companions.

"I have my orders." There was a self-satisfied gleam in the dark eyes as he watched me, and a hint of pride. Couldn't really blame him there. He had just bested an ancient. Few humans could boast that. Probing deeper, I could detect no real malice although there was a faint air of fanaticism surrounding the man. A sense of righteousness. I shook my head. *My Lady, save me from self-righteous prigs.*

"From who?" I asked.

"Why, my bishop, of course."

"Bishop Langley ordered our capture?"

"Naturally."

He still betrayed no fear. The man was confident that I'd do nothing under the threat of harm to my companions. And damned if he wasn't right. I did not know where they were being held or what condition they were in. Somehow I couldn't see Finnegan being taken easily. The man was too well versed in magic. If I were a betting woman, I'd say he was still unconscious. Despite his aid in the past day, I didn't worry overmuch about him. In the scheme of things, the wizard was probably expendable. It was Merry who held the key to all of our survival.

Callous of me? Probably, but when you'd lived as long as I had, you learned to pick your battles and determine the line of importance. I'd prefer the wizard was well. There was something about the human that triggered an unwanted response in me, which I found disturbing in and of itself.

"So you began waylaying every stranger on the off chance that you'd come across a Sithi?"

"Not any Sithi, but you, Lady Riona Northstar. We had word that you were coming."

Damn! It seemed everyone was better informed than I. I'd met Merry and Finnegan in the Crossroads Inn in Memis only days ago, yet word of our alliance appeared to have traveled far and wide.

To what purpose? As of yet, Meredith Sterling's importance had not manifested. Only someone with a Vision would know what her destiny was.

Again, that indicated a Sithi.

Everything was pointing toward the involvement of a Sithi. He or she would have access to Merry's importance, would have the ability to detect and follow my magic, and would have known the power given to the user of a True Name.

As much as I didn't want to admit it, one of my people had betrayed me. The ramifications were horrifying.

"So now what?" I allowed the glow of magic to fade, leaving me in shadow. It was unlikely this mortal could read my expression, but I'd more nasty surprises in the last hour or so than in a thousand years.

"So now we wait for the bishop's emissaries to come claim you."

"Which will be … when?" I came forward out of the shadows. I made sure my expression was amused. I didn't want Brother Morris to know just how worried I was.

"Before the night is out. It seems they've been following you for the past few days."

Were we being followed by half the country?

By my internal clock, I knew we had hours before the dawn. We'd entered the walls of the monastery in early evening, and I'd evidently been unconscious for only a few hours. It was nearly nine o'clock by human reckoning. That left me eight hours to come up with some means of escape.

"Excuse me, but isn't your fifteen minutes nearly up? I certainly wouldn't want my companions harmed because you were chitchatting and tardy in returning to them."

Brother Morris's face twisted with anger, but he still stepped back to the cell doorway, turning to catch the edge before giving me his last parting shot.

"God will see that you are revealed for the abomination that you are and wiped from this world."

"I've heard that before, priest. What you Bible thumpers don't seem to understand is we Sithi are all that stand between you and the Skori."

"Funny you should mention them, elf. They are the emissaries coming to collect you."

Brother Morris slammed the heavy wooden doorway shut, barring it from the outside as I took his information like a blow to my stomach. I rushed the door, my hands grasping the bars of the little window cut into the door. I pressed my face to the iron bars, seeing nothing of the dingy hallway beyond my door. A single torch illuminated the gloom. Searching out, I found the retreating figure of the monk.

"If you allow them within these walls, you will have a bloodbath on your hands, Brother Morris," I shouted after him. The monk hesitated for an instant, then kept walking. "The Skori will not only destroy us, but they will tear apart every living being within these walls. They are the true evil, not us."

The sound of a second door slamming shut was his response,

and I sagged against the door of my prison. Fear clogged my throat for a moment longer before I straightened. This would get me nowhere. I could not let my emotions hamper me. First of all, I had to locate Merry and Finnegan. My blood connection with Merry would make it easy to locate her. Finding Finnegan, if he wasn't being held with Merry, might be a little more difficult, but I'd been in his company long enough to get a feel for his spirit. A bit more of a challenge, but not impossible.

I glanced at the barred door and snorted. A lock was the least of my problems.

Sitting down, I crossed my legs and closed my eyes. Concentrating, I created Merry's image in my mind, adding the emotional and familial connection we shared. All outside discomfort faded. There was a floating sensation as my life-force left my body. Looking down, I could see myself still sitting on the cold stone floor of the cell, unmoving. My expression was peaceful, even serene. Then I turned away from my body and passed through the ceiling to the room above. I realized the cells were positioned in the basement of the monastery, probably along with the storerooms and cisterns.

On the main floor, I hovered for a moment, looking around at the well-appointed room. It was a study with walls lined with books, scrolls, and other odds and ends. The floor was covered with a thick rug, and a fire burned in the rather large fireplace. This room looked well used and well maintained. It was also deserted.

Following the pull of Merry's presence, I passed through the ceiling to the second floor and walls until I found her. She stood in the middle of a small but comfortable sitting room, an open door revealing an even smaller bedroom. It looked more like a nun's cell rather than a guest room. Either way, far more comfortable than my accommodations.

A tall monk was standing just inside the door leading out to the hallway, stance wide, arms crossed over his chest. Obviously a guard. Only one. Good.

Brother Morris paced the center of the room. He must have come straight up here after leaving me. I glanced at the guard and wondered if he was the one instructed to kill Merry and Finnegan if Morris hadn't returned after fifteen minutes.

Speaking of Finnegan ... I glanced around and found him slumped in a chair positioned before the tiny fireplace. Moving closer, I could see he was still unconscious. They must be keeping him drugged. Either he had tried to use his powers to escape or they'd somehow discovered he was a wizard. They were obviously taking no chances with him. He was missing his wet cloak, and his plain gray tunic was still damp at the neck and shoulders. His tangled mass of hair concealed much of his face.

"You're human, Your Highness." Brother Morris's voice drew my attention back to them. He stopped his pacing long enough to glare at Merry. "You're associating with a Sithi and a wizard."

Yep, they knew what Finnegan was.

"They're my friends, Brother Morris. It is of no concern of yours who I choose to associate with."

"Your soul is in peril."

"My ..." Merry began laughing. "It's a hell of a lot more than my soul that's in peril right now. Haven't you listened to a word of what I told you earlier?"

He waved his hand in dismissal. "Dark creatures, pshaw. The elf tried to tell me the same. My instructions are to wait for the arrival of the Skori and hand you over."

"Hand us over to the Skori! You send us to our deaths, Brother Morris. We've been accosted by them in the forest. They're foul, loathsome creatures that delight in murder and destruction."

"My bishop would never condone association with such creatures."

"Your bishop is wrong, and what he is condoning is murder.

My brothers were all butchered by these creatures, Brother Morris. They hunt me for reasons unknown. You are handing us over to be killed."

Brother Morris hesitated, for the first time a look of uncertainty crossing his face, before he shook it off. "You are sadly misled, my child. The elf and the wizard have clouded your mind with their unholy magic."

"No, Brother Morris," Merry said, her head held high, her words calm with conviction. "It is you who has been deceived and misled. The Skori will tear us to pieces and leave no one in this monastery alive. If you release us, we can lead them away from here and save your people."

Again, that hesitation. I was beginning to suspect that the good priest was no longer quite as convinced as he had been. That could only be to our advantage.

I cast around for a means to strengthen his doubt. A slight movement near the fire drew my attention, and I saw Finnegan open his eyes. A glance at the others showed they were unaware of the wizard regaining consciousness. The monk and Merry were in a staring contest, and the burly guard merely gazed ahead into space. Not very alert, which would also be to our advantage.

I floated closer to Finnegan. His eyes were bleary and out of focus, dilated by whatever they'd given him. Drawing on My Lady's magic, I leaned closer until I was eye to eye with him. With care, I sent a thin stream of power into him in an effort to clear the narcotic from his system. As I watched his eyes, I saw them clear with each passing second.

"Can you hear me, Finnegan?" I whispered to him. The other occupants of the room would be unable to detect my presence, but the wizard was far more sensitive than a mortal. "If you can, do not move. The priest will drug you again if he knows you are awake."

Finnegan didn't move for several long seconds, then he gave a barely discernible nod. His dark eyes were now clear and alert. He must have been far more sensitive than I'd suspected, because he was looking straight at me, meeting my gaze without any confusion.

I could almost see the questions churning through his mind as he rallied. Then, in a move that took me by surprise, he closed his eyes and went still. His breathing dropped to a shallow level. It was a shock to see his essence leave his body and join me where I knelt. I'd never known a mortal who could metaphysically leave his body. It was a skill mastered only by the most powerful of Sithi. What other surprises did Finnegan have up his sleeve for me?

"How long have I been unconscious?" he asked when I straightened to face him.

"I'm not sure, but Merry's hair is still damp. I'm thinking a few hours."

"What did I miss?"

"The priest has instructions to hold us until the Skori arrive. I'm not sure, but I do not believe Brother Morris realizes the full scope of his actions."

"Meaning that the Skori will leave no witnesses."

"Exactly."

"Whose orders is he following?"

"Bishop Langley."

Finnegan's expression darkened before he glanced toward the pacing priest. The man's jerky movements betrayed his growing agitation.

"My bishop would never endanger his people," Brother Morris said when he once more paused before Merry. He sounded more like he was trying to convince himself than the woman before him.

"Bishop Langley cares little for those he deems of little consequence."

I winced at Merry's blunt assessment. Not wrong, but she could have perhaps been a little more discreet. As I watched, Morris's expression went from uncertainty to stubborn conviction.

"Your mind has been poisoned, child. You will see the error of your ways when you are taken before my bishop."

"I will not live long enough to meet him, Brother Morris."

Finnegan turned back to me. "We must make the priest realize that he is signing his own death warrant."

"It's doubtful he's ever seen a Skori. If he had, he wouldn't be so willing to deal with them."

The wizard was silent for a moment, his expression pensive. He glanced around the room as if looking for inspiration before his gaze settled on the hearth. The flames now burned low, a fitful flicker that gave little heat and even less light.

Gesturing to it, he asked, "Would you be able to generate an image within the flames of what the Skori are capable of?"

"Perhaps." I thought about it for a moment, then shrugged. "I'm not sure. In this metaphysical form, the power required is beyond me. In my physical body, yes, but it may leave me drained."

"What if I were to lend you my aid?"

That made me stop and stare. This was the second time he'd made such an offer. I'd been strong enough to resist the first time, but now? In this form, I did not have full contact with the Sithi magic that I relied so heavily on. Technically speaking, he should have just as little contact with his spiritual power.

But together? It was an intriguing thought.

"You would grant me control?"

"Yes."

I was stunned, to say the least. I could count on one hand, and still have fingers to spare, the number of times a wizard had voluntarily given control of his powers to a Sithi.

One of those times, the Sithi in question had been my nephew.

I wasn't quite sure what had happened—even Dylan hadn't been able to explain—but the wizard had ended up a gibbering idiot after the experience, and Dylan had been comatose for a week. I could only surmise that the combination of earthen Sithi magic and the human's spiritual magic had spun out of control and rebounded on the wizard. Why it hadn't affected Dylan in the same manner couldn't be answered. After that incident, few Sithi were willing to endanger the few known wizards or themselves.

"Why?"

"We are in need, and I trust you, Riona."

"You barely know me."

"I trust you," he simply said again. His gaze was steady on mine. Warm.

That made me stop for an instant. Why would he trust me? The man didn't know me. Other than traveling nearly a hundred miles together, there was little reason for him to have this degree of confidence in me. Staring into his eyes, I found something in the deep brown depths that caused a shiver to run down my spine ... even in my present insubstantial shape. It wasn't a welcome sensation.

"We do not have much time, Riona."

I glanced at the arguing pair just behind us. He was right. The night waned, and if we were to escape the monastery, we had to do something now.

"This must be done physically," I told him. "My body is in a cell in the basement. Do not do anything until I arrive."

I waited until he nodded and watched as his metaphysical self melted into his body. Assured that the wizard would remain motionless, I allowed myself to return to my cell. It was a bit of a shock returning my spiritual form to the physical. My body had grown cold while I had vacated it. Standing, I stretched a few kinks out of my muscles and again regulated my body temperature before brushing off much of the dust from my clothing. I saw no need to look like a vagrant when I confronted the monk. There was nothing I could do about the blood staining my shirt, but I flicked the dried blood from my streaked hair as I finger combed it.

Glancing at the door, I sent out my senses and discovered the only guard in the small storeroom just beyond the cells. I shook my head with amusement. Brother Morris was very confident with my confinement to leave only one guard. I placed my hand on the wooden door and felt the latch that barred the door. Iron. Again shaking my head, I used my magic to lift the latch, and the door swung open without a sound. The hallway beyond my cell was bare and devoid of any character, lit by flickering torches that did little to drive the shadows back. The short corridor led straight into the storeroom, where I found the so-called guard fast asleep. Another monk, he sat in a chair tilted back against the wall, a cudgel cradled in his lap. With a slight smile, I waved a hand over his face, sending him into a deeper sleep. It was unlikely he'd awaken anytime soon. I opened the door on the far side of the room and found stairs leading upward.

I had little trouble negotiating the passages that led to the main floor. I met few people on the way. Those who I did, I used magic to cause them to glance away as I passed, ghosting my way up to the second floor on silent feet and down the more comfortably appointed corridor. Luxurious in comparison to the lower levels. Tile covered these floors, and tapestries depicting religious scenes dotted the walls. White candles encased in brass sconces lit this hallway, giving the illusion of warmth.

Locating the austere suite where Merry was being held was simple enough. Her blood relationship to me allowed me to find her anywhere. The simply carved door was closed. I already knew there was another monk standing on the other side.

Without warning, I thrust the door open, catching the man from behind and sending him into the wall. Giving him no time to recover, I slammed the door shut and brought my flattened hand down on the back of his head. He slumped to the floor in a boneless sprawl. I didn't spare him any more of my attention. When he awakened, he would have a massive headache, but he was not permanently injured.

"Hold, Rowen—"

The priest was cut off when Finnegan came to life behind him. He abandoned his act and sent out a gust of power that jerked Brother Morris's feet out from under him and sent him crashing to the ground, knocking the breath out of him.

Giving the wizard a nod of approval, I waved a hand and froze the priest's vocal cords. He'd been about to use my True Name again, but this time I would not be caught unaware.

"You are all right, Merry?" I asked as I caught the front of the priest's robes and lifted him easily to his feet. Finnegan straightened his toppled chair, and I thrust Morris into it. The chair rocked back with the force of my push, then settled. We were all treated to a round of glares as the priest tried to speak, his mouth moving soundlessly.

"I'm fine. He means to turn us over to the Skori," she said.

"I know." I turned to Finnegan. "No ill effects of the drug?"

"No, none. Thank you for clearing my system of it."

I smiled. "Any time."

Turning my attention back to the priest, I bent close to him, aware of the fire at my back. "If I allow you the use of your voice, do I have your word that you will not use my True Name?"

The only response I got was a long glare. Then his gaze flickered to the fallen guard, to Merry, Finnegan, and finally back to me. Only then did I get a reluctant nod.

"Do you swear upon your One God?"

Again a glare and a nod.

It was a chance, but I needed him talking. Playing charades had never been a favorite of mine.

"Should you trust him?" Merry asked.

"If he breaks his word after swearing upon his One God, he risks his eternal soul. That oath I will trust."

Brother Morris's shoulders slumped in defeat as he nodded once more, acknowledging the truth of my words. With a gesture, I released his vocal cords. He drew a deep breath and crossed himself. He looked like a man ready to meet his maker.

However, right now, I needed some answers. The night was a-wastin'.

I crouched down next to his chair, my face level with his so I could read his expression as I asked my questions. The flickering flames at my back did nothing to conceal his expression. Not to my eyes.

"Who gave you my True Name?" I felt more than saw Finnegan's sharp look. Did he realize the significance of a True Name? Did wizards possess that Achilles' heel? Doubtful.

"I don't know."

"You got it from someone, Brother Morris."

"I never saw his face. It was another Sithi. A male." He drew another deep breath and met my gaze with unflinching bravado. "He came to me yesterday. He had a missive from Bishop Langley —"

"You're sure it was from Langley?" Finnegan broke in.

"It was in my bishop's hand and had his seal on it. Yes, the message was from Bishop Langley. Over a month ago, I was instructed to watch for and report the presence of any strangers in this area. In this missive, I was instructed to hold you until the Skori arrived."

"Do you even know what the Skori are?"

"Emissaries of Bishop Langley."

Finnegan's derisive laugh made me look at him. "Then you are a fool, man."

A misled fool, perhaps. There were few living who had seen

the Skori up close. Until recently, they'd been the things that went bump in the night. Tales told to scare young children into behaving. Myths and fairy tales.

And oh-so-true nightmares.

"It is he who told me what road you'd be coming up."

"And who told him?" Finnegan murmured to me.

Something I very much wanted to know. If there was a Sithi betrayer among us, I needed to know who he was. In all my centuries of existence, I've never known a fellow Sithi to deliver his brethren into the hands of an enemy. To commit treason. Could the monk be mistaken? By My Lady, I hoped so, but I couldn't think how. Only another Sithi would know the significance of a True Name. This was all pointing toward a collaboration of one of my people with the Dark Brother.

"Do you wish to see these 'emissaries,' Brother Morris?" I kept my voice soft, ominous. I caught and held his gaze. In his eyes, I saw the uncertainty, the faith in his leader, and yes, I saw honor there.

He was a man being torn apart by what he *believed* to be right and what was right.

All that I saw in that fleeting connection, and I felt pity for the man. He was, after all, only human. I marked Merry's position behind the monk's chair and nodded that she should remain there. Physically, she wasn't a match for the man, but she could give warning.

"Let me show you what you are inviting into your midst, Brother Morris. What these 'emissaries' of Bishop Langley truly are."

Getting to my feet, I glanced at Finnegan. Without a word, he came to stand before me. I braced myself mentally and held up both hands, palms out. The wizard mirrored me, holding out his hands until they nearly touched mine. I gazed into his dark eyes, noticing for the first time that he stood slightly taller than me.

Without my asking, I felt the surge of Finnegan's power as he brought it to a peak and then slowly began to feed it to me.

It was an alien magic, powerful in its own right. Quickly, I kindled my own, flung it out to encompass and draw his within its sphere. For an instant, I felt resistance. His spiritual magic tried to overcome mine, struggling against the control I exerted, then something — whether it was his or mine, I don't know — but something gave, and they mingled, fed each other, and built to a crescendo of magic. I could feel the heat of our entwined power as it arced and jumped between us, an electrical charge that echoed and gained strength each time it cycled. I felt it dancing along my nerve endings, setting off sexual yearnings. Yearnings I hadn't felt in hundreds of years. They called to me, whispered promises of power and love.

Feelings I'd suppressed for so long leaped forward and threatened to overpower me. The strain of combining the two magics was incredible, maddening, and for an instant, I feared for him, for me. But then I met his gaze and saw the calm acceptance there. The trust. Something within me relaxed, and the power steadied, became accepting. I found myself able to wield it, at once familiar and alien. I held Finnegan's gaze for another long moment.

Calling on the grace of My Lady, I begged for a Vision. A Vision of a possible future. Turning, I concentrated on the flickering flames of the dying fire. When the power reached a crescendo, I formed a picture in my mind and thrust it into the flicking flames of the hearth. The fire roared as the magic struck it, the light and heat bathing us in its inferno.

Drawing on my knowledge and memories, I fed the images into the fire, the blaze creating and destroying the illusions until finally shapes began to form within the flames.

I heard a strangled gasp behind me but ignored it as I created the image of Skori as I knew them. The massive creatures came to life within the hearth in horrifying detail. No sound came from the slathering mouths, but there was no mistaking the greedy hunger in the red eyes that glowed in the night.

I expanded the illusion to include the monastery, showing the dozens of Skori scaling the walls and attacking the stable hands, leaving none of them alive. The creatures went on to slaughter the horses within the stables before turning their attention on the monastery. I created faceless humans fleeing in horror only to be caught and torn to pieces. Blood ran in rivers over the stone floors, human bodies littering the ground where they fell. Skori fed on those they slaughtered.

I held nothing back from the images, allowing the brutal nature of the beasts full reign.

When I heard wracking sobs behind me, I allowed the illusion to fade. The fire fell back into its fitful flicker as the magic that fed it dispersed.

My shoulders slumped with exhaustion as the power left me. I felt it snap back into Finnegan and heard his grunt of reaction. Hopefully my recovery time would be short. It wasn't a good idea to be weakened at this moment. I couldn't be a hundred percent sure, but under that matted beard, the wizard looked pale, a pinched look about his eyes.

"What I revealed was one future. A future that can very possibly come to be. *Those* are the allies being sent by your bishop."

"I did not know," Brother Morris said, his face cradled in his hands as his body shook with the force of his weeping. "I swear upon my God, I did not know."

"So now you do know, priest. Your bishop's action will cause the death of every living creature in these walls." Finnegan's voice was hard, no evidence of his exhaustion apparent in the rich, resonant tones. Personally, I would have liked nothing more than to lie down and sleep for about a week. Working that combination of magics was at the same time exhilarating and exhausting. Remnants of the sexual attraction lingered, tantalized. I began to see Finnegan in a whole new light and wondered if he felt it.

With an effort, I shook it off.

"If you will allow us to leave without hindering us, we will lead the Skori from this monastery and away from your people," I said, glancing at Merry.

She understood my unspoken hint and edged toward the door leading into the bedroom. I could see our gear where it had been dumped onto the floor. When Brother Morris paid no attention to her, she gathered up our possessions.

"It's too late for that, Sithi. They will be here within the hour."

"Shit," I muttered under my breath, using a word I hadn't used in centuries. My internal clock told me it was a bit after midnight. "C'mon, we have to travel."

"I'll lead you," Brother Morris said. He raised his ravaged face from his hands, his eyes bright with tears. "The west road is washed out, but there's another, less-traveled road that leads straight north. We're an hour from the border of Newland."

Could we trust him? I used a tiny portion of my remaining energy to scan him, seeking subterfuge, but found none. He was sincere.

"Let's go." I yanked him to his feet and pushed him ahead of us, ignoring the still-unconscious man sprawled on the floor by the door. Merry was close on our heels, with Finnegan bringing up the rear.

We met no one in the corridor. It wasn't until we reached the bottom of the stairs that we met another monk. The man hesitated when we reached the first floor, his eyes widening at the sight of Brother Morris.

"Brother?"

"Warn your people to either flee or be prepared to defend themselves," I told Morris quietly. "We can try to lead the Skori away, but they might attack the monastery for the sheer pleasure of it."

"Gather everyone together, Nathaniel. Take them to the sanctuary and barricade yourselves inside. Bring enough supplies to hold out for several days and weapons to defend yourselves."

He glanced toward me. "The sanctuary is part of the old monastery. It was built before the Great Waste and is heavily fortified. Will these Skori be able to break through?"

"If it's too difficult, they may not bother."

"Do it." He didn't wait to see that the man carried out his orders but hurried down the first-floor passage in the direction of the stables. Our steps sounded hollow on the stone floor as we passed from the building and through the open corridor.

The storm had moved on while we were "guests" of the monastery. The tattered clouds were slow to leave the starlit sky; the dying winds left behind an eerie stillness.

I raised my face to the night air, sending out my senses in an effort to detect the presence of the Skori. It took a full minute before I could locate them, but once I had them, I latched on to their spoor. They were still miles away but headed in this direction.

Time was running out.

Chapter Ten

We were on the road, riding hard, when I sensed that our trail had been picked up—a soundless howl of glee punctured the night. My head came up and snapped to the left in the direction of the cry. I felt Finnegan's eyes on me, but no one else reacted. The night was so still I was amazed none of the others had heard that bloodthirsty wail. Despite the near darkness, my gaze met Finnegan's, and I gave a slight nod. The light of the nearly full moon reflected the worry in his eyes. We did not have the defense of an ancient forest around us this time. To allow the Skori to overtake us on the open road was suicide.

Finnegan picked up the pace, pushing our mounts in an effort to put distance between us and our pursuers. Although I had little love for the priest and all he stood for, I would not have those creatures descend upon the monastery. I had far too much weighing on my conscience over the centuries to add the slaughter of defenseless humans. I hoped the Skori found our trail too tempting and would ignore the easy pickings.

"Here. This is the turnoff to the road leading north." Brother Morris reined in his mount where the road forked in two directions. "The road to the right is the one that's washed out. The other will lead you north into Newland."

"Will you come with us, Brother Morris?" Merry asked as she controlled her gelding. The dun danced around in a tight circle. Perhaps the animals sensed what was closing in on us.

"No." He looked at me, knowledge in his eyes. "They're coming, aren't they?"

"Yes. They are less than an hour behind us."

"I will try to lead them down the washed-out road. You go north."

"You'll have no way to escape."

"I know."

"Morris …"

"I've made my peace with my God, Sithi. It is through my folly that my people are in danger and you are hunted." He drew a deep breath and let it out through his mouth. "Deep down, I knew there was something wrong with the orders I received, yet I did nothing but blindly follow. As a result, I not only endangered you and your companions but I may have brought those creatures down on my people."

He shifted in his saddle, and for the first time, I noticed he had a sword concealed under his robes. "I will linger here and allow them to see me. I assume they are bestial enough to give chase after a sighted target." At my nod, he continued, "I will try to buy you time to reach Newland. The border is more heavily guarded, and you will meet with a patrol."

I stared at him for several long seconds. He was resolute. For an instant, I felt shame. I'd viewed the monk as the enemy when he was but an unwitting pawn. A pawn now determined to right the wrong he had done. Thanks to the vision I'd created within the fire, he knew exactly what he faced. Yet he did not hesitate to go to certain death.

"Your God go with you, Brother Morris," I said at last, sketching a deep bow from the saddle before I turned Mysteria toward the road that forked to the left. I gestured to the others to follow me. We needed to race the wind if we were to give Brother Morris's sacrifice the honor it deserved.

"You're just going to let him go to his death?" Merry twisted in her saddle to stare after the monk, her face horrified.

"What would you suggest I do?" I knew my voice was cold, but there was no time for argument. "Hog-tie him to my saddle? No, it is his decision to do this. I will not rob the man of his right to compensate for his wrong."

"But it wasn't his mistake. You heard him; it was Bishop Langley who sent those orders." Her voice rose with each word.

I glanced at Finnegan. Without needing to be told, he brought his mount closer and grabbed the gelding's bridle. When I set off at a ground-eating gallop, Merry's horse was forced to follow. I didn't know what she intended, but I couldn't take the chance that she might follow the priest and try to talk him into coming with us. Time was precious, and it couldn't be wasted on a useless argument.

"If we do not make the border of Newland, Brother Morris's sacrifice will be for nothing." My tone was devoid of emotion.

I ignored Merry's silent weeping. I didn't need to sense the wind to know she thought I was a heartless bitch. And she was right. However, wouldn't she be surprised to know that, deep inside, a tiny piece of my heart wept right along with her?

The road leading north was probably hard-packed during the dry season, but after the winter snows and the spring rains, it was slick with mud. Fortunately, enough gravel mixed in with the soil so the footing wasn't completely dangerous for the horses. The last thing we needed was for one of them to come up lame or worse.

Despite the darkness and the condition of the road, we made good time. The moon finally appeared through the clouds to grant some illumination as we rode in silence. Finnegan no longer led Merry's horse, but she was silent, her chin set. I could feel her determination and her loathing. I knew I'd lost a measure of her regard, but I couldn't let it hinder me. The girl had to be prepared for her future, and if toughening her hide was the price to pay, so be it. I could not let sentiment weaken my resolve.

In less than a half hour, we all heard it. Piercing through the still night air, a victorious howl rang out in the distance. The Skori had seen Brother Morris and were giving chase. The sound came from more than a dozen throats.

I pulled up my horse, turning to look back over the trail, straining to hear more. Faint, so faint that the mortal ear would not catch it, I heard the sound of a horse being ridden hard, away from us. Brother Morris was leading them farther down the right fork in the road. The baying of the hunt was audible to my ears, going on for some minutes before I heard the sound of fighting, of steel on steel.

I turned Mysteria back toward the north, aware that tears clogged my throat. The priest would not last long. Going by the sounds wafting through the night air, there were better than twenty Skori in that pack. It wouldn't take them long to realize they'd been led astray.

"C'mon. We have to move," was all I said before I sent my mount into a swift gallop. Even using my waning magic to give strength to the horses, they could not sustain this pace all night. Our only chance was to reach the border of Newland and hope there was a patrol nearby. A lot of unknowns and trusting in luck. I hated flying blind.

The night narrowed into the here and now. I didn't tell my companions, or even glance at Finnegan, when I heard a final scream that came from a human throat so many miles away. I could only say a silent prayer to My Lady and one to Brother Morris's God. My eyes were dry, and I kept a tight rein on my emotions. Few mortals would have acted as honorably as Brother Morris. He was a man worthy of his God.

The road straightened, and the horses lengthened their stride, manes and tails flying behind them. For long minutes, the pounding of their hooves was the only sound, drowning out the heavy breathing of my companions. I had the lead, my white mare setting a breakneck pace while Merry's gelding gamely followed, and Finnegan's mare brought up the rear. The horses ran in a tight line, bunched close enough that you could reach out and touch one of them. We concentrated on the road ahead, not what might be following behind. The night pressed in around us; shadows became real.

Then we all heard it. A bellow of rage split the air. It caused all of us to glance back with alarm.

"They've just discovered that Brother Morris led them on a wild goose chase," I said, pitching my voice to carry over the steady beat of hooves. "They'll be backtracking now, and it won't take them long to find our trail."

We sped on in the night, the ground open and hilly. I would have wished for better concealment, but we had to work with what we had. The lack of forest allowed us to make better time, but it also made it easier for the Skori to track us.

I sensed the instant the gelding began to lag and fed another portion of my magic into him, giving the horse strength to continue even though the effort weakened me further. I tried to pray to My Lady for additional power, but the pace I'd set made it impossible to concentrate.

An unexpected shadow pressed against my thoughts, clouding them and making them lethargic. I shook my head with confusion. The sensation faded, then returned, stronger than ever.

What was I doing? It was futile to struggle, so why did I try? It was so much easier to stop fleeing and wait for the Skori. That would end my conflict.

The cloud over my vision deepened as dark thoughts continued to swirl through my head. I was so tired, every muscle aching, leaded. I needed to rest. Yes, resting was a good idea.

Without conscious thought, I began to slow, sitting upright in the saddle as I pulled Mysteria out of her wild gallop. The horse tugged impatiently at her reins, fighting for control when I would have drawn her to a halt.

"Riona!"

My attention snapped to the present at the sound of Finnegan's voice. It came from far away, hollow and insubstantial. He was staring at me with puzzlement. Something in my expression must have alarmed him, because the stone at the end of his staff ignited, faint but held at the ready.

"Why are you slowing?"

Confusion clouded my mind for several more seconds before it dissipated to be replaced by a new horror. What had just happened? Those fading skeins of lethargy were alien in nature. Not my own. Not that of My Lady. What had invaded my mind? The touch had been so smooth, slipping in with the delicate precision of a brain surgeon.

Had the Dark Master somehow touched my mind? I was Sithi. It should have been impossible for him to influence me. The fact that it had happened pointed to his strength growing.

"I'm trying to get my bearings."

I caught the tail end of the look Finnegan gave me, but I ignored him. I could not tell them that my thoughts had briefly betrayed me. I could barely admit it to myself. Never in my thousand years of life had I been touched by the Dark Master. How was it possible that he was able to do so now?

I felt defiled.

I glanced toward the east. Although hours from dawn, there was a faint lightening of the night sky, the herald of the morning. We might be safe yet. The Skori found it difficult to bear the sun. Normally they sought shelter during the daylight hours. We needed only to keep ahead of them a few more hours.

I sent Mysteria onward. Now that I was aware of what the Dark Master had attempted, I could guard against it. He would not find it so easy to slip into my thoughts again.

We raced on, meadows becoming fields, small farmhouses set away from the road. An occasional dog barked at our passing but was quickly left behind. I only hoped the creatures would be so intent on us that they would bypass the helpless inhabitants.

We left the farmhouses behind and entered a small wood. The trees grew close to the road, their branches reaching out to catch our cloaks as they streamed out behind us. The waning moon was hidden by the trees, their many branches thrusting us into the darkness of night once more. Not an ancient wood. There was no power here.

Another shriek sounded behind us, closer. Too close. We didn't have much time remaining to us. The labored breathing of the three horses echoed the panting breaths we drew as we rode, leaning low on our horses' necks in an effort to gain speed.

A formation of rocks appeared ahead, the tumbled remains of a large dwelling. Castles or something similar to them had sprung up following the Great Waste. Some of them had already crumbled to slag, and this appeared to be one of them. Large blocks of stone lay about as if thrown by a giant hand. In the uncertain light, I could see weeds and trees growing out of what had once been a sizable room.

I slowed Mysteria as we neared and drew her to a stop, leaping down from her back and letting her continue to the back of the dwelling. Her hooves rang out sharply in the stillness of the predawn morning.

This would have to do. We could go no farther.

"What are you doing?" Merry shouted as the gelding stumbled to a halt beside me. Her voice shook with both fatigue and fear. "Those things are almost upon us."

"Exactly. I don't want to get caught on open ground. This will give us something at our backs."

Finnegan didn't bother to question my actions. He merely dismounted and grabbed his staff in one hand while he untied a sword from his saddle.

"Riona is right, Your Highness," he said as he threw off his cloak and belted the sword to his waist. "We can go no farther. The horses are pushed to their limits. They will come up lame if we continue."

He shoved his mare toward the back of the stones with Mysteria. The blocks stood stacked a good two stories high, perhaps thirty feet across. We stood upon what remained of the flooring, weeds and grass growing between the cracks in the stone. It would offer fair footing when we faced the Skori.

I tossed my cloak on top of Finnegan's and strung my bow. If I could take down a few of the creatures from a distance, all the better. Taking up a space next to Finnegan, I gestured toward the small sword at Merry's side. "Can you use that?"

"My brothers taught me," she admitted as she reluctantly dismounted. She ran a soothing hand down the lathered neck of her mount, perhaps for the first time noticing how spent he was. "I've never fought anything like these Skori, though."

"Then stay back, Your Highness," Finnegan said as he selected the bit of ground to make his stand.

Just as suddenly, we were out of time. Out of the thin stand of trees came the first Skori, hulking creatures slightly darker than the night, pouring down the road at a pace equal that of a horse. The moonlight glinted off bits of armor and drawn swords. The first few hesitated, testing the air as they cast about for our scent.

A shriek of triumph erupted from over a dozen throats when they caught sight of us. Still more swarmed out of the trees. Twenty, thirty, and still more came. My heart sank. Three against two score was impossible odds. I glanced toward my companions, seeing the same realization in their faces. We were going to die here. I steeled myself. But not before we took as many with us as possible.

The Skori were closing in on us. They had all cleared the forest, their numbers substantial. This was no rogue band escaped from the north. This was the prelude of an army. True to my dream, the Dark Master was making a bid for the world, and he was doing it now. There could be no doubt.

Drawing a breath, I centered myself. Reaching for that calm deep within, I grabbed the first arrow and fit it to my bowstring. Finesse was unnecessary. I drew and released. The arrow flew true, sinking into the throat of a Skori. It dropped without a sound. Without hesitation, I nocked and let fly another arrow. And another. Each hit its mark, downing each creature. But for every one that I hit, another took its place. Too soon, they'd be upon us, the distance melting at an alarming rate.

Behind me, I could hear Merry's quickened breathing as the full scope of the Skori numbers hit home. There was no time to wonder how the dark creatures had managed to get this far south without detection. All we could do was prepare ourselves.

Taking a few seconds, I sent a prayer spiraling to My Lady. Asking her, begging her for aid. I closed my eyes briefly and sent my thoughts winging outward in an attempt to seek some sense of My Lady's presence. My magic was at its lowest, depleted.

Peace filled me as I suddenly felt My Lady's focus. The scent of summer warmth wafted over us, driving out the cold of dread. Opening my eyes, I saw Merry glancing around in confusion while Finnegan drew a deep breath, a sense of renewed purpose in his stance.

"*I can only help you when you ask, my Riona,*" came a soft voice in my ear. I nearly looked around even though I knew She could not be there.

"*Will you destroy these Skori, My Lady?*" I sent the thought outward, a new hope rising in my heart as I watched the Skori race toward us. Their long stride closed the distance, leaping over rocks and uneven ground with ease.

"*That I cannot do, my child,*" came the reply laden with despair.

"Those creatures belong to my brother. I cannot interfere."

My heart sank.

"But I can offer aid."

With those words, her presence faded from my mind. Although She was no longer directly with me, I felt the force of her magic fill me. The infusion of power swept away any remaining fatigue and despair. Renewed confidence lightened my heart, and I felt a grin spreading across my face as the Skori closed in on us. I was ready.

A deafening howl erupted from nearly forty throats as the Dark Ones rushed us. They appeared certain of victory over a mere three people. But what they did not count on was one of those people being an ancient Sithi filled with the Lady's grace, and another a wizard.

Flinging my bow aside, I pulled my sword, Viper, free of its scabbard. The sound was a sinister slide of metal on metal, and I positioned myself into a stance of readiness.

Finnegan placed the butt of his staff in the dirt, holding it vertical. He used his staff as a conduit to contain and direct his magic. I could feel the endless well of spiritual magic gather and infuse his staff with power. The rough stone at the tip of his staff glowed. Its brightness lit the night and cast a blinding light over the Skori. For a moment, they cowered from the force of the light, arms thrown up to protect their night-sensitive eyes, but the howl of the leader stiffened their spines, and they resumed their advance. A little slower, a little more cautious.

"Stand behind us, Merry." I had no idea what her skills were with weaponry. The slender sword she carried was an ideal size for her smaller stature, and she held it with confidence. But until I saw her wield it, I was taking no chances with her safety, or ours, by allowing her to face the greater strength of the Skori.

Looking over the horde, I singled out the leader. He, or she, was the one I would take down. It was impossible to determine the sex of the creature. Once it was disposed of, I hoped the rest would fall to disarray. Skori were fierce fighters, but ultimately they were only as skilled as their leader. A cliché, but if you cut off the head of the snake, it was dead. Kill the Skori leader and those linked directly to it were reduced in both power and skill. It was our only hope.

I held back my power until the last moment. They were still unaware of facing a Sithi. When they were a hundred feet away, I stepped to the side of the wizard, raising my sword and calling on the power of My Lady. Bright light blazed down from the heavens, illuminating the scene and adding to the power of the wizard.

Into the ensuing confusion I leapt, bypassing a dozen creatures and making straight for the Skori leader. For an instant, it was caught by surprise, but not for long. With a roar, it engaged me, parrying my first thrust with an unexpected graceful maneuver. I'd fought Skori before, but not in over nine hundred years when the Dark Master had made his first bid for control. Fortunately I'd had centuries to perfect my skill and dodged to avoid its return swing.

Out of the corner of my eye, I saw the wizard swing his staff in a wide arc, the power of his magic forcing the dark creatures to retreat from around us. We'd chosen our position well. The massive blocks of stone prevented the Skori from flanking us. They could only fan out and hope to get past our guard.

I kept the leader in front of me as the others cowered back from Finnegan's light, parrying another thrust before swinging out in an unexpected advance. Viper bit into the sword arm of the creature, drawing blood and a howl of rage from its throat. I danced out of its range, judging that the slice was deep and effective. Brackish blood made black by the shadows ran down its arm and over its hand. I immediately pressed my advantage, closing in and taking a second slice across its other arm. My luck held, and I narrowly avoided its downward swing, its sword catching the material of my shirt and tearing a gaping hole in it.

Unscathed, I twisted behind it, bringing my sword down and scoring a gash down its back. My sword cut deep enough to bare the bone of its spine. Spinning one last time, I swung Viper around and neatly beheaded the creature.

There was an instant of silence before mayhem erupted. Screams of rage and fear erupted from a dozen throats. Only six of the creatures dropped their weapons and fell to the ground, clutching their heads as howls of pain poured from their gaping mouths. Another dozen fled in fear before the light of My Lady. The remaining score stood their ground, the light of my magic combined with the wizard's reflected in their red eyes. I'd hoped for more confusion with the death of the leader, but the odds did improve somewhat.

My sword sang out again, taking the first across the chest as I twisted in the full circle to disembowel the second. I never paused in my deadly dance, using fighting forms that I'd practiced for centuries to dispatch a third and fourth. The wizard used his magic to strike two more, the light of his staff piercing their chests and spreading throughout their bodies, the light leaking from their eyes and mouths before they were consumed and destroyed.

During one twist to avoid a downward stroke, I saw Merry parry a sword and duck under the Skori's swing. Using her smaller size, she slipped under its guard and pierced its chest. I was relieved to see some skill there. A little awkward, a little uncertain, but she'd trained with a master swordsman.

My attention was reclaimed by a Skori who attempted to slip past my guard. I twisted and avoided its thrust. This one wore a jerkin of leather, some oddity in its shape making me suspect it was female. No matter, she would kill me as quickly as any male, and I certainly had no sympathy for the female of the species. They were as deadly as the male, if not more so.

I felt no exhaustion from my exertions, only a sense of exhilaration. This was one of my reasons for being. To serve My Lady in defense of Her land and Her people. I knew the grin that spread across my face was fierce and confident. The creature hesitated for a fatal instant and was dispatched.

I was just beginning to turn when I heard a short cry, the sound abruptly cut off. My grin vanished as I watched Merry go down, a gash blossoming with blood across her shoulder. With horror, I watched as her saber dropped from her nerveless fingers and her knees buckled beneath her.

"Merry!" Ignoring the creatures closing in around me, I rushed to her side. I felt Finnegan falter for an instant, then a wave of his magic cleared the way for me. A surge of magic swept through the night as Skori were flung into the air, their heavy bodies thrown into the path of their brethren to hamper the next wave of attack, as I raced toward Merry. I only had eyes for the Skori that stood above Merry, a wickedly curved blade raised to bring down on the helpless girl.

Uttering a wordless cry, I hamstrung the creature without mercy and brought my sword around to behead it as it dropped to the blood-soaked ground.

Trusting Finnegan to keep the remaining Skori away, I caught Merry before she fell.

"Merry! No!"

I cradled her in my arms, moving the material from the wound to examine it. I caught sight of bone before bright blood welled up in the gash, the edges of the wound gaping and ugly against the whiteness of her skin. It was deep.

"It's not too bad, Riona," she murmured faintly as she gazed up at me. Blood flecked her lips, vivid against her pale face. "I can barely feel it."

"I cannot hold them, Riona," Finnegan shouted as he sent another volley of magic against the Skori. I could only spare him a quick glance. Even I could tell this wave was weakening as his strength began to fail. Time was fast running out.

Frantic, I gathered My Lady's magic and sent it into the small body I held. Her life-force was fading fast, and I had to move quickly. Closing my eyes, I concentrated on the wound, willing it to heal. The flow of blood lessened, and then, with agonizing slowness, the edges began to close. Sweat beaded my brow as I poured still more power into Merry. Everything narrowed to the girl who drew each labored breath as if it were her last.

"Riona!" Finnegan shouted, strain in his voice, but I ignored him.

The wound closed, but it was not healed. Dropping my head to rest against the ragged hair of the girl, I knew I had failed. The injury no longer bled, but something prevented the full healing of My Lady. Only a healer far more skilled than I could save her. As far as I knew, the only Sithi healers were in Minneson City.

Without their skill, Merry was going to die.

Chapter Eleven

Cradling Merry in my arms, I looked up at Finnegan. He stood between us and more than a dozen Skori, his staff held before him, but I could see that the tip of his staff was failing. There was just so much power a body could channel, and the wizard was reaching the end of his endurance. His breath came in gasps, and sweat poured down his face. The distance was getting shorter and shorter each time he flung back the horde.

Glancing down at Merry, I traced the blood staining her shirt and outer jacket. She had followed our example, flinging off her cloak to give herself more freedom to fight. The blood had splattered up her neck and dotted one side of her face. She looked like a child. Small, her complexion pale with tinges of blue beneath the surface of her skin.

Carefully I laid her down on the hard ground, then snatched up my sword and joined Finnegan.

Right now there was nothing more I could do for her. Perhaps nothing more I could do for any of us. But, dammit, I was going to take as many of these Lady damned Skori with me as possible.

With a roar of fury, I swung at the first creature to come close, neatly beheading it. I flung out my free hand, and a burst of magic caught a second full in the chest, flinging it back where it lay unmoving.

The rest backed away, regrouping. Gazing at the hulking mass of heavily muscled bodies, I knew it was just a matter of time before they overran us.

Then I heard it. Over the yammering of the creatures, it came again.

The sound of a trumpet echoed in the distance, so faint, so sweet that at first I thought I imagined it. Then it came a third time, the wind carrying it closer. A battle cry.

I looked toward the hill, the direction our attackers had come from. There, in the west, silhouetted against the night sky, appeared a man astride a massive horse, his mail gleaming. Even as I watched, a second, a third, finally a whole company of horsemen appeared on the crest of the hill, weapons drawn as they assessed the situation below. The sun was just breaking over the horizon, reflecting off mail-covered chests and the helms that hid their faces.

A tall shaft revealed a banner of deep blue. A sudden gust of wind unfurled the long length of material to reveal a white tiger, crouched and ready to attack.

Silence descended over the battlefield. I clearly heard the snap and flutter of the banner as the strengthening wind caught it and swept it back to its full length. It was the flag of Cascadia.

The only other sounds were that of the dying Skori, the creak of leather, and our own heightened breathing as Finnegan and I stood side by side, facing our foes.

The momentary pause was shattered by the battle cry erupting from thirty throats just before the mounted men sent their horses galloping down the hill, their hooves a thunder of sound as they swept closer. The Skori answered that cry with the guttural challenge of their own, most turning to meet this new threat. A few, only a few, looked from one front to the other and dropped their weapons to flee into what shadows remained. I saw three riders peel off in pursuit.

The horsemen never slowed, plunging into the mass of Skori and trampling fully half of them during that first rush. Others dodged between the horses, blades slicing at the humans and animals alike. I saw more than one horseman fall to the counterattack, the screams of men and horses blending in with the howls that erupted from a dozen throats.

I was able to take this all in in a matter of seconds before my attention was reclaimed by the remaining creatures before me.

Renewed strength flooded my muscles, the despair that had threatened to claim me only moments ago gone as a new purpose and hope filled me. My sword darted out to bury itself in the heart of the dark creature that came too close, and I jerked the blade free before it fell. I saw Finnegan gain new strength as well, and the blue flare of his magic shot out to strike the Skori trying to edge past his guard.

The horsemen turned and made another charge, swords at the ready to sweep through the remaining Skori. Their mounts were trained warhorses, skilled with the use of teeth and hooves to render and tear. The wounds they inflicted were grave, fatal. New screams erupted from throats, both human and immortal. Some cut off abruptly as a sword came down to end a life. The horses added their screams to the chaos, some falling with their riders, not rising again. I saw more than one mount on the ground, legs thrashing before going still.

Then, just as suddenly as it had begun, it was over. The new silence was broken only by the groans of injured men and the distressed whinnying of more than one horse as they attempted to rise. None of the Skori moved or made a sound.

The sun broke over the horizon, the morning light bathing the scene as I gazed over the carnage. The torn and mangled bodies of the Skori littered the ground, polluting the purity of the land with their poisonous blood. Lifeless eyes stared upward into the new day. Immortal, the creatures could only be killed by a fatal wound. As I watched, the able-bodied men picked among the fallen, delivering death blows to guarantee the Skori would not rise again.

Looking into the deformed face of one dead creature, I wondered how much humanity had remained within it. They'd once been as human as the rest of us. Humans who had made a bad choice when they'd allowed themselves to be seduced by the evil of the Dark Master.

Human … Merry! My mind froze for an instant. How could I have forgotten her?

I whirled around and found Finnegan kneeling at the girl's side, his hands on either side of her head, the glow of magic casting a blue light over her face. Beads of sweat rolled down his face, mute evidence of the strain he exerted.

I dropped to the ground beside him, watching as he used his power in an attempt to add his healing to mine. Fear shivered down my spine. There didn't appear to be any difference in her condition. Her breathing was shallow, each inhalation drawn with effort. Her wound was grave, but it shouldn't have festered so quickly. Glancing around, I found the Skori who had inflicted the injury. It lay a short distance away, its weapon still in its hand.

Retrieving it, I examined the blade. Something stained the metal, nearly invisible, but my eyes picked it up. Touching my finger to the substance, I brought it gingerly to my nose, catching a sickly sweet scent. Poison? Had to be. Drawing the scent deep into my lungs, I attempted to identify it without success.

"I think there might have been a poison on the blade, Finnegan," I said in a low voice, careful not to break his concentration. He gave a slight nod of acknowledgment.

A shadow fell over me where I still crouched over the Skori, and I went on the defensive. Swiveling around, I brought my sword up. I'd been aware of the humans milling around, checking their wounded and ensuring the creatures were all dead, but in a peripheral way. I'd been far more concerned with Merry to do much more than monitor their movements.

The man had approached me with the sun at his back, but I had little trouble adjusting my eyes to the morning brightness. Straightening to my full height, I topped him by a head, still holding my blade at the ready.

"You're a Sithi," the man said, staring up at me. The helm he wore concealed much of his expression. His breastplate was dented in a couple of places, and a trail of blood ran down one leg where a blade had slashed a shallow furrow in his thigh.

Noting his sword was sheathed, I lowered my blade. "As you can see."

"We don't see many in the west." The man removed his steel-plated gauntlets, then reached up to pull off his protective headgear. Dark hair, damp with sweat, was pulled back in a warrior's braid, revealing the masculine angles of his face. He was beardless, yet there was nothing young in his hard eyes. They spoke of a man well seasoned by battle.

"I'm Kai Tiernan. Captain of the royal guard and emissary from Cascadia." He made a slight bow, deep blue eyes sweeping past me to the wizard and the wounded woman. From Finnegan, I heard another gasp of effort but didn't turn. Until I was certain of this man's intentions, I would not turn my back on him.

"Riona Northstar."

"I am honored, Lady Riona. Cascadia extends greetings to the Sithi people."

I acknowledged his bow with one of my own. "Your arrival was most welcome, Captain Tiernan, and most timely."

"I was given warning of foul creatures hunting this night."

"Warning? By whom?"

"I don't know." His eyes lost focus for an instant before they cleared. I could almost see the remnants of a compulsion in the blue depths. "A woman, cloaked and difficult to see. We were camped about five miles north of here when she appeared and warned us of three travelers in dire need of aid."

My heart swelled. It could only have been My Lady. She'd said she could not directly interfere, but she'd sent in the cavalry. I sent a silent prayer of thanks to her.

"We thank you for your aid, Captain Tiernan. My skills do not run strong to healing, but if I can extend any relief to your wounded men, please let me know."

"That would be most welcome, Lady Riona." Again, his glance went behind me. "But it appears your companion is in the greatest need right now."

"The wizard is better skilled than I with healing. Meredith was slashed with a poisoned blade." This time I turned to look down at the pair. It appeared that Merry was breathing more easily, and there was definitely better color in her face. Had Finnegan managed to leach the poison from her system?

With care, I wiped my blade clean on the remnants of a Skori cloak and re-sheathed it. Kneeling at Finnegan's side, I was careful not to touch Merry. I was conscious of the captain squatting across from us, watching Merry's face with a strange intensity. His dark blue eyes moved over her features, cataloguing each one before sweeping his glance down the length of her body.

When he saw me watching him, Kai shifted his attention to me, but I noticed his gaze slip to the girl time and again. His interest and curiosity were heavy in the air.

"Why would such a large band of Skori attack you?"

Opening my senses to him, I sifted through his emotions but detected no ulterior motive to his question. There was a touch of darkness to the man, but nothing to indicate he was in league with the Dark Master. Then again, I'd been fooled by Brother Morris. The difference was that Brother Morris had truly believed he was working in the name of his One God. He'd been just as deceived as I.

It was probably stupid, but I decided to take a chance with this human. Despite the edging of darkness, his aura glowed with a bright intensity that bespoke of honor and duty. Something had happened in this man's life to affect him for all times. Someday I'd have to find out, if only to keep Merry safe, but for now, my instincts told me he was going to be of great aid to us.

Besides, My Lady would not have sent a man with deception in his heart. He might be able to fool me, but he never would have been able to conceal his true self from Her.

"We're on our way to Newland to aid King Ambrose." I supposed I could give him part of the truth. No need to tell him there was a plot somehow involving Meredith Sterling and that the Dark Master intended to take over the world. That sounded a bit melodramatic, even if it was true.

He shook his head. "I've never heard of such a large band coming out of the north."

"Perhaps not in recent years. But centuries ago, it was not unusual."

Kai's gaze became speculative, and I could almost feel him assessing my age. According to history, the last time the Skori had poured out of the Northern Wastes was well over nine hundred years ago.

"It would explain the absence of the Rangers, Lady Riona. We've been traveling from Cascadia for over two months and have not encountered one."

His news disturbed me. Rangers were generally mix-bloods who chose the solitary way of the guardians of the north, whereas other mix-bloods chose the path of the mage. Were all the Rangers dead, or had they been drawn from their posts? No, it was impossible that they would all be dead. There had to be a good two thousand Rangers spread out from Western Cascadia to Eastern Newland. Because of their mixed blood, Rangers tended to live a longer span than the typical human. Plus their skills were far superior. Given their profession and their close proximity to the border, Rangers were a suspicious lot. I doubt they could have been taken by surprise and eradicated.

"What brings you so far east, Captain Tiernan?"

"I am the emissary sent by my brother, ruler of Cascadia, to learn of the condition of King Ambrose."

So, news of the king's decline had already traveled as far as the west coast. I must have been far more isolated in the Everglades than I'd thought. If suspicion of King Ambrose's condition had traveled that far west, his hold on Newland was tenuous at best.

"There have been Skori raids coming out of the mountains north of us," he continued, "and rumor has reached us of similar occurrences all along the border."

I was about to respond when Finnegan sat back with an exhausted sigh.

"I've done what I can, Riona." Finnegan's voice was weary, defeated. He laid Merry's head back onto the ground. Gentle. Careful. "But it isn't enough. She is still dying."

"That's unacceptable, wizard." A coldness formed in the pit of my stomach, and I heard it echoed in my words. We had not come all this way to admit defeat. But looking at Finnegan's drawn and pale face, I knew he'd indeed done all he could. The man was about to fall over with exhaustion. It took me an instant to come to a decision. My healing skills were not up to this task, but there were others whose were.

Glancing around, I found my cloak. It had been trampled and bloodied in the melee. Nevertheless, I swung it around my shoulders and fastened it. The stink of Skori blood lingered on it, but I ignored it.

Without another word, I turned away and whistled for Mysteria. The mare appeared instantly, her eyes wild with the scent of death all around her. I put a hand to her muzzle to calm her before I swung up into the saddle. It took me a moment to bring her under control as the mare danced around in a tight circle.

"Give me the girl."

Before Finnegan could move, Kai crouched and carefully lifted Merry into his arms, cradling her with an unexpected gentleness. For a long moment, he stared into Merry's pale face, his expression softening, in complete contradiction with his bloodied and battered appearance. I frowned slightly. It was the look of a man struck dumb with love.

With infinite care, he handed Merry up to me, his fingers lingering an instant to brush against one cold cheek. I cradled her across my lap and wrapped my cloak around her. Without being asked, Finnegan found Merry's garment and added its warmth to mine. Probably not necessary since the girl was already burning with fever. I could feel the heat through the thick material.

"Where do you intend to take her?" Captain Tiernan asked, never once taking his gaze from the girl.

"To the Lakelands. The Sithi have healers who can cure anything short of death."

"That's a three-day ride."

"I can get there faster."

"Allow me to accompany you."

"You have wounded men to attend to."

Without looking around, Kai signaled to one of his men who'd been standing close behind him, alert and watchful.

"Lieutenant Crispin."

The man stepped forward and drew his arm across his chest in a salute. Stocky, without an ounce of fat on him, he stood at attention, his helm cradled in one arm. With dark hair cut so short it stood upright, he had a short beard that did nothing to conceal the hard slant of his mouth. Blood smeared one cheek, but he appeared unharmed.

"Aye, Captain Tiernan."

"Make camp and see to the men who are wounded. Our dead are to receive an honorable burial, and you will dispose of the bodies of these foul creatures."

"Burn them," I said.

The captain glanced my way before he nodded and turned back to his man.

"Yes, burn them."

"Aye, Captain." Crispin hesitated for an instant, his gaze sliding to me, where I waited with impatience.

I could feel Merry's labored breathing. The Lady willing, the girl would hold on ... but not for the three days the Captain assumed. I had my own way of traveling that wasn't common knowledge to mortals. My method of Traveling was arduous, and it took time to plan and execute. Most Sithi only used it when the need was great.

Glancing down at Merry, I could not think of a greater need than now.

"With your permission, sir," Crispin finally said, his stance confident and determined, "I would like to leave Jenkins in charge and accompany you."

Tiernan regarded him for a moment, his face expressionless.

"Explain yourself, Lieutenant."

"No disrespect, sir, but our mission is east. Not north. And frankly, sir, I have little trust in elves."

That was very much to the point. And I couldn't fault the man. We Sithi had kept to ourselves for centuries. Many even doubted our existence.

"So you wish to accompany me to the Lakelands to watch my back."

"Yes, sir."

Tiernan spared me a glance, which I returned without expression. It was his call.

"Granted."

"Thank you, sir. I would also suggest, sir, that we take a company of men with us if we are to travel to the Sithi lands."

"And why would that be necessary, Lieutenant?" I spoke coldly enough to chill, but I really didn't care. We were wasting valuable time.

The man met my gaze unflinchingly. Even without using my elven senses, I could see the caution, the distrust in his dark eyes. Behind my blank expression, my mind was turning over his request. It would take more effort to transport the greater number, but the protection of a Cascadian unit might be useful. They were fierce fighters and worth their weight in gold.

"You have my word as a Sithi that no harm will come to your captain or any of his men by our hands," I said as I made my decision. "But to put your mind at ease, you are welcome to bring a dozen men."

Crispin saluted his captain but did not move. "With your permission, sir, I will select a dozen men to accompany us."

Tiernan's eyes turned once more on Merry. "As you will."

"Crispin," I called as the man turned away. He halted, stiff-backed, but did not turn. "Please inform those remaining men that there are perhaps twenty or so Skori still in these surroundings. When I slew their leader, some ran off, but they may gather their courage enough to regroup."

Nodding, he started toward the cluster of men still in their saddles, barking out orders and selecting some of the most able-bodied to accompany us. I noted with approval that he did not leave the remaining soldiers short of protection. There were many wounded, both minor and severe. Had I the skill and energy, I would have made an effort to heal them. But time was of an essence.

I turned toward Finnegan, who was leading his mare and the gelding. He carried my bow and quiver of arrows. Once he was mounted, he secured them to his own saddle. I nodded my thanks.

"Are you up to this, wizard?"

"Where you go, I go, Riona."

The way he said that made me stare. There was almost a double meaning within his words, but his expression was bland when he met my gaze. We sat there gazing at each other for a long moment while the captain and his men made their preparations. Something passed between us. Something I hadn't felt in centuries. Despite the gravity of our situation, it was both exhilarating and disturbing.

Tiernan gave his remaining men a few last-minute instructions concerning the Skori in the area, then he had his dozen soldiers lined up and ready.

"We're ready, my lady."

With an effort, I tore my attention away from Finnegan. The captain had his men lined up in pairs, their horses pawing the dirt with impatience while their riders sat still in their saddles, eyes alert and expressions set. They were a seasoned troop, battle ready and experienced. A few had minor injuries, but nothing to hamper us.

I noticed Lieutenant Crispin positioned himself at his captain's side. The care of the wounded was turned over to the next in command, and the men were already making camp within the shelter of the blocks of stone. Two men were building a fire some distance away while others hitched ropes to horses and used them to drag the dead creatures toward it. Another dozen men were being carried to the camp and carefully laid out.

"Let's go, Finnegan." I wanted to put some distance between us and the camp before I attempted Travel. It was bad enough that these mortals with us would now be aware of this Sithi ability; I wasn't going to display it for those remaining soldiers.

Without another word, I urged Mysteria forward, Finnegan at my side. Captain Tiernan directed his mount up on my other side, and the rest of his men fell in close behind.

"Will she live?" he asked, his voice low. Something in his tone made me glance at him. Although he couldn't have much more than thirty years under his belt, his hard face showed the experience of battle. It was in his eyes, the way his hand lingered on the hilt of his sword and with the thin scar that ran from his left eye nearly to his chin. Captain Tiernan appeared to be a capable leader and perhaps a good man to have at our side during the coming weeks.

"Only your God and My Lady can answer that. But if we get her to our healers, she'll stand a good chance."

Merry drew a hitching breath, a low moan coming from her lips as some measure of pain penetrated her unconsciousness. Using my magic, I delved her body and inspected the results of Finnegan's healing. He'd done a fair job … far better than I could have. I had managed to close the wound, but the poison had penetrated too far for him to halt its progress. I could feel the malevolent quality of the poison, but dispersing it was far beyond my ability.

Touching her mind, I soothed her back into a healing sleep. The ride ahead was going to be rough, and it would be far better for her to endure it while unconscious.

Chapter Twelve

We'd only gone perhaps a mile when I drew Mysteria to a halt in a small copse of trees. The early-morning sun filtered in through the branches to strike the forest floor. For the first time, I appreciated how far along the spring was.

Swollen buds were just bursting to cover the trees with a faint gilding of green. Countless birds called throughout the thicket, while my ears caught the buzz of early bees venturing from their winter shelter into the warmth of the new day.

A stray beam of sunlight fell upon the burden in my arms, and I again checked her condition. A frisson of worry traveled through me. Merry was fading too fast. I couldn't wait any longer.

"Captain Tiernan. Bring your men in close."

I saw the suspicious look Crispin gave me, but I ignored him while I waited until Tiernan had everyone within earshot.

"Now listen to me." I raised my voice as I glanced around at the dozen faces. His men ranged from gray-haired veterans to boys barely old enough to shave. Yet they all possessed that look of experience. "Merry will not survive the three days it would take to reach the Lakelands. We will continue, but when I begin to sing, you must stay within hearing of my voice."

I felt more than saw Finnegan's sharp glance.

"Mists will rise around us," I continued. "But it is imperative that you hear my voice at all times."

"What will happen if one of us falls behind?"

The question came from Lieutenant Crispin. Why wasn't I surprised?

"You will be lost to the mists."

"What is this mist?" Tiernan gave his lieutenant a hard look that silenced the man.

"We do not have three days to spare. What I plan to do is Travel using the Mists of Sithi."

"Ahh," Finnegan murmured under his breath, and I shot him another glance. I got the feeling the man was far more knowledgeable about the Sithi way than I'd suspected.

It again made me curious as to his age and how he'd come by his knowledge. We didn't exactly broadcast our abilities.

"You are aware that our lands are surrounded by impenetrable mists." I directed my question to Tiernan but kept an eye on Finnegan.

"Yes," Tiernan said. "I've heard that anyone attempting to enter your lands is turned back by the mists surrounding it. Those who persist are lost within the mists."

"Correct. However, we Sithi are able to use the mists to bend time and space. By the grace of My Lady and with the use of my voice, I will recreate the Mists of Sithi and enable us to travel the distance to our lands in a matter of hours rather than days."

"Amazing," Finnegan said softly. When I again glanced at him, he shrugged. "I had my suspicions that the Sithi were able to do that, but to have it confirmed … truly amazing, Riona."

"If you're able to do this, why bother going cross-country?" Tiernan asked as he absorbed this information.

"Because it is very difficult to do. And I must know my destination exactly." I looked around the company, deliberately meeting the eyes of each man. "Remember, stay within the range of my voice. If you do not, you are lost. Not even I will be able to find you."

Turning my mount to face north, I closed my eyes and

gathered my concentration. Now was as good a time to begin as any. Sending a silent prayer to My Lady, I began to sing. The song was different from the one I'd used on the ancient forest. This one was ethereal, airy. Again, I sang in the language taught to us by Our Lady so many centuries ago, the words meaningless to the mortals but rich in meaning and beauty to my people.

Concentrating on the image of the Mists of Sithi, I drew power from my homeland, combined it with the magic of the Sithi, and released it into my surroundings. There was a moment of suspended time, of the world— or our little corner of it—holding its breath. Pressure built in the air and was then released.

The gasps from a half-dozen throats was loud in the sudden silence of the thicket. The natural sounds vanished as the first wisps of fog rose from the ground. Ghostly fingers reached higher, spreading and engulfing the party. The sunlight vanished behind a murky wall, and we were wrapped in the mists of another world.

Urging Mysteria forward with my knees, I continued singing, falling into a half trance that still allowed me an awareness of my surroundings. The mist deepened. Beside me, Finnegan's mare kept pace.

"Keep up, men. No one falls behind." Tiernan's voice was hushed as he came up on my other side. I could hear the hooves of a dozen horses close behind as they rode bunched together. No one was willing to risk losing sight of the others.

Even the horses were quiet, only an occasional nervous nicker breaking the near silence as we traveled a mist-covered trail. The ground vanished as I bent time and space to cover miles in minutes.

I was ever conscious of the burden in my arms, cradling Merry close whenever a shudder ran through her small body. I tried not to think about how shallow her breathing was. Traveling the mists was not something you could rush. Not if you ever wanted to emerge from them again.

We traveled this way for hours. The mists made it impossible to accurately gauge the passing of time. I could hear low voices talking behind me, but no one dared disturb me. My singing continued uninterrupted, my voice rising and falling with the rhythm of tune. It was a long wraparound song that allowed me to reach the end and begin again for as long as was necessary.

I was on the twentieth round when I felt a hand touch my arm. Without breaking, I glanced at Captain Tiernan. His face was expressionless, but there was a sheen of worry in his eyes.

"I'm missing a man, Lady Elf," he said softly, careful not to disturb my song.

"How long ago?" Finnegan asked the question I was unable to.

"Lieutenant Crispin just reported him gone this moment."

I closed my eyes with frustration. Damn. Why did humans persist in ignoring instructions? There was no way we could stop and search for him, but if the man was only a short distance away, there was a chance. Faint, but a chance.

Raising my voice, my song rang out in the muffling mist, the sound almost immediately swallowed. If the man was close enough to hear me, I could only hope he would find his way back. If not … there was nothing more to be done. Once disoriented within the mist, the man would wander lost until starvation claimed him. It was not a pleasant way to die.

The other men were calling out in an attempt to penetrate the fog. With luck, they would attract their comrade's attention. In my mind, I prayed to My Lady, asking her to guide the man back to us. I had no idea who was missing, but the thought of anyone lost within these mists brought a sick feeling to my stomach. It'd been my decision to Travel this route, and I felt a responsibility for these humans.

There was a touch of warmth within me, and my song soared to new heights. It was amplified and absorbed by the mist. The men fell silent as I pressed forward, my mare's step sure and confident.

Then, at what seemed a distance, I heard a shout. I glanced around and caught a glimpse of a shape emerging from the fog. The man was young, one of the youngest in the troop.

"Mullins!"

The other men parted their ranks and allowed the wide-eyed youth to ride within their loose grouping. The boy was pale and sweating, a distinct tremble to the hands that held the reins in a too-tight grip. His gelding had a fine sheen of sweat covering his coat, his eyes rolling to show the whites. The boy was lucky his mount hadn't bolted.

"Mullins, you were ordered to remain in sight at all times," Tiernan snapped. Beneath the hard voice, I heard the note of relief. I felt quite of bit of that relief myself.

"Yes, sir. I … uh … had to take a leak."

"I don't care if you pissed your pants. No one is to leave the range of the elf's voice. Is that clear?"

"Yes, sir."

I sagged a bit with relief. As few Sithi had ever allowed humans to accompany them while Traveling over the centuries, I knew of only three other instances where one was lost. None had ever been found again. The man, Mullins, must have been very close to find his way back to us. And very fortunate.

"Keep them close, Captain Tiernan." Finnegan's voice was harsh with emotion. "We may not be as lucky a second time."

He rode closer to peer at the girl in my arms, reaching out to hold his hand above her head as he monitored her condition. A frown creased his brow when he glanced at me.

"Is it much farther?"

I gave him a quick shake of my head as I dropped my voice to its normal range to continue my song. My voice was beginning to grow hoarse. The mists swirled and pressed closer to us, throwing a hazy curtain over the nearest men. We were close to our destination. I could feel the call of my homeland as we drew near. A new song reverberated through my heart, lifting it with gladness and anticipation. It was so long since I'd been home.

Home in every sense. Even before the Great Waste, I was originally from the outskirts of Chicago. My family had had a modest home on the shores of Lake Michigan just north of the city.

A part of me had rejoiced when the Sithi had chosen to make the Great Lakes region theirs. Minneson City was built on what used to be Chicago. As we'd done in New York, we'd converted the numerous high-rise buildings into a small mountain range with a warren of caves below.

Within those caves, we'd preserved much of mankind's arts and treasures. So much had been lost following the Great Waste, but we'd managed to save quite a bit of it and now had these priceless relics well guarded in the caves below our city.

Over the centuries, we'd debated as to whether these items should be returned to humans. Enough of us still retained our own mortal memories to want to keep them safe, while others couldn't care less. We had created our own masterpieces out of each bit of land we'd reclaimed and each exquisite city we'd built within our lands.

I began wrapping up my song, the words taking on a new meaning for me as I felt the difference in the mists. Clasping Merry to me in a comforting hug, I watched as the mists began to tatter and fade. The sun suddenly appeared in an expanse of blue sky, blinding in its brightness.

Looking around at the men, I saw them blink at the unexpected change of lighting. Several crossed themselves as we left the mists and found ourselves on a high bluff overlooking what used to be the southern-most point of Lake Michigan. Here the spring wasn't as advanced as it was five hundred miles to the south. A cold wind blew in off the lake and wound its icy fingers into our cloaks.

With a genuine smile lighting my face, I threw out one arm, gesturing to the expanse of wilderness that lay between us and our destination.

More than one man gasped at the sight that greeted their gaze.

In the distance, the sun caught and reflected off a city of white marble and crystal. Even from this distance, the sight was breathtaking. The many buildings were built directly into the side of the mountains we had created out of Chicago. Structures of white and glass were connected by countless bridges and walkways of white marble. A great waterfall fell hundreds of feet into a pool that eventually fed into the Great Lake.

When you had decades—if not centuries—to create a city, you could go for perfection. Minneson was as close to perfection as I'd ever seen.

The air was alive with the song of birds and the wind playing over the undulating sea of grass that separated us from the city.

"Welcome to the Lakelands. Home of the Sithi."

Chapter Thirteen

Our entrance into Minneson City was met with a strange stillness. The Sithi I saw in the streets fell silent as our party passed, then murmurs rose behind us. That really didn't surprise me. It had probably been a couple hundred years since a mortal had ridden through the shining streets of Minneson City. With better than a dozen humans, we must have been quite the parade.

I recognized a good number of Sithi we passed, but did not pause to speak. Merry's face had taken on a bluish tinge, and her breathing was reduced to shallow gasps, each rattling sounding more painful than the last. Even Mysteria stepped carefully to avoid any jarring motion.

Worry ate at me. Were we too late? Was this beyond even the talents of our healers? I stole another glance downward, nibbling at my lip before I could stop myself. Forcing myself to sit upright, I stared around with a confidence I did not feel.

Hope was all we had. Merry was still alive. There might still be time for the healers to clean the poison out of her wound.

"Riona!"

My name rang out in the near silence, and I glanced to my right. My nephew, Dylan, was just leaving an inn, a look of shock on his face. Seeing him safe ignited a warmth within my heart, and a smile tugged at my lips despite the gravity of my mission. It had been too long since I'd seen my brother's son. Even before I'd left for the Everglades, he'd been missing for a dozen or so years.

Not unusual, but worrisome for me.

"Dylan." I didn't stop but twisted to keep him in sight.

"What can I do to help?" His eyes were on the burden I carried, his sharp gaze taking in the girl's condition at a glance. For an instant, something passed over his face and then was gone. It was too quick for me to interpret. At a guess, I would have said it was malevolent, but the expression he gave me held only worry.

I shook my head. I must have imagined it.

"Run ahead to the Hall of Healing. Alert the healers that I'm bringing in a badly wounded human."

The words were barely out of my mouth before he took off running and darted down an alley in the direction of the Hall. Able to take shortcuts that we could not, Dylan would get there before us. Preparations would be underway by the time we arrived.

Captain Tiernan kept his men close on my heels as we wove our way through the streets. I was aware of their mesmerized stares as they struggled to take in the intricate stonework that surrounded them. Towers soared overhead at impossible heights, gleaming with white marble, some streaked with gold and silver, others of the purest crystal. Even the most mundane inn was constructed using methods far beyond the comprehension of mortals.

Minneson City was breathtaking, its people the epitome of beauty and grace as they flowed through the streets like so many butterflies dancing from flower to flower. Robes and gowns of every shade of the spectrum mingled and parted as we passed.

Ignoring the stares, I continued my steady pace directly to the center of the city, where a perfectly round structure of pure crystal rose above the other buildings. The sunlight bounced off the stone with blinding clarity, catching and reflecting every color imaginable. Belying the early spring, lush gardens of herbs and other healing plants surrounded the structure, their scents perfuming the air to an almost drugging potency. Drawing a deep breath, I could feel a measure of peace steal over me. Bridges spanned waterways, and winding pathways led the way to stone gazebos and pavilions, where it was possible to find a moment of tranquility without disturbance.

The Hall of Healing. Standing approximately six stories high, it was an oasis of calm within the city.

I brought my mount to a halt, aware that the men followed my lead, remaining in their saddles as they stared around in amazement. There were few Sithi within the Healing Gardens. The peace was broken only by the wind and the songs of countless birds.

I ignored all of this, my full attention on the crystal hall before me. Wide, shallow steps of white marble led the way to a pair of enormous doors bracketed by towering pillars. Four figures stood between the pillars, three swathed in robes of violet, red, and yellow, the fourth my nephew.

Relief washed over me. I'd feared that the healers might have been out of the city.

Despite the concealing garb, I recognized Kasia Morninglory, Eleni Foxglove, and Payton Moonlight and felt my hopes rise. These were the strongest healers in existence. If anyone could save Merry, it was these three.

"Bring the human," Payton instructed without moving from his lofty position. I saw Kasia shoot him an annoyed glance before she lifted the skirts of her violet robes and started down the steps, Eleni close on her heels. I managed to dismount without jarring Merry too much. Despite my care, a low moan rose from pale lips. Swallowing my fear, I kept my pace smooth as I began to ascend the steps. We met approximately halfway.

"Let me see," Kasia said as she carefully pulled my cloak from around Merry. Her breath caught when she saw the condition the girl was in. "Bring her, Riona. Quickly. There isn't much time."

Without another word, she turned and hurried back up the steps, her robes flowing behind her. She flung back her hood, and the bright sunlight picked out the mottled brown streaking her white hair. Kasia's hair was pulled back into an intricate braid, revealing the elven points of her ears, numerous golden hoops running down the outer curve from peak to lobe. A sign of her profession.

Without urging, I picked up my pace until I was running up the steps. Merry's weight was nothing to me as I entered the Hall of Healing, following Kasia as she led the way into the sunlit corridor.

"Don't dawdle, Payton," she snapped over her shoulder at the man where he remained with Dylan. "Come with us. This will require all of our skills."

"She's only a human, Kasia."

Sudden fury welled up in me, and I nearly stopped, but Eleni at my back kept me moving.

"All the more reason for you to move your lazy ass," Kasia snapped without turning. "Unless I'm very much mistaken, this girl has taken a Skori wound."

"Skori!"

That got Payton moving. The man was more a scholar than a healer. I'd known him since the Great Waste. In his human life, Payton had been the head librarian of the New York Metropolitan Library. It was through his efforts that so many priceless objects of art had been saved. He was far happier with his nose in a book than he was as a healer. Yet there was no denying his talent in that direction. With Eleni and Kasia, the three of them could heal anything short of death.

Before I continued through the winding hallway, I paused beside Dylan, my glance going down the steps to where the humans were tending their horses. Only Finnegan and Tiernan watched me, the captain going so far as to mount the first step as if to follow. I shook my head at him. This was not the place for a mortal.

"Please escort these men to my home, Dylan. I am extending Guest Rights," I said in a low voice before I continued in the wake of the healers. I saw his eyes widen at my choice of words. He swallowed hard before nodding. "I will be there as soon as possible."

Dylan's gaze left me to travel down the length of the steps to the small band of men standing at the bottom of the stairs. A look of distaste crossed his face so quickly that I almost questioned my seeing it. That was the second negative impression I'd gotten from him. I must be more exhausted than I'd thought.

"I'll take care of it, Riona."

Movement behind me caught my attention, and I found Finnegan a few steps behind me. His appearance was so silent, so quick that I wondered if he had used his mortal magic to appear. Either that or I'd been too distracted by my burden and missed his ascent.

"I go where you go, Riona."

I shook my head before I started down the corridors of the crystal Hall of Healing. My boot heels made a hollow sound on the stone floors. The hallway was wide, easily thirty paces across, the walls plain with few hangings. Niches broke up the unrelieved white, statuary nestled within, each more beautiful than the last.

"I'm finding far more prejudice here than I anticipated, Finnegan," I said in a low voice, conscious of Eleni still at my back. "I need someone to stay with the humans. To run interference."

He hesitated. Eleni must have sensed my need for privacy, because she passed us and joined her colleagues leading the way.

"Please?"

A slight smile appeared in the tangle of his beard. With a low bow, he turned on his heel and vanished through the still-open doors.

I threw a final glance over my shoulder and saw Dylan herding the mortals in the direction of my home. Reassured, I again turned to follow the healers. Their bright cloaks covered them from shoulder to foot. Their appearance was not dissimilar to that of the monks whose monastery we'd so recently left. However, the healers moved with a grace that was lacking in the humans, gliding across the marble floor into the heart of the Hall of Healing.

Impatience ate at me, and I wanted to hurry them along, but I knew it would do little good. The healers did everything in their own good time. I tried to ignore the way Merry's breathing seemed to stop for several heartbeats before resuming with a broken gasp. A glance downward showed that her face was a near-translucent white. Some part of me knew that there was a kernel of awareness emanating from her. She knew the gravity of her condition and was hanging on by sheer will alone.

"Hang in there, granddaughter," I whispered above her head, my voice too low for the healers to hear me. I didn't know if Merry had heard me, but a part of me hoped she had. Perhaps the knowledge of our familial connection would give her something to grasp on to. Only The Lady knew what was keeping her alive.

"Bring her." Eleni stopped at the door at the far end of the corridor and stepped aside, gesturing for me to enter a room at the center of the structure. Sunlight flooded the room, reflected by the countless facets of the crystal that made up the Hall. Rainbows of color streamed across the chamber. It wasn't a large room, but the odd angles and streaming light made it appear larger than it was. A bed—more of a platform—was positioned at the center, where the greatest concentration of energy was focused.

"Lay the human there," Payton intoned in an emotionless voice. Maybe I was being ultra-sensitive, but there was a distinct note of disdain in his voice. Healer or not, I was beginning to dislike the man. Funny how my own attitude had changed in less than two weeks. Other than the few long-standing friendships I had with humans, I'd been viewing them with the same contempt that I was finding here in Minneson City. Perhaps the attitude was infectious among the Sithi. When you were as long-lived as we were, you tended to view mortals as … lesser.

Not an admirable trait.

With extra care, I laid Merry out on the table, keeping my cloak wrapped around her. The protective covering was probably unnecessary since the room held the heat of a sauna as the bright sunlight filtered through the crystal.

Sweat broke out on my forehead before I regulated my body temperature, but Merry shivered despite the warmth.

A glance at the healers showed Kasia moving around the room, lighting candles in tall, freestanding candlesticks, her movements smooth and deliberate. Eleni moved in the opposite direction, mimicking her until more than a hundred candles were lit. Their delicate scent rose to perfume the air, while the two healers paused at a shallow bowl set in a pedestal. I felt the whisper of magic just before the dried herbs within ignited and a thin wisp of smoke rose to mingle with the scents of the candles.

A low hum of sound caught my ears, and I realized that the two healers were singing under their breath, their voices too low for me to understand the words. A glance at Payton showed that he, too, was singing, his deeper baritone complementing the feminine tones. The crystal walls of the healing chamber caught and echoed the song, reverberating in response.

"Are we too late?" I whispered to Eleni as she glided to Merry's side, opposite from where I stood. Without pausing in her song, she carefully removed the cloak from around the girl and eased aside the torn tunic. Her eyes were intent on the wound. Her expression gave nothing away.

"As long as there is breath in the body, you are never too late,

Riona."

I didn't really expect her to answer me, so I was surprised when she paused in her song. Then a part of me feared that my interruption might have endangered Merry.

"The Lady give us strength," Payton whispered as he peered over my shoulder at the wound. The tone in his voice earned him a quick glance, and I saw his stare fastened on Merry's shoulder.

I turned and peered through the gap in the girl's tunic. The wound was swollen and gaping. Darkness lay in the heart of it and radiated outward under the skin as the insidious poison worked its way into her system. Despite my efforts, blood still seeped from the injury, glistening in the bright sunlight.

It was a wonder that we'd made it this far.

"Stand aside, Riona," Kasia said. "There is nothing more that you can do. You've brought the future queen of Newland to us, and we will do everything within our power to save her."

I was unsurprised that Kasia knew who Merry was. I'd long suspected there was more to this woman than her incredible ability to heal. Word had it she had a touch of soothsayer in her.

"Yes, get out and leave us to our work. We will notify you when we are finished." Payton elbowed me out of the way, forcing me to step back as he took my place at Merry's side.

The three gathered around the prone body of Merry, Kasia at her head, Payton and Eleni at either side. Joining hands, they bowed their heads and resumed their song. This time it appeared to mingle with the now-swirling smoke and the heavy scent of the candles. The air thickened until it became difficult to breathe. The vibration of their combined talent was a tangible thing as it accessed the crystal walls of the chamber, drawing on the powers of the earth, spirit, and Our Lady.

Knowing I could do nothing more, I backed out of the room, a part of me unwilling to allow Merry from my sight, but I needed to notify Queen Tesina of my presence and the presence of a band of humans within our borders.

This was not going to be pretty.

Chapter Fourteen

"**Y**ou brought an army within our borders," Queen Tesina Summerfield snapped, icy anger revealed in her narrowed eyes. She sat upright on her crystal throne, back stiff, fury making her face both fearsome and beautiful at the same time. "Have you no concept of what you've done?"

"Hardly an army, Your Majesty." I tried to keep my voice calm and conciliatory. I ignored the presence of the Sithi court gathered within the throne room, which included three types of courtiers—the favored few, those who actually did something worthwhile, and those who hovered at the edges hoping to gain favor. I viewed the third group with contempt. They were what I would have once called ass kissers.

Word had flown ahead of me. While I'd been with the healers, someone had wasted little time in notifying Queen Tesina of my arrival with a band of humans. Whoever that little bird had been, he or she had not done me any favors. The queen had been furious before I'd even entered the throne room.

So far, this interview was not going well. I struggled to keep my voice even and my expression under control. "A dozen men, Your Majesty. Half of whom sustained wounds when they came to our aid."

"Put them out beyond our borders."

"I cannot do that, Your Majesty." Still in my travel clothes, I stood before her, my position at a disadvantage. She sat the crystal throne, elevated above the other inhabitants of the throne room by a half-dozen steps. The courtiers hung on to our every word, avid anticipation in more than one face. I was not among the favorites within the queen's court, but my age and experience put me far above them. That rubbed many the wrong way. I was aware of Laurel Westward edging closer and turned to give her a cold look. The youngling and I rarely agreed on anything. Hell, I could say the sky was blue and she'd argue. Definitely not my ally here.

Richly dressed in a gown of pale green velvet, Laurel made me conscious of my travel-stained attire. Not that it mattered. It was a little tough battling Skori and remaining fresh and unscathed. Still, I couldn't help but compare her intricately styled hair with my own tangled mess. Carefully selected jewelry was woven into the mottled mass, the light catching the emeralds and causing them to flash with every movement of her head.

Irritation added fuel to my glare. It was enough to make her back off a few steps, but it wouldn't last. Like sharks with blood in the water, my enemies were circling. One of the main reasons why I had been gone so long from Minneson City. The politics were worse than contemporary Earth. We certainly had more practice at perfecting the backstabbing.

"There is a good chance that the Skori who attacked us were not the only party on the hunt." I was forced to return my attention to Queen Tesina and ignore the courtiers. "I would be sending these men to their deaths."

"And I should care?"

Shocked, I stared at her. The queen of my people sat upon her throne, every inch the regal monarch. Dressed in rich silks of gold, she was beautiful as all Sithi were with her high cheekbones, pale complexion, delicately tipped ears. Like the rest of us, her hair was losing its winter whiteness as spring wove streaks of golden-blond within her thick, waist-length tresses. A crown of golden laurel leaves circled her brow, the design echoed in the necklace at her slender throat.

But I was noticing something different about Tesina. When had she lost the final vestiges of her humanity? When had she become so cold and contemptuous of what she once had been?

Even more disturbing was that, in her face, I saw a possible reflection of myself. A little more than a week ago, I'd been ready to turn my back on humanity and retreat to the solitude of my home.

What had changed that? The answer was easy. One little human. A mortal who reminded me of what I once had been. A mortal who was even now being saved by our greatest healers. Hopefully.

"I have extended Guest Rights to them, Your Majesty. Is the hospitality of the Sithi so lacking that we cannot honor our invited guests?"

"You've extended Guest Rights?" Her voice dropped to a hissing whisper. Fury flared in her amber eyes for an instant before she regained control. "You've been too long from Sithi, Riona Northstar. I've been calling our people home in preparation of closing our borders."

"Closing our borders?" Another shock. This was unheard of. True, no human or Skori could enter the mists without a guide, but to close our borders would be to close off the mists to all but the Sithi. Even with a guide, no mortal would be able to pass through.

I glanced around at the courtiers who had by now given up all pretense of interest in other matters. From their various little groupings, they watched Tesina and me with avid attention. Men and women who were present in the throne room for one reason or another were now riveted to the discussion between our queen and me.

My glance swept over them, noting their fine dress and careful grooming. They all wore the look of complacency. None of them had been laboring on Our Lady's behalf. I doubted many of these Sithi had been out of our lands in decades, if not centuries.

"We cannot close ourselves off from the world, Your Majesty." I didn't bother lowering my voice. Let them all hear. I was beyond caring. The two guards who stood unmoving at the main entrance watched me with alert eyes, weapons always at the ready. Did they care about my opinion? I cast a contemptuous look over the assembled courtiers and found one or two nodding in agreement with me. So I wasn't the only one to disagree with this plan. But so few appeared to share my view.

Deciding to take a chance, I stepped closer to the throne, putting one foot on the first step of the five-step dais upon which it sat. I felt more than saw the guards stiffen.

"My Queen," I began in a calm voice, loud enough for all to hear. "I was honored with a Vision granted by Our Lady while in the custody of the monastery."

"A Vision."

I erased the frown that threatened at the skepticism in her voice. Although rare, Visions were not unheard of. I wasn't accustomed to being doubted.

"Our Lady led me down the shining path that we all once took so long ago." A murmur of voices rose behind me. "But instead of a door, I was led to an arena where there appeared three beings."

The murmurs grew louder until a sharp glance from Tesina silenced them.

"One of them was Our Lady. The other two were her siblings, the One God of the humans and the Dark Lord of the Skori."

"What did they look like?"

The question was asked in a hushed voice, and I looked over my shoulder at the young Sithi who'd posed it. Young by our standards, Marnius Willowisp was only three hundred years old. His eyes were wide with wonder and fear.

"I could not see their faces but could identify them by robes and attitude." I turned back to Tesina. "Everything that is happening is connected. The deaths of the Newland heirs, King Ambrose falling into madness, the Church of the One God growing in ambition. The Dark Master is stirring and making a bid for control, Your Majesty."

I quickly shared the rest of Vision I'd been given by Our Lady, omitting a few details that I felt had no bearing on the present situation. I didn't feel a need to repeat my bold questions of Our Lady, nor to give her True Name. These were gifts given to me, and I treasured them, hugged them to my heart.

Tesina listened in silence as I concluded those portions I felt important to convince my people of the danger we faced.

"We cannot ignore the outside world, My Queen. Especially not now."

"What do we care of the politics of mortals?" Tesina asked, her voice cold and distant. She looked down her nose at me from her elevated position. As usual, her superior attitude pissed me off, but I struggled to conceal it. Now was not the time.

"The politics of mortals are directly related to ours, Your Majesty. What affects one eventually affects the other."

"Other than to persecute us, humans have little use for us. After all that we've done for them, this is the thanks we get."

"All that we've done for them?" Disbelief colored my words as my voice rose. The noticeable drop in the volume behind me alerted me that the initial shock had worn off and we were once again the center of attention. I was beyond caring. "We labor for Our Lady, Tesina. Not for ourselves or for any mortal. They merely gained the benefit of our labors."

"And what thanks did we get?"

"What thanks did you expect? Have you forgotten, Tesina, what it was to be human? Have you forgotten that you were once an accountant before the Change?"

I suppose I shouldn't have brought up our past life. For some of us, these things were better forgotten, but I never forgot what I once was. The daughter of a farmer, a wife, and a mother. Still, some of us hadn't completely accepted a life of servitude. Even now, when our labors were all but complete. The last of the pollutants had been transformed; any lingering vestiges of the Industrial Age had been eradicated. Our Lady was pleased. The woodland abounded with game, and the harvests were rich—for both elven and human.

"Despite what we've become, we can never forget our roots, Your Majesty. It colors everything we do and everything we are. We have no choice but to involve ourselves in the politics of mortals. Sooner or later, they affect us."

The remaining murmur of voices had whittled to silence during my argument with Tesina.

The look I received from the queen should have frozen the blood in my veins, but I returned her glare with one of my own. I was too old to back down. Perhaps this wasn't my most diplomatic moment, but I was past caring.

No one had dared speak to our queen in such a manner in centuries. But I dared. My age gave me certain rights where Tesina was concerned. Not that she, my contemporary, would see it that way. Especially since it had been a close contest between us for appointment to her position.

The difference was, I hadn't wanted it. I never wanted to rule. I was far more interested in roaming the land, watching the changing world, interacting with the mortals she found intolerable. It was not in my nature to sit upon a throne and rule a people.

However, the direction Tesina was taking the Sithi was making me rethink my position. If only to advocate for a ruler more fit for the position.

Tesina ignored me for the moment, waving one of her personal ladies forward. The woman, more of a girl by our standards, went down on her knees before our queen, holding out an elaborately carved bowl containing a dozen different types of apples. Tesina inspected the fruit with careful consideration, making me wait several minutes before she selected an apple perfect in shape and color.

I stared at the red and gold apple for a moment. It reminded me much of my present ruler. Perfect on the outside, but who was to say that the inside matched its beautiful exterior? I wondered how long this attitude had been going on. The changes that had occurred during my century-long absence came as a surprise. A nasty one.

"You will perform for us tonight, Riona," she said at last before she bit into the fruit with a sharp snap of her teeth. Her words were careless, but there was nothing unmindful in the look she gave me. "Since you insist on giving these mortals Guest Rights, we shall show them that the Sithi are not completely without manners. They will join us for dinner and entertainment."

"I ..." I stopped. I'd been about to say that I intended to monitor Merry's progress with the healers, but this wasn't a choice Tesina was giving me. It amounted to a command. I'd already overstepped the boundaries with my public comments about her attitude with the humans. She was reasserting her authority over me.

"As you command, Your Majesty." I bowed deeply, arms sweeping wide. "May I withdraw and see to my guests?"

She waved me away, and I backed up a few steps before turning and striding down the length of the throne room. I didn't look right or left, aware of the stares following me from the courtiers.

I knew my abrupt dismissal was deliberate. It was another childish power play that Tesina excelled in. Still, it didn't matter. I thought I'd achieved a little bit of good here. The public report Tesina had pressed me to make had enabled me to alert the Sithi court of our danger.

Whether she liked it or not, Tesina was forced to pay attention to the outside world.

Chapter Fifteen

I tucked myself in an alcove in the corner of the ballroom. Heavy velvet curtains concealed my presence, allowing me to observe the room's occupants with a minimum of notice. Strumming my fingers across the gitar, I absently tuned the instrument while my glance moved over the faces of the gathering. The entire Sithi court was present in all their glory and over-the-top finery. Flashes of every color imaginable were visible as the crowd undulated from one end of the ballroom to the other. The wine flowed freely, and laughter echoed from every corner of the room while the sound of crystal clinked as toasts were raised.

Such beauty and grace were the things dreams were made of.

And such a farce.

Near immortality had its downside. We were not quite invincible. Like the Skori, any fatal injury could kill us. We just didn't age. Unlimited time and opportunity made for a whole lot of boredom for those who didn't keep busy with outside interests. Hence another reason I was away so often.

A motion to my right caught my attention, and I glanced toward the entrance of my hidey-hole. Kai Tiernan and his men paused under the great archway, looking over the ensemble. Stunned amazement painted the faces of his men as they stared at the ebb and flow of Sithi moving about the ballroom, the kaleidoscope of color and beauty mesmerizing the humans.

The captain's expression never changed. I found that

interesting. The sight of the Sithi court in full regalia was not something any mortal had seen before. Not in a thousand years. Yet Kai Tiernan appeared completely unimpressed.

As their court raiment had been left behind during our wild ride to save Merry's life, the mortals had been given a selection of clothing to choose from. To a man, they'd chosen plain hose and tunics in dark colors, somber compared to the flamboyant court. Somehow, Kai had acquired an overcoat bearing the symbol of Cascadia, the crouching tiger on a sea of blue. Beyond a dagger strapped at their belts, none of the men bore weaponry.

While his men stood clustered, Captain Kai looked at ease despite his disadvantage within the ranks of the Sithi gathering. A hawk among the peacocks. I watched as he ran his gaze over the throng, a hint of amusement in his manner. Either a brave man or a foolish one. Each and every one of my brethren might appear foppish, but appearances were deceptive. If the occasion called for it, they would kill without hesitation or remorse.

Gauging Kai's expression a moment longer, I decided he wasn't a fool. He appeared casual, but his gaze was watchful and cautious. He wasn't about to underestimate the courtiers thronging the ballroom. No matter how pretty they appeared.

Queen Tesina was absent, of course. No surprise there. Tesina liked to wait before making her grand entrance. The vast hall was decorated in celebration of the new spring. Sprigs of new growth adorned numerous crystal vases, many in flower and perfuming the air with their rich scents. Winter tapestries had been removed, replaced with scenes depicting the coming summer. The ceiling overhead appeared to open to the night sky, the glass so clear that the stars glittered like jewels against the black velvet of vast space.

"Humans at the royal hall." Beyond my velvet concealment, someone paused, contempt coloring her voice. "What's next? Horses in our bedchambers?"

I went still, my fingers above the strings. I didn't recognize the voice.

"I was almost surprised when Queen Tesina allowed it," a second voice answered, and I recognized the dulcet tone of Laurel Westward and made a slight face.

"She should have abandoned them to the mists."

"Don't be silly. The mortals are Riona's pets." Laurel laughed, but there was little amusement in her tone. "Although she and the queen may appear to be adversaries, Queen Tesina doesn't dare oppose Riona openly. Riona would win every time."

So, Laurel was more observant that I'd given her credit for. I'd have to remember that. And she was quite correct. Our standing among our people and the powers bestowed by Our Lady were too closely entwined for Tesina and me to ever go to war. While we rarely agreed on anything, Tesina was, for the most part, a fair ruler. It was a role she enjoyed, and more power to her. I had no desire to challenge Tesina.

Besides, sometimes I thought she enjoyed our sparring as much as I did. Who was I to deprive either one of us of that pleasure?

"I must say, though"—Laurel's voice grew thoughtful—"the captain is quite attractive. For a human."

Her companion's laughter held a touch of scandalized incredulity. Not originally human, then. Born a Sithi and possessing all those prejudices that were becoming so predominant. Arrogance and superiority. Some Sithi needed to be reminded of their roots.

I waited until the voices passed on before I once again ran my fingers over the strings of my gitar, realizing in an absent sort of way how much I'd missed playing. A hybrid of a guitar and a bittern, it was smaller than a standard instrument of old yet had the same tone and feel. I had never been much of a musician in my mortal life, but I'd been required by my parents to learn the piano. The long years of immortality encouraged outside hobbies, and I'd found a very real talent with the gitar.

Still, despite the preservation spell I had cast upon my home, a century of neglect had left the instrument sorely out of tune.

That same preservation spell had caused a bit of trouble when I'd finally returned to my home after leaving Queen Tesina. I'd found Finnegan and the humans milling around the meadow just outside the overgrown gardens, attending their horses and cleaning their gear. Dylan had vanished, leaving my guests stranded outside my home with no way of breaching the spell I'd placed upon it before I'd left for my final assignment in the Everglades.

I supposed I shouldn't have been surprised that Dylan had been unable to reverse the enchantment, and I shouldn't have expected him to. As far as the Sithi go, he was fairly weak when it came to magic. I wasn't sure why My Lady had limited his powers so long ago, but it wasn't something I was about to question. But it was something I knew he resented. She must have had a good reason.

Still, to leave my guests without a means of refreshing themselves… That went beyond rude. I'd have to track Dylan down later and have a few words with him. My nephew's manners appeared to have gone missing over the centuries.

A slight smile curved my lips as I continued to tune my gitar. It felt good to be home. Despite the politics, there was nothing more peaceful, more satisfying than being surrounded by your personal stuff. Most of the structure had been built into the side of a hill with only the front made of stone and wood. I'd built it in the Tudor style I'd always admired. The inside was lavish with highly polished wood-framed smooth plaster painted in warm colors. It was lit with crystal sconces that held elven light, positioned to reveal the fine art and delicate figurines I'd collected.

With each city we'd restored to pristine woodland condition, the Sithi had cleared out any objects of art or anything of value with the intention of preserving them. By old human standards, we were beyond rich in the reclamation of old artwork and statuary. Some Sithi collected jewels and precious metals, and others took great delight in preserving old documents and books. The original Declaration of Independence was carefully stored under a preservation spell by Payton Moonlight. A former librarian, he was obsessed with the preservation of old books and documents. Deep underground, he had accumulated an incredible collection of ancient books, many from his former place of employment in New York's Metropolitan Library. I'd always been partial to Disney collectibles myself, but who was I to debate great art?

I shook off the thought and strummed an intricate melody to test the tuning of my strings. The pure notes wound their way through the crowded room, causing more than one Sithi to pause to listen. Despite Tesina's edict that I perform tonight, it wasn't a chore. I enjoyed playing. Along with the piano lessons, my family had insisted on singing lessons, and back then I'd had a fair voice. With the blessings of My Lady, my talents had now surpassed those of mortals and most Sithi. My voice was now mesmerizing.

I shook back the flowing sleeves of my tunic to allow myself freedom of movement as I began a melody I had written centuries ago. My court clothes might be a little out of date, but what did I care? Fashions came and went, but plain old hose and a well-cut tunic with boots never seemed out of place in any gathering. My leggings were plain black but of a fine material, and my knee-high boots were polished to a high sheen. A short cape of dark red brocade fell down my back, embroidered with fanciful creatures and held in place with a fine silver chain. I'd braided my hair into an intricate arrangement of knots, noticing that the winter white tresses were nearly overtaken by the pale blond of my spring color. Soon the blond tresses would fade into the dark brown of the summer season.

Concentrating on my music, I was nevertheless conscious of

my surroundings. The sound level rose and fell as the crowd of guests, friends, and court parasites waited for the arrival of the royal party. There was a sense of anticipation in the air. I wasn't sure if it was because of the humans and how the royals were going to react to them or something else. Either way, I was determined to keep my eyes and ears open.

Tesina's husband and consort was an ancient by the name of Fallon Summerfield. I'd never known what his original name was, but I believe he'd once been a detective with the LAPD. A fitting mate for a queen who battled court intrigue at every turn. Unfortunately, they'd never had children, and I'd already heard some whispers of Tesina either stepping down or naming her successor. Rumors so far, but I'd found rumors usually held a whisper of truth.

I knew this gathering was ostensibly in celebration of the arrival of spring. A special time in both the Sithi and mortal worlds when the crops were in and the people prayed for a good harvest.

Compared to the humans', the Sithi celebrations were normally conducted in a more sedate fashion, with quiet contemplation, feasting, and, yes, there would be drinking and dancing far into the evening. We were so long-lived that we tended to savor our celebrations, make them last days rather than hours.

A motion caught my eye, and I noticed a tall human enter the room. For a moment, I couldn't place him. I didn't recall seeing him among the captain's guard. Watching him, my fingers stilled once more on my strings for an instant before I continued to strum the tune. Something about him …

My head continued to turn to follow his progress. My gaze wandered down a broad back to linger on a very nice backside. The dark hose he wore beneath a short cape hugged a nice, tight butt and emphasized muscular legs.

It took me a full minute to realize it was Finnegan I was

admiring, and I felt my eyes widen with astonishment. He'd taken the time to bathe and had his hair cut and his beard trimmed close around his jaw. Without the matted mess of beard to conceal his lower face, his features were strong and compelling. Viewed from this angle, I could see that he was handsome, sensuous lips curved into a half smile as he approached Captain Tiernan.

My gaze traveled over the rest of him, noting that he'd disbursed with the voluminous robes that concealed much of his body. Dressed in the short cloak, more of a cape, of the deepest blue edged with silver, he cut a very fine figure. His hose were black and stuffed into shining black boots trimmed with silver. His tunic was snowy white, against which his tanned skin stood out, his beard appearing more white than gray. It was amazing what a decent bath and fine clothes did for the man.

A ripple of hushed whispers followed in his wake, but he ignored the stares as his dark gaze swept over the vast room. He was searching for someone, and I was hoping that someone wasn't me. I wanted to remain incognito for a bit longer while I scoped out the lay of the land.

He reached Kai Tiernan, and the two men nodded to each other in recognition. I watched from my alcove as he paused to speak with the Cascadian. If I used a touch of magic, I could pick up their conversation, but a man of Finnegan's talent would immediately detect the intrusion. Plus it was rude. For all I knew, they were discussing the merits of wine versus beer.

I strummed my fingers over the strings of my gitar, playing a soft tune to accompany the rise in conversation. A few guests glanced around to locate the source of the music, but I was well concealed in my alcove. I wove my way from one song to another, using a touch of enchantment to enhance the sound so that it reached the farthest corners, soft and unobtrusive.

I saw Finnegan glance in my direction, a glass of wine in his hand. Somehow he detected the source of the magic in the room.

From where he stood, he was unable to see me, but he raised his glass in the direction of my alcove. I smiled to myself, impressed despite myself. He really was quite powerful. And astute.

My fingers flew over the strings, drawing a lively tune from the gitar as I relearned the many songs of my own youth. Normally a small band would be performing for this gathering, but Queen Tesina had commanded my performance. It might have been flattering if I didn't know that Tesina viewed this as a punishment.

Evidently she had forgotten how much I loved playing and would much rather be here in this alcove than mingling with the other guests. Making small talk and pretending to be interested in the current goings-on of the court was far more of a chore than my current occupation. I'd already managed to ferret out the bulk of the gossip circulating the palace and the surrounding city. Currently, my only interest was in the condition of one small human. I'd left word with the healers to contact me the moment they completed their own brand of magic. Or, the Lady forbid, Merry took a turn for the worse.

"Any word on Merry's condition?" a voice inquired in a near whisper from the other side of the curtain. The words were an echo of my own thoughts.

Shock caused me to stumble over a chord before I found my rhythm again. I had allowed my attention to wander for a moment and missed the wizard leaving Tiernan's side. Beside me, the velvet material moved, and Finnegan slipped into the alcove. He held two glasses of red wine, wordlessly holding one out to me until I paused long enough to take it. He then moved to lean against the far wall and gave me a smile that made my heart skip a beat. Why hadn't I noticed how attractive he was? I should have been able to see beyond his disguise.

Probably because we had spent most of our time fleeing for our lives. This close, I could still feel the remnants of the combined magic we'd utilized in the monastery, the sensation an erotic prelude. Again, I felt that long-forgotten flutter in the pit of my stomach.

"No. The healers did send word a short time ago that she appears to be resting." After relieving the dryness of my throat, I set the glass aside and bent over my gitar, allowing my braid to fall over my cheek and conceal much of my expression. What was my problem? He was human; I was Sithi. I couldn't recall the last time a mortal had affected me this way. Or another Sithi, for that matter. Not in centuries.

It was unexpected and unwelcome.

"I was warned that she's not out of danger yet, but the healers are confident she is over the worst." Trying to ignore my hormones, I concentrated on both my playing and the conversation.

"Thank God," he murmured, closing his eyes for an instant before opening them to pierce me with a sharp stare. His eyes definitely held more than just inquiry. A warm emotion gleamed in that chocolate-brown gaze. I guess I, too, cut a better figure in court regalia than I did in worn travel clothes.

He took a seat on the far end of the bench where I sat, leaning back against the wall and putting a foot up on the velvet cushion. He cradled his glass of wine in his hand, watching me.

"And how much trouble are you in for harboring us?"

Well, I'd never once thought that the man was stupid. He apparently had a keen understanding of court politics—whether human or Sithi. I dropped my gaze back down to my gitar but could feel the weight of his gaze on me. I wanted to avoid an answer but knew we'd probably dance around the subject until I gave in.

"Let's just say the queen was most displeased. I've extended Guest Rights to you and the captain's men."

"Guest rights?"

"Yes. By Sithi law, that gives you free run of the city, and any Sithi asked is required to give you aid and courtesy." I paused. "But it also makes me responsible for any actions on your part."

He was silent for a moment, and I concentrated on the ebb and flow of the conversation outside our private little sanctuary. There was a sense of intimacy in our secluded location, and I had to concentrate on my playing to avoid more than one carnal thought.

This made no sense. I'd had lovers in the past, but always Sithi. I hadn't had a human lover since the death of Ian. I'd told myself so many centuries ago that I couldn't go through that again. Watching a loved one age and die while I remained ever young. My heart couldn't take that pain.

"How many mortals have been extended this honor?"

My attention snapped back to Finnegan. He had two fingers pressed against his lips as he watched me, idly swirling the red wine in his glass, his eyes unreadable.

"Mortals? As far as I know, very few."

"Ah. An honor." He nodded and fell silent for a long moment, listening to my playing as he sipped his wine. "I couldn't help but notice a certain ... chill in the air when we arrived. Was that my imagination?"

"No." How much to tell him? I did feel a certain loyalty to my people. We kept stuff from mortals, but right now, how much of a connection did I feel for my brethren? I'd been gone for more than a hundred years. So much had changed in that short span of time. This self-absorption, the isolation that Tesina was advocating. It didn't feel right. This was also not something that had happened overnight. Was I just as guilty of being so self-absorbed that I hadn't seen it coming? I should have. With our appointed tasks all but complete, there were a lot of Sithi with nothing but time on their hands. Yes, with the aid of the Rangers, we made sure the Skori were held in check, but this was the first time they'd been stirring in centuries. From what I could see of this crowd, my people were woefully unprepared for the coming storm. Tesina needed a wake-up call.

Did I feel some discomfort in criticizing my people? A little. But this was Finnegan. For some reason, it felt right revealing to him something I would never say to another. Again, it was unexplainable.

Chapter Sixteen

Uncertainty was not an emotion that I'd felt in a long time. Or perhaps, something I hadn't acknowledged. I'd almost forgotten what it felt like. Yet with Finnegan staring at me, I felt a shift in my emotions. I'd always felt a kinship with my human self. A certain affinity to what I'd once been. Unlike a good number of my people, I could never forget my roots.

"We Sithi tend to keep to ourselves."

"Only for the past five or six hundred years."

His words were droll, and I nearly struck a sour note before I returned my concentration to my music. For several long moments, I played, moving from one tune to another while my mind worked furiously. Had it been that long since the coldness had first set in? Had it been a gradual thing? Something that'd crept up on my people? Something I'd just never noticed?

I glanced through the curtains at the flowing colors as dancers swirled past my hidden sanctuary in step to the music I was providing. I watched as Sithi created intricate patterns of graceful movement, coming together and then separating. The conversation was overly loud; the laughter sounded forced.

It struck me that it was almost a parody of life as we'd made it.

Why had it taken me so long to realize this?

I glanced over at Finnegan, a strange moisture forming in my eyes. Something else I hadn't felt in years. He was watching me with warmth. Understanding.

"I …"

I wasn't sure how I might have responded, but a fanfare of trumpets stopped me from continuing. The dancers halted and the conversation dwindled to silence. I set aside my gitar and swept the curtain open. No one looked at me or Finnegan. Everyone's attention was at the end of the ballroom.

We were close enough to have a clear view. An honor guard of twelve stood at attention just inside the enormous double doors of the ballroom entrance. Their polished mail gleamed in the muted lighting, hands on swords, the other across their chests. Tall, they were comprised of six men and six women, all of them hard-faced beneath their helms, eyes never resting in one place.

They were impressive, but the entering couple captured every eye. Dressed completely in white, Queen Tesina was spectacular, and I heard Finnegan's breath catch in his throat. I spared him a glance and couldn't fault his stunned expression. Tesina's pale brown hair was swept up into an intricate arrangement, curls falling artfully about her slender neck. Diamonds were sprinkled throughout her hair, sparkling with each turn of her head, while a fortune in the same stones draped her throat and adorned her delicately pointed ears. The pure white gown left her shoulders and a good portion of her bosom bare, hugging her slender figure lovingly before falling to the ground to sweep behind her in a long train.

Her husband and consort, Fallon Summerfield, presented an equally impressive figure. An ancient, he was tall, muscular, and stunningly handsome. His gaze swept over the assembled throng with cold attention. I saw his eyes continue over me, pause, and then come back for an instant. His expression never changed, but I was certain he gave me the slightest nod of acknowledgment before he continued his perusal of the room.

His right arm was outstretched to allow Tesina to rest her hand upon it, while his other held the leash of what was once called a

Russian wolfhound. How they managed to hold the breed true after all these centuries was a mystery. Most of the domestic pets that had survived the plague had turned feral and interbred to a point where their origins were impossible to trace.

My gaze left the enormous dog and returned to Fallon. The man wasn't a fool, and if it weren't for Our Lady's decree that the Sithi throne was always to be held by a woman, he would have made a good king. More than once, his counsel had tempered Tesina's occasional rash decrees.

In a wave, the entire court sank into curtsies and bows as the royal couple swept into the ballroom. Captain Tiernan and his men followed suit, bowing low as Queen Tesina and Prince Fallon came abreast to them. Tesina paused, her cold glance brushing over the humans.

"You are welcome to the Sithi Court, mortals," she said, the ice lacing through her words giving lie to the greeting.

So, she was going to hold to Guest Rights. I was almost surprised. Despite the law, I'd fully expected her to find some way to circumvent my invitation. My glance dropped to the dog. He was watching the humans with intent, a low growl rumbling from deep in his throat.

"Your Highness." Kai Tiernan straightened from his bow, standing tall in his borrowed clothes. While his men looked star struck and slightly ill, he showed no sign of discomfort. After a brief glance, he ignored the hound. "I wish to thank you for your hospitality."

"I understand you are residing with Riona Northstar. You are comfortable?" Prince Fallon asked, his expression warmer by several degrees than that of his wife. Tesina turned to look ahead, dismissal in her expression.

"Yes, Your Highness. Thank you."

"If you have need of anything, do not hesitate to ask."

With another nod to the mortals, he continued down the aisle to the two thrones at the end. The wolfhound stared after the humans for another second before the prince tugged his leash and he turned to follow. Prince Fallon handed his wife up to the larger throne before taking his place at her side.

The entire court rose to their feet and faced the royal couple. The silence continued as everyone awaited the pleasure of our rulers.

Tesina looked over the hall, her gaze arrogant as she swept it over her court, resting an instant on the humans before her green gaze snapped toward me and my wizard companion. I couldn't begin to guess her thoughts. Raising her chin, she clapped her hands together twice.

"Let the celebration continue," Queen Tesina announced before she took her seat upon the golden throne. Prince Fallon followed her example, the hound dropping to the ground at his feet, his head up, watching both Sithi and human with equal intensity.

"Riona Northstar! Music."

Well, that was my cue. Leaving the velvet curtains open, I resumed my seat, the gitar cradled in my arms. I'd given this quite a bit of thought since Queen Tesina had commanded that I perform tonight. Of the attitude of the court and the direction I saw the Sithi was heading. With the humans present, I knew just which song I wanted to sing. Something to remind the ancients of who and what we were. Something to spur their memories.

"Open the window, please," I murmured to Finnegan as I bent over my instrument. If they hadn't blocked out all of their humanity, the ancients would recognize this song. The younglings would think it a curiosity but would hopefully wonder and ask questions. Mostly, I hoped to get my message across to Tesina and Fallon.

Finnegan opened the casement, and the fresh night air flowed in as I began the opening bridge, the notes ringing out in the still, silent hall. Using my magic, I wove an enchantment to enable all to hear my music.

I close my eyes, only for a moment, and the moment's gone.
All my dreams pass before my eyes a curiosity.

It was an ancient song, written and sung by a group called Kansas. It was ironic that only now, a thousand years later, did its words reveal their true meaning.

I poured my heart into the music, my voice rising and falling, rich and true in the continued silence. There wasn't a rustle of movement, nothing to distract from the spell I was weaving with my song. The night air poured in through the open window, a counter measure to the music, amplifying the sound and the emotion behind the words. A perfume of herbs and other sweet flowers flowed in with the rich scent of magic. I nearly missed a note as I felt the grace of My Lady behind that wind, the fresh purity picking up the tune and enriching it beyond my talent.

Dust in the wind. All they are is dust in the wind.

I sang as never before, the wind and the magic weaving through my music and holding all spellbound. I glanced up once and met the eyes of my queen, surprised, and yet not surprised, to see tears glistening in their green depths and trailing down over her smooth cheeks. Looking out over the assembled court, I could see raw emotion covering the faces of the ancients, confusion mixed with sorrow in those of the younglings. Few had dry eyes. The humans listened as raptly as the Sithi, held mesmerized by my music and the magic woven by My Lady.

As the final notes faded away, the night wind died, leaving a quiet so profound that none dared to break it. No one moved, no one appeared to breathe.

"A beautiful song, my lady Riona," Finnegan finally murmured in a low voice for my ears only. "One wrought in meaning, I think, for you as much as for all others. Both Sithi and human."

Queen Tesina was on her feet, rage wiping away the emotion

so raw on her face only moments before. Color rose high in her cheeks, and fury quivered in every line of her body. Prince Fallon was also on his feet, but his face revealed no expression. He placed one hand on his wife's arm, but she shook it off.

"Get out, Riona! Get out now!"

Raising my chin, I stood, tucking my gitar under my arm.

"As you command, My Queen."

I bowed slightly, almost an insult, yet I refused to grovel. I felt no remorse in what I'd done. It had been necessary. I exited the alcove, Finnegan at my side. My glance swept over the assembled court, daring any to offer me censure. Many met my gaze unflinchingly with nods of approval, tears still tracking down smooth cheeks. In more than one pair of eyes, I saw a new awareness. In others, confusion.

Good.

Without a word, I started down the center of the ballroom, a path opening before me. I wasn't halfway down when I heard it. Softly at first, someone began to clap, then another and another. Before I reached the double doorway, the entire court was applauding. I paused just before the doors and turned. Tesina still stood on the dais in front of her throne, new fury sweeping over her face as her court cheered me.

And something else. Even from this distance, I saw fear in her eyes.

Chapter Seventeen

In silence, Finnegan and I walked through the dark streets of Minneson City. Beyond the sound of our boots striking the cobblestones, there was little to be heard. The cool evening wind carried distant conversations, but nothing nearby. High overhead, a nighthawk called out … the sound lonely in the night. The stars appeared equally cold and distant.

The captain and his men had been prepared to accompany us, but I urged them to stay. Just because I was banished from the festivities didn't mean they had to miss out on this opportunity to witness a Sithi celebration. Finnegan merely fell into step beside me without asking. Although I wouldn't admit it, I was glad for the company. Lonely? Me? Nah. Besides, I was more than a little intrigued by this new Finnegan. Not good, in my opinion.

My home wasn't far from the royal palace, so the walk was a pleasant one. A companionable one, for the most part, but I was also irrationally nervous. No question as to the source. This new awareness of Finnegan was both disturbing and unwelcome. Since I'd evolved into Sithi, I'd rarely felt any attraction to a mortal. I almost wished he'd remained the scruffy, bedraggled wizard I'd first met. Now …

I stole a glance his way and found him staring straight ahead with a slight smile on his lips. Lips that were well shaped and tempting. Tracing his profile with my gaze, I felt a shiver of renewed awareness travel down my spine.

His hair was brushed back from a strong forehead, falling down over his shoulders in a thick wave. The trimmed beard enhanced rather than detracted from the masculine beauty of his face. The dimness of the evening only added a measure of mystery to this man.

He carried his staff, the stone on its tip catching and reflecting the globes of elf-light placed at intermediate spaces along the walkway. He must have retrieved it before we'd left the palace. The faint click of its butt hitting the ground was nearly drowned out by our footsteps.

To distract myself, I looked up at the star-strewn sky. It was an amazing night. Clear, with only a faint chill in the air. We turned down a street that held a popular inn, light spilling out of the windows and the sound of music and laughter within. I was about to suggest stopping in for a drink when an awareness of a different type swept over me, and I stopped.

"What is it?" Finnegan asked when he halted beside me.

"I'm not sure." I cast around for the source of my discomfort, but all appeared normal. An alley was directly across from us, dark and empty. A burst of laughter came from the inn only a few doors away; dancing shadows crossed the windows in accompaniment to the music. I glanced upward at the roof line, finding nothing above. Only the glitter of countless stars against the velvet blackness of night.

I drew a deep breath and blew it out. My imagination? Could've been. I was about to continue on to the inn when a scraping step snapped my attention back to the alley, and a trio of Sithi emerged from the shadows, cloaked and silent. Something in their manner was disturbing, and I felt a wave of magic spike the air. Their faces were concealed in cowls, and the dim lighting made it impossible to guess at their identities, even with my enhanced eyesight. Two of them held unsheathed swords, the blades reflecting the glow from the elven lights.

I hesitated, scenting the magic as I attempted to identify them, but a wave of malevolence roiled over me, staggering me with its foul stench. This wasn't the magic of Our Lady. It was like nothing I'd ever felt before.

The figure in the front made a gesture with his free hand, and a ball of light appeared. It was similar to elven light, white but with veins of red and black running through it.

"Get down!" Finnegan shouted and shoved me to one side as the cloaked figure flung the ball at us. Deadly and silent, it missed me by inches, striking the stone building behind me with the wet sound of a rotten melon breaking. Like liquid fire, it flared before winking out. A shallow hole with burns dripping down the stone was the only testament of its acidic composition.

Finnegan swept his staff before him, the blue stone igniting, the light spilling over the cloaked figures. The shadows and the hoods pulled over their heads concealed their features. The light of Finnegan's staff should have penetrated those shadows. They must be using an enchantment to hide their identities.

These thoughts ran through my mind in seconds as I took a defensive stance. But for the gitar slung over my shoulder, I was unarmed. Without hesitation, I swung it around just as one figure darted forward. Steel struck the wood, cracking the fragile instrument, but it kept the sword from reaching me. I didn't have time to mourn the loss of my gitar as I pivoted on one heel, slipping under his guard and bringing the instrument up as hard as I could. The gitar swept into the darkness of his hood and smashed into his face where his chin should be. The wood disintegrated with the force of my blow, and the Sithi crumbled to the cobblestones.

Quickly I backpedaled to avoid the third figure. He leapt over his fallen comrade, his sword narrowly missing me. Without hesitation, I dropped and swept out my leg, catching him by surprise. As he went down, I felt a rush of air from the left and dove away in time to miss another one of those deadly balls of poisonous light. Rolling, I sprang to my feet just as Finnegan swept his staff forward, the light bursting from the tip to catch my attacker full in the chest. He didn't have time to scream as the wizard's magic sank into him and ignited. Within seconds, he vanished. There was nothing left to mark his passing.

A snarl of fury gave me an instant of warning before our final assailant sprang to his feet with a catlike grace, and we both whirled around.

"Interfering bitch," he bit out before he brought both his hands together, that malevolent light igniting between his fingers, the stench of corrupt magic heavy in the air.

Acting on instinct, I gathered my own magic and created a ball of pure energy, flinging it at him just as he released his. The two lights collided with the force of a small explosion, igniting the night. The concussion flung both Finnegan and me backward, and we hit the opposite building with enough force to knock the breath out of us.

For an instant, I saw stars. The stone was hard against my back as I slid to the ground. Shaking my head, I tried to clear the spots from my eyes, frantically seeking our final attacker, but he was gone. The shadows of the night swallowed him up.

I became aware of people pouring from the nearby inn, many calling out, but the ringing in my ears was too loud for me to understand their words. Hands caught my shoulders, and I immediately went on the defensive, but before I could strike, Finnegan's face swam into my view. He appeared uninjured, for which I was grateful. In fact, staring at him, at that moment, I don't think I'd ever seen anything more wonderful.

I took stock of my condition before I let him draw me to my feet, leaning against his strength. Bruises, some abrasions. Nothing broken. Lucky.

For several heartbeats, I allowed myself the luxury of his

warmth. Drawing a deep breath, I nestled against the fine material of his tunic, enjoying the play of muscles that flexed under my cheek before I forced myself to push out of his arms.

His embrace was far too comfortable. I didn't know if it was my imagination, but I could have sworn I felt the brush of his lips against my forehead. When I glanced up into his dark eyes, his expression revealed nothing.

For an instant, I was tempted to use my magic to delve his emotions, but refrained. Frankly, I was too burnt out to even make the attempt. Besides, did I really want to know? Maybe, maybe not.

When I was certain of my balance, I turned toward the dozen or so Sithi who had gathered around us. Several were eyeing Finnegan with suspicion, while others were bending toward the fallen body of our remaining assailant.

"Stand away from him," I called out as I hurried forward to put myself between them.

"What is the meaning of this?"

The commanding voice drew my attention, and I saw a half-dozen guards approaching from the direction of the main gates. I recognized the commander. Not an ancient, Mauren Oakwood was a veteran of many battles along the northern borders. He was taller than most Sithi, clad in leather rather than the more ornate garb of the palace guard with him. He presented an intimidating figure. Not many people messed with Mauren.

I spied a golden badge on his right shoulder, marking him as a member of the palace guard, which was a surprise to me. The palace guard was the last place I would have expected to find a man of Oakwood's experience.

"We were attacked on our way home," Finnegan said as he bent to retrieve his staff. The stone was once again a dull sheen, his magic subdued.

"By Sithi?" Disbelief colored Mauren's voice.

"I don't think they're Sithi."

I went to the body of the man I had downed with my gitar, and I nudged his hood back with my foot. The material fell back to reveal the face of a stranger. Lifeless eyes stared upward, his head twisted at an unnatural angle. I had broken his neck with the force of my blow.

I knelt at his side, my magic held at the ready. Weak though I was at the moment, I wasn't about to be taken by surprise. Extending my senses, I could detect no life in the body and relaxed slightly. He was no longer a threat.

With a sigh, I straightened and found Mauren beside me, his dark eyes examining the dead man at our feet.

"I don't recognize him." The commander glanced around the gathered crowd. "Does anyone here know this man?"

Most heads shook in denial, but one woman stared at the dead man, recognition in her eyes. Horror swept over her face as she nodded. Mauren gestured for her to come closer. It was with obvious reluctance that she obeyed.

"You know him?"

"Yes." Her whisper was barely audible. "His name is Jaren Moonlight. He went missing nearly a decade ago. He was engaged to my daughter ..." Her face crumbled with pain, and she turned away. A man came up and put his arm around her shoulders and steered her back toward the inn. A low murmur of shock rose through the onlookers. At a nod from the commander, the palace guards began to disburse the crowd.

Mauren gestured to one of his men. "Take her statement. I may need to speak with her daughter."

The guard snapped a salute before following the woman into the inn. Mauren waited until we had some privacy before he turned back to me. The hardness of his face gave nothing away, but I'd been around too long to be intimidated. I was aware of Finnegan at my back. Somehow I found comfort in that knowledge.

"Did anyone here witness the attack?" Mauren asked in a low voice.

"No."

"What happened?"

"As the wizard said, we were walking to my home when three men emerged from the alley and attacked us. We were unarmed, but I managed to dispatch this one." I gestured to the dead man in front of us. "The second one met with Finnegan's spirit magic."

At the commander's nod, I didn't bother to elaborate. He'd been around long enough to recognize the wizard's power. I noticed that the glance he gave Finnegan held a measure of respect and caution. "And the third?"

"He used some sort of magical energy." I hesitated. "Not the magic of Our Lady. It had a malevolence to it. When his power met with mine, the concussion blinded us long enough for him to get away."

"Would you recognize him if you saw him?"

"No. I never saw his face."

Mauren turned back to the dead Sithi, staring down at him with a troubled look on his hard face.

"This is Sithi. Yet not," he said softly, half to himself, before he closed his eyes. I felt him reach out with his magic to examine the dead man. After only an instant, his eyes snapped open as his breath hissed in through his teeth and he jerked back. "Unnatural. This was once Sithi but is no longer."

"What do you mean?"

"I've ranged the northern border for centuries, Riona Northstar." He glanced around the sparse crowd and signaled his men closer. Mostly to allow us privacy from the remaining civilians. "This has the feel of a Skori," he said in a soft tone, his words more of a growl.

"Skori!" I looked at the dead creature with new eyes. I didn't bother trying to delve him myself. I was too weak, and besides, I trusted Mauren's judgment. Physically, what was once Jaren Moonlight looked Sithi. Delicate features, pointed ears visible through pale mottled hair. Yes, but there was a difference, slight though it was. A cast to his features that wasn't quite right. A shadowing of wrongness. He'd obviously been Sithi. What had happened?

"How could something that reeks of Skori possibly penetrate the mists?" I kept my voice low, but alarm shivered through me. That should be impossible. The mists had been created centuries ago through the grace of Our Lady. They were our defense and our strength. No Skori could pass through them. The mists were tuned to our nature and would repel the evil creatures.

"I do not know, Lady Riona. But I mean to find out."

I stood, moving away from the dead man with a feeling of revulsion. How could this Jaren Moonlight possibly have the corruption of Skori on him? Had the other two also been infected with the perversion? And were there only three of them?

"Are we free to go?" I asked the commander. "We will be at my home for tonight."

"If I have any further questions, I'll seek you out."

I turned to go, but the captain stopped me.

"It may be prudent to house the mortals at the palace for tonight, Lady Riona."

I was unsurprised that he knew about my guests. Rumors flowed fast and furious when it came to the unusual.

"Will the queen allow it?"

"They are under Guest Rights. Their safety is the duty of all Sithi. I will send a message to the palace."

With a nod, I turned to leave, aware of Finnegan joining me. The humans would be safer in the palace. Commander Mauren would see to it.

My gaze fell on the ground where the second attacker had

stood, but nothing remained of him. Not even a grease spot on the paving stones. The wizard's spiritual magic had utterly destroyed the man, leaving nothing behind. This was the work of the benevolent One God? Somehow the knowledge that the wizard could so thoroughly eradicate someone was disturbing. I didn't think I had the power to do what he'd managed with so little effort. So little apparent effort, I mentally amended as I noted the tight lines around his eyes, the paleness of his face. Finnegan wasn't quite as steady as I'd thought.

Something must have shown in my face, because a frown lit his brow, and he studied me before he drew himself up straight. His face dropped into expressionless lines.

"Riona?"

For a moment longer, I stared at Finnegan, trying to reconcile this man and the companion I'd spent the past week traveling with. What did I know about him? Nothing. He'd appeared out of nowhere, conveniently at the same inn where both Merry and I had met up.

Happenstance? I wasn't so sure anymore. Still, prognostication was not impossible with humans. Particularly ones that might share elven blood. I'd known a few wizards in my long life. But not one as powerful as the man before me.

"Riona."

"How did you know to come to that inn in Memis?" My question was low. We were far enough away from the palace guards for privacy. Nevertheless, I glanced in their direction to make sure we would be unheard, even by the superior Sithi ears.

He hesitated, a shadow of indecision crossing his face before he gave a slight nod. I noticed that his own glance went to the guards. He wouldn't speak here. Too many ears.

"C'mon," I said. "Mauren knows where to find us if he has more questions."

I should have felt wary, but somehow I couldn't quite bring

myself to distrust Finnegan. He'd had a reason for being at the Crossroads Inn. I very much wanted to know what it was.

We walked in silence, both buried in our own thoughts. A part of me was alert to any renewed attack, while the other was turning over the events of the last hour.

Our assailants had been lying in wait for us. How had they known we would be passing that way? Granted, it was the most direct route from the palace to my home, but what disturbed me was not so much the location but the timing. How could someone have known that the queen had dismissed me from the royal party so abruptly? Again, it could have been a matter of lying in wait, knowing we'd be passing this way sooner or later. But then we probably would have been accompanied by Captain Tiernan and his men. The odds would not have been in favor of our assailants. So it stood to reason they had known it was only Finnegan and me walking this route. So again, the question—how had they known?

Answer? A spy in the palace. Someone who'd sent word that I was leaving at an early hour. Seemed logical.

"Things are moving faster than I anticipated."

Finnegan's words jarred me out of my thoughts.

"Than you anticipated?" I kept my tone even, allowing none of my reawakened suspicions to leak through.

"You have your sources of information, Riona, and I have mine."

"Mine is from My Lady."

"And mine is through My One God."

Shock stopped me in my steps, but his hand came under my arm and urged me forward. His touch sent a wave of warmth through me. Magic? I didn't think so. Or if it was, it was a very different sort of magic.

Automatically, my feet obeyed his urging, taking me toward my home. I had to shake off the warm sensation and concentrate on the matter at hand. I hadn't told Finnegan about the Vision I'd had with My Lady. I was under the impression that Yahweh, the One God, was neutral in this conflict, yet here was Finnegan admitting that he was taking his orders from Him. Interesting.

"Someone revealed our location to Brother Morris and provided him with your True Name," Finnegan continued as we reached my home. We paused at the small gate. There were two houses on either side of mine, but neither was close. We tended to give ourselves space.

I automatically released the spell I used to deter any visitors and led the way in through the gardens. The stasis spell only worked so far, and the gardens were wild and overgrown after so many years of neglect. I really had to do something about that. The thought was irrelevant, which only went to show how scattered my wits were.

"Now we're attacked in the heart of your city—"

"Where, if anywhere, we should have been perfectly safe," I finished. Opening the door, I invited him inside. The evening's events had evaporated any earlier thoughts I might have had about a romantic tryst. A foolish notion, but the thought had crossed my mind. More than once.

"It can mean only one thing." I closed the door behind us and continued into the sitting area. Dying coals in the fireplace illuminated the room. An unnecessary but comforting warmth. I paused long enough to rebuild the fire. Elven light would have sufficed, but there were times when I found the warmth of a fire necessary.

"The Skori are infiltrating our ranks. The Dark Master is subverting the Sithi."

Chapter Eighteen

"Is that possible?" Finnegan's tone held no fear, no censure, but when I turned from the hearth, I saw the evidence in his face. The lines of weariness at his magical expenditure had morphed into lines of tension, his manner wary and, for the first time, uncertain. I couldn't be one hundred percent sure, but it was the impression I was gaining.

"I wouldn't have thought so, but I cannot deny the evidence before me."

Although I kept my voice even, inside I was terrified. The thought that the Dark Master could subvert my people was incomprehensible.

For all our immortality, we were first of all human. With all the same human foibles and needs. It was possible not everyone shared Our Lady's vision of the future. I thought back to that night so many centuries ago, the night I'd chosen My Lady. I remembered the temptation of that black door, the pulsating passion and promise of power.

Were the Sithi still susceptible despite the protection of Our Lady? Was that promise of power still as tempting now as it had been then? Even knowing what we did? Knowing what the followers of the Dark Master were destined to become?

I shook off the question and glanced at Finnegan. He was watching me, the tension still in his face.

I couldn't think of anything to say.

"Tea?" I asked.

"Yes, please."

Drawing a deep breath, I left him and made my way to the kitchen. I had to think. Finnegan was working under the auspices of his One God, just as I was working under the direction of My Lady. From the sound of it, to the same goal.

So much for Yahweh remaining neutral.

I wondered if My Lady knew about this. Was it possible they were working together and pretending impartiality to throw off the suspicions of their dark brother? At this point, anything was possible.

The preparation of tea was a mindless task, allowing me to indulge in my less-than-cheery thoughts. A flick of my finger set the copper kettle to boiling while I found the canister that held tea. A woefully meager supply. I wondered if I'd be in Minneson City long enough to replenish it.

Somehow I doubted it.

A thought niggled at the back of my mind. Something in the manner of the third Sithi. The one that had gotten away. Something had felt vaguely familiar about him, but I couldn't quite put my finger on it. Unfortunately, I'd been away from the Lakelands far too long for the memory to surface. It could have been anyone. I sincerely hoped it wasn't someone I'd known. The thought of any Sithi forsaking the light for the Dark Master made my stomach twist.

"How long do you think Merry will be in the infirmary?"

I stiffened. Damn, but that man could move silently when he wanted to. Turning, I found Finnegan standing directly behind me. The flickering elven light threw shadows over his face, making his expression difficult to read. The knowledge that we were alone in my home lent an intimacy to my little kitchen, and I felt a resurgence of awareness. I could tell myself that any type of relationship with a mortal was doomed from the start, but my awakening hormones belied that reasoning. Hard to shut down hormones when they'd taken an interest.

"Hard to tell." I concentrated on the teapot, trying to get my emotions under control. This was completely unacceptable. "The injury she took was near fatal. She cannot be moved for at least a fortnight."

"Do we have a fortnight?"

"No. I don't think so."

"So what is our next move?"

"I'm not sure about *our* next move, but I need to see King Ambrose."

"Despite the state of his mind?"

"He holds the key to this. I feel it in my bones."

Finnegan put a hand to my hair, smoothing it back from my face. I shivered. I didn't know if it was the remnants of adrenaline, but my body came to life with that simple touch.

"Then we go to Newland," he said.

"You would be safer here."

"Will I?"

The doubt in his voice pinched my brows together, but as much as I wanted to, I couldn't dispute his words. An hour ago, I could have argued the point, but no longer. Not after that unexpected attack.

There was at least one compromised Sithi on the loose. No telling how many others had given over to the Dark Master. Like rats in the walls, they crept unseen, but the potential damage was immeasurable.

The question was, how did we flush them out? And how could Merry be kept safe while we traveled to Newland? Would our departure draw them after us, or was Merry also a target?

A warm hand slid under my chin, and my thoughts scattered. I was tall, but Finnegan topped me by several inches. I gazed up into those chocolate-brown eyes, seeing the warmth and something else. Something that called to me, igniting a heat deep within. My breath caught, and a sense of anticipation threatened to overwhelm my good sense.

He bent close, and his lips brushed lightly over mine. Soft. Testing. I felt the kiss to the tips of my toes. It awoke something within me that I'd thought was dormant. Was this a good idea? No, probably not.

I wanted to respond. Oh, how I wanted to. I hadn't felt this type of closeness in so long. Hadn't even been aware of how lonely I was. It was tempting beyond words. But I put a hand to his chest and held him off when he would have pulled me closer.

"No, Finnegan. This isn't wise."

"Why?" His voice was a whisper of sound. Intimate, and I almost groaned. This man could seduce with his voice alone.

"There's no future."

"Because you're Sithi and I'm human?"

"Yes."

He pulled away, putting distance between us. Both physical and emotional. I felt the loss of his warmth, and something inside me cried out. His expression went stony.

"I would have thought you were above that prejudice."

"I have no prejudice against humans." Did I? As of two weeks ago, I might not have been able to dispute his claim. Yes, it was an out, but not one that I could take. I couldn't leave Finnegan with the belief that I looked down on mortals. It was a coward's way out.

"Think about it. I'm immortal. I will never age." I pulled away from him and walked to one of the round windows that faced out onto the deserted lane in front of my home. I could see no movement in the night and used the reflection of the interior to watch Finnegan. "You are human. You will eventually grow old and die. If I were to form an … attachment to you, I do not think I could bear to watch that happen."

My voice dropped to a whisper toward the end. It suddenly struck me that I already cared too much. How was it possible? I'd known this man less than a fortnight, during very trying circumstances. Somehow he had wormed himself into my life and, perhaps, already, my heart.

"I cannot change what I am, any more than you can, Riona."

Through the glass, I watched his reflection as he approached me from behind, tensing when his hands curved around my shoulders. Despite my avowal, I leaned back against his strength. Sometimes I was so tired of being alone, but was I ready for this?

Could I just live for the moment and forget about the future? Centuries ago, I'd lost one man I loved to age. What would it do to me to go through that again? If this was just sex, that would be different. But I suspected it would never be *just* sex with Finnegan.

His body slid along my back, distracting me from my thoughts. Through the glass, I could see the look of tenderness cross his face, and something within me melted.

"I understand your fear, Riona," he whispered against my hair, his breath teasing the escaping tendrils and tickling along my neck. When his hands tightened, I knew my shiver of reaction didn't go unnoticed. "I'm a wizard. My life expectancy is far longer than that of a normal human."

"But you will age and die."

"Yes."

"Hence the problem."

My joke sounded lame to my own ears, yet something inside flared with expectation. It was an emotion sadly lacking in my life. Giving in to my desire, I turned and linked my arms around his neck, without a word, pulling his face down to capture his lips with mine. At the same time, I opened my senses to him, reading his desire, his need. The softness of his lips was a heady aphrodisiac for the senses, at odds with the harsher curves and angles of his face. Sliding one hand down to the hard plane of his chest, his heart beat steady against my palm, seemingly in time with my own.

Releasing his mouth, I angled my head to run my tongue along the curve of his lips, relishing his unique flavor, drawing his scent into my lungs. Like a strong drink, it went straight to my head.

What started out as an impulse quickly evolved into a conflagration of need. For that moment, I didn't want to care about anything beyond the feel of this man against my body. Wanted him in a way that I hadn't wanted in centuries.

My breath left my body when his hands glided up my back and his finger slid into my hair. As he released the bindings, pure sensation spiraled up my spine to ignite nerve endings that'd been dormant. The brocade of his tunic was smooth under my hands when I slid them over his chest. His beard was soft against my face as I brushed against it, enjoying the texture against my skin. His lips slid along my throat, pressing a tantalizing string of kisses before he lingered at my pulse. I felt his fingers brush against the tips of my ears, and a new jolt of desire swam through my system. Either this man had made love to a Sithi before or he instinctively knew where our most sensitive nerve endings were located.

My blood sang with sensation as I found his scent and drew it deep into my lungs. It was an intriguing combination of herbs and spices with a hint of the wine he'd consumed earlier.

Unfortunately, the taste of that wine went a long way to clearing my head and reminding me of the events of this evening. I went still.

Opening my eyes, I found myself staring out the window over Finnegan's shoulder. The sky was streaked with red and gold, heralding the dawn.

"Riona?"

This wasn't right. We had the dark cloud of evil hanging over our heads. There were plans to be made. Arrangements for our departure and assurances of Merry's safety that I had to procure. Why did I feel like time was running out?

With a massive effort, I controlled myself and drew out of his arms. His reluctance was obvious as he gazed into my eyes, but I also saw the knowledge and understanding.

"We have bigger problems than this, Finnegan."

"Agreed. As much as I'd like to say otherwise." He smoothed my loosened hair away from my face before he leaned forward once more and stole a long, lingering kiss that left my lips tingling and me regretting my stupid common sense. "When I make love to you, Riona, I don't want it rushed. There will be time enough for that in the future."

"Will there be a future?"

He rested his forehead against mine. The smile in his chocolate-brown eyes warmed me in ways I wouldn't have thought possible.

"There will be a future. I want an entire night with you and many nights after that. I want to explore every inch of your body and indulge in every manner of pleasure."

Damn, the man could seduce me with words alone. Suppressing a shiver, I pulled free of his embrace.

But not before I felt him draw a deep breath, saw when he regained control of himself. I could sympathize because I was having the same trouble. I wanted nothing more than to jump his bones and the future be damned.

But I had duties. Several lifetimes of duties. It was a hard habit to break. Merry was important. Finnegan was important. If what we knew about the Dark Master was true, the fate of the world as we knew it was in jeopardy. That was important, far more so than my own desires.

More was the pity.

With a sigh of regret, I put a little distance between us. There was much to plan, and the dawn was breaking. I doubted either one of us was going to get much sleep. Between the wild ride, the battle with the Skori, and the trip through the mists, we'd had little sleep in the past forty-eight hours. I didn't know about the wizard, but I got grumpy if I went more than seventy-two hours without sleep, so I was still good to go.

Getting to Newland wasn't a problem. As long as the mists were present, I could access them to Travel.

"Will Merry be well enough to travel?"

The question drew my attention back to the man. He was leaning against my kitchen table, arms crossed over his chest. A chest, I noticed, that was broad with the hint of muscle beneath the brocade of his tunic. How had the man concealed such a tempting physique these past few weeks?

"No. The last word I received from the healers is that she's stable, but her condition is still precarious. The poison has traveled deep."

"But she will recover."

There was a hint of a question at the end of the comment.

"They believe so."

He closed his eyes for only an instant. Long enough to make me wonder. What else was Finnegan privy to? He'd admitted to working with his deity, which still surprised the hell out of me given their vaunted noninterference rule.

"What aren't you telling me, Finnegan? What's going on?"

His expression didn't change, but I caught a flicker of something in his eyes. Secrets. Great. Just what I needed. Particularly from a man I'd so nearly made love to. From a man I trusted. I'd always had a hard time with the whole trust issue, even as a human.

Silently, I pled in my mind, *don't make me regret the trust I'm placing in you, Finnegan*.

He hesitated, and I opened my senses to him ... and found nothing. Damn! Bloody wizard was adept at hiding his emotions and thoughts. Not that I could read the thoughts of mortals, but I had the ability to sift through the emotions to get a pretty good handle on what they were thinking. With Finnegan … *nada*.

"Sit down, Riona."

That didn't sound good, but I did as he asked. The chair I pulled out scraped on the smooth slate floor, loud in the silence of the dawn. He waited until I dropped into the seat before turning away to complete the tea preparation. The tea that had been forgotten during the intimate distraction. I licked my lips, still tasting him.

The kettle steamed as he tossed a handful of tea leaves into a ceramic pot that was probably older than he was. When he added the water, the scent of herbs and black tea filled the kitchen. Between that and the fire blazing in the hearth, it was a cozy scene. Why didn't I feel soothed?

I let him root around my cupboards to locate the mugs. Honey sat in the middle of the square table I'd made centuries ago. I glanced around my kitchen as Finnegan brewed the hot drink, seeking to find comfort in it. The roof was high and curved, whitewashed with dark beams. Hooks were imbedded in many of the beams. Normally, bundles of herbs hung from them, but they were empty now. A ceramic sink with a hand pump stood across from the wide hearth, and other than a hutch that held crystal glasses and ancient crockery, there were few pieces of furniture. Cabinets and cupboards filled the rest of the walls, some of them glassed to display the treasures I'd collected over the centuries.

A steaming mug appeared in front of me. Startled, I glanced up to find Finnegan looming over me as he placed the cup on the table. Drawing a deep breath, I calmed myself and spooned honey into my mug.

I waited until he took a seat across from me before raising my mug to my lips, inhaling the pungent scent before taking a cautious sip. The drink ran down my throat, warming me and making me aware of how tense I'd been.

"Well? Let's have it." Fortified both mentally and physically, I fixed him with a steady glance. "How did you know both Merry and I were going to be in that inn that night?"

Finnegan didn't answer at once, taking a sip of his unsweetened tea before setting it down.

"A couple of months ago, I did a scrying."

Well, that explained much. Sithis had Visions; wizards did scryings. It was a difficult art, and only the most powerful attempted it. There was a real danger of your essence getting sucked into the metaphysical vortex and of losing yourself while your physical body wasted and died. Not a pleasant way to go.

"So you had the right time and the right place and managed to track us down."

"I think you realize how important Merry is to all of this."

"I sort of got that impression."

He flashed me a half smile that just barely reached his eyes.

"Her birthdate makes her a focal point. For what, we don't know."

"We?"

He merely gave me a look. Ah, yes. He was definitely working in conjunction with his deity. I wonder if My Lady knew about this. I suspected she didn't.

Now came the question. Did I tell her? Or was she already aware of this little bit of news through my thoughts? I was never quite clear on how much she gleaned through our connection or how often she was in my mind. Did some divine ability allow her to know what I knew, or did it need to be a conscious effort on her part to discover what I knew?

The thought should have been intrusive, but it wasn't. It was just one of those facts of life, as far as I was concerned. You know, the whole working in mysterious ways and all that.

"We think Merry is going to be used to tear the fabric of this millennium and open the way for the Dark Master."

"How is that possible?"

"It shouldn't be. From what I understand, the three deities were placed in charge of our world and other worlds. By yet a higher power."

Great. Now there was yet another element to consider.

"Each was given the option of running this world in whatever manner he or she saw fit. My One God was given the first opportunity, and for several millennia, he did well."

"Up until the Industrial Age."

"Yes."

Why wasn't I surprised that the wizard had knowledge of a period of time that was long gone? A time that had taken place centuries before his birth.

"Had the world continued on the path it was taking, mankind would have destroyed itself. The seeds had already been planted for a catastrophic world war. The first two wars in the early twentieth century were a mere shadow of what was coming. Had the third war erupted, the devastation to our world would have been irreparable."

"But the release of the plague prevented that from happening."

"Correct."

I wanted to ask who'd released the plague that had destroyed such a high percentage of mankind, but did I really want to know? Morbid curiosity pushed me.

"Who caused the plague?"

"It was the Dark Master who caused the Great Waste."

There was an answer I hadn't expected. Deep in my heart, I'd always suspected My Lady was responsible. I hadn't wanted to believe that, but it was to her benefit that it had happened, and I said as much.

"No. The three siblings saw where mankind was heading, and plans were made to divert that course. The biggest argument was in the manner of that diversion. However, the Dark Master took matters into His own hands and released the plague. Once it happened, My One God and Your Lady could not stop it. You will recall that every adult human was given a choice shortly after the purge."

How could I forget? I gestured for him to continue.

"If the Dark Master had gained sufficient followers over Your Lady, it would be He who would have ruled this millennium, not Her."

A shiver of fear traveled up my spine at the thought. Who knew what horrors the Dark Brother would have wrought?

"You seem pretty chummy with your One God, wizard." My cup was empty. Something that surprised me. I didn't recall drinking the rest of my tea. I reached over and picked up the teapot, pouring myself a second drink. "If I remember my original religious training, it was my understanding that Yahweh worked in mysterious ways. Never really coming straight out and revealing his plans."

"Yahweh?"

"That is the name of your One God, isn't it?"

"Yahweh," Finnegan whispered as a look of wonder came over his face. It dawned on me that he hadn't known the name of his deity. Maybe I wasn't supposed to tell him, but the damage was already done.

It really shouldn't have surprised me. I'd recently learned the given name of My Lady, and I'd been around considerably longer than Finnegan.

"Did your One God give any hint as to how Merry is the catalyst to all this?"

"No. He didn't know." He seemed to shake himself out of his inner thoughts.

So much for all seeing, all knowing.

"Did He have any suggestions of what we should do now?"

"No."

"Helpful," I muttered into my drink. Setting the mug down with a thump, I leaned forward. "From what I can see, everything that happens through our deities appears to be by choice. I became Sithi through choice. The Skori were created through choice. And your ancestors remained human through choice."

"Yes."

"Then it stands to reason that whatever occurs through Merry will be through choice."

He was quiet for a long moment. "It would seem logical."

"So what do we do? Ensure that any choices Merry makes are the correct ones? And how do we know which are right?"

Too restless to sit, I stood and moved around the kitchen, pulling open cabinets to check the extent of my stores … or lack thereof. Pretty pitiful. It appeared that my cupboards were bare. I'd have to replenish our supplies before we set out tomorrow. My mind continued to work as I made a mental list of our needs.

The future stakes were high. It was a gamble beyond anything ever before seen with the world as we knew it at stake. No pressure. Nope. None at all.

What exactly would happen if the Dark Master took over? The annihilation of humans? Could he possibly destroy the Sithi? Could the Dark Brother eliminate or kill his siblings? So many questions and no answers.

Uncertainty didn't sit well with me. I liked action. Sometimes I liked everything in black and white. Preferred things in black and white. You knew who the bad guys were and what needed to be done.

Getting into the middle of a family feud might not be the smartest move in the world. Particularly if said family were deities.

Chapter Nineteen

Everything was ready. The captain and his men were waiting outside with the horses, our supplies assembled, and Finnegan was at my side. I had one last task before we left Minneson City.

"We are safe within our borders, Riona. The Skori cannot penetrate the mist," Queen Tesina said, her tone cold. Despite the need to protest her assertion, I held myself still. Over her right shoulder, Fallon Summerfield put a hand on her, his touch calming her. I watched as she drew a deep breath and let it out. Saw the effort it took to regain her composure.

The throne room was nearly empty, but there were the usual parasites lingering within the halls. A good number of them had appeared after I'd requested an audience with the queen. Morbid curiosity. Probably hoping to see her ream me out for last night's audacity.

"You have Commander Mauren's report," I said. A movement out of the corner of my eye caught my attention, and I saw my nephew enter the throne room. He gave me a slight smile and nod before I turned my attention back to my monarch. "You know what attacked us last night. Perhaps the Skori alone could not, Your Majesty, but if subverted Sithi have the power of the Dark Master behind them, they can and will penetrate our defenses and see to the annihilation of our people."

"You dare much."

"Damn right, I do." I closed the distance between us, as close as I dared. Perhaps closer than was wise. Out of the corner of my eye, I saw Summerfield stiffen, and the guards positioned on either side of the throne put their hands to their weapons. Dylan closed the distance and positioned himself at my side, opposite Finnegan. His wordless support warmed me. I'd barely seen him since my return and missed his companionship.

"We cannot relax our vigilance, Tesina." I kept my voice low. I would prefer to keep this argument between us, but asking her consort to leave was impossible. And I wouldn't demand that Dylan and Finnegan leave. I could, however, ensure that the courtiers heard nothing. With a wave of magic, I created a bubble of privacy around us. Immediately, all sound vanished save that in our private sphere. The rustle of cloth when Tesina shifted on her throne, someone's heightened breathing. I almost frowned, thinking it was Finnegan who appeared nervous, but a quick glance showed it was Dylan who was glancing around with unease. When he caught my stare, he offered a sickly smile and a shrug. I dismissed his odd behavior. No time now.

"It was complacency that allowed the Nazi Holocaust to occur nearly eleven hundred years ago," I began. "I will not stand by and watch the Skori sweep over the mortals. They cannot defend themselves against the horde. Nor will the Skori halt with the humans. The Dark Master wants the world. Our Lady revealed his plans to me."

"I am the queen of the Sithi." Tesina stood. Taking the steps down from the throne, she got in my face, her own flushed with anger. "The Lady should have come to me."

"Since when does Our Lady allow one of us to dictate her actions? She has taken a great chance warning me."

"Riona …" Dylan touched my arm, and I drew a deep breath. Recriminations would not sway Tesina.

"My apologies, Your Majesty. This is not the time or place for this argument."

Summerfield leaned forward and whispered something in Tesina's ear. Although I was close, I could not hear his words, but they had some effect on the queen. She resumed her seat, slumping in her throne, her hands gripping the arms of the chair.

"What would you ask of me?"

I'm sure surprise flashed over my face before I could control it. That she gave in so easily …

"I need assurances that Meredith Sterling will be protected."

"She is under Guest Rights."

"Beyond Guest Rights."

"You are pushing, Riona."

"I will see to her safety, Riona," Dylan put in quickly when tempers would have flared once more.

I glanced at my nephew, gratitude warming my heart. "Thank you, Dylan." I returned my attention to the queen. "Merry is one of my human descendants, Your Majesty, and according to Our Lady, a catalyst of all that is happening."

"Very well. She will be taken care of. Beyond Guest Rights. The heir to Newland will be guarded."

"Your word on this?"

"You have my word."

"Thank you, Tesina."

"Do not thank me, Riona." Her head dropped for an instant, and I felt a sense of sorrow touch her emotions. Then she raised her chin again, regal persona in place. Her beautiful eyes flashed with green fire, and her lips were drawn in a tight line. "Last night you reminded me of things I'd rather forget."

"Our one-time mortality is not something we can forget, Teresa." I used her True Name in a soft voice. "It is what makes us what we are and what we will be."

Releasing my magic, I stepped back, sweeping a bow to her, respect evident in the depth of my courtesy. "I will entrust the life of the human, Meredith Sterling, to your hands, My Queen, and to your care, Dylan."

I made it clear to the listening audience that my ruler had my trust. "I will continue to Newland to do what I can for King Ambrose and to investigate the connection of the mortal Church with these dark times."

"Go. Take your human companions and leave our land. I will not close the borders until your return."

I bowed again. That was the best I was going to get. I had to be satisfied with it.

I didn't know if it was my imagination, but it seemed the mists were reluctant to free us. The final notes of my song died, and a silence fell over our little party as the vapors dissolved under the bright sun.

Glancing around to ensure that everyone was present, I dismounted, concealing my unease under the pretense of checking Mysteria's cinch. From the corner of my eye, I watched as the last of the mists receded. Was there something wrong with our barrier, or did it somehow sense danger within its borders?

Or was my imagination working overtime?

"We're about fifteen miles outside the Canada City," I said as I made unnecessary adjustments to my mount's tack.

"Why didn't we come out closer to it?" Lieutenant Crispin asked as he ran a hand over his damp brow. Going by the paleness of his face, the man still wasn't comfortable with the Sithi mode of travel.

Call me set in my ways, but I wasn't accustomed to someone questioning me. Nor did I like it. I gave Crispin a level look before I swung into the saddle. But then I gave myself a shake. It wasn't his fault that humans were harboring this growing animosity for my people. That road ran both ways. Evidenced yesterday in the

Sithis' reaction to humans in the Lakelands. Were these prejudices new or something encouraged by outside sources?

I kept my tone even as I responded to the lieutenant.

"Less chance of a local farmer or villager getting caught in the mists when we emerged." I was familiar with this area. At least, I used to be. It had been a number of years since I'd been here. It was probably blind luck that we emerged from the mists in an unsettled area. But I wasn't about to admit that to Crispin.

"We have a ways to travel before nightfall."

"Better to announce our presence." Kai Tiernan signaled his banner man to unfurl the standard of Cascadia. The strengthening breeze caught the blue material, snapping it to its full length until the crouching white tiger, which had been the symbol of the West Coast for centuries, was revealed.

It also reminded me that Kai Tiernan was a prince of that realm. He may have been traveling to Newland at the behest of his king, but his rank of captain did not detract from the fact that he was third in line for the throne of Cascadia. I knew the king had two sons, and it didn't seem likely that Kai would ever ascend the throne. However, in these troubled times, one never knew. Look what had happened to Newland. There had been better than four members of the Sterling family in line for the throne. Now it had fallen to one young girl.

I stared at the banner for another minute before turning my mount to the east. The road was wide enough for Finnegan to bring his gray mare alongside Mysteria, and after a minute, Captain Tiernan joined us at my other side. For the first time since meeting the man, he appeared hesitant.

"Will Princess Meredith be safe, Lady Riona?"

"Just Riona, please, Captain."

"Then I am Kai."

I allowed a slight smile to curve my lips. Despite his hardened exterior, there was much about the captain that I liked.

"Under the guard of my queen, she will be safe."

"Far safer there than traveling with us," Finnegan commented from my other side, and I glanced his way. He'd exchanged his finery of the night before for a gray woolen cloak. The quality of the pale material was far superior to the garb he'd donned when I'd first met him, stretching over broad shoulders to conceal a mouth-watering physique. I again felt a flush of sexual awareness and found myself regretting what I'd passed up last night. With these uncertain times, would that have been so bad?

"What is her role in all this?" Kai asked, not looking at me. His question snapped my attention back to the human.

I studied the hard lines of his profile. This was a man used to command, to hardship. I knew little about him beyond my experience of the past day, but my senses told me much about him. I could feel the honor and integrity of the man.

Plus, I could sense his interest in Merry Sterling. It went deep.

"Through the circumstance of her birth, she is a catalyst. A culmination of centuries of decisions."

"What do you mean?"

"From what I can discern, the three deities are bound by the decisions made by mankind. Fate ordained Meredith Sterling's birth centuries ago. It is her decisions that will determine the direction these events will take."

As I said these words, I realized the truth of them. Our fates were in the hands of a young woman who'd barely reached her majority. It was a disquieting thought for me. It also made me wonder at the wisdom of leaving Merry in Minneson City. Was it the right decision? With the evidence of Sithi corruption, should I have entrusted her safety to my brethren?

Considering my options, there had been little choice. She was too ill to travel, and it was imperative I get to Newland and assess the situation with the king and the bishop. I had to know if the men who ruled Newland and Florida were compromised. And, if so, what steps I would need to take to circumvent any damage done by the Dark Master.

"But what exactly is her role?"

I was snapped back to the present. "That I cannot say. My Lady is unable to reveal that to me."

We continued on in near silence, the jingle of harnesses and the occasional murmur between the men the only sounds. The lack of conversation didn't bother me. I'd gone decades without the sound of human voices. The peace was usually welcome. This time I was left with my thoughts, which weren't quite as welcome. They refused to center on any one subject but jumped from Merry, to Sithi prejudices, to Finnegan, even to Dylan. It was an unsatisfying use of the silence.

Sunlight filtered down between the interlocking branches overhead, and a slight breeze carried the scent of woodsmoke. Automatically, I scanned our surroundings, finding evidence of farms scattered throughout the valley we were traveling.

Yes, the area was more populated than the last time I'd been here. The wildlife less prolific. I sensed the presence of deer, fox, and even some more exotic mammals that had adapted to the North American environment. Funny how survival encouraged adjustment.

I allowed my thoughts to wander, falling into a sort of half awareness, dismissing my useless ruminations and staying cognizant of my surroundings. The warmth of the sun receded from my consciousness, and what little conversation there was fell away. The rhythm of Mysteria's gait lulled me into a waking dream, my body moving with her smooth gait.

"You must beware, Riona."

"My Lady?" I was startled, but not enough to emerge from my trance. I was aware of everything around me, but in a vague, peripheral sort of way.

"Humans can be possessed by the essence of my dark brother. I suspect King Ambrose may be compromised."

"*Possessed!*" I didn't know that could happen. "*How is that possible?*"

"*The soul must be open and willing. My brother cannot take control otherwise.*"

"*My descendent would never turn to the Dark Master.*"

"*Every mortal is vulnerable to temptation. A mirror will reveal a possession.*"

A mirror? We used mirrors to communicate across distances, but to use it to expose a Skori possession? I shook off the thought. Something else to think about later. I had bigger questions.

"*What of Sithi?*"

"*No. Normally I am able to protect my people from such enticement.*"

"*There were at least three in Minneson City who were compromised.*"

I sensed sorrow before the emotion was suppressed.

"*Yes, I know. As I said,* normally *I can protect them. Over the centuries, there are those who chafe over the tasks I set for my people. Who have allowed my brother into their hearts.*"

"*Do you know who they are?*" It would be a great help to know who my enemies were. Whether human or Sithi … anyone who embraced the Dark Master was a danger to us all.

"*My brother has blocked their presence from me. I can only guess.*" She must have sensed my next question because She continued without hesitation. "*I will not name them, Riona, until I am certain of their identities. I will not have my people unjustly accused.*"

I would have liked to argue, but I knew it would do little good.

"*He should not have been able to turn my Sithi. Our rules do not allow for infringement on each other's people, but Saytan is a greedy deity. He does not hesitate to break the rules, no matter what the consequences.*"

Saytan. That was the name of the Dark Master? Apparently mankind had had his name correct all those centuries ago when he was called Satan. It made me wonder at other past involvement with the three deities that had never made it into the history books or religious beliefs.

"How will I know if a human is possessed?"

"You will know. And Riona ... beware the shadows."

Her presence faded from my consciousness. I was once again aware of my surroundings, of Finnegan's questioning glance. I merely shook my head. I would tell him later. Right now I had a lot to think about. My Lady's last comment, for one. *Beware the shadows*. What did that mean?

We were close to Canada City. It was with more than a little fear that I wondered what I'd find there.

Chapter Twenty

After two days, I was tired of cooling my heels.
Facing a wide expanse of windows, I stared out over the palace gardens, appreciating but not really seeing the floral abundance.

The greenery called to my Sithi senses, to the point that I had to resist the urge to leave the cold comfort of the audience chamber and wander the graveled paths. Instead, I remained here, in the palace, waiting on the pleasure of King Ambrose.

Or, I should say, the pleasure of Bishop Langley.

During the past two days, I'd managed to eavesdrop on enough palace gossip to discover that it was Austin Brannigan, the king's chancellor, who was running Ambrose's schedule … with the bishop hovering like a dark specter behind him, directing his puppets.

Despite our daily messages requesting an audience, we'd wasted five days sitting at our inn, awaiting our summons to the palace. When we'd finally received one, we'd been made to blow the last two days waiting in the audience chamber while numerous other dignitaries, both major and minor, had paraded past us and into the inner sanctum of the throne room.

My patience was at an end. I was tempted to throw off my glamour and storm into the throne room, but in the end, caution won out. As far as Langley knew, our party was an embassy sent by Cascadia to meet with the king of Newland. I'd carefully altered my features to pass myself off as a male human, one of Captain Tiernan's lesser officers. When I looked in a mirror, I saw a young man with short blond hair, fuller in the face, with a hint of whisker. It was unnecessary to make many alterations to my figure since I was small-breasted to begin with and, in a uniform, could pass for a young man who hadn't quite reached his full maturity. The only addition I made was to broaden my shoulders a bit to give the impression of heavier muscles.

Looking over the gardens, I didn't turn when I felt Finnegan join me at the windows.

"You realize that seeing you in this disguise is rather disturbing," he said in a low voice.

I slanted him a quick glance. "In what way?"

"I never found myself attracted to a man before."

I stared at him for a brief moment, then amusement pushed my irritation aside. After our brief interlude nearly a week ago, we'd both been careful to keep our hormones under control. This was not the time or the place. But a reckoning was coming. We both knew it. The anticipation was making it all the sweeter. It had been far too long since I'd made love, and with luck, nothing important had atrophied.

"Don't worry. All the necessary parts are still female."

"That's a relief."

Captain Tiernan wandered over to our side, using the light from the wide windows to conceal his expression from the guards positioned at the wide double doors that blocked our access to the ruler of Newland. His hard face held a bland emptiness that could have meant anything. Curiosity had me opening my Sithi senses. I detected the myriad of emotions his expression concealed. Amusement, resignation, and more than a touch of annoyance. In the face of the insult being extended to him, the man was far more patient than I was. No king, not even one as strong as Ambrose, ignored the presence of an embassy of a fellow ruler. Wars had been started over less.

"The king has been informed of our presence," he said. I noticed that his eyes were rarely still. The only betrayal of his impatience was the way he continued to watch the other occupants of the room. "There are few who would ignore the arrival of a wizard and the Cascadian embassy. They don't realize they have a Sithi in their midst."

"It was a bit of a surprise to find all Sithi banned from the palace." Hence the reason I was using a glamour. "We have always been welcome here."

Another grave insult. I could just imagine Tesina's reaction if, and when, she heard about this.

"If King Ambrose isn't in his right mind, he may be listening to those who counsel the ban," Finnegan said, his voice low. His caution with being overheard was justified. The room might be large, but it was made up of hard surfaces … marble floors, stone walls. All of which echoed the conversations of unsuspecting occupants.

"Well, we know the bishop is here in the palace."

Kai's comment drew my attention.

"Langley is no doubt the reason we're still waiting in the anteroom rather than the throne room." The man hated Sithi with a passion and evidently viewed wizards with the same low regard. The Cascadian contingency was probably despised by association. Nevertheless, the insult ran deep.

"According to my sources …" Finnegan began.

"Sources?"

"I do know some people within the palace."

"Why doesn't that surprise me?" The smile he gave me was guileless but fooled no one. Least of all, me. "So what do these inside people say?"

"I was informed this morning that Bishop Langley has been at the palace for the past two months. Apparently, he's playing on the king's grief and has Ambrose nearly convinced that he should install one of the bishop's top men as temporary monarch until King Ambrose recovers from the tragedy of losing his sons."

"That bastard," I muttered under my breath. "It's highly unlikely that Langley will release his hold on Newland once Ambrose is recovered."

"Very true."

"The man is despicable."

"I do not know much about the politics of the Eastlands," Kai began after absorbing these tidbits of information. "But since Newland is a monarchy, wouldn't it be impossible for the Church to take control?"

"Once Langley has a grip on Newland, he will never let it go," Finnegan said as he, too, turned to put the light of the window at his back. His glance swept over the room, noting the position of the other occupants, lowering his voice further until even I could barely hear him. "Even if King Ambrose recovers, once the bishop has his man established, it may be impossible to displace him. King Ambrose will become a puppet monarch."

Finnegan shot a glance over his shoulder toward the guards at the door. "There is also other talk in the palace. Of dark creatures that roam the night. For the past two months, representatives of towns and villages from as far north as Nova Scotia have been arriving to petition the monarchy for help. People have gone missing; entire families are found dead."

"Skori."

"Cannot be anything else. My sources also told me that a small band of Rangers came through here a week ago, seeking an audience with the king. They were turned away and banned from the city."

Now that was news. Few possessed the freedom of the Rangers to come and go as they pleased. Sithi and Rangers might not always get along and tended to view each other with a certain degree of distrust, but their position as guardians of the north made Rangers sacrosanct where we were concerned. They had an uncanny ability to sense Skori, something they no doubt gained from their Sithi blood.

"But how are the Skori getting past the Rangers?" Kai asked.

"That I would very much like to know."

The fact the Skori had appeared in Memis and followed us nearly into Newland was disturbing. In the thousand years of my existence and even during the Skori wars of 455 N.A., they'd never managed to penetrate that far south.

"Have you had any word from your people?" Finnegan asked. His change of subject drew me out of my troubled thoughts and thrust me into a new line of problems.

"Not a word."

Instructions had been left for regular reports on Merry's condition. Even if Queen Tesina closed the Sithi borders, the healers would have little trouble contacting me with the use of a mirror. It was an imperfect art but adequate for communicating over great distances. I carried a small one at all times. About the size of my hand, it was more than effective. Other than an initial contact the first day we'd entered Canada City, it had been strangely silent. That was a bit worrisome.

"She's sure to be safe within your lands." Despite his words of reassurance, there was a gleam of doubt in Finnegan's dark eyes. I couldn't blame him. That same doubt was worming its way into my thoughts.

Before I could respond, a movement through the windows caught my eye, and I turned my attention back to the gardens. A woman left the vast greenhouses situated along the east wall of the courtyard and stepped onto the gravel path. She moved slowly, the way an elder would. But this was no elderly woman. Young, lovely. An air of tragedy surrounded her as she wandered aimlessly through the garden.

From where I stood, I could see that she was finely dressed in a gown of dark gray, the material long enough to sweep along the gravel. A sheer veil covered her face, but it could not disguise the golden-blond of her hair nor the porcelain delicacy of her features.

As I watched, the glass doors opened a second time, and a child dashed out. The woman turned and, with a sharp word, caught the boy's hand and hurried him down a path edged with dense foliage. It was the way she glanced around in a furtive manner that piqued my interest. That and the glimpse I had of the boy. There was something very familiar about his near-black hair and his slight build.

Making a quick decision, I glanced again at the closed double doors leading into the throne room. At the guards who stood on either side. Again, I was struck by how young they were and began to wonder where all the more seasoned soldiers were. I could discern no sound beyond the thick doors. If the past two days were any indication, we'd be waiting here for the rest of the day until we were dismissed to return to our lodgings.

And I wanted a closer look at that child.

"I'll be back shortly," I told Finnegan.

"Where are you going?"

"Just checking out something in the gardens."

Without waiting for his response, I left the audience chamber, passing two finely dressed courtiers in the wide corridor. They paid me no heed as I took a hard right and found the small door I was looking for. The palace had been fashioned centuries ago and carefully laid out. I knew each room and passage intimately since I'd had a hand in creating this edifice over six hundred years ago. During a particularly prosperous time in history, my descendent, Marcus Sterling, had requested that I help with the design of a palace to reflect the wealth of Newland.

Using the Schloss Neuschwanstein of ancient Germany as a rough model, I'd designed a soaring palace that sat like a jewel on the craggy cliffs overlooking the Atlantic Ocean. A bit ostentatious, but Marcus had been delighted.

It didn't take me long to reach the doors leading out into the gardens. The freshness of the air was welcome after being cooped up inside for the entire morning. Spring on the East Coast was always milder than in the Midwest, and I welcomed the warm sun on my face as I paused to get my bearings. These gardens had undergone quite a change since the last time I'd been here. The original design had been altered to reflect the taste of the present head gardener and the times.

Although they were enclosed by massive walls, the gardens still had a wild feel to them. An ancient feel. At least this portion of the original gardens was intact as per my instructions centuries ago. The oaks, elms, and maples trees, hundreds of years old, grew massive by the grace of Our Lady. I remembered many of them as saplings, having personally planted a great portion of them.

I made my way along the twisting paths, reacquainting myself with old friends and meeting new. I ran my fingers over the wild azaleas and rhododendrons, pausing briefly to admire their vivid colors. In this sheltered area, they bloomed early in the season, an explosion of reds and pinks. Dark ferns littered the undergrowth along with foliage of every type, some native to this area, some imported in centuries past.

I was impressed. These gardens couldn't compare to the bountiful beauty of Minneson City, but they weren't bad for a human effort.

Because of my initial effort, there was old magic here. No one would ever guess that this site had once been a toxic dump. When the plague had hit, so many people had died that there'd been no one to shut down the factories and nuclear reactors. As a result, many parts of the country were contaminated and rendered poisonous. It had taken us weeks to render this soil fertile once more.

I paused beside a particularly impressive elm, running my hands over the gnarled trunk as I spied my quarry. The woman sat on a bench a short distance away, the child standing before her. She clutched both his shoulders, her manner urgent as she spoke to him in a low voice.

"You know better than to come outside during the day, Louis. Someone might have seen you."

"But I was tired of being indoors, Mama. There's nothing to do."

"You must be careful at all times. No one must know that we're here in the palace."

The boy straightened his thin shoulders. He had to be all of ten years old, yet he tried to appear grown.

"I know, Mama. I was very careful. I used the secret passage from our tower. No one saw me come outside."

"Except, perhaps, me." I dropped my glamour as I stepped away from the tree. The woman came to her feet with a small cry of alarm, her hands tightening on the boy's shoulders before she thrust him behind her. Her fear lasted only seconds before she raised her chin and tried to block my view of the boy with her body, but it was too late. I'd already gotten a good look at the child. All arms and legs with a shock of curly dark hair. It was the ice-blue eyes, however, that gave him away. There was no mistaking them. He was the spitting image of Lionel Sterling at that age. Lionel Sterling who had been slain and whose family had vanished.

"Who are you? What do you want?" The woman made a show of aggression, but she couldn't disguise the tremor of fear in her voice. Through the sheer material covering her face, her dark eyes were wide with alarm, darting in several directions as if in search of an escape.

"Don't worry." I made no move to come closer. Sending my

senses outward, I inspected the gardens for any other intruders, but other than a pair of gardeners at the far end, there was no one else in the immediate vicinity. "You're quite safe with me. If I'm not mistaken, you are Bianca Sterling. Wife of Lionel Sterling."

Her gasp was audible, and new alarm swept over her face. For an instant, she appeared to be on the verge of fleeing, but a maternal protectiveness came over her, and she stood her ground, her beautiful expression set in lines of determination. Despite myself, I was impressed. I'd never met Bianca Sterling, but here was no delicate porcelain doll. This was a woman who had somehow escaped a Skori attack, made her way here to the palace, and remained hidden for what must have been months.

There was a movement at her waist, and a small face peered around her skirts. A pair of blue eyes stared up at me with fascination.

"You're a Sithi, aren't you?"

"Louis!"

"Not to worry, Lady Sterling." Careful not to alarm her further, I approached. After giving Bianca another reassuring nod, I crouched down until I was eye level with the child. "Yes, I am. And you must be young Louis Sterling."

"How do you know that? Did you use your magic?"

"Not at all. I heard your mother call you by name, and I must say you look just like your father when he was your age."

"You knew my father?"

For a brief moment, sorrow swept over me as I thought of the young man as I'd seen him last. He hadn't even reached his majority yet. At the age of fifteen, Lionel had been a daring boy, yet mindful of his position. I'd lost so many people whom I'd cared for over the centuries that I sometimes wondered if it was worth the emotional turmoil to allow mortals close to me. Their lives were so fragile, so short.

"Yes, I knew your father." I glanced up at Bianca, seeing the pale smoothness of her cheeks through the veil. It was amazing she was alive. According to Merry, her siblings and their families had all been slaughtered. How had Bianca and her son escaped? The Skori had to have sent someone to ensure the demise of the entire Sterling family. Finnegan had mentioned the rumor that after Lionel had been killed, his family had vanished. How had the two of them made their way here? Aware of the continued danger, Bianca had somehow concealed their presence in the palace.

A very amazing woman.

Another thought struck me as I stared down at the child. With Louis alive, he stood in line for the throne of Newland. Ahead of Merry. She did not need to take up the crown.

The Vision I'd had in the forest did not need to come to pass. There was another path to the future. Wrapped in this one small child.

Chapter Twenty-one

Determination leant me strength as I stormed past the other petitioners scattered throughout the receiving room. Finnegan must have been watching for my return because he was waiting at the little door I'd used to the gardens. He didn't say a word at my appearance, merely dropped into step with me. Tiernan took one look at my face, at my lack of glamour, and took up the position to my left, Crispin close on his heels. Neither asked questions although both must have been aware that something momentous had occurred in the gardens.

The whispers started as soon as I reentered the receiving chamber.

"Sithi!"

"Sithi has returned to the palace."

"There is hope."

"Sithi filth."

For an instant, my step faltered, and I glanced to my left, locating the human who occupied the shadows in a corner. Given the brightness of the room, those shadows were unexpected. And unnatural.

My elven eyes easily found a man of middle height huddled there, his body swathed in the monkish robes that depicted his affiliation with the Church. Although his face was hidden by the cowl of his robe, there was no missing the fanatical light of conviction in his eyes. He was a new occupant to the audience chamber. I definitely would have noticed him earlier had he been present. Funny how fear and ignorance knew no era. It was apparently human nature to be prejudiced against what they didn't understand.

"Be careful, little mortal." I whispered the words, using my magic to carry them to the man. "Angering a Sithi is very unhealthy."

Fear, and something else, spiked the air, but the man drew himself to his full height. A height that still fell well below mine. The shadows around him seemed to thicken, distorting his shape, making him appear bulkier. I frowned but sensed no magic, malignant or otherwise.

"Unclean heathen. The One God will smite you from this Earth, Sithi."

The Church seemed awfully fond of that word *heathen*.

"Your One God has no say in the matter, mortal."

Why was I arguing with this nut case? Besides being a waste of time, we were gathering an audience. The guards at the door came alert, and the other occupants of the room halted all conversation to watch our confrontation with morbid fascination.

The man overcame his fear long enough to step into my path, arms spread wide as if to halt my advance into the throne room.

"Man shall rule the Earth for all time!"

I didn't have time for this crap. Any minute now, the guards were going to call in reinforcements. The extra numbers would not halt my entrance into the throne room, but I'd rather not destroy portions of the king's palace to get there or harm the humans who sought to block me. I turned away from the monk.

A tingle down my spine alerted me to the presence of My Lady. There was a sense of movement, and Finnegan yelled a warning just before the monk tackled me, carrying us both to the floor.

I absorbed the bulk of the strike, my head crashing onto the stone. My teeth drove into my tongue, and blood flooded my mouth.

For several seconds, I saw stars, but I shook off the pain. Gathering my arms under me, I heaved the man off of me. He flew several feet, then slid along the polished floor until he came up against a pillar.

Leaping to my feet, I flung out a hand. Bright light shot from my palm to strike the monk full in the chest. The force of my magic pinned him against the pillar, his robes flat against his skinny body. The cowl fell back to reveal an unremarkable face. Stringy dark hair, a slightly bulbous nose. A face I would see every day in a crowd and not take due notice. The smell of him, on the other hand, would announce his presence ahead of time. He smelled like he hadn't bathed in weeks, if not months.

I shook my head. My vision faded in and out. Hitting my head must have been more damaging than I'd thought. Shadows edged out of my peripheral vision and then engulfed me. The sunlit room vanished as I closed the distance between myself and the monk.

Giving my head another shake, I realized that the shadows were real and definitely unnatural. I was trapped in the midst of them.

As the deranged monk watched my approach, the expression on his face went from fury to shock to horror in the space of seconds. He seemed to be struggling against something other than my power. His head thrashed back and forth as he tried to say something, but all that came out was a litany of "Oh God! Oh God, oh God, oh God!"

Keeping him pinned to the pillar, I saw something strange ripple across his skin. A wave of movement made his face bulge and his body swell, the material of his robes suddenly tight where before it had been loose. His mouth opened in a rictus of agony as his eyes rolled back in his head until only the whites showed. His scream of terror and pain echoed off the walls, deafening.

The shadows closed tighter around us, blocking out the sunlight, enclosing us in a cloak of gloom. The sudden foulness of the unnatural twilight froze me for a moment, a shiver of fear traveling down my spine.

My alarm turned to horror as the monk's skin began to split, blood spurting from a dozen wounds. His screams were cut off as his face ripped open and something began to emerge. Blood sprayed in every direction as the creature shook off the remnants of its host, covering me with human blood and gore.

Horrified, I watched a Skori emerge from the remains of the human body. Somehow it had taken possession of the monk. Literally, not in the metaphysical sense. The robe was in tatters around the massive creature, revealing leather crisscrossing its crest and a sheath strapped to its back.

From a pasty face streaked with the monk's blood, dark, soulless eyes focused on me with deadly intent. The slit of a mouth drew back in a snarl as it drew its blade and advanced. I could see nothing beyond the engulfing shadows, had no way of knowing how far the gloom extended or what had become of my companions and the other petitioners still in the room.

These thoughts barely registered before I leaped back, avoiding the swing of the sword by inches. The creature was fast, no hesitation as it reversed the direction of its blade for another strike. I ducked to one side, my foot slipping in something I'd rather not think about. I nearly lost my head as I dodged again.

"I look forward to tasting Sithi flesh once more." Its words were guttural, barely understandable. Wholly unexpected. I could count on two hands the number of times I'd heard a Skori speak intelligibly. Not that it mattered.

I was unarmed. We all were. It was one of the requirements of an audience with the king that we leave our weapons at the inn. Fools that we were.

I kept the Skori in front of me as I circled, backing up with care. Its dark eyes never left my face as it paced me, confidence radiating off of it.

"You will be delicious."

I ignored its words. The shadows moved with it. I realized it was the shadows that allowed it to function during the daylight hours.

The gloom swirled around the two of us so thickly I didn't have a clue as to where Finnegan or the Cascadians were. Muffled shouting came from somewhere, but my sense of direction had been distorted. Dizziness swept over me. A strange lethargy threatened, and my vision blurred for several precious seconds.

I stumbled. Pain ripped across my chest, but it barely registered. My mind moved sluggishly, and I realized something in the unnatural gloom was weakening me. My experience with Skori magic was limited since they rarely used it, preferring to defeat their enemies with brute strength.

The Dark Master must have decided it was time to share His knowledge in his unsanctioned move to usurp My Lady.

A flash of movement sent searing fire running down the length of my left arm, the pain sharp and immediate. I staggered back. The creature had scored me twice as my mind wandered. If I wanted to survive this, I had to stay alert, push back the weakening shadows, and focus. Ignore the burn that ran from my collarbone to my right breast, the blood dripping down my arm.

The bastard was toying with me. As I watched, it ran a finger along the blade, bringing my blood up to its mouth to lick it. Again, a look of pleasure crossed its face.

I took a quick inventory of my injuries. The slices weren't deep enough to incapacitate me, but they hurt like hell. A glance at the blade showed it appeared free of the poisons that Skori were fond of using. Lucky me.

I kept the creature in front of me as I backed toward what I hoped was the doorway leading into the throne room. The guards who'd flanked that door were the only two who possessed weapons.

Dodging another swing, I slammed against the stone wall. Risking a glance to my left, I saw the ornate framing of the wooden archway. But no guards. Of course they'd taken their weapons with them when they'd abandoned their post.

"Now you die, Riona Northstar."

It took me a few seconds for its words to sink in. Not only did this creature know who I was but it'd known I was to be here today. The Dark Master had targeted me specifically.

The knowledge that a deity was taking such an unhealthy interest in me should have terrified me. Instead, it hardened my resolve and went far in shaking off the narcotic shadows. The Dark Brother would not find me easy meat. If He wanted me, He had to work a helluva lot harder than this.

I feinted to the left in an attempt to draw the Skori's attack. As it shifted its stance, I dropped to the floor and struck, swinging my leg out to sweep the creature's legs out from under it. But when I tried to brace myself, my left arm gave out. Instead of dropping the creature, I only managed a solid blow to its knee. The strike buckled its leg and threw it off balance, the sword swinging wildly.

I heard a solid *thunk*, and I glanced up to see the blade stuck in the wooden frame surrounding the doorway. With a snarl, the creature spent precious seconds trying to free his weapon.

Taking advantage of its distraction, I leaped to my feet and drew deep on my magic, shoving my right hand against the creature's chest. I'd never tried this maneuver before, but Finnigan's defense in Minneson City had inspired me. I focused all my energy on my hand, seeing white light flare. It flashed from my palm straight into the Skori's body, sinking into its blood-streaked chest.

The Skori flung back its head, shrieking. Light burst from its mouth and eyes, growing brighter and brighter until the creature was consumed by it. When the flare faded, it took with it the shadows that had concealed the creature, leaving nothing behind but a greasy spot on the marble floor. A grim smile stretched my lips. Not as neat as spirit magic, but just as effective.

Weakness swept over me, and I dropped to my knees. The vast amount of magic I had expended left me drained. As the adrenaline dissipated, the pain of my wounds burned. I knelt, stunned for a moment before awareness of my surroundings returned.

The shadows had vanished, leaving the room as bright as it had been moments ago. What had seemed like minutes had happened in seconds. Finnegan was still in the center of the room, his staff held at a defensive angle, the blue stone glowing bright. Kai and Crispin stood at his back, crouched in defensive positions. They must have been as blind as I when the shadows converged. But they were unharmed, thank the Lady. Now I knew what my Lady had meant when she'd said to beware the shadows.

"Riona."

Finnegan reached my side and fell to his knees in front of me, dropping his staff with a clatter. With gentle fingers, he touched my cheek, his face pale. The feel of his hand on my face was soothing, and I allowed myself to lean into his caress for precious seconds. Then, with care, he edged the sliced tunic away from my upper chest, inspecting the slash. Even that light touch caused my breath to hiss in between my teeth before I turned my attention to my wounds.

One advantage to being Sithi was our ability to heal swiftly. The slash was shallow, already closing. The wound on my arm was deeper, and pain burned its way into my consciousness.

Using the remnants of my magic, I sent a wave of healing through my body and felt the knitting begin. Skin binding, cells tingling, pain lessening. By tonight it should be gone.

"No poison," I said.

He closed his eyes. "Thank God."

"And the Lady." Again, I allowed myself the luxury of leaning against him for a moment. The fight had been short and vicious, but it had left me as weak as a kitten. "What I want to know is how the hell a Skori managed to possess the body of a human."

"And how was it able to withstand the daylight," Finnegan added as Kai and Crispin reached our side.

"It was the shadows," I said. "The Skori is somehow able to use shadows to travel. Much like the Sithi uses the mists."

Finnegan frowned. "Then they should be able to appear anywhere. Anytime."

"Not necessarily. It takes a lot of magic to manipulate the mists. I can only assume shadow is much the same. My understanding is that the Dark Master is stingy with his power. There cannot be many who can use the shadows."

I glanced around the room, not surprised to find it nearly empty. Two mortals were huddled in the corner, clutching each other and weeping. The guards were nowhere to be seen, and the door to the outer hall was open.

I wanted to believe they'd gone for help, but given their youth and apparent inexperience, I was more willing to bet they were still running.

My glance went to the inner door leading to the throne room. Granted, it was thick and sturdy, but surely someone would have heard the commotion through it. The screams alone from the other petitioners should have alerted those within that there was something happening beyond that room.

Anger gave me strength to climb to my feet. Finnegan followed suit, no doubt ready to steady me should I stumble. But I had no intention of stumbling. Sending a brief prayer for renewed strength, I felt My Lady's response. Magic flowed into me, sweeping away the pain and fatigue. Relief made me sigh, and I straightened my shoulders.

I wanted very much to know what was going on in that throne room. Without another word, I headed for the doors. Pushing against them, I was unsurprised to find them locked.

Anger washed over me and gave me strength as I waved my hands outward. The doors burst open, rebounding against the inner walls before the force of my magic cemented them to the walls of the throne room. A quick glance around showed more guards within. Older, more experienced, they stood at various points in the room yet didn't move when I made my dramatic entrance.

Frowning, I took in their vacant expressions. They'd been spelled. Small wonder no aid had come during the attack.

It also meant I had another enemy within this room.

"Keep an eye on them," Finnegan said in a low voice to Kai and Crispin. It was a nice feeling to know that someone had my back.

What little activity there was inside the vast room stuttered to a halt as I led the way down the length of the red-and-gold-patterned carpet. I only had eyes for the small party at the far end of the room, assessing and cataloguing each occupant as I closed the distance.

It might have been easy to dismiss the guards as being no threat, but someone in this room was controlling them. Someone who could either release them from their trance or order them to attack at any second. I had to trust my companions to give me warning if that should happen.

Ignoring the few sycophants scattered throughout the room, I focused on the man at the far end. The hushed voices faded from my consciousness as I saw my descendent clearly for the first time in over twenty years. Seated upon a marble throne of white shot through with silver and gold, Ambrose Sterling, the ruler of all

Newland, was an old man. No, this went way beyond the trappings of an old man.

Despite the weak sunlight slanting through the skylights set high in the ceiling, a dark miasma hung over the dais that housed the royal throne of Newland. My heightened magic allowed me to see it clearly. Not the same as the shadows that had engulfed me a short time ago, but something dark and deadly nonetheless. My caution jumped another notch as I started forward.

This was not the king I remembered. Even from this distance, I could see his sunken eyes, his face pallid except for where his cheeks burned with an unnatural fever. His steel-gray hair hung in greasy strands about his head, matted, filthy.

I fought to keep the shock out of my expression. This wasn't the same vibrant man who'd ruled Newland for decades with fairness and a firm hand. This was a pitiful shell of the man I'd once known.

Was it only the loss of his sons that had broken him so? Or was it something more?

I suspected the latter.

I sent out a delicate stream of magic to investigate the occupants of the room, but it was rebuffed. The shroud of gloom seemed to absorb and neutralize my reading. Something dark was at work here. Question was, where, or who, was the source?

The heels of my boots made no sound when the carpet gave way to an intricately tiled floor. The image of a great sun was etched with tile below the dais, the skylights overhead picking out the gold with blinding clarity. If there were Skori here, they were deep within their host bodies in order to withstand the brightness of the streaming light.

Two more guards stood at the bottom of the dais. Dressed in the black and green uniform of Sterling, they stood as still as statues, their eyes as vacant as their comrades' but heavily armed.

I'd been a fool to let the outer guards strip me of my weapons.

I'd known we'd be entering a potentially hazardous situation yet had allowed my need to see King Ambrose to outweigh my instinct. It was a mistake I would not make twice.

"How dare you!"

The voice boomed across the distance that separated my party from the throne. There was a movement behind the throne, and a figure clad entirely in white and gold stepped forward until he stood before the king.

"You dare pollute the king's inner sanctum with the filth of your presence."

A bit melodramatic, but I'd come to expect nothing less from James Langley. I turned my attention on the man, allowing a sneer to curve my lips. Bishop Langley was tall, handsome by human standards, and possessed a presence that helped make him the head of the human Church. Golden-blond hair was brushed back from his forehead and half-concealed by a pontiff-like hat. I could only guess that a painting or photo of the last Catholic pope must have survived the centuries. His robes were of the purest white, ingrained with threads of gold and silver to make them shimmer.

Compared to the man on the throne, Bishop Langley looked pure and godly. But I knew that within the perfection of the trappings, rot had been growing steadily over the years. Question was, how deep was the infestation, and was there an outside influence?

"Give it a rest, Langley. The king is ill and requires healing."

"By you? You will not be allowed to lay your cursed hands upon King Ambrose."

Reaching under my tunic, I palmed the small mirror I had secreted there. According to My Lady, if a human was possessed by the Skori, the mirror would reveal it. Seemed to me that Langley was a likely candidate. I couldn't sense the presence of a Skori now, but then I'd had no warning of its possession of the monk in the receiving chamber.

There had to be something about them being concealed within a human host that confused my senses. I needed to get close enough to catch his reflection in the little mirror I held. We were still about three meters from the dais. Too far to use the mirror.

"Don't be ridiculous, Langley. How long has the king been in this state?"

I deliberately left off an honorarium. If he insulted me, I would respond in like. Petty? Maybe.

"Since the Sithi destroyed his sons."

That was a rumor I was tired of hearing.

"The sons of Ambrose were not killed by Sithi. There is no doubt it was the work of Skori."

"You lie! There are no Skori. They are a rumor invented by the elves to conceal their vile acts."

"The sad thing is, he believes it," Finnegan murmured at my side. He'd been so still I'd almost forgotten his presence. I glanced over my shoulder to see the captain and his lieutenant following the exchange in silence, their faces revealing none of their thoughts.

"Langley is not a stupid man. Misguided and narrow-minded, yes, but not stupid." I kept my voice low before I turned back to assess the man before me. "There must be some advantage for him to perpetuate the belief that Skori do not exist."

My eyes picked out the minute changes in the bishop that had not been present the last time I'd seen him. Though still a man of beauty, new lines scored across his forehead and down either side of his mouth. There was a darkness about him, a gleam of near madness in his brilliant blue eyes. Even his elegant trappings of power could not conceal the growing pollution on his soul.

A flutter of movement stirred the velvet curtains behind the throne, drawing my glance. But when I looked, the material was still. Sending out my senses, I found a presence there. Someone was hidden. Not Skori. At least I didn't think so. I should have sensed that immediately, but even that wasn't a guarantee.

Calling on the grace of My Lady, I felt the brush of her presence, and her magic flared deep within me. I was exhausted from my earlier battle, but I felt a new infusion of much-welcomed power course through my veins. The added strength allowed me to ignore the aches and pains that wracked my body.

"I ask permission to approach the throne, Sire."

"Do not allow it, Your Majesty." Langley stepped back to lean down. His whispered words were clear to me. "She will bewitch you with her pagan ways."

"Hardly pagan, Langley." With an effort, I kept my words wry, my expression amused. Hard to do when you were injured and looked like hell.

Without awaiting permission, I closed the distance, allowing my magic to flare to counter the bishop's stench. He stumbled back two steps before he caught himself, his eyes wide with revulsion. Gathering his rich robes around himself, he straightened to his full height. All Sithi were tall and willowy, so he fell short.

His attempt at regrouping would have been laughable, but I knew him to be a dangerous adversary. Bishop Langley had been in Newland for months, with access to the king. His influence must have been considerable.

I was also getting tired of being negated to the level of pond scum.

Halting before King Ambrose, I presented a bow, one leg extended, my arms sweeping wide. The mirror was fitted in my palm, concealed from the pair before me.

"My Lord King Ambrose. I bring you greetings from Queen Tesina of the Sithi." My words were smooth, and the whispering halted as those present strained to hear.

I ignored the courtiers. Most were vultures circling the wounded, but some might be of assistance once I weeded out the useless and the opportunists.

King Ambrose betrayed no awareness of my presence. His chin rested on his chest, eyes half closed. Drool escaped the corner of his slack lips, and he mumbled softly under his breath. His richly colored robes were wrinkled and stained, as if he'd been wearing them for days, if not weeks. His gray hair was so knotted and wild that I couldn't tell whether he wore his crown.

"Where is the princess Meredith?" Langley asked, his snide tone regaining my attention.

I would have ignored his question if it weren't for the look on his face while he waited for my response. There was a flush on his high cheeks and a lascivious gleam in his eyes. His flush deepened when he noticed my stare, and his mouth curved into a sneer before he leaned close to whisper something in King Ambrose's ear. I stared at him for several seconds. Just long enough for him to squirm before he seemed to realize it and drew himself straight.

"Why would you think I could know where Meredith is?"

"Do you deny it?"

"I deny nothing. I'm curious."

"We had … words before she vanished. She said if no one was going to do something, she would. That she was going to find the Sithi. Strange you appear shortly afterward."

I continued to stare at him, not speaking until he again fidgeted.

"You appear here in the palace," he said again. "I can only surmise you are the abomination she located."

Personally, I was getting a little tired of being called an abomination … particularly to my face. Langley really needed to expand his vocabulary.

Still, it was interesting that Merry had said nothing of this conversation.

Langley stepped forward.

"Again. I demand to know where Princess Meredith is. She is to be returned to us."

"To us?" I arched one brow in an inquisitive manner. "I understand her importance to her father." My glance flickered toward the wreck of a man sitting on the throne. "But you, Bishop Langley, have no claim on her."

A flush climbed higher on his cheeks. It was tempting to let the man squirm a bit more, but that would be petty, wouldn't it? Finally, I capitulated and gave him an answer.

"She is safe, Bishop," I said.

"Where? With King Ambrose ill, she must take up the reins of rule."

Careful to keep my expression neutral, I sent out a light probe to read his emotions. If he was possessed by a Skori, I didn't want to alert it to my suspicions. Barely suppressed excitement colored the air around the man, intermixed with caution and more than a touch of lust. Yes, he wanted Merry to take up the reins of rule, but with him at her side, whispering in her ear, no doubt taking it further.

Interesting. So the oh-so-holy Bishop James Langley coveted Merry Sterling. Was it because she was a beautiful young woman, or was it she was now destined to be queen? Either option was reason enough to whet his interest. And, apparently, his appetite.

"Not to worry, Langley. She is being well taken care of."

I was close enough to get a feel for the presence I knew was concealed behind the curtain. Opening my senses further, I was hit by the miasma that kept interfering with any accurate reading.

Someone was there ... male ... which was all I could determine.

"Your Majesty." I dismissed Langley and turned my attention to Ambrose. "Your Majesty, can you hear me?"

The king opened his eyes fully to reveal the same pale blue color as his daughter's. Something coherent moved behind the vacuous look before he straightened and glanced around.

"Merry? Is that you? You bring word of your brothers? When will they arrive? It has been too long since I've seen them."

"No, Your Majesty. It is not Merry. It is Riona of the Sithi."

"Lady Riona, eh?" Ambrose glanced up and found me. He was worse than I'd feared. His face lit into a temporary animation that faded even as I watched. "Welcome, my lady Riona. Too long have you been gone from my court. Do you bring word of my sons?"

"No, Sire. I regret that I've heard nothing of them."

The light went out of his eyes. In the contemporary expression of my former life, we would have said the lights were on but no one was home. As you watched, you could see the intelligence fade. From the distance of perhaps a meter, I tried to untangle any one emotion in the ruler of Newland, but they kept slipping away, ranging from elation to disappointment to … nothing.

Or perhaps it was Langley's emotions that were interfering with any accurate reading I might make. Carefully opening my magic further, I attempted to untangle the situation.

The myriad of emotions emanating from Langley was a stench on the air. Ambition, lust, greed … all a rancid tangle. He tried to keep me in his sights, but his glance kept sliding toward the king. At one point, he nodded, as if listening to a silent voice. Alarm slammed through me, and my stomach clenched.

I heard Finnegan draw a sharp breath. Risking a glance over my shoulder, I expected to find his attention centered on Langley, but his gaze was on the blue velvet curtain that framed the throne. Without taking his eyes from the material, he gave me a slight nod. Perhaps he detected something that was eluding me. I had to trust his instincts in this matter. If there was danger behind that curtain, he was sensing something I wasn't. Was Langley the threat? Or was there more than one?

According to Finnegan's sources, Langley was ignoring the rule of Florida to devote all his time to the acquisition of Newland.

The question was, why now?

Was it because of Merry's coming of age? Was she the catalyst to his metamorphosis? Was it merely the ambitions of an ambitious man? Or was he an emissary of the darkness?

Mentally shaking my head, I returned my attention to the present, my disquiet growing. I'd be foolish to underestimate him. Or to give him more credit than was his due. It was a fine line I walked. I needed to get close enough to catch his reflection in the mirror without his being aware of my intent.

But he was too close to King Ambrose. I couldn't risk a Skori attack if he proved to be one.

"It is imperative, Sire, that you take up your rule and train your daughter to follow." Now was not the time to mention another potential heir. One who was right here in the palace. I put one foot on the lowest step but made no move to climb the remaining five.

The glow of my magic reached Ambrose and bathed him in its healing light. I felt My Lady feed more energy into me, infusing me with power and boosting my healing abilities. It washed over him, lifting some of his grief and clearing his mind.

"You must face the fact that your sons are lost, King Ambrose," I said. "You must prepare ..."

"The king must do nothing, elf."

Langley's insults were becoming tiresome. Yes, we were elves, but it was well known that we preferred the title of Sithi. By the Lady's grace, we'd been around for a thousand years, and through it all, we'd labored to the benefit of humans. Once in a while, when I came across mortals like Langley, I could almost appreciate Queen Tesina's attitude toward mortals.

Right now I had to concentrate on King Ambrose. The effects of my magic were already visible. He was sitting up a little straighter, and the lost hopelessness was fading from his eyes. Now that I was close enough to concentrate my power, I could feel an outside source feeding his sorrow. Wave after wave of rancid magic was coming from someone nearby.

And they were not emanating from Langley.

Chapter Twenty-two

Twisting slightly, I glanced down at my mirror, angling it so Langley's reflection was visible. I wasn't sure what I expected to see, but his all-too-normal human reflection was not it. There was something odd, though. A veil of darkness lingered over him, outlining him until there appeared to be an aura of shadow surrounding him.

Was this the beginning of a possession? Or was it the Dark Master's way of harvesting an already corrupted soul? Either way, Bishop Langley had not been possessed by a Skori.

Yet.

Langley was staring at the king as I continued to send my magic into him, healing him. With the added strength of My Lady, I was able to counter the darkness.

The film all but vanished from over his eyes. With an added twist, I began to remove the filth of weeks that clung to his face and clothing. Slowly, the man I remembered emerged from the miasma of evil that sought to engulf him. The shadows surrounding him reluctantly gave way before the light of My Lady, clinging to him with tenacity but retreating by slow degrees.

"What are you doing to the king?" Langley's tone was hushed.

"Pushing out the darkness seeking to possess him. I suspect with the deaths of his sons, King Ambrose's soul was left vulnerable."

"How dare you use your foul elf power on him. King Ambrose is a man of the One God."

"Who doesn't seem to be doing much at the moment."

Probably an unfair charge given Finnegan's presence at my back, but the bishop's hypocrisy was really getting on my nerves.

From the corner of my eye, I saw Finnegan edge closer to Langley. The man was too busy watching me and the king to notice the wizard's approach. For an instant, I thought Finnegan meant to take out Langley, but just as the last of the shadows left the king, an enraged scream came from behind the curtain framing the throne. The heavy material was flung aside with a force that ripped it from its moorings and sent it crashing to the ground.

Without thought, I placed myself between the king and the figure that was even now ripping its human host from its body. I had an instant to recognize the king's counselor, Austin Branigan, before he was literally torn to pieces. The Skori that emerged was bigger than the first one I'd fought. Uglier, too.

With strips of the counselor hanging from him like a grisly cloak, the creature stood at about seven feet, taller than even me and heavily muscled. Blood covered its pallid face. Its red eyes burned with fire and hatred. A hatred that shifted from me to the man who sat vulnerable in the throne behind me.

"Get him out of here!" I shouted before I flung myself forward.

I caught the creature around the waist and bore it to the ground. We landed among the velvet material of the curtains, and I scrambled to get purchase, but his skin was too slippery from the blood and gore that were all that was left of Branigan.

With my arms around its waist, I felt the long sword it had sheathed along its back. Out of its reach. Sinewy arms wrapped around me, squeezing until I thought my ribs would crack, fetid breath washing over my face.

I gagged at the smell of rotted flesh.

The Skori made a guttural sound deep in its throat before it opened its mouth. Teeth bit into my shoulder, and I screamed. Pain ripped through me as it worked its jaws, tearing through tendon and muscle until it struck bone.

My left arm dropped useless to my side, losing whatever purchase I had on the creature. My right arm was slipping free.

Rolling, it was on top of me. It pulled back, my blood dripping from its mouth. Soulless eyes stared down at me, satisfaction evident in their red depths.

That more than anything fired my fury. With my right hand, I reached up behind it and grabbed the sparse length of hair, yanking its head back.

"Riona! Your eyes!"

There was movement behind me, and a corner of the blue velvet was flung over my face. My first instinct was to free myself, but I'd recognized Finnegan's voice and released my grip on its head. Using my body, I bucked the creature upward. Not to fling the Skori off of me, but to make it a better target.

Through the thick material, I saw a blue streak flash over my head and strike where the Skori had been. I heard it scream, and then its weight was gone.

Despite the protection, the brightness of the wizard light seared my eyes, blinding me for precious seconds. Then there were hands on me, someone pulling the material off my face. Looking up into Finnegan's beautiful face, I smiled. He returned my smile, at the same time palming a small blue crystal into a hidden pocket within his tunic.

Then the pain hit me, and I couldn't bite back a cry. My entire shoulder was a burning mass of agony. Pain washed over me, and I had to fight to keep my last meal down. Elves did not barf.

I looked down at my left shoulder. From what I could see, a huge chunk had been gnawed out of it. The blue velvet had sopped up some of the blood, and through the raw flesh, I could see the gleam of bone before new blood welled up and spilled over.

"It's bad, Riona," Finnegan said as he carefully moved the collar of my tunic. Even that slight movement sent waves of pain radiating over my shoulders and down my back. I suspected my shoulder bone was cracked.

I knew the injury was bad, and I hurt like hell. Still, I wasn't worried. Already I felt heat radiating from my core. My Lady would heal me ... hopefully before I lost more blood. I was feeling light-headed. Like barfing in public, fainting would not improve the Sithi image.

"Hold still."

Like I was going to move? Finnegan tried to be gentle as he tore my tunic, exposing more of the wound. A short cry escaped through my clenched teeth. With an effort, I refrained from snarling at him.

Besides the chunk gnawed out of my shoulder, I was sure there were claw marks across my back and numerous puncture wounds. I couldn't even determine the state of my ribs over all the other pain.

I must have gotten soft. I hadn't been this beaten up for centuries. Then again, when this day had begun, I hadn't exactly expected Skori to start crawling out of humans.

As much as I wanted to lie there for another couple of minutes —hell, a couple of years—I didn't have that luxury.

"Help me up."

"You need a healer, Riona," Kai said.

I glanced to my right to where the captain squatted on his heels a short distance from me. He looked disgustingly whole. His blond hair wasn't even mussed.

"He's right, Riona," Finnegan said as he tore a strip from his tunic. With care, he pressed it to my shoulder in an effort to staunch the flow of blood.

I hissed at him, baring my teeth.

"No time."

By the Lady, I wished my wounds would at least heal enough to stop bleeding. I closed my eyes as a new wave of dizziness swept over me.

Gritting my teeth, I made it to my knees, swaying. I looked up at Finnegan. "Please."

He gazed into my eyes for what seemed a long moment but was actually seconds. I'm not sure what he saw there, but he sighed and leaned down, taking my right hand and carefully helping me to my feet.

Agony ripped through me. New blood poured down my chest, darkening the ruin of my tunic. That damn Skori had really done a number on my shoulder.

"Where is King Ambrose?"

"I'm here."

Relief filled me, and I closed my eyes for an instant before looking up to see Ambrose Sterling appear in my line of vision. His eyes were clear and alert, his body held erect. He looked more like the man I'd known years ago.

I sent up a silent prayer of thanks.

Ambrose must still have an important role to play.

Rather unusual given the rules that seemed to surround the three siblings with their strict hands-off policy. Should My Lady be lending me the strength and ability at this level to help a human? Given my history with the rulers of Newland, I wasn't about to argue. I was just happy to see my descendent restored to his former self.

"Your Majesty." Bishop Langley pushed forward, elbowing me out of the way, causing a new wave of pain to cascade through me. "You are unhurt."

Damn, it was so tempting to just pop the man. His aura still pulsed with darkness, but it had the feel of a shadow that was trying to find a way in. Not one that had already gained entrance.

The man was on the brink. And needed to be watched.

"Still believe the Skori are a myth, Bishop?" The comment was a little petty, yes, but it was satisfying to be able to say *I told you so*.

Langley straightened, wrapping his robes around himself as if warding off a chill. "The Church must meditate on the recent events."

"Recent events?" Was the man mad? "Wake up and face reality, Jimmy-Boy. You just came face to face with your worst nightmare. You say your Church believes in the devil? Well, let me introduce you to one of his demons."

I waved a hand toward the grease spot staining the marble. Being able to rub his face in cold, hard facts was one of the few highlights of my day.

"The Church must send a party north to negotiate with these Skori. We must save their souls."

I could only stare at him in disbelief. There he stood in his pristine white, not a scratch on him, while I was bloodied and torn, and he was spouting soul saving?

"Skori don't have souls, and they don't negotiate. If you send an expedition north, you'll get your people back in little bits and pieces."

I turned my back on him. The man was hopeless. If the savagery of the attack hadn't convinced him, for all I cared, he could hide his head in the sand long enough for some Skori to come and cut it off.

If I didn't do it first.

"Your Majesty, how do you feel?"

"Lady Riona, you have my gratitude." Ambrose took my good hand in both of his. He drew a deep breath, as if drawing clean air for the first time in months. "I could feel the tentacles of corruption winding deeper and deeper into me, but I could do nothing to stop it."

"When did it start?"

He looked away, a frown coming to his brow.

"The night I was informed of the deaths of my sons."

"A door was opened," Finnegan said.

We both turned to look at Finnegan. He stood close at my side, probably ready to catch me when I keeled over. The blood was trickling to a halt, but the loss was making itself felt. Dizziness clouded my vision, the darkness of unconsciousness threatening to overwhelm me.

"Counselor Branigan was able to plant the seeds of darkness, using your sorrow as the way in," Finnegan continued.

"God has seen fit to save you, Your Majesty."

Langley really was a pain in the ass. I knew for a fact that his God had nothing to do with the king's restoration, but I wasn't going to get into an argument of semantics with a fanatic. I'd done that in the past with Langley, when he was but a lowly monk. So long ago. He'd only gotten worse over the years.

The look King Ambrose gave Bishop Langley told me that he wasn't buying that, either. Good man.

"Before the death of your sons, the rumors of violence and death you chased across your land had a foundation of truth, as you can see, Your Majesty." I gave Langley a cold look before I turned away from him. I hurt too much to give him much attention. It was becoming an effort to remain on my feet.

From behind me, I felt waves of hatred emanating off the so-called holy man. Though tempted to teach this miscreant a lesson, I was not here to educate rude imbeciles. Langley would be dealt with if and when he got in my way. I had little doubt he would in the very near future.

"Where is my daughter?"

The question threw me for a moment. Given his recent state, I was surprised Ambrose was even aware of the fact Merry was gone. Now he was staring at me with clear eyes. The eyes of a father who had lost everything and who was now grasping at what was left.

"Your daughter is safe."

King Ambrose sighed, relief in the exhalation. Despite my weakness, my curiosity was aroused. According to Merry, she was being used to attract the highest bidder in the marriage mart. The look on Ambrose's face told me that his affections for his daughter ran deep. With all the political games played by the nobility, was it possible that Ambrose had been concealing the depth of his love for Merry? Something I had to think on at a later date. Right now I had to figure out what kind of damage control was necessary.

How long had the king been in his debilitated state? I had known Merry for only a bit over two weeks. Going by the damage I'd witnessed, King Ambrose had been mentally incapacitated for a couple of months, at least. What edicts or commands had been issued during that time? And by whom? My glance flickered to Langley. Him? A very disturbing thought. Or by the recently deceased Austin Brannigan? Again, disturbing. How long had Brannigan acted as a host to the Skori? More questions without answers.

"Merry is presently under Guest Rights with Queen Tesina of the Sithi."

"Thou shalt not suffer a witch to live."

"Oh, puh-leese." I actually rolled my eyes as Langley quoted an old passage from the Bible. "Save it, mortal, for someone who cares."

"With your dark ways, you brought this evil upon us."

"In case it's escaped your notice, I didn't come out of that fight unscathed."

"This is a Sithi trick to lull us into trusting you."

"Enough!"

King Ambrose bellowed out the order, causing us to fall silent. I could feel color rising in my cheeks. Light! Here I was indulging in a petty argument—again!—with a Bible thumper. I knew better than this.

"Forgive me, Your Majesty." Langley made an elegant bow.

I clenched my teeth with frustration. Here I stood, sliced and diced, while he stood there in all his pristine glory. Sometimes there wasn't any justice in the world.

Ambrose gave us both a glare, again reassuring me that the man I knew was in full control. I merely inclined my head with respect. I answered only to My Lady and my queen. Descendant though he might be, the laws of a mortal held no sway over my actions.

"As I was saying, Your Majesty, Merry is safe. She was injured in an encounter with a band of Skori."

"How badly?"

"Bad enough that she could not travel." I hedged my answer. The last time I'd seen Merry, she'd still been unconscious, but our healers had reassured me she was slowly recovering.

I felt rather than saw Finnegan's glance, but he remained silent.

"She is now my heir. She must be returned to Newland."

"When she is able, and when it is safe."

Ambrose appeared to consider my words. As a rule, Sithi did not lie, but we'd long mastered twisting the truth. I didn't know if he was aware of young Louis Sterling's survival, but I wasn't about to bring up his presence here in the palace. There were too many ears.

"You say she is under Guest Rights?"

"Correct."

"Then she will be safe within your borders."

Finnegan stirred at my side, drawing attention to himself. "I would not be so sure of that, Your Majesty."

All eyes turned his way. Looking more closely at him, I noticed he had not completely escaped injury during the battle with the Skori. There was a cut across his cheek, and his tunic was stained with what I hoped was my blood. As far as I could tell, Finnegan didn't have the self-healing abilities of a Sithi.

"Why do you say that, wizard?"

"I fear the Dark Master may have reached all levels of our world. Even the Lakelands may not be completely safe."

I wanted to argue with him, but I couldn't. Personally, I would rather he hadn't brought up the possible danger. The breach in our security already had too many people aware of it. It would have been best to keep it from King Ambrose, particularly within the hearing range of Langley.

"My queen pledged Merry's safety. She is far better protected there than with us." I had to believe that. "We came here to see to your health, Your Majesty. And to determine whether the Skori have penetrated your borders. Evidently they have."

"Princess Merry will be returned shortly?"

The question came from Bishop Langley, something in his voice capturing my attention. Suspicion sharpened my senses, and I did another sweep of his emotions.

It was an intrusion of privacy, but I had no qualms when it came to the bishop. I had sensed the depth of his interest earlier whenever Merry's name was mentioned, an interest that far exceeded that of a man of God intent on saving a soul.

His interest was unacceptable, as far as I was concerned.

Over the centuries, a lot had changed with the mortal Church. Their priests and monks were allowed to marry, but they were held to strict morals. I had no problem with the sex part, but the thought of someone like Langley lusting after one of my descendants was nauseating.

"She is not for you." I used a touch of magic to whisper the words in his ear, excluding the others in the room. The bishop's face paled as he swung his attention back to me, knowledge blooming in his eyes when he realized I was aware of his passion for Merry. "She will never be yours."

Black hatred flared to life in his eyes, drowning out any lust or even fear. Langley had been my opponent for years. Now he was my enemy.

Chapter Twenty-three

Gazing into the bottom of my nearly empty tankard, I made a face. I knew better than to use alcohol to try to deaden my senses. It didn't work. Sithi weren't particularly susceptible to fermented drink. Still, after I don't know how many tankards of ale, I was carrying a faint buzz. Better than what I usually achieved. The owner of the establishment was certainly delighted with the amount of coin I was parting with.

The pub I was sitting in was rough, smoky, and loud. Perfect. Just what I needed at this moment. We'd been in conference with the king and, unfortunately, Langley, for hours, discussing the situation, making and discarding numerous plans.

The only thing I revealed about Merry was that she was safe and in the care of Queen Tesina. I thought it best not to let her father know how badly she'd been wounded. I did tell them my opinion that Merry was somehow a catalyst to the events that were occurring, but that I could not fathom in what way. The Dark Master wanted her for some reason, but I had yet to determine what.

I would have much preferred the absence of Langley, but he'd been adamant in being present. With the destruction of Branigan, the miasma of darkness surrounding the bishop had dissipated somewhat. In the end, he had added a few pertinent thoughts to the discussion. Much as I hated to admit it, some of his input might prove helpful. Eventually.

Glancing around the dingy pub, I sighed. There were maybe a dozen patrons here, male and female, most of them rough-looking. While Canada City was a prosperous city, there were always the more questionable characters to be found. The Gray Goose was just one gathering place for them. It was off the beaten track and in need of a good cleaning. Maybe even a fumigating. A place I could remain incognito.

I'd renewed my glamour, making minor changes to appear more threatening than the young man I'd portrayed at the palace. I didn't need anyone noticing I was Sithi and, bolstered by drink, challenging me. It'd happened in the past and never came out well for the human.

My all-but-closed wounds still ached and itched. That tended to make one irritable. A mood that suited me perfectly. The constant fussing of my companions had soured what remained of my temper. Listening to the snide remarks made by the bishop had pushed me to the limit, and the way Finnegan and the Cascadians had been hovering over me had caused me to flee the palace in search of peace.

Kai and Crispin had elected to stay at the palace. As representatives of Cascadia, they had a duty to their ruler. Meetings with King Ambrose along with various members of his cabinet were being arranged. But Kai had assured me he would keep his eyes and ears open for any hint of further Skori infiltration.

Though King Ambrose had tried to convince Finnegan and me to remain at the palace, I'd felt the need to return to our lodgings. But once there, I'd found myself too restless to stay.

Something was going to happen tonight. I just didn't know what.

While Finnegan had been freshening up, I'd escaped out the back door of the Wayfarer's Inn and made my way to the Gray Goose, finally achieving a measure of peace and quiet. The wizard was going to be very unhappy with me, but at this point, I just didn't care.

As I raised my tankard to my lips, someone settled at my table. Glancing up, I saw a figure shrouded in a cloak. The scent of fresh flowers reached my nose, and I frowned. A woman.

"I don't recall inviting you to join me." My tone was deliberately threatening. After the day I'd had, I did not want company in any shape or form. If this was a doxy, she was in for disappointment. Another glance at the cloak dispelled that notion. It was way too fine.

Peering into the depths of the hood, I could not penetrate the shadows concealing her features. Extending my senses, I ran into a blank wall.

"Riona."

Shock held me immobile for an instant before I allowed my mug to drop to the table with a solid *thunk*. It tipped over, and the remainder of my drink dribbled onto the scarred wood. I hardly noticed.

"My Lady." The words came out in a strangled whisper. Color swept my face as I recalled my earlier thoughts.

Two white hands raised and pushed back the hood of green velvet. Once again, I was staring into the beauty of My Lady. Her rich russet hair fell about her shoulders, crowned with wild flowers and leaves. Her clear blue eyes held mine with warmth and love.

This was the first time She'd ever come to me in the flesh. Always before it was in dreams or a Vision. Never this way. I wanted to reach out and touch her, to see if she was really here, but I didn't dare.

I dropped my gaze to my hands. My fingers were gripping each other so tightly the blood was squeezed out of them. I'd been incredibly rude.

"Forgive me, My Lady. I did not know it was you who joined

me."

"There is nothing to forgive, Riona." Her words were a soothing balm on my nerves. "I cannot linger, my child. Time is racing."

"What happened?"

"We have been betrayed. One of my own has chosen to follow my Dark Brother."

I steeled myself. "Who?"

"Dylan."

Dylan? I sat stunned for a long moment. No! Not Dylan. Not the only family I had left from when I'd been human. Deep within my heart, a part of me cried out. Another part was not surprised. I'd known that Dylan was unhappy. Had known for a couple of centuries. But this? To betray, to scheme and open his heart to darkness?

"My Lady." There was a note of begging in my voice, of rising despair. Pain ripped through me, leaving me beyond pride. I didn't want to believe this. "Please, tell me you are mistaken. Please. I beg of you."

Her beautiful face was sad and hard at the same time. Compassion for me, fury for the one who'd turned.

"My brother boasted of his conversion. I searched, but I cannot see into his heart, Riona. It is closed to me."

"Which points to his guilt." I said the words with a listless acceptance.

He was my brother's son ... my human brother's son. The only survivor of my family from the plague that had taken so many from me. During the Dream so long ago, he had chosen to follow the path of Our Lady, to become Sithi. His turning had been a spark of joy in my life when my second husband had died and I'd been forced to turn from my children to save myself the pain of watching them age and die as well. Dylan had been at my side, my support, my bastion of strength.

"Yes."

That one word shuddered through me, and I closed my eyes. The interior of the Gray Goose receded from my consciousness. The raucous laughter and voices raised in argument meant nothing to me. I wanted to crawl into a dark corner and curl around my despair.

My nephew. I'd known Dylan when he was Daniel John Starsky. I'd watched him grow up, become a man. He'd been with me when the plague had struck, helping me bury first my husband and then my two children. Together we'd nursed and eventually buried his parents, my parents, my other siblings. Our lives were tied together in ways totally incomprehensible to any other.

"There is no doubt?" I reached out an imploring hand, not quite touching her, wanting to. Realizing what I was doing, I pulled back and hugged myself around the waist, rocking back and forth. The pain was tearing me apart. "He is Sithi. Can you not turn him back?"

"Once my brother is chosen, there is no going back. You are always given choice, my child." Her voice caused me to look up, gazing into her compassionate eyes through a veil of tears. They were so deep and wise. I knew they were looking into my soul, seeing my confusion, my agony.

"You chose to follow me, and you have done so without question, my darling Riona. Dylan—" Her face hardened for an instant. "No, he is Dylan no more. Daniel also chose to follow me, but he chafed under my rules and requirements. Because of his arrogance, I have always limited his magic. I fear I may have misjudged, child, and he has allowed himself to be seduced by my brother."

"Why wait until now? Why serve you for a thousand years and then turn to darkness?"

"My brother grows strong. He is recruiting followers, both

human and Sithi. The Sithi he gains will become his generals, his leaders. He is a master of lies and seduction. His arsenal is vast. His temptations great."

"But to tempt Dylan …"

"He gained Daniel for a purpose, Riona."

I went still as her words washed over me. Pushing aside my pain, I tried to think. What purpose could the Dark Master have to seduce a Sithi of moderate power?

Dylan … no, Daniel, could have been an ancient, an elder but for the restrictions Our Lady imposed upon him. Had that fact chafed at him all these centuries? Had he felt cheated in some way? My Lady accepted all who chose her, but I knew she limited the degree of power given to those whose character she found unworthy of Her full grace.

Daniel had been hotheaded as a boy, somewhat demanding and selfish as a man. When he'd chosen to follow Our Lady, I had been elated. I would never be completely alone. Deep down, I'd always known he hadn't earned all the Lady's gifts, but I'd never wanted to admit it. Doing so would mean I'd have to admit that he should have remained human. I'd wanted this choice to be the right one. To never lose another loved one.

What use would the Dark Master have for a Sithi of moderate power? Power that My Lady had withdrawn? I went still.

"Me," I whispered as realization struck and new pain ripped through me. Fear accompanied it. There were few things I feared, but to attract the personal attention of the Dark Master was enough to make the strongest quake. "Your brother wants me."

"Yes, Riona. My brother seeks to either convert or destroy you."

Danae reached across the small distance separating us and put a hand beneath my chin to raise my face to again meet her gaze. It was the first time My Lady had ever physically touched me. Her hand was soft, warm. A thread of power traveled from her hand to my chin, spreading slowly over my face and down my neck to permeate my body. Some of my pain and fear receded, leaving behind a measure of peace that allowed me to think more clearly.

"Why? Why would your brother seek me?"

"Can you not guess, Riona?"

A brilliant light surrounded My Lady for a moment, green with the power of all growing things of the health of the earth and the strength of the sun. A quick glance around the pub showed no one was paying any particular attention to us. We were within our own protective sphere. Some of the dinginess seemed to have vanished under the presence of My Lady. The patrons were less raucous and more reflective.

"You are my prize, Riona. When you chose to follow me, I knew you would be my greatest Sithi."

That brought my focus back to her.

"Tesina ..."

"Sits on the throne because you declined to do so. Tesina is an able leader, but she is not the true ruler. You, Riona, are the true ruler of the Sithi."

"I never wanted to rule."

"I know. Which is why the matter was never pressed. But now your hand is forced, my child. Tesina will not be able to hold back the darkness. She is not strong enough, nor does she have the right. Only you can lead the Sithi to aid the humans in this hour of need."

I shuddered as the dread sank deep into my soul. I didn't want this. I didn't want to rule. I wanted to remain unfettered by the restrictions of rule.

I realized this was exactly what Meredith Sterling had felt when I'd pointed out her destiny. How arrogantly I had waved off her objections. How childish I was now acting. My Lady said we always had choices, but sometimes choices were thrust upon us and we had to take up the challenge or all was lost. Ultimately, my choice as to whether or not to rule had just been taken from me by the Dark Brother and with the knowledge that all might be lost if I did not choose to rule.

I'd always known Tesina was an adequate ruler but not a strong one. She and I had never seen eye to eye. Her out of jealousy, me out of an unconscious disdain. She handled the rule of the Sithi in a manner lacking in true leadership. She could not and would not lead the Sithi to help the humans. Her threat to close our borders showed that. Even though after the Dark Master defeated the humans, He would turn His attention on our people. She refused to acknowledge the danger that threatened both of our races. Her shortsightedness could cost us the world and all we loved.

My Lady's strength continued to seep into me, slowly, in a steady stream. I realized she was infusing me with the strength of the Sithi far beyond what she'd ever bestowed on any other.

I gazed into her gentle eyes, saw my realization reflected there.

"Yes, Riona," she said in a soft voice, the tone caressing my nerves and calming my sudden fear. "I am bestowing my full strength upon you. My one worthy child. You will have the ability to call my magic whenever you desire and feel no weakness, no fatigue."

"Why?"

"Because you must be strong to face the armies of my brother. He will not expect me to do this."

"Will he not also give strength to a chosen champion?"

"No. My brother is very possessive of his power. He does not willingly share it. Why do you think his people are magically weaker than mine? He relies upon their brute strength rather than share his magic."

I could feel the magic coursing through my veins, stronger and stronger. It bordered on pain as it crested and fell, adapting me to accept the full scope of My Lady's magic. I could actually feel the cells of my body adjusting, evolving. Looking down where our hands were clasped, I saw my own reshape itself slightly, appearing more slender, graceful. There was a pearlescent glow to my skin, one that traveled up my arms. Heat rose up my chest and into my face.

A particularly strong wave broke over me, my body snapping upright, my spine arching as I drew in a gasping breath. My last sight of My Lady was her gentle yet satisfied smile.

Then I became a creature of magic. No longer true Sithi ... something else.

Chapter Twenty-four

When I came to, I was face-down on the table with a full tankard clutched in my hand. For a long moment, I didn't move, trying to assess my physical state. Dizzy, yes. Disoriented, that was there. Ill, most definitely. Every nerve ending in my body tingled, zapping me with little sparks of electrical currents. Every inch of my skin felt sensitized, any aches and pains remaining from my wounds gone, as if they'd never happened.

Opening my eyes, I stared at the scarred wood inches away as I relived those last moments with My Lady. There had been a flash of light, searing pain, and then nothing. I could feel her magic running through my veins. I felt drunk—something I hadn't experienced in eons.

What had she done to me?

Blinking several times, I gathered my wits to raise my head. The dim room swam before coming into focus. For a moment, there was a sense of vertigo. My elven sight was sharper yet. The shadows held no secrets, and I could see the tiny spider weaving a web in the deep gloom of a far corner of the room. The dinginess of the Gray Goose was made even more so with this augmented eyesight, the dust and grime coming into startling clarity as I looked around.

Memory slammed into me. Holding up my hands, I could see that they still glowed with that pearlescent gleam. Concentrating, I was able to dim the light until my skin looked almost normal.

What other physical changes had been wrought upon me? Touching my face, everything felt normal, but there was a new leanness that I hadn't possessed previously. I didn't have my mirror, so I couldn't check.

My gaze went to the chair opposite me.

I was alone at my table. My Lady was gone. Had that been another Vision? A dream?

Everything appeared much as it had been moments before. Had it only been moments? Looking around, I was pretty sure I was missing a chunk of time. It was still night, but the patrons were in a deeper state of inebriation. The laughter was louder, more raucous. The few light-skirts were openly plying their services, displaying their wares to potential customers. The dice game going on in the corner had a new group of players, and the drinkers arguing at the bar had several additions.

By my reckoning, better than an hour had passed.

Glancing at the tankard still in my hand, I started to raise it to my lips, then hesitated. My cup had been empty just before My Lady had come to me. Had an enterprising waitress refilled it, or had My Lady provided it to restore my senses?

Sniffing it with care, I could not detect anything foreign added to it.

"Go ahead. I didn't put anything in it," came a voice behind me. "It's perfectly safe."

My shoulders stiffened, but I didn't turn. I knew that voice. Why wasn't I surprised my nephew had tracked me down in this little hole-in-the-wall pub? There was a sense of inevitability to this confrontation. Perhaps it was what I'd been expecting all evening.

I left the drink untouched and twisted in my seat to find Daniel a scant meter behind me, leaning against the wall, arms crossed in an indolent pose. He straightened and came around the table, turning the opposite chair around before he straddled it. His expression was open, friendly. No different from the countless times we'd shared a drink in a pub over the centuries.

Easing my cloak to one side, I surreptitiously loosened my sword from its scabbard. Whatever he wanted, I didn't think he meant to kill me. Not yet, anyway. If that were his intent, he'd had the opportunity to slip a blade between my ribs before I'd regained consciousness.

"I don't recall inviting you to sit down."

"Not even for a little family reunion?"

"You're no longer my family."

"Ah, She told you. My Master told me She would." Reaching for the tankard, I deliberately upended it into the rushes covering the floor. I set it down with more force than necessary, and there was a sound of finality to it.

"Why?" My composure slipped, and the single word came out in an agonized whisper.

Daniel gave me a lopsided grin, one I was so familiar with. One I'd seen since he was a little boy. My heart shattered a little more.

"How 'bout power? A little old-fashioned ambition?"

"You sold your soul to the devil."

"Isn't that a bit melodramatic? The way I see it, I exchanged one taskmaster for another. One who can give me more power than you can imagine, auntie dear."

"Don't call me that. You abdicated that right. You are no longer Dylan, nor are you Daniel. What do you call yourself?"

"Damon. It has a nice ring to it, don't you think?"

Appropriate. A close association with the word *demon*.

He leaned closer, peering into my face.

"What happened to your eyes? They're different. When you changed into an elf, they were that weird aqua-blue. Now there's a ring of gold around them."

News to me, but I said nothing, just continued to stare at him. I'd already noticed his eyes. They were an obsidian-black.

Physical proof of his own alliance.

My fingers curled around the smooth handle of my sword, and I gathered my magic, feeling it rise from my core in a nova of power. As far as I was concerned, there was no need for an intervention or trial. Once turned to Skori, there was no going back. Damon was now my enemy.

Magic traveled over my skin, tingling with a strength I'd never felt before. Next to this power, my sword was superfluous.

"I wouldn't do that, Riona." He shook off his fascination with my eyes. "If you look around, you'll notice that I have my men positioned at various points in the room. They have orders to slaughter every human if you make any threatening moves."

That froze me. Carefully, I scanned the dingy room with my newfound ability. In the deepest shadows, I found shapes too large to be human. Two were seated at remote tables, another standing beyond the reach of the candlelight, and a fourth near the doorway. A trick of the light caused more than one pair of red eyes to glow in the darkness. How had they entered without my knowing? I should have sensed their foulness immediately.

Reining in my power, I sat back. There was little doubt he would do it.

"Smart girl."

"What do you want?"

"Join me."

For a moment, I stared at him. Stupefied. Then I laughed in his face. Did he truly expect me to mindlessly betray everything I was because he asked it? His face darkened with anger as I continued to laugh. Using amusement as a cover, I built a very subtle spell and sent it throughout the room. A tiny whisper would sound in the ear of every human, telling them it was time to go home. Near the bar, three friends finished up their drinks and tossed coins onto the counter. With much laughter and argument, they staggered to the door and vanished into the night. One of the light-skirts tugged at the arm of her mark, and together they left for her dwelling.

Careful to keep my attention on him, I leaned forward to brace my elbows on the table.

"You have got to be kidding."

"You have no idea of the power the Dark Master possesses. What He has to offer."

Damon leaned closer, an urgency in his expression, tension in his voice. This close, I could see a sheen of sweat covering his face, could feel his eagerness. This close, I could also smell the air of foulness that surrounded him. His corruption. It made my stomach turn and my anger burn brighter, but I controlled it. I had to keep him talking.

"Besides lies and betrayal?"

"I've been charged with contacting you …"

"Recruiting, don't you mean?"

"Okay, recruiting."

"Save it. Not interested."

So far Damon appeared unaware of the trickle of humans leaving the pub. I'd timed the spell to home in on a few mortals at a time so there was no grand exodus. Little by little, people finished up their drinks and began to wander out of the pub. The bartender gathered up an armful of dirty mugs and made his way into the kitchen.

I kept my focus on Damon. It was easy to view him with all the dispassionate disdain that I felt. I'd had time to absorb the pain of his betrayal. Was able now to see him only as the traitor he was. Besides the color of his eyes, there were already other changes taking place. Subtle so far. Tendrils of darkness surrounded him, and he was losing that graceful Sithi look we were blessed with, his features already taking on the brutish cast of the Skori. I had the feeling he wouldn't change completely —he was destined to be one of the Dark Brother's generals. He could not be allowed to become one of their mindless hordes.

"C'mon, Rowena ..."

"That's Riona to you," I snapped. "You've lost all right to use my True Name." Making a slight gesture with my fingers, I enacted a spell that would make it impossible for him to repeat my True Name. With the full power of My Lady behind me, the spell was a simple one. A mere flick of my wrist.

An ugly smile twisted his lips as his dark eyes gleamed with malice.

"I'll call you whatever I wish, Row ..."

My name was choked off as he gasped for breath, his voice dying as his throat closed. I watched him struggle for breath for nearly a full minute before I tied off the spell. He slumped to the table, struggling to draw in gulps of air.

The shadows stirred, but I ignored them. I had each Skori pinpointed. I'd know the instant they moved. And I was ready.

I leaned closer, until our faces were inches away. "You will be unable to say my True Name. You will be unable to write it down or even think it. Each time you attempt to do so, your throat will close for a little while longer. I estimate you will be able to attempt it at least five times before your throat is closed permanently."

"You are breaking Your Lady's covenant." The breath he drew was harsh, his voice rough as he looked up at me. The hatred in his eyes should have shocked me, but knowing what he now was and what he was capable of ... No, I was beyond shock.

A worm of pain again wound its way into my heart, but I steeled myself against it. His choice had been made. My nephew would not hesitate to serve me up to my enemies, preferably with an apple in my mouth.

"My Lady does not advocate senseless killing. But she does allow us to kill our enemies."

"I'm not your enemy, Row— Riona." Urgency colored his words as he leaned closer, cutting off his use of my name when I raised one brow. I'd told him the truth. The spell I'd placed upon him would eventually kill him if he betrayed my True Name again. Wise of him to realize that.

It also made me realize who'd given my True Name to Brother Thomas. Was it also Damon's behind-the-scenes work that had nearly destroyed King Ambrose? And what of Langley? The miasma of darkness that had hovered over him, looking for a way in. Was this all attributed to Damon? As good of a guess as any.

"We can work together, Riona," he went on, his voice still low and urgent. "My Master can give us the world. All you have to do is deny Your Lady and follow Him."

I couldn't believe he was doing this. "You're mad," I whispered. The stench of his corruption again permeated the air, turning my stomach. It was the scent of decay. "Can you even hear your own words?"

"I know that Your Bitch has used us for centuries, giving us useless tasks and hard labor with little or no reward. She has allowed these puny mortals to persecute us while she did nothing. We are far superior to them. They're nothing but a blight upon this world."

"Have you forgotten that you were once human?" I knew there was no way to change him back to what he once had been. He had made his choice. The fanatical light in his eyes spoke of wholehearted loyalty.

"I try to forget what I was, Riona. A helpless, mewling mortal who mindlessly followed a god who cared nothing for us. I thought with choosing the Goddess, I would be given unlimited power."

"If it was power you wanted, why didn't you choose the black door?"

He looked away for an instant, and I drew my breath, afraid he'd notice the absence of humans. When he again met my gaze, I saw nothing to indicate his awareness.

"I was too afraid. Then. What I didn't know was I'd exchanged one life of servitude for another when I chose the green door."

"Don't play stupid. There was never any secret of our mission when we turned Sithi. Our duty was to clean up the mess left behind by the Industrial Age. Once that was accomplished, we were free to do as we wished."

"Are you free, Riona? Will Your Bitch release you from her servitude?"

I couldn't respond. I knew She wouldn't. She'd revealed to me that my destiny was to take up the reins of rule, and with that final task, I would never be completely free. Something within me had always known this but struggled against it. Now? Necessity was forcing my hand, and I was prepared to do my duty.

"You can't even deny it, can you?"

"I know what I must do, Damon. Do you?"

Movement at the door captured my attention, and I glanced up to see Finnegan appear. Shock held me immobile for an instant. What was he doing here? For that matter, how had he found me?

With a fatalistic inevitability, I watched him pocket a small blue crystal as he started toward my table. He carried his staff with him, but the stone on the end was dull and silent.

I didn't want him here. I didn't want him anywhere near Damon or the several Skori scattered throughout the room.

A quick glance around showed the last pair of mortals leaving through the front door, and satisfaction hummed through me. At least they were safe.

Now if we could get out in one piece. I had few illusions left after listening to Damon. Once he realized there was no way I was ever going to turn, he'd kill me. And no doubt take Finnegan with me.

As this thought crossed my mind, Damon followed my glance, and his face lit with satisfaction.

"Ah, the lover. You really are slumming it, aren't you, Riona?

Granted, a wizard is a step up, but still ..."

I didn't bother to respond, watching as Finnegan scanned the room, his eyes pausing on the deeper shadows before he started toward us. His hand slipped back into his pocket.

With my newfound level of magic, I sensed his caution as he took in the situation. Nothing showed in his face as he crossed the room and pulled up another chair.

"Sorry I'm late," he said as if I'd been expecting him. Removing his gray cloak, he folded it over the back of his chair before arranging himself with his back to the wall, his staff cradled in his arms. The position gave him an unimpeded view of the room. By now, there were no humans left in the Gray Goose. Even the bartender had found a reason to vacate the premises.

"A messenger arrived at the inn about an hour ago. I knew you were waiting for word."

I had no idea what he was talking about but let nothing show in my face. Instead, I watched Damon's expression. The flash of confusion was brief before he concealed it behind a mask of confidence.

"So you're Riona's pet human."

Finnegan snorted. "Hardly a pet. I have more uses than that. I don't believe we've been formally introduced. I'm Finnegan."

"Damon."

"Ah ..." Finnegan's glance cut to me for an instant before he returned it to the man to his left. "Formerly Daniel and formerly Dylan. Now what? Chief toady?"

A snort of laughter nearly escaped. I couldn't believe my ears. Finnegan was actually baiting a minion of the Dark Master. I would have been more worried if I hadn't noticed the spark of color that appeared in the stone at the tip of his staff. I'd seen that magic in action. It was a formidable defense. Plus, there was that stone he'd stashed in his pocket earlier. I wasn't sure what type of power that gave him, but if it was anything like the stone he kept on his staff, it gave him an extra measure of protection. I hoped. I got the feeling we were going to need it.

Damon's face darkened with anger before Finnegan's contempt, and he started to say something when one of his Skori grunted something from the shadows. The sound was loud in the silence of the room.

Whatever it was, it caused Damon to glance around, for the first time realizing the inn was nearly empty.

"Very clever, Riona. Do you actually think this is the extent of my army? I have Skori situated throughout the city. One signal from me and they attack anything that moves. It'll be a wholesale slaughter."

Did I believe him? Did I dare take a chance? I sent out a pulsating wave. An hour ago, I couldn't have done this, but now, with the blessing of My Lady, my power enabled me to search the city and pinpoint any threats. My senses swept over the city, searching for those foul pockets of life that would betray a Skori.

And found nothing.

"Nice try. Beyond the four in here and the two inside the alley to the west, there are no other Skori in the city."

Damon paled an instant before anger replaced his stunned expression. A flash of red appeared in his eyes, making them glow.

"Kill them!"

I sprang out of my seat. Using the momentum, I grabbed the edge of the heavy table and flung it into Damon. It crashed into him and drove him to the dingy floor. I didn't wait to see if he was injured. Drawing my sword with one hand, I pulled at the tie securing my cloak and flung it from my shoulders to give myself freedom to move.

Out of the corner of my eye, I caught the flow of shadows and turned in time to see the four Skori converging on us.

Whirling, I went into a defensive crouch. I felt rather than saw

Finnegan move behind me, and a flash of blue light streaked past me and caught one of the Skori in the chest. The creature screamed, the sound echoing in my ears as the light consumed it. When the blaze faded, there was nothing left.

Another Skori came at me, and I ran my blade through it. The steel slid between the plates of hardened leather covering its chest, piercing the creature in the heart. No finesse necessary. This was survival.

Something solid barreled into me, slamming me against the wall with a force that cracked the plaster. My sword flew from my hand, skittering across the floor to disappear beneath a table. The weight behind me pinned me to the wall, my face pressed against the rough surface.

Even without my blade, I was far from helpless. One of my greatest advantages was that neither Damon nor Saytan were aware My Lady had infused me with the full scope of her power. The magic I had to call was far beyond anything any Sithi had possessed in the past.

Fetid breath bathed the side of my face as it tried to wrap clawed hands around my throat. The Skori at my back was going to rip out my throat. Putting my hands against the wall, I levered myself to arm's length and got one leg up against the wall. Using all my strength, I pushed against the wall, slamming against the creature. We both flew backward, over a table, and into the large hearth, where a fire still blazed.

The Skori took the full force of the fall, landing among the burning logs. It screamed as flames licked at its flesh, the clawed grip loosening enough for me to pull free. Turning within its arms, I grasped its head and slammed it against the stone wall at the back of the hearth. There was a crack as its skull shattered, and its grip fell away from me.

Heat licked at me, and I leaped back, scrambling out of the hearth as the flames consumed the dead Skori. Drawing a deep breath, I nearly gagged. The stench was overpowering. The movement shot pain through my throat. I put a hand to my neck, and my fingers came away with blood. The scratches were shallow, but they stung like hell. It beat a torn throat.

Finnegan!

Whirling around, I searched the room. Where was Finnegan? I'd been so intent on the Skori attacking me that I'd lost track of the other combatants. There was movement behind an upturned table, and a Skori rose, blood splattered across its upper chest and face. Its eyes glowed red as it looked at me, and horror held me immobile. Whose blood was that?

I managed one step forward when a flash of blue light shot up from behind the table and caught the Skori in the head. For an instant, the creature was illuminated in a halo of blue before it disappeared.

With a low cry, I scrambled over fallen chairs, flinging them out of my way, and rounded the table, my heart pounding. Finnegan lay crumbled on the ground, covered with blood. So much blood.

But he was alive.

Dropping to his side, I carefully turned him until he lay on his back. The movement caused him to bite back a sharp cry, his lips pulling back in a grimace of pain. I was relieved when his eyes opened.

"Where is he?" he asked. His voice was breathy, causing me to frown.

"Who?"

"Damon."

I looked around. Stupid of me to let my guard down. Searching the shadows, I found nothing. I sent out my senses, but I couldn't feel him. Unless he had the ability to cloak himself, he was far from here.

"I think he's gone."

"I managed to wound him before that Skori caught me from behind." He moved his head, and a thin stream of blood escaped the corner of his mouth.

"Lie still."

"I don't plan on moving." His words were ground out from between clenched teeth. "How bad is it?"

As I pulled back the blood-soaked front of his tunic, I sucked in a sharp breath.

His chest was a ruined mess. Deep scratches marred his body from neck to belly, exposing torn muscles and tendons. A rib poked through his skin, glistening with blood. By the sound of his breathing, I knew one of his lungs was punctured.

"It's bad, isn't it?"

"Yeah."

No sense in sugarcoating it. The man was far from stupid. A sense of despair swept over me as I assessed the full extent of his injuries. They were far beyond my healing capabilities. I was going to lose him.

"Here."

His voice was faint, strained. I looked into his pale face, saw the knowledge in his eyes. Glancing down at his hand, I caught the gleam of blue. The small crystal glowed. Deep within the jewel, a light pulsed. It took me a moment to realize it was throbbing in time with his heart. As I watched it, the light stuttered, dimmed, and then brightened.

A spark of hope flared to life. Curling his fingers around it, I brought his closed fist up to his chest. If there was ever a time for his One God to take a stand, this was it.

Inhaling, I centered myself, drawing on the magic from deep within. When I opened my senses to the power, it swept over me in a torrent. Its strength took me by surprise and nearly made me lose control. How could I have forgotten the additional power My Lady had graced upon me? It was a wave that threatened to overwhelm me as I rode it out.

That tiny spark of hope flared brighter. Would it be enough?

Closing my eyes, I wrestled with the wild magic, allowing it to ebb and flow as I learned the full scope of its strength. Strain tightened my muscles as I fought to bring it under control, to master it. The ugly little room receded as light and power filled me to the point of pain. Little needles of agony stabbed into my flesh, feeling like volts of electricity dancing along my nerve endings.

In the midst of the smell of blood and death, the scent of fresh flowers touched my nose, and my hands felt hot, the power sweeping from my body to concentrate there. My eyes snapped open, and I looked down. My hands were glowing with a green light. There was an answering flare of light from the blue crystal clutched against Finnegan's chest. The two colors swirled around each other to create a brief vortex before absorbing each other to become a rich shade of turquoise.

The color of my eyes.

Taking a deep breath, I reached out and laid my glowing hands on Finnegan. The light flared for an instant before it sank in his chest. I pressed more firmly, feeling the heat knit together torn flesh and muscle. The freely flowing blood tapered to a halt as the skin healed from the inside out. Concentrating, I urged the cells and platelets to produce new blood, speeding the process as I drew deeper and deeper on the magic flowing through me and into the wizard.

Color came to Finnegan's cheeks, and he drew a deep breath. I was relieved to hear the air pass into his lungs, the sound no longer labored and shallow. His heart beat strong and steady. When his lids fluttered and rose, I could have wept.

Releasing my grip on the magic, I let it dissipate, feeling a wave of weakness wash over me. Fortunately, the effect was temporary, passing almost immediately.

Finnegan stared up at me for a long moment without speaking. The look in his eyes touched something deep within, my body responding to his heated expression. I didn't know if it was the remnants of the magic flowing through me or that special connection that I'd found with the wizard, but it was as if I'd found something precious. Something to be treasured and protected.

Then he blinked, and the moment passed, shattered by reality.

I felt his muscles tense, and I put an arm around him to help him sit up. The slide of his boots on the debris-strewn floor sounded loud in the silent room.

"How do you feel?"

"Good." He paused to look down at himself, the blood still staining his tunic and breeches. "Better than good. I thought you said healing wasn't your specialty."

"I got a little bit of help."

"What happened to your eyes?"

Again with the eyes. I really had to find my mirror.

"Let's just say I was blessed with a little help from My Lady, and this is a side effect."

He continued to stare into my changed eyes a moment longer, a touch of wonder in his own.

"They're beautiful," he murmured, and I felt color rise in my cheeks before I shook it off. We'd just been in a battle to the death, and I was blushing like a child. He must have sensed my thoughts because his gaze left mine to range over the destruction of the pub. Tables and chairs were little more than matchsticks, and there were substantial cracks in the plaster of one of the walls. Courtesy of me being thrown into it.

"They're gone?"

"Yes. Four of the Skori are dead, and Damon has vanished."

"Damn. We need him."

"Why?"

He took my free hand in his, the look in his eyes telling me that I wasn't going to like his next words.

"Merry is missing."

Chapter Twenty-five

I stilled. Merry! I think my heart actually stopped for an instant before the adrenaline kicked in. New tension flowed into my muscles as I unconsciously drew on my magic, feeling it flow into me. This time it was effortless. No wild, uncontrolled flare. The infusion steadied me and allowed me to think past the initial shock.

"What happened?"

I couldn't believe how calm my voice sounded. As if I stood outside myself, my mind assessing the situation, comprehending the potential disaster.

Finnegan held my glance for a long moment. I felt he knew what was going through my mind. He probably did. Despite knowing me for less than a month, the man was astute at reading me.

"A small party arrived at the inn earlier this evening. Led by a Sithi by the name of Captain Joran."

"High in the queen's guard. Second only to Commander Mauren."

"Riona." He hesitated again, his fingers tightening around my hand. "Queen Tesina is dead."

I could only stare at him. Tesina? Dead? My mind was having difficulty wrapping around that.

"How?"

"She was found this morning. Torn to pieces."

"Shit!" A shudder traveled through me. I might have had my differences with Tesina, but I'd never wish such a fate on anyone. She'd been a friend for centuries before our personal disagreements had driven a wedge between us.

"It was in the palace. There was no sign of a break-in or a struggle." His fingers tightened around mine. "No one else was harmed."

"Thank the Lady." I looked down at our linked hands, my stomach twisting. For the first time in a very long time, I felt tears come to my eyes, making no effort to wipe them as they spilled over and tracked down my cheeks. "Poor Tesina."

"Merry had been with her the night before. Joran was on duty and says they'd been talking deep into the night. That was the last Merry was seen. No one saw her leave the palace or the city."

"A search was made?"

"According to Captain Joran, Commander Mauren ordered a house-to-house search, and an accounting for every Sithi was made. Besides Damon, there are about nine Sithi missing or unaccounted for."

"Recruits for the Dark Master?"

"Mauren seems to think so. He spoke with the healers after Merry was discovered missing. Healer Kasia Morninglory informed him that Merry had been keeping company with … Dylan, now Damon."

"Damon!"

"Yes. Two days after we left, she was well enough to get up and move around a bit. Evidently Dylan was her constant companion while she convalesced. Kasia was becoming concerned that his attention may have been a bit … familiar."

"Son of a bitch!"

"She kept a close eye on the situation, but there were times when they disappeared for a while. Something else Kasia mentioned …"

"What?"

"At times, there was a feel of magic surrounding Merry after these outings."

"He enchanted her?"

"Kasia seems to think so, or at least suspect."

Not a difficult magic to perform. But to what end? The contempt Damon showed for his human roots made it clear he'd have little interest in a mortal lover. The thought of his filthy hands on Merry made my stomach clench, and for an instant, I saw red as fury sprang to life. It took me a moment to wrestle it down enough to think clearly.

"As of yesterday, she'd been completely healed and released from the Hall of Healing. According to Joran, either Tesina or Dylan was probably the last one to see her."

"And Tesina is dead." My mind leaped to the obvious conclusion. "Damon knows where she is."

"How long has he been gone?"

Glancing around, I found a small clock on the mantle of the fireplace. The coals had nearly burned themselves out. Only a faint red glow peeked out of a pile of gray ash. The candles lit earlier were melted down to stubs.

"It's nearly four o'clock in the morning." The confrontation and battle had been so short and vicious it seemed more time should have passed.

"He has an hour on us." Finnegan looked around and located his staff. Miraculously, it had escaped damage during his fight with the Skori. "You said earlier at the palace that the Skori used shadows to travel. Much like the Sithi used the mists. He could be anywhere by now."

"Maybe not. As I said, according to My Lady, his master is possessive of his powers. Traveling by shadows must draw a lot of power. Damon may not have the juice to use them again."

"How many Skori would he have with him?"

"Beyond the four we destroyed, he had only two others in the alley. If he had more outside the city, I'm unaware of them."

"Can you track him?"

Earlier this evening, I would have said no. But with the added boost of power provided by My Lady, there was no telling how far my reach was. Only one way to find out.

Centering myself, I sent out my senses, searching for the spoor of evil. It was strongest in the pub, of course, where violence had left a lingering signature. Like a hunting hound, my senses latched on to a trail that led from the pub and into the street, discerned when he'd been joined by the two Skori and had taken off through the streets, heading north. Mentally, I followed the trace until I was certain he had headed for the Northgate.

"Damn, we need to stop back at the inn for our horses."

"They're stabled one street over. I brought your mount when I came in search of you."

"Excellent." I was already heading out the door, pausing only long enough to drop several gold coins into one of the pewter mugs behind the bar. Not much I could do about the damage we'd done to the pub, but the coins should be more than enough to take care of the repairs.

"He has a lead on us, but we should be able to catch up. His Skori will be unable to travel during the daytime hours."

Dawn was close. A faint pearling of light to the east heralded the coming day. This early, we met no one as Finnegan led the way to the stables that housed his mare and Mysteria. The horses were in the first stall just inside the stable doors, still saddled.

"I didn't think we were going to be long, so I didn't have the stableboy bed down the horses. That confrontation with Damon was unexpected."

A rustle of movement overhead caught my attention, and I glanced up to find a bleary-eyed stableboy staring down at us. I could only imagine what he was thinking as he took in our torn and bloody appearance. All sleep left his eyes to be replaced by alarm.

"For your troubles," I said and flipped him a coin to quiet him.

"A Sithi," he whispered in awe.

Finnegan had the horses out of the stall and waiting on the street by the time I joined him. Taking up Mysteria's reins, I swung myself into the saddle. With one last glance up at the slowly lightening sky, I turned my mount north and began following my nose. The taint of evil was still strong on the morning air. Following Damon should be easy.

And when I caught up to him, there was going to be hell to pay.

The city was silent as we passed through, and I drew a deep breath, enjoying this brief respite. The bakers and haulers would be stirring soon, setting up for the day's trade, and the early-morning tradesmen would soon be swarming over the now-deserted streets. The hooves of our horses echoed on the cobblestones, the jingle of their tack loud in the predawn. The air was fresh after the events of the evening.

"Merry isn't the only heir to Newland," I said at last, breaking the silence as we neared the Northgate. My voice was low. Not that I expected anyone to overhear me, but caution had been bred into my bones.

I felt rather than saw his quick glance but kept my attention on the street ahead of us. The streetlights cast pools of light at intervals, their flames flickering within their glass casings. On one side street, I caught a flicker of movement and turned to see a Lighter extinguish the series of lights lining the lane. "Lionel Sterling had a son."

"Louis."

I shot him a glance.

"You know about him?"

"I know of Lionel's son. I assumed he was killed during the Skori attack."

"No. He and his mother are hiding in the palace." Finnegan had to know this in case something happened to me. "Louis is about nine years old."

"And the heir to Newland."

"Correct."

"What use would Damon have with Merry if she isn't the heir?"

"He may not know of Louis's survival. For that matter, the Dark Master may not be aware of his existence." I'd given this quite a bit of consideration. Speaking those thoughts out loud helped coordinate them. Despite what we'd been led to believe, I was pretty sure that the deity siblings weren't all knowing, all seeing. "If that's the case, as heir, Merry would be valuable to them. If they find out Louis is the heir, her usefulness may come to an end."

"And they'd kill her."

"Yes." I pursed my lips. "But there is still the matter of the date of her birth and the significance of the coming century turn. Her usefulness may extend beyond her claim to the Newland throne."

Fear slid over me. Yes, Merry was my descendant and, therefore, family. Beyond that, in the past few weeks, she had become important to me. I'd come to value her as an individual and a friend.

But her importance extended to the fate of Newland. She was vital. That much I sensed. My enhanced magic gave me a feeling that it was imperative we keep her safe. Was it part of the Vision I'd had a couple of weeks ago? Or was it pure instinct?

No way of knowing, at this point.

In short order, we arrived at the Northgate and pulled up at the tall portcullis. It was still shut tight. I glanced to the right.

Through the window of the guardroom, a faint light glowed, the sight warm in the chilled gloom. Beside the window, the small gate stood open, the door ripped off its hinges. There was no sign of the gateman. Staring at the destroyed gate, I had a brief hope he'd fled his post when Damon and the Skori had come through. That hope vanished when I caught sight of a lifeless hand just visible beneath the splintered wood that was once the small gate.

"No time to notify the authorities," Finnegan said as we stared down at the hand. "He'll be found soon enough."

I nodded. Giving the poor man one last glance, I turned Mysteria toward the open gate, ducking down as I rode through. The rough stone on either side brushed against my legs, and the low archway caught at my hair. After about three meters of thick stone, we were on the other side of the guardian walls of Canada City. Walls that rose ten meters in the air and blocked out the lightening sky.

I raised my face to the sky. Unerringly, I sensed the direction the Skori had taken. Their trail led straight north. The Skori were easy to sense, but Damon's trace was a bit more difficult to pinpoint. His was more of a feeling of wrongness. Closing my eyes, I memorized the taint, fairly confident I'd be able to follow Damon wherever he fled.

He was not going to escape me again.

After an hour of hard riding, I couldn't say whether we'd gained any ground on our quarry. They were moving fast. Almost as if they knew they were being pursued. Or determined to beat the lightening skies.

Glancing upward, I tried to gauge the time we had left before the Skori were forced to go to ground. And the question was, where would they go? In open woods, they'd be limited. A farmhouse might do, but that would leave them vulnerable.

Giving it a bit more thought, I stiffened.

The caves of Old New York.

The caves were a perfect place for Damon and the Skori to hole up for the day. Worse yet, deep within the caves and protected from the sunlight, the Skori could continue traveling north without delay.

Not many people were aware of the extensive cave system that existed beneath their feet. How had the Skori discovered one of our greatest treasures so far from their lands? I shook my head. Simple answer.

Damon again.

Although he hadn't been one of the Sithi involved in the restoration, he had to be aware of their existence. And had planned to use it as an escape route.

Without hesitation, I turned Mysteria westward. There were several entrances to the catacombs, some of which were known only to a few. Entrances that Damon would have no knowledge of.

The one I had in mind opened several miles into the caves. With luck, we might come in ahead of him and cut him off.

"They turned west?" Finnegan asked as he followed my lead.

"No." Putting my heels to my mount's flanks, I quickly explained about the caves and my plan to head them off.

"And if their numbers have increased?"

"Then we deal with it when that time comes."

I didn't want to think about the possibility that Damon may have had additional Skori hidden in the caves. The scent I'd been following was that of only a few creatures. There was no hint of greater numbers. But who was to say there weren't more concealed in the protective darkness of the caves?

So many questions. So many possibilities. Most of which I didn't want ... or couldn't deal with right now.

Chapter Twenty-six

I remembered where the entrance was.

Getting in was another matter. Centuries of growth had changed much of the terrain, rendering it unrecognizable.

I stared at the thick foliage that covered the stone of what had once been the skyscrapers of Philadelphia. The caves extended all the way up the East Coast to what was once Hartford, Connecticut. We'd made it a point of connecting the entire system. I think the idea at the time had been to ensure that the Sithi had a place to withdraw to if there was ever a need. However, once we'd come to an agreement with the humans to accept the Great Lakes region as our own, this sanctuary had become unnecessary.

"When was the last time you were here?" Finnegan asked as he watched me pace back and forth in front of the cliff face.

I shot him an annoyed glance. He was sitting on a large boulder, one leg drawn up to his chest, his arm resting on top. He looked as comfortable now as he had a half an hour ago when I'd had to admit my uncertainty.

"What year is this?"

"That's what I thought."

"Centuries do tend to cause a few changes." I turned back to the impenetrable wall of greenery. Sumacs, oaks, maples, thorny blackberry bushes thrown in for good measure ... countless other species of brush that had had nearly a thousand years to grow unhindered now concealed what used to be a bare wall of stone.

"What if it's blocked by a cave-in?"

"It won't be. We used magic to preserve this entrance."

"Can't you use magic to locate it?"

"You're not helping, you know."

"What would you have me do? This is Sithi magic. My spirit magic will do little good."

Something twinged at the back of my mind. Spirit magic. In its own way just as powerful as my nature magic.

"It was a combined spell, using the magic of a dozen Sithi," I murmured as I tried to grasp the significance of my stray thought. Something was …

"Then how was Damon able to get in?"

"I'm not sure. On his own, he should not have been able to. But if the Dark Master gave him aid …"

I trailed off as the sun broke past the low-lying peaks to the east. The morning was well along and a reminder of how much time I was wasting here. Damon and his merry band of creatures were getting farther away with each passing moment.

Putting my fists on my hips, I stared up at the greenery. The mountain range wasn't tall, but in places, it was deep. We'd transformed the old subway system in New York City into a vast underground lake. This section wasn't nearly as deep, but it was a labyrinth of passageways. Unless you knew the way, it was easy to get lost.

If I were lucky, Damon would find himself trapped within the caves.

I glanced again at the lightening sky. Enough wasted time!

Closing my eyes, I narrowed my concentration, closing out the sounds around me, drawing on the peace of the birds heralding the dawn, the gentle breeze that teased my hair where it was loosened from its braid. The faint scent of the ocean miles away. The soft sound of Finnegan's breathing as he waited with infinite patience.

Which made it all the more annoying. Time to try something new. Something I was still hesitant to access.

Centering myself, I found the reservoir of magic that resided deep within me, locating the unfamiliar strength that My Lady had graced me with. It was still too new for me to feel comfortable or to know the total extent of the power. I'd had a sample when I'd healed Finnegan, but I sensed what I'd experienced had been just a teaser. What My Lady had done to me far outstripped anything a Sithi had ever been capable of.

I just wasn't sure what to make of it. Just as I didn't know what to make of the change in my eyes. Finnegan described the outer gold ring and seemed fascinated by it.

Shaking off the thought, I drew on that deep reservoir of power and sent out a probe, feeling my power penetrate the thick foliage and crawl along the stone wall. Like a sonar, it found every crevice and gap in the cliff wall. There had been numerous rockslides during the past centuries, but then my magic struck and resonated off of an impenetrable barrier.

"Ah. There it is," I murmured as I located the entrance. Satisfaction thrummed through me. I should have tried this an hour ago.

Closing my eyes and using a wave of my new magic, I silently asked the centuries of growth to move aside. There was a rustling of movement, and the pathway opened to reveal the archway we'd created so many centuries ago.

At Finnegan's sharply indrawn breath, I opened my eyes to see the doorway etched into the solid stone wall. Graceful vines were carved into the rock, winding up both sides of the doorway and over the top. They were so lifelike it was difficult to tell where the natural vines ended and the Sithi-made ones started.

Finnegan came off his boulder in one smooth movement to stand at my side, his expression intent. The air seemed to be holding its breath; stillness surrounded us. Within the shadows cast by the mountain, the doorway glowed with a power of its own.

"Incredible."

Finnegan's reverent voice drew my attention for an instant before I returned my gaze to the doorway. I'd found the doorway, but without the help of my brethren, would I be able to open it?

Taking a deep breath, I approached the doorway. The power pulsing from it tingled over my skin and ignited my nerve endings. It stood about seven feet high and half as wide. Looking at it, I could see that we'd subconsciously designed it after the door we'd chosen to serve so many centuries ago. That door had been a thing of beauty, and we'd tried to replicate it. By comparison, it was a poor attempt, but even this was pretty damned good.

"I can't do this on my own," I said as the wayward thought I'd had earlier began to jell. This entrance had been created by a dozen of the strongest Sithi combining their magic. With the added power of My Lady and the spirit magic of the wizard, would I be able to do what a dozen Sithi had done? Holding out my hand, I waited until he took it, his warmth spreading from my fingertips to my heart. "I'm going to need your spirit magic."

"It's yours."

No hesitation. No questions. I liked that in a man.

I heard him murmur a prayer under his breath, and I felt the wave of magic that swept over him. Different from mine but some points of similarity. I could tell that it was given through the grace of his One God and that it was drawn from everything spiritual. From there, it branched off in directions I couldn't guess at.

Where our hands were joined, his glowed blue. Calling on the grace of My Lady, I drew on that deep reservoir of magic within myself and felt it well from the center of my soul. My hand glowed green, circling, mingling, and finally joining with Finnegan's power to flare into a spectacular teal.

Directing our combined power, I sent it against the portal, watching it splash against the stone and then absorb it. The gray stone glowed brighter, the color bleeding to teal. There was a moment of silence before a crack appeared down the center of the seemingly smooth stone surface and the doors swung inward. There was no eerie groaning of sound or shower of dirt or debris like in a long-ago movie. Just a silent opening that beckoned us.

With the rising sun behind the mountain range, this part of the valley was left in shadow, the dim light extending only a few meters into the cave. We'd cut stairs into the stone for the first hundred meters, then the stone dissolved into the natural cave.

From where we stood, there was little to see.

A tentative peep from a hidden bird broke the silence. The forest creatures were awakening, and time was wasting.

"Well? Shall we?" Finnegan asked as I continued to stare into the darkness. Without a word, he released my hand and flicked a finger against the blue stone on his staff, igniting it to throw a beam of light over the shadows.

Raising my hand, I produced a ball of white light. The combined power dispelled the remaining shadows and revealed the hollowed-out walls leading into what had once been massive skyscrapers.

Without another word, I led the way down the corridor. Again, there was no dirt or debris, though the caves had been sealed for nearly a thousand years. Magic was a wonderful thing.

We traveled maybe a half an hour before the corridor opened into a vast cavern. Our combined power threw light over a cave system that hadn't been seen in ages. Stalactites and stalagmites glistened with water, jewel colors reflecting off of our light. They looked like they'd had eons to form instead of a mere thousand years. There was nothing to hint that these had once been the interior of manmade structures.

The scrape of our boots was loud in the silence, faint echoes bouncing off the walls where the caverns opened and soared far above our heads.

"Beautiful," Finnegan breathed, his tone reverent. I glanced at him to see the echo of that awe in his face. He was staring up at the stalactites that stretched up into the darkness, lost to the distance. The drip of water was the only sound.

"Thank you."

"The Sithi created this?"

"Technically speaking, this is the creation of Our Lady. We were merely the instruments through which she worked." As I stared around us, a new appreciation bloomed inside. "I have to admit, though, the idea of converting ancient buildings into a cave system came from me."

"Nicely done."

I smiled. Yes, I was proud of this bit of work. We'd avoided the cities for a long time after the plague outbreak. The sight of millions of rotting bodies had not been a pleasant experience. We'd waited until everything had been cleared by scavengers or deteriorated naturally before beginning the conversions. The millions of skeletons had been crushed to dust and returned to the soil. Ashes to ashes, dust to dust ... and all that.

As we moved farther into the cavern, I felt my senses come alive. There was no fear of losing my way within this labyrinth. My own personal magic was an intricate part of this wondrous place. I could close my eyes and literally feel my way through it. Which was one of our greatest advantages.

Without hesitation, I turned right, leading Finnegan farther into the maze. To give him credit, he didn't hesitate to follow me. Most men—and women—would feel the press of countless tons of solid rock above them. Finnegan betrayed no sign of unease. If possible, my estimation of him rose.

I sent out my senses, searching ahead of us for any hint of life, any hint of foulness that would betray the presence of the Skori. I was fairly certain Damon couldn't have gotten ahead of us, but the delay of searching for the entrance had set us back. No telling where Damon and his merry little band might be.

Glancing around, I realized this might be a good place for an ambush. There were few entrances in this portion that traveled deeper into the caverns and east toward the ocean. They would have to travel through this cave to continue north.

Instinctively, I placed my feet carefully, mindful of the echoes that could betray our presence. Without being told, Finnegan emulated my actions, our passage silent but for the brush of our clothing, the sound of our breath.

Time lost all meaning as we crossed the vast expanse, but I felt its passage by the position of the sun far beyond my sight. We must have traveled for nearly an hour when we heard the muted sound of a roar. I knew what was ahead.

As we came around the corner of a massive column of stone, we were greeted with the sight of a vast underground waterfall. The ceiling soared into darkness, the water falling from the shadows, over rocks and debris, to feed into a great underground river. It was the Hudson River of old. We'd redirected its route underground to eventually flow into the ocean.

If I remembered correctly, the route Damon and his band had taken should bring them into this cavern, close to where we positioned ourselves. The falling water should disguise any sound we might make while we waited.

Glancing around, I spied the crevasse through which Damon should emerge. Drawing a deep breath, I couldn't make out any hint of Skori. That wasn't a guarantee they hadn't already passed. The falling water might have dispersed the scent of their passage.

As I moved closer to the opening, I looked above and found a narrow ledge positioned slightly to the right of the crevasse. Perfect.

I gestured to a series of stalagmites angling off to the left of the passage. "You take them from the left, and I'll take them from above."

Finnegan followed the direction I indicated and nodded.

"As far as I know, there will only be Damon and four other Skori. We have to take them out here." I paused before I speared him with a ruthless glance. "Leave no survivors."

I felt a twinge at the necessity of killing my own nephew, but there was no going back. He was no longer Daniel nor was he Dylan. He was Damon.

"Find a good position and douse your light," I whispered as I moved toward the crevasse. With a leap, I cleared the five meters and landed on the ledge. It was a bit narrower than I'd anticipated, but I could easily balance myself on the slip of stone. I took care to brush aside any debris littering my perch so that none could accidentally rain down below.

I waited until Finnegan dimmed his staff and faded into the shadows of the nest of stone before I made my ball of light disappear. Darkness surrounded us, so deep that a mortal couldn't see his hand in front of his face. My superior Sithi eyesight allowed me a measure of sight. Faint, but I was able to discern shapes within the shadows.

"Now we wait."

Chapter Twenty-seven

The wait was short but stretched my nerves. Balanced as I was on my spit of a ledge, it was impossible to find a comfortable position. The fall of water was loud to my ears, and even my Sithi vision couldn't keep Finnegan in sight as he somehow merged with the shadows to become invisible. Waiting wasn't my forte. I could remain still for hours, but it wasn't my favorite pastime. I found myself shifting and had to force myself to stop.

Then I caught it. A stray scent. A feeling of evil assailed me, bringing me to full alert. The sensation grew stronger with each passing second.

Picking up the pebble I'd reserved for this reason, I lobbed it in Finnegan's direction. Within the shadows, a darker shape shifted, and I sensed his acknowledgment. Crouching lower, ignoring my discomfort, I waited, tension thrumming through my nerves.

Moments later, I was rewarded by the scrape of boot against stone and the faint sound of someone stumbling before swearing viciously. A gasp of breath caught my ear, and I frowned.

Something wasn't right.

A glow of red appeared below me, growing stronger as the sound of their passage became louder.

"Keep her quiet, fool. Riona is here somewhere. I can feel her."

Damn. So much for the element of surprise.

One by one, the Skori emerged from the crevasse, Damon in the lead. He entered the cavern cautiously, a glow of red suspended over his hand to light his way. I glanced toward Finnegan, but he was invisible. I suspected he was using his own brand of magic to disguise his presence.

Tensing, I prepared myself, waiting for the final Skori to enter the cavern before I acted. Finally, I caught sight of it just as it paused below me and gave the rope he carried a vicious tug. Another gasp ended on a curse as the final figure emerged into the flickering light.

My breath caught in my throat when I recognized Merry. Her hands were tied before her, and she was being dragged behind the Skori. Clothing torn and soiled, she stumbled into the cavern and looked around. Bruises marred one side of her face, and I could see a smear of blood where her lip had been cut. From where I stood, her injuries appeared minor, and I allowed myself a measure of relief even as fury threatened my control.

The red flickering light revealed an odd mixture of determination and despair in her expression. My heart went out to her.

As I watched, Damon tensed and halted. Raising the ball of red light above his head, he slowly circled.

"I know you're here, Riona. Come out, come out wherever you are. Why don't you come out and play?"

Fool that I was, I'd hesitated too long. It'd given him time to confirm my presence.

With a deep breath, I drew my sword, careful not to make a sound. My care was probably unnecessary, the muted roar of falling water covering the slide of steel as Viper left its sheath.

I stole a glance in the direction I knew Finnegan to be, then I leapt from my perch. Air whistled past my ears, and I hit the ground and rolled. Coming up in a crouch, I slashed the first Skori across the throat. The creature fell back with a gaping wound. Whirling, I dispatched the second, the force of my blow slicing across its abdomen and neatly spilling its intestines onto the cavern floor.

There was a flash of blue, and a third Skori vanished as Finnegan hit it with his wizard's light.

I'd just twirled around, searching for Damon, when a bolt of power slammed into me. Red light surrounded me, and I flew back, pinned against the stone wall with a force that left me gasping, struggling to draw air into my lungs. Once the stars cleared from my eyes, I tried moving, but my limbs were pressed against the hard stone at my back. Straining against the force at my throat, I was able to turn my head and see a band of red light shackling my wrist to the cavern wall. Going by the pressure on my other wrist, legs, and waist, I could only assume a similar restraint bound them.

I was effectively pinned. A bug on display. Straining was useless. The malevolent light rendered me helpless.

"It would be so easy, Riona." Damon stepped into my line of sight, his dark face gloating. In his hand, he held my sword. The impact had spun it from my grip. Putting the edge to my throat, he leaned closer. "I could so easily slit your throat, and there isn't a damn thing you can do about it."

He could, too. I was completely vulnerable. Well, not quite. I had my magic. Carefully, I began to build my power, slowly, subtly. I didn't want to alert him.

"Tell your pet human not to move or I'll kill you."

A quick glance toward Finnegan showed him standing perfectly still beside Merry. He'd dispatched another of the Skori and had cut through Merry's bindings. She leaned against him, her head on his shoulder as she worked blood back into her hands. In the light of his spiritual magic, she looked a little worse for wear, the bruises standing out in stark relief. The blood on her face and clothes was dried, so no recent wounds. Her spirit was intact. The look she shot toward Damon held pure murder.

"Are you all right?" I asked her.

"That bastard …"

"Tsk, tsk." Damon interrupted in mocking tones. He didn't take his attention from me as he stepped closer, my blade pressing a little harder against my throat. "Such language from a young lady. Whatever would Papa say?"

It was a relief to know Merry was physically unharmed. And madder than hell.

I gave Finnegan a slight nod.

"Would your master allow you to kill me?" I asked with a hard-won calm. "You were pretty insistent earlier that I join with the Dark Brother. Seems to me he wants me alive for some reason. Wonder what that could be?"

I pretended to consider options, all the while watching Damon's expression. In the dim lighting of the cave, I could see further changes in his features. The graceful lines of his jaw were thickening, squaring off, his dark eyes glinting red, reflecting the light of his illumination. He already possessed some of the Skori features. I wondered how far he would evolve. Then decided I'd make sure he was dead before he got that far.

At my words, rage sent color into his pale face, and his expression twisted into real evil.

"I know what he wants you for, Riona. Can't you guess? You now hold the power of the Bitch in you." He laughed despite my blank my expression. How could they have known that My Lady had graced me with her full power? His next words froze the blood in my veins. "Obviously, he cannot mate with his own sibling, but he can mate with her Chosen One. Through you, He'll gain the most powerful magic known."

My mind went blank as horror hit me. This had never occurred to me! Or, I was willing to bet, to My Lady. The Dark Master coveted me because of the power instilled by his sister. Had this been his plan all along?

Real terror ripped through me as the full scope of the plan

formed in my mind. The power that My Lady had bestowed upon me had made me vulnerable in ways neither of us could have guessed.

"Through you, He will have the power of his sibling and the ability to take His turn at making this world into His."

Damon's gloating expression went a long way toward calming me. I drew a deep breath in an effort to control the terror that threatened to scour my mind. Furiously, I built my power to a peak, ready to blast him to hell and back. I had to keep him talking. Discover if this was the full scope of the plan.

"Hmm. Wonder what that'll do to your power base." It was a real effort to keep my voice mild, to conceal my fear. "From what I can tell, your master made you all sorts of promises that he has no intention of keeping. Remember, he's better known as the Father of Lies."

The blade at my throat wavered, its sharp edge nicking my skin. A thin rivulet of blood ran down my neck, the sight attracting Damon's attention. His gaze followed the progress with an almost hungry look.

"My Master has given me far more power than the Bitch ever did."

"Carrot and the donkey."

The blade pressed a little harder against my neck. If I swallowed hard, I'd slit my own throat.

"I could so easily end it here, and there would be no usurping of my power."

"You could, but wouldn't your Master know it? I hate to think what he'd do to you if—and when—he discovered you'd betrayed him. Seems to me he isn't particularly forgiving."

My glance went to Finnegan and Merry again. The girl was inching toward a sword. By the looks of it, it had come off of a fallen Skori. There were two surviving creatures, but they remained unmoving. Only their hungry red eyes followed the conversation back and forth. I wondered how much they understood of what was occurring and decided they probably had a pretty good idea.

Finnegan's immobility drew my attention. He still had one hand on Merry's arm, as if supporting her, but there was a glazed look to his eyes that told me he wasn't all there. What was going on? Had he been injured by a tainted blade? Running my glance over him, I didn't see any injuries.

New worry ate at me. More so when I saw his fingers tighten on Merry's arm when she would have pulled away to reach for the sword. He was restraining her. Why? A glance toward the Skori showed they were paying scant attention to the humans, their eyes hungry for blood. Sithi blood.

I amped up my magic another notch. It glowed within me, but none of it danced along my skin to give away the full power I held. I had to time this right.

"What use do you have for the mortal?" I asked. There was no need to make my question sound casual. He already knew Merry was important to me.

The smile he gave me was more than a little smug as he pulled the blade away from my throat. I was able to breathe a little easier while he casually inspected the blade.

"You can congratulate me, Riona. I'm going to be a father."

"*What?*"

"Just as my master has a use for you, so does he have one for your little mortal. Can you imagine it? A child who is Skori, Sithi, and mortal. All three powers bound up in one. Does the old word *Anti-Christ* come to mind?"

"You raped Merry and got her pregnant?" I glanced at the girl and found her staring at Damon with hatred twisting her face.

"No rape was involved. Although ..." His smile was truly evil. "That would have added spice to the act. No, young Merry was under the impression she was being wooed by that other mortal,

Captain Tiernan."

"You bastard." Merry strained against the hold Finnegan had on her. "You tricked me."

Frowning, I had difficulty wrapping my mind around these ramifications. It explained much. Damon's interest in Merry while in Minneson City, the disappearances into his care that had had Kasia Morninglory concerned. The scent of magic that surrounded her when she'd returned. The Dark Master had covered most of his bases. All except one. He was counting on his brother taking no action to interfere.

I shot a concerned glance toward Finnegan, but he still had that glazed look on his face. What was wrong with him? A fine sheen of sweat dotted his brow, and his lips moved silently.

"Your surprise when you discovered you'd just given your virginity to me was delicious," Damon continued, his laughter echoing throughout the cavern. "You may never be the same. You'll probably never be satisfied to have sex with a mortal again after sampling Skori flesh."

"What makes you think I'd ever keep a child a creature like you fathered?"

"You have no choice, lover. A spell has been enacted to ensure your death should you attempt to end the life of the child."

It only took a second for me to confirm his claim. My senses found and inspected the spell he'd placed on Merry. Dark magic. I couldn't hope to counter it.

My fury was building to a peak.

"Think about it." Damon started to turn back to me. "I only had to tumble her once and voila … mission accomplished. I got her knocked up on the first try. Damn, I'm good!"

With a screech of fury, I unleashed my magic, tearing myself free of the invisible bindings, and leapt toward Damon. The surviving Skori called out, starting forward. Without hesitation, I flung out both hands. A beam of white light shot from my palms and engulfed the last two Skori. There was an instant of suspended animation before they vanished, no trace left behind.

Damon was still turning toward me when I started forward. He brought up my sword and would have caught me across the chest if I hadn't ducked and swung my leg out to sweep his feet out from under him. He anticipated the move and leaped, leaving me off balance. Rolling out of his reach, I bounded to my feet in time to avoid his next slash.

Dancing a couple feet away, I prepared my next bolt of power, determined to end this once and for all.

"Stop!"

"Riona!"

Chapter Twenty-eight

The power behind the command and the fear in Merry's voice as she called out froze Damon and me, leaving us staring at each other. For an instant, all that could be heard was the pounding rush of water as it tumbled from the shadows high overhead.

As one, we turned toward Finnegan. Shock shivered through me when I saw he had his arm around Merry, holding her immobile with the tip of his staff at her throat. The blue tip glowed, throwing an eerie light over her frightened face. The glazed look was gone from his eyes, but his expression shifted from determination to indecision and back again.

"An Anti-Christ cannot be born," Finnegan said.

"Don't do anything stupid, mortal." Damon straightened from his defensive crouch, a note of caution in his voice and in his expression as he lowered my blade.

"Riona?" Uncertainty colored Merry's voice and face. Looking at Finnegan, I was pretty sure he wasn't dissembling to provide me with a distraction. He looked deadly earnest.

"What are you doing, Finnegan?"

"My One God will not allow this child to be born."

"That isn't His choice." One thing I'd learned about the rules controlling the siblings was that free will was the cornerstone of their existence.

In the moment of silence, a warm breeze flowed over my face, bringing with it the scent of fresh flowers.

"*The child cannot die.*" The words were whispered, so close I almost turned to see if My Lady was standing behind me, but I didn't dare take my attention from Finnegan.

"*What should I do?*"

Even as I silently asked the question, I saw that Finnegan's hands were shaking, a sheen of perspiration covering his face as his attention turned inward.

"My Lord, please do not ask me to do this. I beg of you."

"Master, he's too far away. I would never reach the mortal before he killed her."

It took me only an instant to realize both Finnegan and Damon were speaking to their deities. Just as I was.

"*My Lady?*"

I sensed her hesitation before renewed determination flooded through me. "*You must allow me to possess you, Riona.*"

Sharply, I sucked in my breath. Possession? A part of me balked at the idea, but at the same time, I realized She was going to take a hand directly. Something I'd thought was forbidden.

"*It is the only way to stop my brothers.*"

Before I could make a decision, I saw a change come over Finnegan. He stiffened, and his eyes glowed blue—the same color as his crystal stone.

"Riona?"

"Don't move, Merry." I sensed we were all balanced on the edge of disaster. This was out of our hands.

A quick glance at Damon showed he, too, was changing, his eyes glowing red, his face contorting.

Dear Lady. They were both being possessed by their deities.

"*Take me, My Lady.*" With that, I surrendered my free will to my Goddess. I trusted her. Implicitly and without question.

The scent of the forest grew overpowering before a flood of heat permeated every cell in my body. My vision faded into a myopic tunnel, and a roaring filled my ears. These discomforts were nothing. For an instant, I thought I was going to burst into flame; the pain was excruciating. As quickly as it had swept over me, it was gone. I felt my consciousness shuffled into a corner of my mind as My Lady took control of my body. I was a bystander, able to view the events, unable to take part.

"Stop, Yahweh," She/I commanded, stepping forward with a grace foreign to me. "You cannot destroy this mortal, nor the innocent child she carries."

"Do not interfere, Danae. The child cannot be allowed to live."

"She's mine," Saytan/Damon commanded, his bearing regal and demanding. His face was changed, narrower, his skin darker than before. His eyes were an eerie red. My sword dropped from his hand, landing with a clatter onto the stone floor of the cavern.

"Through no choice of hers, brother." Danae/I rounded on Saytan/Damon. "You were well aware she would have never allowed a Skori to lay with her."

Danae/I glanced toward Merry. Her confusion was a palpable thing as her eyes darted from one to the other. There was nothing I could do to reassure her or explain. The blue stone didn't waver from its position at her throat, but by the same token, nor did Yahweh/Finnegan act.

"We are allowed to work through our minions."

I nearly missed the exchange and snapped my attention back. The faint whine in Saytan/Damon's voice grated on my nerves. Could a deity be petulant?

"This is my millennium. You have no place here, brother."

"I was robbed of my time."

"You forfeited your turn when you released the black plague during my millennium," Yahweh/Finnegan said. For the first time, I saw anger in his face. A good thing, I thought. As far as I was concerned, this One God had been too lenient toward the Dark Master.

"Enough," Danae/I said, my voice commanding. "This is my millennium and subject to my rules. I will take charge of the girl and her child."

"And do what?" Yahweh/Finnegan did not move, nor did he shift his staff from Merry's throat.

As I watched, I detected indecision in Finnegan. I was pretty sure it came from Finnegan and not Yahweh's possession of him. Had his possession been of his free will, as mine was? Or had his One God taken control when Finnegan had hesitated to do his bidding? I willed him to break free. Was that even possible?

"The child she carries is an abomination."

"Not necessarily. The child has the right to the same choices all of our followers are allowed. She will be raised without our interference to make her life's choices."

She?

"And consider this, brothers. The child Merry carries is a combination of everything that we are. Perhaps she is destined to exist. If you destroy that, you may destroy all."

"You don't know that."

"Nothing is certain. Only the Maker has all the answers."

Again, I saw hesitation in Finnegan's face before it twisted with something close to agony.

"No! I will not be a party to this," he cried out in his own voice. He wrenched the blue stone away from Merry's throat and released her. In a violent gesture, he flung his staff away. It landed meters away, clattering against the stone to vanish into the shadows. "I will not commit murder in your name."

For a long moment of silence, no one moved, then a blue glow surrounded Finnegan, so bright I squinted. Finnegan threw back his head and screamed, the sound echoing off the cavern walls. As the blue light faded, Finnegan collapsed unconscious to the ground.

Fear ate at me. For an instant, I struggled with My Lady to

regain control of my body and go to him.

"*He lives*," My Lady whispered to me. Relief made me hesitate and again surrender my will to her.

Free, Merry stumbled into my embrace, her body shaking with reaction and fear. Danae/I hugged her, offering wordless comfort and protection. "You are safe, child."

"The mortal belongs to me," Saytan/Damon screamed as he closed in on us. I'd almost forgotten him, but My Lady evidently hadn't. I could feel her anticipation when Damon reached for Merry.

Thrusting the girl behind us, She/I grasped his arm and yanked him close until we were nose to nose.

"Merry is the direct descendent of one of my Sithi. She is under my protection and will be given into the care of Riona Northstar." Her/my voice became intense and dropped to a growl. "And remember this. You will not covet, nor possess, my champion. Riona will never be yours, brother. Do you understand me?"

"What use would I have for one of your Sithi?"

"Do not play innocent with me. You waited until I infused Riona with my full power and then planned to steal her from me. You are playing your games from two fronts."

"Perhaps stealing would not be necessary. Perhaps she would prefer my patronage."

"Never!" It was my voice that emerged from my mouth. I felt more than saw the shock reflected in Saytan/Damon's eyes. "I am loyal to My Lady. I would never forsake her."

"There. You have your answer." Danae quickly resumed control as I relinquished it. I had the feeling she was better equipped to handle her sibling should things go south. In this case, I would be a liability.

"If you want your worthless minion to survive this day, you will release him, brother." Her words were low, intense. "If you are in possession of Damon when I destroy him, there is a good chance that you will also cease."

Though my eyesight was distorted, I caught a flash of fear in Saytan/Damon's eyes. I couldn't tell how much of that fear belonged to Saytan or to Damon, but with a scream of fury, he wrenched himself free of our grip and backed up several paces. Hatred blazed in his eyes as he enfolded himself in shadow and vanished.

I took three steps after him before My Lady stopped me. Frozen, I couldn't move; the only sound was the falling water.

"*You let him escape.*" I was furious. We'd had him literally within our grasp, could have ended this once and for all.

"*Despite my threat, I am not allowed to harm my brothers,*" She said, her words penetrating my anger. "*We are—all three of us—a part of each other. To destroy one is to destroy all. Just as the child Merry carries is a combination of Sithi, mortal, and Skori. She carries a piece of each of us within her.*"

"*What does that mean?*"

"*At this point, even I am uncertain. I only know that this child holds a destiny to either unite or destroy all of our people.*"

That didn't sound promising.

"*What must I do?*"

I felt affection flow through me, warm with Her love.

"*My Riona. Ready to do whatever necessary.*" Green light edged my peripheral vision, and I felt her presence within me fade. "*I am charging you with protecting Merry and the child she carries.*"

As the green glow dimmed, so did My Lady. I regained full possession of my body, her departure so abrupt I stumbled, unprepared to control my limbs.

"Riona?"

Merry caught me around the waist, supporting me while I regained my balance. For a moment, I leaned against her, allowing myself a measure of unfamiliar comfort. Given the difference in our heights, it should have been awkward but wasn't. Then awareness took over, and I pulled away. Stumbling over to Finnegan's still body, I dropped to my knees. With shaking hands, I turned him over, my fingers searching for and finding a pulse at his throat. Relief flooded me. It was strong and steady.

"What are you doing?" Merry asked, alarm in her voice. I heard her scramble for my sword, the blade sliding against the stone as she brought it up. "He tried to kill me."

"Not Finnegan. His deity." I didn't spare her a glance.

"The One God?"

"He took possession of Finnegan and tried to force him to carry out His bidding."

Merry went still, her expression stunned. I barely registered her reaction because Finnegan stirred and opened his eyes. I was relieved to see they were their normal chocolate-brown color. But seeing the stark despair in their depths, I drew him into my arms, twisting so that he was sitting with his back against my chest. I ran my hands down his chest, offering comfort. I didn't need to see his face to know the chaos of his emotions.

"Are you all right?"

"I feel like I've been soundly beaten."

"Looks like it as well."

For a minute longer, he leaned on me before he pulled away and got to his feet, swaying slightly. I followed, but when I offered support, he waved me off, his gesture rough.

"I denied Him." Finnegan's face twisted with anguish. "I couldn't do it."

"He would have had you kill me," Merry broke in. Her voice shook, and it took me a second to realize it was with anger rather than fear. The look in her eyes when she faced us was hard. The grip she had on my sword was knuckle-white. "He is my God as well. The being I follow tried to have me killed."

What could I say? It was true. The One God was worshiped by all mortals, and He'd basically put a hit out on one of his followers. Still, I had to attempt some damage control.

"There's an old saying: God works in mysterious ways."

"What does that mean?"

"It means your One God was testing Finnegan. If He'd been earnest, you wouldn't be here."

Yeah. Right. Like I believed that. I couldn't believe the crap I was spouting, but I couldn't allow Merry to go on believing her deity wanted her dead.

"So it was all a test?" Her words were soft. Pensive. I was relieved to see some of the anger fade from her eyes. It wasn't much of a fix, but it might do for now.

But first things first.

I took Finnegan's arm and urged him closer to the underground river, using the sound of running water to cover my words.

"What exactly happened?"

"I denied Him." The anguish hadn't faded from his eyes. His face was haggard as he ran his hands over it, wiping at a vision only he could see. "I thought if I allowed him to possess me, I could not blame myself for murdering an innocent girl and child. I was wrong."

He looked at me, and with a soundless sigh, I drew him into my arms, hugging him to me in an attempt to offer what comfort I could. I never wanted to see that look in his eyes again. It went beyond pain and betrayal.

"Choices," I whispered.

He pulled back far enough to look into my face.

"We're always given choices, Finnegan. Right or wrong, what we do is through our own free will." I took his face between my hands. I understood his internal struggle. "That unborn child will have a choice. Yes, she or he will be a combination of Sithi, Skori, and mortal, but the child will also be raised to know right from wrong. Its choices will be made, and we will be there to either support or oppose them."

"I don't want this child."

I turned to find Merry behind us. She had joined us where we stood at the river's edge.

"I hate it. I hate the thought of carrying it." Her voice shook with the strength of her emotions. Tears glistened in her eyes and spilled over. "I hate the fact it isn't Kai's child."

I closed my eyes, feeling her anger and her pain. What could I tell her?

"Damon wasn't bluffing, Merry. The spell he placed upon you is very real and not one I could counter. If you end the child's life, it will end your own."

She was silent for a long moment, studying her hands. Finally, she looked up, determination in her expression. Tears still streamed down her face, making tracks in the dirt that covered her cheeks. The bruises and lacerations stood out on her pale face.

"Very well, Riona Northstar. I'll carry this child. But the instant it's born, I want it gone. You can do what you want with it, but I want it gone."

"As you wish."

That was probably the best I was going to get.

Without hesitation, I accepted the responsibility. How could I not? Despite the circumstances of its existence, this unborn child was my descendant and therefore under my protection.

I had no way of seeing into the future. I had my doubts that My Lady even knew what the future might bring. This was going to be a case of nature versus nurturing. I could only do my best and hope.

What this child might mean for mankind, I hadn't a clue. But it was a chance I was willing to take.

ABOUT THE AUTHOR

Born and raised in Southeastern Wisconsin, Liz Kreger was number eight of ten kids. Reading and writing became her escape, somewhere she could give her imagination free rein.

A longtime fan of science fiction and space operas, Liz also fell in love with paranormal romance and fantasy, and always wrote in the genres she loved.

Liz passed away after an eighteen year battle with cancer in late November 2014, but her pure, joyful spirit lives on in the hearts of her friends and family, and in her books.

www.ingramcontent.com/pod-product-compliance
Lightning Source LLC
Chambersburg PA
CBHW071048250626
47159CB00002B/402